We Made It All Up

We Made It All Up

MARGOT HARRISON

LITTLE, BROWN AND COMPANY

New York Boston

Copyright © 2022 by Margot Harrison
Title page art © Brilliant Eye/Shutterstock.com
Emojis on pages 56 and 57 © Intellson/Shutterstock.com

Cover art © 2022 by Peter Strain. Cover design by Jenny Kimura.
Cover copyright © 2022 by Hachette Book Group, Inc.

Little, Brown and Company
Hachette Book Group
1290 Avenue of the Americas, New York, NY 10104
Visit us at LBYR.com

First Edition: July 2022

Little, Brown and Company is a division of Hachette Book Group, Inc. The Little, Brown name and logo are trademarks of Hachette Book Group, Inc.

The publisher is not responsible for websites (or their content) that are not owned by the publisher.

Library of Congress Cataloging-in-Publication Data
Names: Harrison, Margot, author.
Title: We made it all up / Margot Harrison.
Description: First edition. | New York ; Boston : Little, Brown and Company, 2022. |
Audience: Ages 14 & up. | Summary: Celeste Bergstein moves to a small town in Montana to escape her past, only to become embroiled in her new hometown's twisted secrets when the school's star athlete—who is also the subject of Celeste's writings—is found dead at the mouth of a cave.
Identifiers: LCCN 2021032561 | ISBN 9780316275767 (hardcover) |
ISBN 9780316275668 (ebook)
Subjects: CYAC: Secrets—Fiction. | Authorship—Fiction. | Self-destructive behavior—Fiction. | Hazing—Fiction. | Revenge—Fiction. | LCGFT: Novels.
Classification: LCC PZ7.1.H375 We 2022 | DDC [Fic]—dc23
LC record available at https://lccn.loc.gov/2021032561

ISBNs: 978-0-316-27576-7 (hardcover), 978-0-316-27566-8 (ebook)

Printed in the United States of America

LSC-C

Printing 1, 2022

To my sister, Eva Sollberger,

the first one who ever listened to my stories

Now

Joss Thorssen spins the bottle, and then we persuade him to kiss each of us. "Okay," he says. "Okay."

It shouldn't be okay, but here on the dark mountainside, with the lights of town winking far in the distance, maybe it is.

He starts with Vivvy, because she's the closest. When his head dips toward her, a fist clenches in my chest—envy or excitement, I don't even know. Though I've never kissed Joss, barely touched Joss, in some strange way I still feel like he's mine and *she's* mine, too. We're coconspirators, Vivvy and I. He's what we conspire about.

I force myself to watch as Vivvy closes her eyes. Joss kisses her on the right cheek, the left cheek, corner of the lips, forehead. Soberly, ceremonially, like a holy man performing a rite. Vivvy's face has gone as still as a waxwork.

Then Joss rises, staggering a little on his bad ankle, and walks around the fire to Seth, his foot swiping the bottle on the way. When he spun it a few minutes ago, it pointed at Seth, who sits with his back to the valley. Now it points up the hill toward the cave entrance.

The mountain breeze is scathingly cold, but the liquor is a furnace in my chest. Vivvy has grabbed her phone again and started tapping, and I wonder how she can concentrate on anything but what's happening right now.

Seth flinches when Joss touches him, as if he expects to be hit. Then he goes still the way Vivvy did, eyes closed.

Joss repeats the exact sequence of kisses he gave Vivvy. It's over in three seconds, and he's on his feet again, swaying unsteadily toward me.

I brace myself because I've only been this close to him once, and yes, I've imagined this, but not *like* this. When Joss's fingers close on my shoulders, when I smell him—the realness, the bigness, the alien musky maleness of him—I stop breathing or moving. My eyes stay open, unseeing.

Right cheek, left cheek, beside the lips, between the brows. I feel it but I don't. My skin is ice. He smells of motor oil and weed.

I'm about to exhale when Joss's head dips again, his pale hair brushing my cheek. He kisses me full on the lips, his warmth resting there just long enough for sensation to rush back into all my nerve endings. My limbs melt. My lips move.

And then his are gone, along with his warmth and his smell and the itching sense of his closeness. I close my eyes and feel the liquor rush through me, dilating my blood vessels. Already it seems as if I just watched that happen instead of living it.

Joss kissed the new girl. Joss kissed the weirdo. What a twist!

When I open my eyes, Joss is limping toward the line of cedars that screen the cave entrance. "Gotta take a leak," he says, sounding weirdly satisfied. "Vivvy, you got another bottle?"

Vivvy opens a bottle and puts on a log. Flames jump in the pit, red against the vast darkness of the valley. I don't want to think about the almost smugness in Joss's voice, so I grab the bottle and take a swallow of something that tastes like mouthwash, then a swig from my thermos of tea for good measure.

I can't look at Vivvy. My face is flushed, and I feel like I'm grimacing, but maybe it looks like a wild, triumphant grin.

Seth lurches toward the bottle, blocking the fire and the stars. "Joss chose you," he tells me.

The lone frail birch on the slope is dropping its gold-coin leaves, and decay is thick in my nostrils. Did Vivvy hear that? No, she's busy with her phone again. I hand Seth the bottle, shake my head. "It doesn't work that way."

Any minute Joss will come back. I still feel his lips, my warmth opening to his, the burn of his stubble. Do I want to be chosen?

I don't do self-inserts. I am not the heroine of my stories, and this started as a story—my story and Vivvy's.

Then Joss whistles and calls my name, and I see Vivvy's head jerk hard to the side, and I don't care how the story's supposed to go.

I rise and go to the nook between the cedars and the cliff. His hand emerges from the dark and pulls me inside, where the dirt is bare and fine and soft and you can't see the town's lights, only the stars.

And just for a moment, I think this was always supposed to happen.

Then

The first thing I noticed waking up each morning in Kray's Defile was the quiet.

No grumbling of trucks, no sirens, no laughing gangs of students headed to the corner *dépanneur*. Just a cool, layered stillness that felt thick enough to slice.

It was quiet as I showered and dressed and ate toast and peanut butter at the breakfast bar. Our rental house was the first actual *house* I'd ever lived in, and it didn't disappoint, with its breakfast bar and laundry room and even a wood-paneled basement rec room that looked like nobody had done any recreation in it for the past fifty years.

We were down to the heel of the stale white bread that Dad had picked up at a mini-mart on his commute from Billings. I shoved it into the toaster, remembering how Mom would bring home a bag of bagels three times a week from our favorite bakery in Montreal, chewy and slathered with sesame seeds. I put "shopping trip" on my mental list. Surely there had to be a supermarket with whole-grain bread within forty miles?

This town was a way station, I reminded myself, stepping out onto the overgrown lawn. Not my home.

Sometimes where you are is just a step on the way somewhere else—Dad taught me that. All academics know it, he said. He was here for a temporary, grant-funded job, in this place you could pass in a blink on the interstate, and I'd chosen to leave Mom and come live with him for a fresh start. In two years, I'd be off to college—anywhere away from Montreal. Next year maybe I'd get my license and commute to Billings for college courses. Though having my own car still felt like a pipe dream, and the roads here...

They were so long. So lonely. So much empty space.

As I walked to the bus stop, a neighbor came out and picked up her newspaper, her hair in a majestic style I hadn't seen outside of old movies. She called to me: "Hi, hon, is your dad at home?"

"He's off early, Ms...." I didn't know her name. I should know her name.

"Well, I have a little tip for him. If he looks in the book under 'lawn care,' he'll find Carlsson's, but they charge an arm and a leg..."

I stopped listening closely. She just wanted to talk about her nephew, who was taking a break from college and would mow and trim for a song.

She thrust a slip of paper into my hand. "Tell your dad. He won't regret it."

So this was a place where people noticed your lawn. We'd never had one before.

I stashed the paper away. Maybe I should call the nephew; Dad wouldn't remember to do it himself.

It was quiet on the bus: lots of pasty-white faces, flannel shirts, headphones. No eyes on me, and that was a relief; I didn't want to be the one thing that was out of place here, like our overgrown grass. I kept my eyes to myself, hoping my light blue T-shirt and jeans were neutral enough.

In nearly a week at this school, I hadn't spoken to anyone except Sarah Blessingham, my assigned physics lab partner.

When I stepped off the bus, the air surprised me as it still did sometimes—a fresh whoosh in my lungs, making my heart pound and my eyes tear. I swung around, and there, across the road from the school, was the mountain pass, the "Defile" itself, looming over the town like a craggy granite iceberg.

It was so enormous, sharp-edged against the blue sky, that I wanted to stand on the sidewalk and stare. To take it in. But people pressed past, shoulders and elbows brushing mine, pushing me onward.

A fresh start. A way station. None of it is any use if you can't blend in.

The school lobby was all people yelling, grabbing, exchanging phones to share photos, whooping with ear-shattering laughter. I kept to the edges, skirting two scarecrows dressed in blue-and-yellow jerseys that stood propped against the trophy case, each holding a hockey stick. ON THE ICE, said one jersey. FEEL THE SPIRIT, said the other.

Hockey was big at my school in Montreal—hockey is big in Montreal generally—but this "spirit" thing was new to me. On the way to my locker, I passed three giant hand-painted "spirit" posters, then two knots of girls wearing pastel uniforms. What was their sport? I couldn't tell.

It was like walking into the past, or into one of those soapy high school shows where everybody gets excited about sock hops and harvest dances. Maybe that was why people looked past and around me. I belonged to another time, another plane of reality.

Physics. Trig. Spanish. Lunch. Health. I had simple rules: Sit in corners and back rows. Don't raise your hand. Do speak when called on. Blend in.

Clock hands bounced like twitching muscles, and it was time for AP English.

Ms. Linney didn't quite fit in here, either, which made me like her. She had a weird hair-dye situation going on: butter yellow at the crown of her head and brown looped into a basket shape on her shoulders. I stared at her nude, glossy lips as she handed back quizzes and bantered with the boys in letter jackets. They didn't seem to think her hair was weird. Was *my* hair weird?

"It's time for our first Shakespeare monologue victim. Ah, yes. The brave Mr. Thorssen. Mr. Larkin, I believe you're in the director's chair today?"

Over the course of the semester, we'd all have to do an oral presentation in pairs, actor and director/coach. Memorizing and reciting Shakespeare was nothing new for me, but I dreaded doing it here. People might think I was showing off.

I didn't know the name of the slender boy who sat in the designated "director's chair" in the front row, but I knew Joss Thorssen. If Kray's Defile High was a soap, he was the star. His broad shoulders filled out varsity letter jackets, royal blue and marigold yellow, and people were always fist-bumping him and yelling, "Thorssen!" I'd heard him say he signed up for the earliest possible monologue slot so it wouldn't interfere with his hockey season.

Now he had to become Richard, murderous Duke of Gloucester.

Standing before us, Joss clenched both fists and stared at the floor like he would rather be about anywhere than here. " 'Now is the winter of our discontent / Made glorious summer by this sun of York...' "

He trailed off, and a few people chanted "Yeah" encouragingly.

" 'Now are our brows bound with victorious wreaths; / Our bruised arms hung up for monuments...' " Joss's fists had loosened, but he still spat out the words like he was in a race.

My lips moved, silently reciting the speech along with him. He'd skipped some lines, and "bruised" should have had two syllables.

Joss went on, and I sensed a growing tension in the room, like we were all holding our breaths for him to reach the finish line and stop mangling the words. " 'I, that am curtail'd of this fair proportion, / Cheated of feature by dissembling nature, / Deform'd, unfinish'd—' "

"Dude," said a tenor voice. "Sorry to interrupt, but you're killing me."

It was the "director." His legs sprawled into the aisle, his mouth twisting sardonically. If I had to guess, I'd have placed him toward the bottom of the Kray's Defile social hierarchy—skinny and corpse-pale, with greasy black hair and a ripped T-shirt.

"C'mon, dude." The director pulled himself upright, planted

8

both elbows on his desk. "Are you even *thinking* about the words? You sound baked."

The room filled with brief, appreciative snickering, followed by abrupt silence. We weren't supposed to laugh at Joss.

Ms. Linney said, "Keep it respectful, Seth. Observations, not judgments. Would you like to stand up and explain how *you* see the character of Richard?"

"Do I have to?" The director—Seth—hauled himself to his feet. Joss stared stoically at a spot just below the windowsill.

"So this guy, Gloucester, Richard, whatever. He's all privileged and, like, born to a noble family. But he has a hunchback, and everybody in his world has a problem with that. Girls aren't into him. Even dogs bark at him."

Joss continued his study of the wall. Around me, people were tensing. Maybe they were afraid Seth would make them laugh again.

"All because of his physical appearance. Which isn't his fault." Seth's words came quicker and louder, like he was determined to get a rise out of Joss. "You need to get *inside* Richard, not just say the words. Have you ever felt like everybody hates you?"

A girl tittered. Someone in the back muttered, "Look in the mirror, freak."

My cheeks burned. We all knew it wasn't Joss who was the outcast, with his corn silk hair and firm jaw. And we knew Seth was taunting Joss for a reason—because no one thought he'd dare.

At last, Joss looked up. He had what some girls call "puppy

dog eyes," guileless blue and droopy at the corners, a little lost. "Sure, I've felt that way," he said, as if it were another line he was reciting. As if he knew he had to say it, but he wasn't 100 percent sure what it meant.

"You've felt like a monster?" Seth took a step, another, closing the distance between them. His voice rose. "Seriously? Richard freaking hates himself. Do you have the slightest clue?"

"But you just said—" Joss couldn't seem to finish the thought. The full blush on his pale cheeks and neck made quite the spectacle.

"Aw, now he's done it," a boy muttered behind me, like he expected Joss to haul off and punch Seth.

I half expected that, too. What I didn't expect was what happened: Joss's lips pressed together, and he took a stutter-step and sank to his knees. On the floor. In front of Seth.

A girl in my row gasped theatrically—one of the pretty ones. Beside her, a weedy little girl with a pale, bunched-up face just stared.

Nobody spoke. Joss swayed on his knees like he was considering getting up again.

Seth took a step back. He moved like he hated his body, but his eyes were as blue as Joss's, with long lashes that made me think of willows at dusk.

Joss's fists clenched. "I *know* you think I'm a monster," he said in a small voice. "I may not know much, but I know that."

"It's some kind of psych," whispered the boy behind me. "Thorssen's gonna pound him, watch."

Ms. Linney cleared her throat.

Seth said, "Monster. You said it, not me."

Joss rose in a blur and towered over Seth, his whole body coiled with rage. "Why are you on my ass all of a sudden? What the hell is your problem?"

"Okay, boys, can we please—"

"You got it." Seth backed away from Joss, audibly gloating. "You finally sound like Richard. You want to strangle me, you want to pound me into next week, so give it a try. Stop pretending to be *nice*."

"Stop it," I said.

It was my first time speaking in class in Montana without being called on. Heads whirled to look at me. Even Joss turned, his body going still.

My mouth was dry, my breath a weak gust in my throat. "You're pushing him too hard. When you push actors too hard, they shut down."

That's what a girl in my McGill drama workshop told Frank, our director, after he asked me creepy questions in front of the whole class. Maybe it would work here, too. Maybe not.

"He doesn't look shut down to me," Seth snapped.

Joss didn't move. The girls were all staring at me, especially the weedy one. She had a short blond bob like a twenties flapper, and she wore a Victorian blouse with a cameo brooch.

Ms. Linney jumped in: "That's an excellent point, Celeste. Pushing too hard *is* counterproductive. Seth, could you express your critique in a way that's less—"

But Seth had had enough. "You're so full of shit, Joss," he said, backing toward the classroom door. "You may not be

11

deformed in a way people can see, but you're an asshole, and you'll always be an asshole, and you're just too dense to—"

The bell rang.

Seth vanished into the corridor. Some of the large, letter-jacketed boys tried to go after him, but Ms. Linney stopped them short with a frantic spiel about the assignment.

I got up as unhurriedly as I could and walked to my locker. My mouth was dry, and something pressed against my throat and chest, making it hard to breathe. My feelings tended to make themselves known by wrapping around my neck like pythons, never announcing their names.

You'll never be an actress if you don't let yourself feel, Frank said in my memory. *A fascinating face, but your emotions terrify you.*

Frank was always pushing me, like Seth had pushed Joss just now. Always wanting me to feel. I'd come here with Dad rather than stay with Mom so I could stop feeling—stop worrying about boys not liking me, and about grown men liking me too much. To blend in and just be for a while.

As I worked the locker combination, a silvery voice said, "That took balls."

It was the weedy girl with the bob. Up close, her eyes were whitish-green like lichen, and her mouth didn't look like it should have "balls" coming out of it. She added, "Somebody needed to slow Seth down before he got in real trouble. He's not a bad person."

I nodded noncommittally, already ashamed of the role I'd played in the classroom. This was none of my business.

But she kept right on talking: "When Joss was down on his knees, and Seth finally looked at him, I honest to God thought they were going to kiss."

Could I have misheard her? The scarecrows and spirit posters weren't the only retro thing about this school; I hadn't seen a single rainbow banner or pin, or a same-sex couple holding hands, and nobody ever discussed pronouns. "Are they, uh...a thing?"

The girl shook her head, looking satisfied to have gained my attention. "Joss's always been with girls. But I mean, c'mon, that wasn't a regular fight. That was a special, steamy fight. That was psychodrama."

My mouth must have been hanging open, because she added, "Don't tell me you weren't thinking it."

I lowered my gaze to the spearmint-green linoleum. I was thinking it *now*, okay, visualizing Joss pulling Seth into a passionate kiss, but that didn't mean she knew anything about me. She couldn't hurt me.

"You're from the city, aren't you? Out of state somewhere?"

Before I could deny it, she stuck out her hand. Her grip was spidery and strong, and she seemed older and younger than me at once, her eyes glittering.

"I'm Vivienne Kray," she said. "Vivvy, if you insist. Sorry I weirded you out; I do that to people sometimes. See you around."

13

Now

My head pulses. Cotton candy clouds wreathe the horizon, the newly risen sun shining through them like a promise. I was promised something.

My back hurts, resting on something hard, and the night comes back in a flash—but not enough of it. The cedars, the cliff, spin the bottle, the smell of rotting leaves, Joss's lips on mine.

I sit up, pain shooting down my spine, to find I'm on a park bench. My head is a fragile jellyfish laced with throbbing veins. My limbs feel light and weak.

I don't remember walking down the hill, yet here I am in the little park on Vivvy's block, with two benches and a sandbox full of dead leaves. Under the bench I'm on, I find my duffel bag with the extra sweater, flashlight, and thermos of tea. I don't remember putting it there.

Can alcohol do this to a person who's never been drunk enough to pass out? What about alcohol that's been sitting in a musty basement for fifteen years, maybe growing all kinds of exotic mold? I should be terrified, but more than anything I feel *new*, rebooted, like when I woke in the hospital after having my appendix out, with a black hole in my head where the last several hours should be.

My head swims again as I stand up and gaze down on Kray's Defile, the drab grid of five east-to-west streets and four north-to-south ones. The dogs are barking, the chain saws and leaf blowers growling to life, in this town with one stoplight, where all friendships can be traced back to preschool.

I am still new here. I still don't belong.

The shiny sky says, *But you do. Joss chose you.*

I remember a little more now. The cliff wall—jagged, cold, solid. Grass brushing my calves. Joss's hands pushing me against the wall, urgent but not rough, and my hands all over him, too, tugging him closer. The fire bright through the chinks in the cedars. Blood singing in my ears, higher pitched than the last febrile crickets. Joss smoothing back my hair: "Mmm. Soft."

"Vivvy's going to kill us," I whispered to him.

"Why?"

Without Vivvy and the stories we wrote together, I would never have been here, but I couldn't tell him that. And the stories weren't about me and Joss, they were about Joss and Seth— kissing. Healing each other with soft words and touches. Hopelessly in love.

I wanted to touch him all over, and touching him was holding my hand over a flame, feeling that tantalizing, tickling warmth that was almost burning. Any second it might start feeling like the last time I was this close to someone—but not yet. Not yet.

I remember shivering, my jacket too thin for the night. I remember Joss removing his own jacket to reveal a chamois shirt—"shammy," he called it—and peeling the shirt off and holding it so I could slip my arms into the sleeves.

I remember the snug, rough feel of his jeans under my palm. The raised surface of his ram's-head belt buckle. Light kisses tracing a path from my mouth to chin to neck. I remember wishing it wasn't too dark to see the color of his eyes. Did they really look like sea glass or a bay, and were the flecks coffee-dark or gold? We'd never been this close. I wanted to write his eyes better.

I remember his pulling away and my feeling relieved and the next instant achingly empty. *Is this how it feels to want someone? Is this how it's supposed to feel?*

Then Joss said, "I'm wasted, but this is good," and he came back to me. Warm hands on my waist, under my shirt. Soothing breath in my ear. My hands slipped around his waist, too.

And then—nothing. A gaping black hole where the rest of the night should be.

———

At home, I tug off my jacket and find his chamois shirt still underneath. This is why I didn't freeze sleeping on that bench.

I take it off gingerly, as if it might rip. Looking in the mirror, I spot two delicate pinwheels of broken capillaries on my neck, my throat. Did his mouth make those? I remember his mouth, remember throwing my head back because it felt good, but somehow I didn't expect it to leave marks. The rest of my clothes seem pristinely undisturbed, and that, I admit, is a relief. The black hole can't hide anything too bad.

The chamois shirt is faded blue, almost gray, and as soft as I remembered. The left cuff is missing a button. I raise it to my face and inhale, and yes, it smells like him.

———

Vivvy calls eight times. Then she starts texting, which means she *really* wants to reach me, because Vivvy considers texting a barbaric way to have a conversation. Each time the phone buzzes, my throat tightens, and my right thumb goes numb—a reflex from the days when Frank was stalking me. But today all my texts are from Vivvy:

Are you okay? Home safe?

Is it okay I left you up there at the cave mouth? Was so cold. Have you talked to HIM today?

I almost block her so I won't have to read them anymore. When I blocked Frank, he started texting again from another number, and then another.

I google *Can you black out if you're not an alcoholic.* The answer is yes—it's all about how fast you drink and how well your body handles it. Maybe my liver is a dud.

When I took off my clothes to shower, I found two big bruises, one just above each elbow, and now I can't stop imagining someone dragging me somewhere. Joss wouldn't have done that, though, any more than he would have abandoned me on a park bench. Besides being the golden boy, the hockey star, Joss is decent. I know how it feels when someone doesn't read your body, doesn't notice when they hurt you, and he wasn't like that.

On Halloween, in the scare-house in Vivvy's basement, he held me close for an instant after I screamed, but not too close. He could tell where to stop.

I huddle on the couch in an afghan, willing Joss to text me and fill in the blanks in my memory. Just one tiny text: *Hey, sorry I booked last night. Mom had an emergency. Vivvy help you get home?* It can be a flimsy excuse, I won't care.

I don't feel ready to talk to anyone about the gaping hole in last night, but at four twenty, with the sun poised for its quick slide into darkness, I can't keep ignoring Vivvy.

I'm alive! Sorry I scared you. Just been sleeping.

At home??? Alone???

Is she imagining Joss and me cuddled up together? My throat fills with bile. *Yeah. I got kind of sick after you left. What about you, you ok?*

Vivvy feels fine, but she starts apologizing on overdrive and googling to see if "old brandy" can poison you. I purposely keep my symptoms vague. I hold Joss's chamois shirt draped across my arms, rocking it like a baby, remembering how he gave it to me to keep me warm.

She keeps bringing the conversation back to Joss. *So you haven't seen HIM today?*

No.

What happened last night???!!! Before you got sick? Hold on, calling.

The phone rings, and this time I pick up and tell Vivvy a story I hope is the truth, or close to it.

In this story, after Joss and I talked and made out a little, I

18

started feeling sick and told him I needed to get home. Joss said he'd be right behind me; he needed a smoke to "clear his head." I staggered down the hill and fell asleep on the park bench.

My story is just sexy enough without being embarrassing. I embroider it, speculating that Joss's friends might have been partying in the cave. Maybe he joined them, assuming I was with Vivvy. In this story, there are no bruises, no black holes.

"Has he called you yet?" she keeps asking excitedly. "Has he texted?"

This part I can't lie about. "Not yet."

Vivvy keeps fixating on the sexy part, like she's shipping Joss and me for real now, like she thinks he chose me, too. "Tell me as soon as he does, okay?"

I promise I will.

Then

TWO AND A HALF MONTHS AGO
(FRIDAY, AUGUST 30)

The day after the Shakespeare debacle, I looked for Vivvy at school and spotted her with the book, wearing a navy dress with a lacy Peter Pan collar and Mary Janes. She smiled at me in a distracted, dreamy way.

After school, Dad texted to say he was working late again in Billings. At home, I tried to start my homework, but all the lawn mowers on the street seemed to be burring at once. So I went for a run on the wooded trail along the upper edge of town.

Soft dirt muffled my footfalls as I jogged up the hill, thighs pumping and lungs straining. The woods were so quiet that the scramble of a squirrel in a thicket made me jump. Trees met overhead in places, blotting out the streaky blue sky.

What if I came around a curve and barreled into a grizzly? Running in the city, on the Mont-Royal, I always had other people in sight, but here—

Branches thrashed ahead. Not a bear, though—a boy. He lurched out from between two scrubby pines, zipped down the bank, and fell into step beside me.

What on earth? His long legs kept pace with me effortlessly, yet he faced straight ahead as if he didn't see me there. Should I run back down the trail? Into the woods?

With strange men, my first impulse is to freeze, always. Mom taught me that when I was little. When I was about five, and we were taking an elevator way high, a man got on and said something I didn't understand. Mom shrank into herself, as quiet and tiny as a field mouse. *I'm not here, you don't see me.* I stayed quiet, too.

After that, I noticed she did the same thing when strange men approached her on the street or in the Metro. Later, I learned to freeze, too, whether men were catcalling me or just looking too hard. I was prey, hoping the predator would get distracted by something else.

But out here in the middle of nowhere, the boy wasn't going to get distracted. What, then? I staggered to a stop, my heart hammering and my bangs soaked with sweat.

The boy stopped, too. He was tall with a halo of pale blond curls—and now I recognized him from my Spanish class. *Thank God.* He always spent at least half the period on his phone without the teacher seeming to mind, so I'd assumed he was a grad student observer. Maybe he just wanted to say hello.

A voice from above yelled, "Celeste! Stop it, Bram!"

A girl perched in the fork of a pine with her bare legs dangling. She was wearing baggy shorts and a big T-shirt, so it took a moment to recognize Vivvy. Then I went limp with relief.

"Why are you acting like a weirdo? Are you trying to scare her?" she asked the boy, sliding easily down from the tree. "She's just trying to have a run, not collect a stalker."

The boy stood with his arms crossed, seeming not to enjoy eye contact any more than I did. "I'm not stalking anybody. I think I can take a run on land my family owns."

"You own it?" I asked stupidly, still panting.

"Yep." Now he did smile, but his gaze still didn't meet mine. "All the way up to the defile trailhead."

"Don't mind him. Everybody uses this path; we couldn't keep people off it if we tried." Vivvy picked her way down the bank, bending to scoop up an armful of prickly green boughs. "Bram, this is Celeste. She just moved here. Celeste, Bram is my twin brother. He's the genius in the family."

I could see the resemblance in their pale, downy hair and their twitchiness, but Vivvy was at least a foot shorter, and she had no trouble looking me in the eye. "Nice to meet you," I said.

Bram nodded. "I'm not actually a genius."

"We're going to green up our parents' graves," Vivvy said. "We do it a couple times a year. Want to come?"

Words stuck in my throat. I couldn't imagine losing both of my parents. "I—" I gestured up the path to indicate the urgency of my run, as if I were training for a marathon and not struggling to cover five K. "I'm so sorry."

"Now you're the one acting weird, Viv," Bram said. "You don't just invite somebody to meet your dead parents."

"Why don't you?" She cocked her head, not looking like a grieving person at all.

"She's going to think we're tragic orphans."

"We are tragic orphans."

"I'll come," I said, partly to stop the argument and partly because I was curious.

The cemetery was three blocks down the hill from the trailhead, within earshot of downtown traffic, surrounded by mossy stone walls and the severe bulk of a Lutheran church. I helped carry the evergreen boughs, which made me feel useful, though my hands were sticky with sap by the time I deposited them at the foot of a plain granite headstone. Jonathan Weston Kray and Jennifer Enright Kray, both dead for the past fifteen years.

"They went down in a plane over Lake Michigan," Vivvy said. "We don't remember them."

Bram let his branches fall to earth. "I do."

He spread out the boughs with stiff, careful motions. His sleeves were rolled up, his forearms tanned and strong, and again I felt that shock I'd experienced when he began running beside me. But he didn't seem like the pushy type, the "stalker" type, and that was a relief.

"He's always trying to convince me he remembers practically back to the womb." Vivvy bent and helped arrange the branches with a care that belied her casual tone. "I know this seems weird," she went on, "but in our family, cutting down the Christmas tree is the big ritual, and supposedly Dad proposed to Mom while they were hanging fir boughs over the mantel at his parents' house. They didn't like flowers because they die so quickly."

"Isn't that the point?" I tried not to look at Bram, but I couldn't ignore him, either. "I mean, the flowers go quickly because life does, right?"

"Memento mori." Finished with her arranging, Vivvy gestured for Bram to kneel beside her in the grass. I did, too.

She crossed her hands neatly in her lap and closed her eyes. "Um. Mom and Dad. I don't exactly pray, and I don't exactly know you, except in the way you know somebody whose flesh and bone and skin are part of yours. But I know I would have liked you, and sometimes in dreams, I hear your breathing inside of mine."

She went still for a moment, as if trying to hear it, and I was sure then her jauntiness was an act. She'd probably been trying to impress me because she thought I was a jaded city girl.

"Like a flame you lit in me," she finished. "Thanks."

She popped up, not waiting for us to follow. Her eyes had a brightness I remembered from our very first meeting at the locker, an intense focus like a herding dog's, as she asked, "Have you been to the roadhouse yet?"

Did roadhouses exist outside of old movies? I shook my head, feeling but not seeing Bram's grimace as he said, "Count me out."

"Nobody asked you, party pooper." She shot me a smile. "It's kind of retro and kind of pathetic, but you should come tonight."

I didn't realize it was an invitation until we parted ways and she called to me—Bram was already a block up the hill—"I'll pick you up at eight."

I started to give my address, but Vivvy said, "I know where you live. Everybody does. Do you know how long it's been since anybody new moved here?"

Walking home, I imagined eyes peering between the curtains of the ranch houses. How many other people in Kray's Defile had noticed me without saying a word?

Now

A slip of paper floats from my locker. Mint-green, hand-sized, scalloped on the bottom. Block printed with angry letters: *HE DOESN'T EVEN REALLY LIKE YOU, SLUT.*

I stare at the paper, my heart thudding as my eyes film over. The PA system crackles, something about an unscheduled assembly.

The words are cold fingers on my bare skin, creeping toward the bruises hidden under my clothes. I've never been called a slut before and never expected to be, given that I don't have anything to do with boys, but that's not the important thing.

Somebody found out. Someone knows *something*. Joss must have told. Unless Seth... but no, Seth isn't this petty, this jealous. After saying *he chose you*, he wouldn't call me that word. And the note isn't Vivvy's style at all.

As people laugh and shout and redirect each other, heading for the gym instead of first period, I listen for an undercurrent of whispers. *That's her.* I look for narrowed eyes sizing me up, cutting me down. *He could do so much better.*

Nothing. People look through me, just like in those first

weeks of school. I crumple the note in my fist, stuff it deep into my backpack, and follow the crowd.

The gym booms with voices. It takes me long minutes to get through the bottlenecked door, my palms moistening. I want to go somewhere and hide, but running away now will only make me stand out.

Inside, the din is worse. I can't find Vivvy, so I tramp up to the highest tier of the bleachers and find a seat near the end. Down on the gym floor, the county sheriff stands beside Vice Principal Caffrey. Vivvy's aunt is the undersheriff, and I recognize the sheriff by his short stature and his way of standing, like a spike planted belligerently into the ground.

As the last stragglers settle, Caffrey taps the microphone. In the back of my mind, a small voice keeps repeating, *Please don't look at me. I'm not a slut, I'm not, I'm not. I just . . .*

I tell myself I'm still looking for Vivvy, but okay, maybe really I'm scanning the crowd for Joss.

He isn't with his usual jock brigade, or with Sarah Blessingham and Halsey Halstead and the other powder-puff football girls where they huddle on the bottom tier. Halsey is glowering. Everyone in this room knows she and Joss used to sit together at every assembly—her snuggling close, arm around his waist, content as a cat with a full can of tuna. Not everyone knows why that changed.

Caffrey taps the mic a second time, and conversations bleed away. He clears his throat and introduces Sheriff Palmer.

Is it time for another lecture on just saying no to drugs (they rarely mention anything stronger than pot), or have more trophies been stolen from the case in the lobby? This school seemed so cute and retro once, but a slut-shaming note in a locker isn't a TV plotline. It's my life.

The sheriff keeps darting his head for emphasis, making his words cut in and out. "Small town...news spreads fast... wanted to inform you before..."

Where *is* Vivvy? And Joss? My hair hangs limp in my face, full of split ends.

"...passed away."

Something comes loose in my stomach. Confusion ripples through the crowd, people leaning over to whisper, "What did he say?" No one seems to have heard the entire sentence.

"Who?" another person asks.

"A student."

"Who?"

Caffrey grabs the mic. A thought forms in my head, solid as granite: *Please don't let it be Vivvy.*

"I regret to tell you the student whose remains were found yesterday was Joss Thorssen."

The room shifts, a photo rotated wrong, a nightmare of fluorescents reflected in raw, wet eyes. For an instant, they're just words, an idea, a possibility being tossed out into the universe: *What if Joss dies? How's that for a plot twist?*

Then it's real. The thread connecting me and Joss, the waiting-for-his-text thread, breaks. I feel it still attached to me, dangling in cold emptiness.

A girl in my row picks up a half-knitted scarf and holds it against her mouth, whimpering. Heat gathers behind my eyes, but part of me just freezes, too numb to feel anything yet, listening to the sheriff try to answer the questions people keep shouting at him from the bleachers. "Sunday afternoon," he says to one person. And to another, "Near the west entrance to Kray Cave."

That's where we were Saturday night. Wait, did Joss die *there*? Between Saturday night and Sunday afternoon? But how—?

Joss whistles behind the cedars, and his whistle splits the fabric of the world, fire and trees and sky. It splits me into two people, now and then. Before, I was watching; now I'm part of the story.

It's real. The gym pixelates and whites out as if my brain has a bad connection. My right thumb goes numb. I bow my head, cover my ears, and count to calm myself: *un, deux, trois, quatre.*

Sheriff Palmer is telling a thick-necked hockey player that no, he can't provide details, but yes, he believes they're dealing with a homicide. He pauses to give the word its full impact before urging anyone who was in or around the cave entrance on Saturday night to come to the office, where his team will be stationed all day. He reminds us that Fish and Wildlife has posted the cave off-limits. Then Caffrey is back at the mic, talking about condolences and grief counseling and how Joss was an amazing athlete and human being, and the words flow through me and out the other side.

All I can think about is the chamois shirt hanging from my closet doorknob—how it felt (*soft like his lips*), how it smelled (*sweet like weed*). How I meant to bring it to him today, but I didn't.

Almost like I already knew.

Then

The roadhouse was ten minutes from town over the bleakest roads in the world, so much rolling yellow grass on either side, the asphalt felt like a mirage. Kray's Defile itself was small and safe-feeling and pure nostalgia, but the Big Sky stole my breath, spinning me into smoke and wind. I wasn't sure I could live with this much space, so I hunched myself tight.

Being with Vivvy, though, made me want to unfold. She was so *here*. I tried to focus on everything she was telling me: how the town was named after her family, because her ancestor, Josiah Kray, had explored the nearby defile in the 1800s. How she worshipped Edna St. Vincent Millay, Dorothy Parker, and Flannery O'Connor and took wardrobe cues from them. How Flannery O'Connor once described a car as "rat-brown," and that was why Vivvy bought the vintage Chevrolet Impala we were driving in—it was that exact color.

Shayna's Hi-Life Roadhouse was half diner and half bar, though it looked more like a barn from outside. Inside, the whole dusty room teemed with twinkling fairy lights, moth-eaten animal heads, and novelty signs. The regulars at the bar wore sturdy coveralls and cowboy hats. From our booth by a shuttered window, I smelled them—acrid tobacco, horsey mustiness.

Normally I'd be nervous around these grizzled men, but Vivvy acted like we were in her living room. When the server arrived, she ordered a Sidecar.

"Nope, Viv. Unless you want it virgin."

Vivvy leaned forward, elbows on the table. "Pretty please, Rayette. I want to impress my new friend. She's from the city."

"Uh-huh." Broad-hipped, cowboy-booted, all attitude, Rayette turned to me. "Hon?"

The word "friend" pinked my cheeks. "A coffee, please."

"Make it two. Lots of creamers." As Rayette vanished, Vivvy scrubbed her fingers through her short hair. "There goes my attempt to be cool."

"This place is cool enough," I said.

"I know it's dead now, but wait. Everybody comes here after the game."

"Game of what?" There'd been a line of cars at the stoplight when Vivvy picked me up.

"Football. Hockey season doesn't start till October, but it's mostly the same crowd. Okay, so which city are you from? Were you there your whole life?"

"How'd you know I'm from a city?"

"Your clothes. The scarves especially."

I hadn't realized it was so obvious. "Montreal, and yeah." Images and sensations came in a rush: canals flashing past as I pedaled my bike, snow-covered spiral staircases. Musty classrooms, dressing rooms, backstages. Clammy leggings, stinging snow, fear.

"Oh my God, for real? You're not even American? Do you speak French?"

I gave her the whole spiel: My mom spoke English, my dad spoke French, I spoke both, they'd been divorced forever with joint custody, and my dad had a job at MSU studying the local bat colony.

"Oh, the bats in the cave. It's right up the hill from my house, but we're not allowed to go in there since the state got all excited about them."

"Yeah, he said some locals had issues with that." Specifically, Dad said the inhabitants of Kray's Defile liked to use the cave-riddled interior of the mountain as "their own personal taproom and toilet." But I didn't want to bore Vivvy with my dad's strong opinions about the fragility of cave ecosystems, so I was relieved when the ambient noise swelled to a roar.

A crowd of high schoolers was wedging the door open and spilling into the dining area. They blocked my view of the bar with their broad shoulders, letter jackets, streaky-blond pony-tails, arms trailing around waists and dipping into pockets.

Go still. Blend in.

Vivvy didn't seem perturbed. She clearly wasn't hearing the voices I heard in every whisper or shrieky laugh: *Oh my God, what's she wearing? Have you ever seen her smile?*

"See her over there?" Vivvy stirred in the extra half-and-half Rayette had brought her.

I reminded myself I was the observer now, not the observed. "Who?"

Aside from my lab partner, Sarah Blessingham, I couldn't tell the newcomers apart: pert girls, beefy boys. They moved as if glimmering pathways in the air guided their every gesture, like they never had to wonder *Do I walk wrong? Sit wrong? Is my laugh too loud? Is my smile too goofy? Too inviting? Should I just STOP?*

"That's Halsey," Vivvy said, still discreetly pointing. "Her real name's Melinda Halstead—Joss's girlfriend."

I pushed away a shred of disappointment—of course Joss Thorssen had a girlfriend—and examined the compact bottle-blond talking to Sarah. While Sarah dripped sweetness, this one had a laugh that made my skin crawl.

"If this were a TV show, he'd be with Sarah," Vivvy said. "She's junior class treasurer, born again, volunteers with Meals on Wheels. But Sarah's a pushover. Halsey knows how to get what she wants."

I nodded. There's nice-popular and mean-popular. They tend to pair up so the second kind can do the first kind's dirty work.

Vivvy indicated a broader girl, almost stocky, with a husky, authoritative voice. "And that's Halsey's friend Cammy, the Rizzo of the group."

"You know *Grease*?"

"Oh God, yes. Musical, not movie, please."

I filed away the info that it was safe to reference musicals with Vivvy. "What are those weird uniforms they're all wearing? With the hair ribbons?"

"Powder-puff football. It's what you do when you're popular but not acrobatic enough for cheer. Sporty but want to emphasize that you're cute."

I wished she'd lower her voice, but no one seemed to notice. A few of the girls sang out, "Hey, Vivvy!" and Vivvy sang, "Hey!" right back. I tensed, but no one stopped to chat or asked who I was. With my frowzy black hair, heavy eyelids, and thick brows, I might not belong in their world even as an outcast—an oddly freeing thought.

Somebody put a dance mix on the jukebox. A sly-faced, lanky, redheaded boy grabbed Rayette, twirled her, and pulled her into a dip. She swatted him with a whisk broom.

Halsey yelled, "Oh yeah, Tan! Work it! Maybe she'll give you a beer."

"Tanner McKeough." Vivvy sipped her coffee. "He's our starting right wing. One of Joss's besties, and Halsey's second cousin or something. Kind of a dick, but he brings the drama, and this crowd needs that."

She indicated a burly, mop-headed boy. "Gibsy, the goalie. The unintentional comic relief."

"Is Joss here?" I ventured.

"Not yet. But look who is."

This time her gaze flew over the heads of the rancher barflies to a pair of flickery neon signs that said STALLIONS and FILLIES. A slight figure slouched there, arms crossed tightly. Seth Larkin.

"Is he friends with these people?"

"Friends?" Vivvy said. "Try supplier."

"Drugs?" I wasn't sure I wanted to know. Criminal or not, Seth was the person in the room I felt most akin to.

"Just weed, I think. He gets it from some creep who works at the meatpacking plant in Brickerville. Everybody here buys from Seth."

She sounded so breezy, I wondered if she bought from Seth, too. Then I noticed her pinkie tapping her coffee mug, a nervous metronome, and I knew the casualness was just an act. Maybe she wasn't like me, but she wasn't like them, either.

"Vivvy, hey!"

"Hey, Celeste!"

Astonished that Sarah remembered my name, I smiled as hard as I could. She was with two girls Vivvy hadn't bothered to ID, all of them in the periwinkle-blue powder-puff uniforms, all talking at once:

"Have you looked at the homework yet, Vivvy?"

"Did you miss the game?"

"Oh my God, epic takedown. Brickerville's *bleeding*."

After what felt like a hectic five seconds of conversation, they all turned in a flurry of skirts and sang their goodbyes. They hadn't said anything that wasn't 100 percent nice, but my palms had gone clammy. My eyes flitted to the restroom signs—Seth had vanished.

Kids kept coming in, the door still wedged open by bodies. I muttered, "Right back," and made my way past the bar to the Fillies' restroom.

At least there was no line yet, no tittering in the stalls. I splashed cold water on my face. Would Vivvy hate me if I asked to go somewhere else?

She wasn't like these people, she borderline-mocked them, yet she didn't seem scared they'd see the difference and turn on her. Maybe it was a small-town thing. But small towns always have scapegoats and pariahs, don't they?

The restrooms occupied a corridor off a small foyer that led to the roadhouse's back door. Crypt-deep voices from the foyer stopped me in my tracks.

"What the fuck, Thorssen. You meet a bear?"

"Halsey get rough during a special moment?"

Guffaws. And then a softer, abashed laugh that I somehow knew was Joss.

I pressed my back against the wall of the corridor so they couldn't see me but I could half see them. Broad shoulders in letter jackets plus a piece of ratty carpeting and a cigarette machine that was probably installed in the 1970s.

They were all so big. Athletes. Town heroes. Man-sized boys who could get away with anything.

"I went in the hole for my stuff and tripped coming out." Joss's tenor voice again. "Busted my eyebrow."

"Looks like you got coldcocked," one boy said.

"Ah, he *tripped*," another said in a mocking whine. "Tough to walk in high heels, huh?"

"Cut it out, Gibsy." That was Tanner again.

I inched toward the foyer as Tanner lifted Joss's chin, holding his face into the light. "That cave, she keeps kicking your ass, man," he said with a weird solemnity. "Better learn to respect her, proxy boy."

"Fuck you, McKeough."

As Joss shoved Tanner away, I finally saw what they were all looking at. A lattice of Band-Aids above Joss's right eyebrow didn't quite cover the edges of a nasty gash. A bruise glowed on the same temple.

He's not perfect. He can be hurt.

Ice prickled down my thighs, followed by a flush of heat. I looked away and wanted to look back, the same way I'd felt in class when Joss knelt in front of Seth. My own temple throbbed gently as I imagined raising my hand to Joss's face and dabbing the dried blood away.

"I just think it's funny that the only fights you get in are with rocks," Tanner said. "Hit of Jim Beam?"

Brandishing a flask, he led his friends past me into the main room. I froze, but they didn't look at me, except for Joss. When I raised my eyes, his lips were curved in a faint smile.

"Thanks for that thing yesterday," he said.

Before I could think of a reply, he grinned—not a mean grin—and vanished with the rest of them.

And I was left alone in the ugly little foyer that still smelled like them: weed, musty basement, liquor, and sweat, sour and sweet at once.

Now

As we shuffle out of the assembly, the businesslike tromping of hiking boots drowns out the sniffling. Sarah Blessingham sits on the lowest tier of bleachers with a boy's head in her lap, stroking his hair.

Where's Vivvy? My legs carry me automatically toward first-period physics—past the admin offices, where Sheriff Palmer now stands blocking the doorway, deep in conversation with the principal.

Students give him a wide berth, some freshmen skittering comically close to the wall. Small as he is, the sheriff has a way of looking at you as if you're a cockroach, making you draw in your shoulders and avert your eyes.

He beckons to someone in the crowd, and for an ice-cold moment I think he means me. But then I see Halsey trudge toward him, pretty and heart-faced and scowling like she's mentally debating the option of shattering his tibia and making a run for it. Not exactly the face of a grieving girlfriend, but then, she and Joss haven't been together since October.

The sheriff extends his arm, ushering Halsey into the offices. I turn my eyes to the wall and keep walking.

Halsey's bitch face has jogged the memory of the note in my locker. *Someone knows something.*

Someone could tell, which means Vivvy, Seth, and I should come clean. We need to go to the office and tell Palmer we were with Joss outside the cave on Saturday night, and why. I should do it right now, but I *can't*, not alone, because I don't know how to describe what happened. I don't know how to say it in words the sheriff will understand.

For now I just want to sit in physics and stare at the soapstone counter and let its light-absorbent blackness absorb me, too. But there are eyes on me, and when I turn and see one of Joss's friends, I freeze.

Freezing, always freezing, whenever they get too close or look at me wrong—drawing myself in tight and pretending nothing's happening. Not boldly meeting their eyes, not asking what they want, not doing a clever song and dance to keep them at arm's length, just going numb. It never really helps at all, but here I am doing it again, as Joss's friend plunks down beside me and says, "Shit, are you okay? Can't believe it."

He's a big, rangy hockey player with shaving scars and raw red eyes. Patrick something, someone I've never spoken to in my life. His huge hand closes on top of mine, and if I could, I'd jump up and run.

I don't know you. What does he think? What has he heard?

Patrick must sense my terror, because he releases my hand. "It's gonna be okay," he says. "They talk to you yet?"

The sheriff. A cold hand squeezes my throat and jams my breath. "No." I exhale for four-count, then try to make my voice sad but not *too* sad. "I didn't know Joss all that well. I only came here in August. What about you?"

"Wait. Weren't you guys, I dunno…kinda together or something?"

My right thumb and pinkie have gone numb. It takes me a moment to gather myself, to remember everything I learned in acting workshop, and to look Patrick in the eye. "No. We never even really hung out. We were just getting to know each other." *Despite what that note says.*

Whoever wrote the note felt like they had a claim on Joss. It could be Halsey, for sure, or one of a dozen girls with crushes on him. It could even be Seth, *maybe*. It wasn't Patrick, but if he thinks we were "together," who else does?

He looks confused. "You're the French girl, right? The one who sang that song in French?"

He's talking about the *Les Mis* audition. My right hand hurts; I look down and realize I'm gripping it with the left, digging short nails into the webbing between thumb and forefinger.

"Joss really liked your singing. And at the Halloween party, I thought—"

I interrupt, trying to sound sympathetic and detached at the same time. "Joss was always really sweet to me. I can't believe he's gone. But there wasn't anything like that."

Part of me is still in denial, telling me Joss is up there hiding behind the cedars, playing a trick on us all. But the other part of me, the calculating, frozen part, knows I'm in grave danger.

If Joss told his friends where he was going Saturday night, soon we'll all be hauled into the sheriff's office. I can already see the disgust mixed with titillation that would crinkle Sheriff Palmer's eyes if he heard about spin the bottle and everyone kissing, and the disbelief that would narrow them as I told him about the black hole in my memory.

I'm done with letting old men ask me questions about my sex life. Done forever.

"But..." Patrick looks confused.

Mr. Portman switches on the SMART Board and raises his arms like an orchestra conductor, commanding our silence.

"So, you and Joss, you really weren't, like...close?"

You don't really know anything. You don't. I shake my head. He keeps staring at me, and I stare back, frozen again.

Once, in Montreal, as we walked past an enormous, lit-up ice sculpture, Frank said to me, "You could live in there. Princess of a frozen castle."

That's me right now: frigid. Here in my castle of ice, where I can pretend I'm safe, I'll go over everything that happened, everything that led to today, until I figure out what to do.

"Celeste?" Patrick is whispering now. "You okay?"

I nod, then shake my head. "We weren't close. No."

But he won't be the only one asking questions, and I can't stay frozen forever. If someone points a finger at me and says I killed Joss, I need to be ready to tell everyone what really happened.

Then

know Joss just got there," Vivvy said in the car, pulling out of the roadhouse lot, "but I couldn't take game night a second longer."

"Same here." Relief flooded me, along with a traitorous hint of disappointment, because Joss was still back there. Joss had told me thank you.

"Before we were so rudely interrupted, I wanted to ask you something. Why didn't you stay with your mom instead of moving to a dump like Kray's?"

My hand went instinctively to my phone. Sixty-eight days had passed since the last text from Frank.

There was no way to tell her I couldn't be in the same city with a man, a grown man, who claimed to love me. Who thought I owed him something because he'd built up an image of me in his head. *You remind me of a depressive Chekhov heroine.* I couldn't explain to anyone how hard it was, when you met that person on the street, not to start becoming the thing he wanted you to be.

So I said, "I want to go to college in the States"—*the very best college, far, far from home*—"and my parents thought being here would help. Plus, my mom's always getting new boyfriends, and I'm kind of done with that."

"Your mom sounds like my Aunt Valerie. She's dated practically every eligible person in town, and that's *person*, as in all genders. She just likes dating."

"That's so weird," I said, and then realized that came out wrong. "I mean, not liking people of all genders. Liking dating."

"The part *I* think is weird is liking people, period. I mean, not that I hate people, but I'm very selective."

"Me too, I guess." Warmth in my cheeks. Was she trying to tell me I should feel lucky she'd selected me? I did, but it made me wonder what she wanted in return.

"Val just thinks all people are fascinating. She even had a thing with the mayor, and he's super old and gross."

Now I knew why I felt safe being open with Vivvy; she was one of those people who liked to be the biggest sharer in the room. "Beware of gut spillers," my dad told me once. "They'll spill your secrets, too."

But I was up for the risk. Talking about myself gave me a dizzy rush, like turning in circles under the big sky.

"You saw Joss in there, right?" I asked. "Did you see his bruises?"

She gasped. "What bruises? He was too far away, and Halsey was all over him. Tell me!"

I told her everything I'd seen and heard, including Tanner

42

McKeough's taunting. "He called Joss 'proxy boy.' Does that mean anything?"

"Maybe it's a hockey thing." Vivvy shot me a birdlike glance. "They get bruised up all the time, but you think this was different?"

"Maybe." I told her what Tanner had said about the cave, implying Joss hurt himself in there. "I thought Fish and Wildlife posted it."

"Like they care. If they want to get wasted in the cave, they'll get wasted in the cave. And Joss lives right down the hill from the entrance." Her voice was tight with excitement, and it made something fizz inside my own chest. "Want to see?"

⸻

We surveyed Joss's house from behind a giant juniper bush, surrounded by the keening of late-summer cicadas.

It wasn't like he was in it. We weren't stalking him.

The house stood weathered and unpainted: three modest floors, a front porch, and a slate roof. Behind it, the mountains hulked, enormous against the darkness. The Ford F-150 in the dirt driveway sported a gun rack.

"Joss's truck is way older," Vivvy whispered. "A pickup. See the attic? That's his room. Not what you expected, right?"

I peered up at an oily reflection that might have been a window. "Not really."

"Things have been rough since his dad died." Vivvy wrapped her arms around her knees. "Mr. Thorssen was the county sheriff back before my aunt Val got there. When Joss was little, his dad gave him a ram's-head belt buckle because Joss is an Aries, and now he always wears one. He has, like, ten identical buckles."

To get here, we'd walked a quarter mile straight uphill from the highest paved street of Kray's Defile—Vivvy's street, she said—using scrubby bushes as cover. Below us winked the grid of the town. Above, yellow grass sloped upward to the jagged mammoths on the horizon.

Hollow mountains, full of pitch-dark passages and bats. *That cave, she keeps kicking your ass, man.*

All evening I'd been avoiding the topic of Joss and Seth. Vivvy had put the image of them kissing in my head when we first met, and if she went there again, I might blush so hard she'd think I was actually obsessed with them.

But now, as we crouched there like a pair of spies, I didn't care. "So, I mean, is there an actual reason Seth acted like that in class? Did something happen with the two of them?"

Vivvy kept her eyes on the house. "When we were in middle school," she said, "this bully Nate Carlsson went after Seth, and Joss decked him. It was pretty spectacular, blood and everything. After that, I'd see Joss and Seth together on the jogging path. We'd all hang out. I think maybe Seth was selling Joss weed, but they never smoked when I was there. I never saw them together anywhere but the woods, and then I stopped seeing them."

"Did they have a fight?"

She shrugged, like the story made her tired and sad. "No idea. I was never really friends with them individually. Just in that one place, together."

"And is Seth actually..."

Bang! A door slammed open. Footsteps thudded on the splintery wood of the porch.

I flattened myself to the earth. Beside me, Vivvy curled into a ball.

A broad-shouldered, slightly bowlegged man strode across the yard, beneath a floodlight, into a shed. He emerged with a clinking six-pack and grunted his way back up the porch steps.

"That's the stepdad," Vivvy said after the door closed behind him. "Let's go back to the car."

We crept back down the hill to the little park where Vivvy had parked the Impala. She cranked her window wide, and air whooshed in as she drove the three blocks to my house.

"I could afford a better car than this," she said. "When Mom and Dad died, I got their trust. But I suffer for style. Anyway, to answer your implied question, yes, Seth likes guys. He told me that much when Joss wasn't around. He also told me he doesn't expect to do much about it till college, because the pickings are slim in the Defile."

"I can see how that would be." I knew how Seth felt, waiting for his real life to start. "So, Joss's stepdad. Do you think he could have...?" I imagined the bowlegged man cuffing Joss on the temple, knocking him sideways. *The only fights you get in are with rocks.*

"Joss could kick his ass. But maybe. I'm skeptical of the cave story."

"His friends were joking about Halsey hurting him in the heat of passion." The phrase made me blush; why was I such a prude?

Vivvy snorted, rolling to a stop in front of my rental ranch house. "She'd hurt him, all right. But she'd probably scratch her name on his back with her nails to claim him."

I cringed. "You don't like her."

"I don't care one way or the other about Queen Halsey Halstead. I'm just a student of human nature. Check this out." She scrolled on her phone and thrust a photo in my face: Halsey and Joss in a locker room, him dressed for hockey and her in the powder-puff flippy skirt. Halsey had an arm wrapped around Joss's waist, gazing adoringly at him. Joss had a spacey smile, his attention drifting out of frame. "Happy couple, huh?"

"He doesn't look too into her," I conceded, opening the car door. She was probing me, gauging my response—my skin itched with it. "Why do you have that?"

"Because I fantasize about Joss."

I turned back but couldn't see her expression, only her shrug as she went on. "I mean, duh, I already basically told you. And I'm not embarrassed, because having fantasies is normal and totally different from acting on them—which I don't, by the way. Sexually, I mean. Not yet. I'm still figuring all that out."

Something about this speech made my throat go dry. I'd never heard a girl my age admit she didn't have "it" figured out already.

The only way I knew to be safe was to keep myself in lock-down, a princess sealed in ice. But when Seth called Joss out in front of the class, I'd felt heat roiling inside me, seeking escape. Whether that heat had to do with Seth or Joss or both of them, I didn't know, but now I wondered if it was okay just to feel it. *Fantasy. Not real.*

Imagine feeling okay to feel.

"I'm figuring it out, too." I slid out of the car so I wouldn't have to meet her gaze.

As I crossed our gauntlet of whispering cottonwoods, Vivvy called, "I can tell we're going to be friends."

Now

All morning I've been looking for Vivvy. Suddenly, at my locker after third period, there she is, her tiny fingers firm around my wrist and her gray-green eyes fixed on me. "Has Sheriff Palmer called you in?"

The halls are still reverberating with grief and gossip and speculation, shock waves moving outward, but no one else has assailed me the way Patrick did in physics. I shake my head.

Vivvy mouths, "Outside."

It's lunch hour, so we slip behind the big juniper bush on the edge of the unofficial smokers' area, shivering against a stiff breeze.

We look at each other, and then we're both really shaking. Her image blurs.

"How?" Because of her aunt being the undersheriff, Vivvy often knows things before other people do. "How did it happen? Have you heard anything?"

Her voice seems to come in fractured pieces like the sheriff's through the bad mic, only it's because she's trembling. Or because I am. "Someone hit him—just once, they think, and not that hard. But sometimes that's enough."

I raise my hand to my right cheek. The one I sometimes slap hard enough to sting. "How long have you known? Since yesterday? Vivvy, I was waiting for him to text this whole time."

Vivvy's eyes fill with tears. It's only the second time I've seen her cry. "I should've called you," she says. "I'm so sorry. I heard yesterday night, but after that I just couldn't..."

She looks like she might fall, so I wrap my arms around her and let her hide her face against my sweater. "I know. I know."

While she wipes her eyes and catches her breath, I decide not to tell her about the note. It might freak her out, and it could be a coincidence, a case of bad timing, nothing to do with Saturday night. It could even be meant for someone else.

"We should trash all our stories," Vivvy says when her voice is steady again. "Delete everything. If you have hard copies, burn them."

"What are a bunch of stories going to prove?" Delete and burn my Joss/Seth stories? I wrote them. *We* wrote them. You don't just snap your fingers and annihilate a fic-verse.

Vivvy looks quickly to the right and left. "They prove we were fixated on him."

"Everybody was fixated on Joss. Anyway, people saw us with him." Patrick, for instance. "At your Halloween party."

She blows her nose. "The whole town was at my party."

"I know." Joss told Patrick things, though. "Do you think Joss could have told anybody where he was going Saturday?"

"No! His friends think we're lame. *We* didn't even know if he'd show."

Funny to hear her say that now, because she'd always insisted he would. In class last Thursday, she mentioned to Joss we'd be up at the cave mouth on Saturday with a couple of bottles of "vintage liqueurs." To hear Vivvy tell it, he said, "Cool, I'm there," but I had my doubts. Joss was just off crutches after his Halloween injury, and the hill is a hike.

On Saturday, we walked up from town as light faded in the west—my arms full of blankets and my duffel; Vivvy with the liquor bottles and a thermos of tea for each of us; and Seth with the firewood. We built a fire, and Vivvy opened a bottle of throat-scorching booze she'd pinched from her ancestral stash in the cellar.

And then we waited.

When Joss arrived, well after dark, things were awkward at first. I remember wondering if he was only there because his team was playing a home game and he couldn't bear to watch from the stands. Or because he knew Seth would have weed.

Spin the bottle wasn't his idea. We'd all drunk way too much by the time that started, except for Vivvy.

"Someone could have seen us up there," I point out. Only a few people live on the slope, but it's treeless until you reach the cliffs, as exposed as a stage.

"No one's reported it yet." Vivvy knocks on the wall of the school, though it's concrete. "We'll deal with that when it happens. *If.* I'll monitor as well as I can via Val. So far, they know Joss was up there with the fire, but that's it. We'll talk to Seth. He won't say anything."

Seth. I've barely had time to think about him. "There was so much weirdness between them." I haven't forgotten how Seth flinched when Joss first touched him, even though he knew that was the plan, sort of.

"Seth left first, Celeste." Vivvy looks right at me. "As far as we know, *you* were the last person with you-know-who."

Suddenly I'm shivering harder than the November chill justifies. "You know I'd never hurt J—you-know-who. Or anyone."

Vivvy's narrow face goes intent, like when she's thinking out the next plot development in a story. "I know that. I just—we have to think about this like cops, okay? Just the facts. Yesterday, why'd you take so long to text me back?"

"I was waiting for Joss to text me." I'm suddenly very aware of my hands, one clutching a pen and the other fiddling with the scarf that hides the hickeys Joss left on my neck.

These hands have turned Joss into fiction without his permission. They've wandered all over his body and stroked his chamois shirt. Under my clothes are bruises he may have left there, and in my brain is a black hole that may never be filled.

These hands have slapped my own cheeks, releasing the pent-up stress of my body, but they didn't hurt Joss. I know that.

Vivvy reaches out and clasps my pen hand. "I'm just saying, be careful. You're so weird sometimes, Celeste, the way you just seem absent. And people notice."

Tears build, a painful tightening between my eyes. It's not the first time she's said things like this; once, she told me I reminded her of a house with all the lights off during an air raid. An inhabited house impersonating an empty one.

"Fine, then. I'm on my own with this."

"That's not what I mean!" She grasps both of my hands now, looking up into my eyes. "You left him up there having a smoke, and that's the last time you saw him, and you're telling the truth. I *know* that."

"Maybe I should tell the sheriff. Maybe we should go together." Much as I hate the idea, Sheriff Palmer knows Vivvy. He trusts her.

But the moment the words are out, I can see she thinks I've gone off the deep end. Her face is pale and pinched, horrified. "Val would be so pissed off at me," she says. "And can you imagine explaining what happened, Celeste? All of it?"

"Okay," I say. "Okay, you're right. I don't want to do that, either."

She releases her breath and says in a small voice, "We'll talk to Seth. That's what we'll do."

We plan to meet in the woods after school. She'll slip a note in Seth's locker, leaving no digital footprints, and we'll stagger our arrivals so we aren't seen together. I try to appreciate these elaborate precautions, so very Vivvy, and not to think about what will happen if she finds out that my story—the story I told so well that I almost believe it myself—is a lie.

The black hole in my head seems to expand with every minute that passes, the air screaming around it, the world disappearing inside. I need to fill that void in my head where the rest of Saturday night should be, and I need to do it by myself. Vivvy is a good writing partner, but this story is mine.

Then

The day I wrote my first story was the same day I got a new text from Frank, after hoping that was over for good.

One word from you would mean the world.

I deleted the text and wedged the phone between the couch cushions, my hands ice-cold. Pressure rose in my head, and I felt a thread tugging at me, a connection I thought was severed. *How can you ignore someone who loves you? What if nobody ever loves you again?*

Though Frank was nearly two thousand miles away, I rose to close the curtains. Paced back and forth, hugging myself, feeling that *need* mount in my head, that tightness desperate for release, and then, before I knew it, I was slapping my own cheek.

Not hard, never hard enough to bruise, but the sting was as clean and blissful as a glass of ice water. The pressure started to bleed away. I did it again, and as I raised my hand for a third, my dad's Civic rumbled down the street. *Thank God.*

Dad strolled in from the garage, loud as always, like he

half expected to catch me at something, which he never would. "Hello, hello!"

A woman followed. Younger, with long black hair, wearing jeans and one of those chamois shirts everyone seemed to own here. Dad overenunciated his English words as he introduced her: "Celeste, this is Amy Elder. She monitors endangered mammals for Fish and Wildlife, such as our bats."

Amy had a firm handshake. "So you're the actress."

"That's something I used to do. I'm thinking about finance now." Specifically, I wanted to make enough money to own and live in my own private sanctuary for rescue animals, but that would sound childish.

"But you're still in high school? I would've guessed junior in college."

"Yup." Ever since I turned twelve and shot up to my current height, adults had been astonished I wasn't one of them.

I used to like it. I was flattered when Frank thought I was over eighteen. "But you're so mature," he'd insist. "So brilliant. Such a quiet composure about you."

I wore clothes that would stand out at those acting workshops— a red dress, or a black tank top with spaghetti straps, or tall black boots. After years of hiding at school, I was trying out something, I guess. The college boys glanced at me and quickly away, as if I were a dissected frog. Frank kept looking.

He rarely paid special attention to me in class, in front of the others—he was too smart for that, I see now. But when we met by chance at a Pre-Raphaelite exhibit at the Museum of Fine

Arts, he followed me through the halls, talking and talking. He insisted on buying me lunch.

In his mind, I think, we were close to the same age—starting out in life, sensitive and vulnerable. In his mind, he wasn't as old as my mom's boyfriends, or nearly as old as my father.

Even back then, I thought I understood the whole situation better than he did. Aside from class time, I really spent only one afternoon and one evening with him—trapped by his eyes and his smile and his attention, forced to wait till he was done. Like a princess under a spell, I knew what he was doing was wrong and I didn't want it, but how do you say no to someone loving you when you don't know if that'll ever happen again, your whole life?

Vivvy would have said no anyway. Vivvy would've laughed in his face—and thinking about her felt good, like a firm hand in mine.

Dad ducked into the kitchen and returned carrying a wine bottle. "Celeste, I'm headed over to Amy's apartment so I can teach her what a *vrai* decent merlot tastes like. Back by eleven. Would you mind holding down the fort?"

Same phrase he used whenever he disappeared in the evenings. My dad was nothing if not consistent.

I did mind this time, because of Frank's text, but I smiled at Amy. She'd asked Dad about me—he wouldn't have told her all that on his own. She must like him.

As their laughing voices faded into the garage, I wondered what she saw in him. A French-accented Jewish Canadian with romantic dark eyes? A sophisticated professor? Maybe she liked hard-core bat nerds with strict rules about what you were supposed to do in caves.

What she probably didn't know yet was that if you were a human being and not a bat, my dad would notice your existence only up to a point. Over the years, he's asked me now and then if I have a boyfriend, as if I were a normal girl with killer makeup skills and friends to text with and a selfie gallery. Every time I said, "Not yet," but I wanted to throw up or cry.

Alone, I flipped through the channels while scrolling on my phone. Shiny dishes. Turbo-moms in clean kitchens. A cartoon bat flopping haplessly until antidepressants turned it into a happy bluebird. Men with guns. Girls selling jewelry. Men with gavels.

A text message popped up from Vivvy. *I hate texting. We should never text.*

I typed some *Ha ha, I'm dead* emojis. But no, she was testing me to see if I was worthy of a real conversation. I deleted the emojis. *Call me, then.*

Bram's right here. Awkward. So, you think Seth noticed Joss at the roadhouse last night? Those bruises?

Before I could reply, she did it herself. *This is going to sound weird, but I can't stop thinking about Seth seeing Joss all bruised and then feeling guilty about how he went off on Joss in English class.*

I tried to make it into a joke. *Maybe he offered Joss a first aid kit.* ☺

Heh. Oh God, now I can't get that image out of my head.

Heat rose in my face and chest, because now I saw it,

too—Seth swabbing Joss's temple with a warm rag. Gently, the way I wanted to.

I doubt that's actually what happened.

Let me have my fantasy. ☺

I wasn't sure I agreed with Vivvy that fantasies could be safely separated from reality. But things I myself couldn't physically do, like be a boy kissing another boy—maybe it was a little safer to fantasize about those.

As soon as I set the phone back down to focus on the TV, it started buzzing with a call, and my right thumb went numb the way it always did when something triggered my anxiety. Was it Vivvy after all, or was Frank calling me now?

Neither. Just Mom from Montreal with a million questions.

How was school? How was Dad? Was the town really that small? Why didn't I post more pictures? How'd I been sleeping?

"Eight hours a night." I grabbed the laptop and checked for new texts, but Vivvy had gone silent. Maybe she was embarrassed.

"No chest pains?" Mom asked.

"No."

"Does it feel better not to be acting anymore?"

Focused on the computer screen, I took a moment to hear the question, but then it hit me like a wrecking ball out of a blue sky. She thought acting was the problem. She thought *I* was the problem.

"How do you know I'm not acting?" My voice turned mean. "Maybe I'm trying out for all the plays."

Mom always talked about acting as if it were a dangerous addiction. Too big, too loud, too many feelings—which was exactly why I loved it. Onstage, I had permission to laugh, to shout, to shriek, to cry, to flirt, whatever the script and director ordered. No holds barred. No consequences. So I used to think, anyway.

"I guess I assumed," Mom said meekly.

"You shouldn't assume things."

And we went on like that, my voice hard and nasty and hers sweet and calm and understanding.

Here's why I always understood that Frank was trouble: My sweet mom's life has been one Frank after another. When she was my age, she "dated" her high school teacher—her word. He brought her flowers. "I know now he was abusing me," she said when she told me this story. "But back then, we didn't have the words. Things were tough for me at home. I thought I was escaping. I thought I was in love."

That was my first clue that love could be dangerous.

I never thought I was in love with Frank. I don't know if it was fear or curiosity or something worse, like wanting the attention, but when I was around him, I just couldn't seem to move away.

"I wish you'd tell me why you're so upset. It was just a question. I'm here, Celeste. I'm listening."

For a second, I wanted to tell her everything, but that would be like stabbing her in the gut. She'd told me the story about her teacher so I'd know better, the way any good mom would. But when I was put to the test, I reacted exactly the way she had.

So I apologized to her, and we said stiff, nice things the way we usually did these days, and we hung up. I checked my texts again. Nothing.

My cheek itched. That pressure built in my head, and I needed somewhere to put the want-to-smash-things I felt when I thought about Mom and Frank and me and how I should have been better, stronger. Laughed at him. Been more like Vivvy.

I started a new message. *Sorry, Mom just called. God, I'm sick of her. I came here to get away and I still—*

No. I held down the delete key and watched the lines disappear, along with the inconvenient questions they might raise.

Instead, I opened a Google doc and wrote a title: "First Aid." And then I wrote a story.

I started out typing fast, eager to fire off something to Vivvy, but when I realized the story was going to be longer than a few paragraphs, I slowed down. As if the story were a sweltering summer evening and I had to be careful not to move too fast, or the heat might rise from my chest to my face and paint me a telltale red.

Drop by drop, the pressure bled out of me.

Seth swung open the door of the roadhouse john and froze. Joss Thorssen was bent over the sink, looking at himself in the mirror.

It was Friday evening, but the game rush hadn't arrived yet. The two of them were alone.

Seth almost turned to leave. These days, he did his best to ignore Joss and his jock friends, and Joss ignored him right back.

But that afternoon in class, when Joss had started reciting the Shakespeare monologue like a robot, Seth couldn't take it anymore. Joss was messing with him somehow, he just knew it. And he'd lashed out.

"How's it hangin', asshole?" he growled now. He was about to add a mocking "Putting your face on?" when he saw what Joss was actually examining in the mirror.

A jagged, bloody gash across his eyebrow. Above it, a bruise on his temple.

"Get a good look," Joss muttered.

"What happened?" The snark had bled out of Seth's voice.

"None of your goddamn business." Joss's eyes were empty.

Seth opened his backpack. "I got first aid stuff. Let me clean that before it gets infected."

He was pretty sure the bruise came from a blow, not a fall. His mom had a boyfriend once who was a mean bastard, so he could tell the difference.

But who could have kicked the ass of the crown prince of Crap Reviled High (his private name for it)? Joss had no enemies, unless Nate Carlsson was still pissed at him for that day back in grade seven when Joss practically broke Nate's nose to stop him from bullying Seth.

Seth hadn't thought of that day in ages.

"You carry a first aid kit?" Joss asked incredulously. But he leaned back against the counter so Seth could reach the wound.

"My mom's a nurse's aide, remember?"

Seth squeezed Neosporin onto a piece of gauze and gently swabbed Joss's forehead. No boy should have eyelashes like that—or eyes like that. Close up, they were blue-gray like the sky above the ocean, flecked with cinnamon and gold.

Seth had never seen the ocean, but he hoped to someday.

Joss flinched. "Ouch!"

"Don't be a wuss." Seth taped gauze over the wound, trying not to look at Joss's eyes again. He could feel sweat slicking the roots of his hair.

"Thank you."

Suddenly Seth was staring directly into those pools of harbor and sky, as if Joss had worked a magic compulsion on him. He said, "I'm sorry about what happened in class. Don't know why I was such an asshole."

"It's okay. I get it."

"You get what?"

"I deserve it. My friends are dicks to you, and I don't stop them."

Seth felt his cheeks go hot. To cover it up, he said in a preachy PSA voice, "I guess we all learned a lesson here."

Joss straightened, examining his bandaged face. "So, anyway, I tripped and face-planted getting out of my fucking car, if you can believe it."

I don't. Somebody hurt you.

*But Seth nodded—he'd keep Joss's secret. He remem-
bered they'd been friends once.*

Maybe Joss remembered, too.

My head was strangely light now, as if I were drunk, and I
didn't pause between writing the last line and sharing the doc
with Vivvy. I couldn't. I just hit the button and imagined elec-
trons flying off into the ether, soaring on radio waves, bearing
my fantasy—*our* fantasy—straight into Vivvy's brain.

Now

After school, I put on running clothes and jog down the street, past Vivvy's house, up her driveway to where a dark wedge of conifers looms against the mountains.

The place we call "Middle-earth" is several yards off the running path, through a twiggy chokecherry thicket. Despite the name Vivvy and Bram have given it, there's no verdant moss there, no hint of New Zealand—just spiny trees, yellow grass, and stone. The rock ledges towering among the ponderosa pines suggest stairsteps, and there's a place where the setting sun turns the stone into a sauna.

Vivvy and Seth are sitting in that hot spot, both on their phones. He shivers visibly in his black denim jacket, legs drawn to his chest. She looks like a small girl lost in her long coat and tall shearling boots.

Seth puts down his phone and stands to help me onto the narrow ledge. Closer, I see the swollen eyes, the angry hue of his nose, like he's been blowing it too often. He knew Joss better than I ever did, but somehow I didn't expect him to be so upset. He didn't seem happy when Joss "chose" me.

I like Seth, but he's always been more Vivvy's friend than mine.

"This fucking day," Seth says as I settle between them.

I can't tell if Vivvy has cried again, even when she removes her after-school glasses and polishes them. But when she says, "Look," pulling out a tiny notebook, there's a deep-down quaver in her voice.

She goes on: "I'm freaking out, too. I couldn't sleep a single hour last night after I heard; it was like getting sucked into *The Twilight Zone*. But we have to be smart, okay? We have to agree on what we'll say happened on Saturday night if we have to say anything."

" 'We'?" Seth hunches into the rock. "Why don't you two start by telling me what happened, because I have no idea. I was the first to leave." His glance shoots to Vivvy. "You *saw* me leave."

Vivvy taps her pen on the notebook. "I was the second. When Celeste left, Joss was still up there, and he was fine."

Together we tell Seth the story I told Vivvy on Sunday, the lie I'm now stuck confirming. As I go over the events again, real and imagined, I remember what I said to Joss behind the cedars: *Vivvy's going to kill us.*

Could Vivvy have heard that? Probably not, and anyway, I was being silly. Dramatic. Vivvy never minded when Joss showed signs of liking me in a way he didn't like her. Shipping Joss, imagining him helplessly in love, was her passion; whether it was Joss/Seth or Joss/Celeste barely seemed to matter.

Still, I wish I hadn't said it. The words have a bad ring now.

Seth's blue eyes meet mine. "You must have been really

wasted to pass out in the cold, in that park. Worse than you looked."

His doubt sinks deep, like the chilling wind. I wish I knew where the headache and the bruises came from, too, but my body is sensitive; my capillaries burst easily. I can never be sure how I'll react to things. "I don't drink much. That's probably why."

"What are you saying, Seth?" Vivvy asks.

Seth hugs himself tighter, bare hands under his armpits, peering at the weak bronze light slanting through the pines. "I'm trying to figure out what happened."

"If we start doubting each other, we're all screwed."

I keep my voice level. "It's okay. I was the last one with him. I get it."

I will keep saying those words till they don't frighten me. I will not let them see my fear.

But Vivvy's cheeks have gone bright pink, and when she tries to speak, something guttural comes out. She takes off her glasses, wipes her eyes, clears her throat, and says, "You *don't* get it. Either of you. You don't really know how he died yet. I do."

Homicide. It makes me imagine Joss lying on his back in the cold dirt with a golf club making a dent in his skull. Clean and bloodless, like the murder victim in a board game. "You told me someone hit him, just once."

"Right. That's what they didn't tell us in assembly, what I heard Aunt Val say on the phone. He was hit a single time with something—they think it had a flat surface. So not a rock, and bigger than a hammer. Whatever it was, they haven't found it."

Her eyes fly to me as if we share a secret about this—as if I should know what's flatter than a rock and bigger than a hammer. I have no idea.

Seth keeps asking questions. Vivvy chews her lip, fiddling with her glasses. "Like I said, just one blow. It was a freak accident. The medical examiner thinks there was a cerebral hemorrhage—bleeding in the brain."

Seth presses his forehead to his knees. I feel it, too—the eggshell fragility of my skull. The terrible, jellylike tenderness of the brain that made Joss Joss.

Vivvy says, "I just think of him dying up there in the cold, alone. I can't stop thinking about that."

"Stop it," Seth says, the words ending in a sob. I've never touched him before, but now I slide over and wrap an arm around him, because I need to hold someone as badly as he does. Maybe worse.

Seth presses his face against my coat as a cold wind lashes our perch. Before I can stop myself, I meet Vivvy's eyes. *Look at me. I'm not absent. I'm here, doing what normal people do.*

She's crying. I look down at Seth—it's easier.

So many times I've imagined stroking Seth's blue-black hair—not as myself, of course, but as Joss. In my stories, my hands become Joss's big hands, calloused and soft at once, soothing and steady.

Now my fingers hover above Seth's head, but they don't touch. This is a real person, not the version of him we made up. I didn't imagine his hair would look as oily as it does. I can't imagine a fraction of what's in his head right now. But I did imagine his shoulders would shake as he leaned against me/Joss, and they do.

Then

When I opened my locker after lunch, an envelope tumbled out.

Inside was a thick ivory card with the monogram *VSK*. Spiky, painstaking, almost calligraphic handwriting: *Tea at my house. See you in the parking lot after school?*

My face twisted into a grin. Vivvy could have texted, but she'd chosen to do this. I was being courted, but not in a sinister way: a friendship courtship, as harmless and breezy as a summer dress flapping on a clothesline.

Eleven minutes after I shared my story with her, she'd written back: *I NEED MORE OF THIS. NOW.* I never would have dared to show that story to anybody but Vivvy, and she didn't disappoint me. On the day she showed me her parents' graves and confessed to her fixation on Joss, she gave me her trust, a tiny fire kindled in her heart and transferred to mine.

Now I would enter her sanctuary.

The Kray house anchored the peak of town where the streets ended, a looming pearl-gray Victorian with a slate roof and chocolate-brown trim. Vivvy parked the Impala on the street outside. We stepped through an iron gate and a massive door into a foyer that looked like a museum in need of donors. One wall was dominated by a swooshy painting of a pretty, nude, young redhead doing an interpretive dance with the Eiffel Tower visible through a window.

"That's my granny," Vivvy said. "When she was alive and young, obviously. Are you shocked?"

"More impressed."

"Right? A famous artist did that when she lived in Paris. Granny died three years ago."

"I'm sorry." We walked down a passage covered in coral-and-pink-striped wallpaper.

Vivvy tilted her chin as if to keep her grief at a distance, but she didn't put on that fake, jaunty tone she had in the cemetery. Maybe she trusted me a little more. "Granny was our legal guardian and raised us. Then Aunt Val took over."

The kitchen sported ancient mustard-colored appliances, a woodstove, and a stone fireplace so large I could walk into it. Combined with the Kray twins' tragic orphan story, it made me feel as if I were in another century.

A scrawny, turtlenecked young woman eyed us from the radiator, book in hand. "Has anyone seen my coffee?"

"If your coffee's sitting somewhere, Fiona, it's probably cold." Vivvy put a massive stainless-steel kettle on the range.

"Don't care if it's cold. Need it strong." The woman's glance darted back to me. "Who's this?"

"Celeste Bergstein. She's from Montreal, and your coffee's right here, dummy."

Today Vivvy wore a fitted black sweater and a string of pearls—a glamorous librarian. She said, "Celeste, this is my aunt Fiona. She has no manners, and she walks around with books and cold coffee. It's called being a grad student."

"Your dad must be Leo Bergstein. The new chiropterologist at MSU." Fiona shook my hand as if I were royalty.

"Yeah, that's him."

Before I could find out how she knew offhand the term for a guy who studies bats, Fiona choked and spat out her coffee. She marched into the passageway and shouted upward, "Val! Valerie Kray! How dare you?"

Vivvy rolled her eyes.

"What?" A bellow came from above, as deep as Fiona's voice was reedy.

Footsteps thudded down a back staircase, and a door opened to reveal a broad, beautiful woman over six feet tall with gleaming chestnut hair, wearing full makeup, a sheriff's-department uniform, and a pissed expression. This must be the aunt with the overactive love life.

Fiona fished something from her coffee and held it up accusingly. "A fingernail! I made a positive ID, since it happens to be Dresden blue. So don't call in forensics to try to clear yourself. When you clip your nails at the table, they fly! They have wings, Val!"

"Don't leave your coffee on the table while I clip my nails." Val caught my eye and smiled as if we were coconspirators.

"It's not civilized behavior to groom in eating areas! But we aren't civilized here, are we?"

"I was just thinking the same thing." Vivvy took Fiona's elbow and none too gently steered her out of the kitchen. "Don't you have some footnotes to write?"

"Sorry about the shouting," Fiona called back to me. "We don't have a lot of guests."

"Speak for yourself, Fee!" Val gave me a friendly nod and thundered back up the stairs, singing a snatch of "On the Street Where You Live" from *My Fair Lady*. Maybe that was where Vivvy got her musical expertise.

Alone again, Vivvy and I listened to the kettle boil. The house's old timbers echoed with the two aunts' contrasting voices.

"I told you my family was weird." Vivvy poured steaming water into the teapot. "Well, you probably guessed that when you met Bram and me in the woods, but the aunts are on another level."

"I like them." Grandstanding, eccentric people make it easy to be invisible; they suck up all the attention. "Is Val really the sheriff?"

"Undersheriff. Which isn't saying much, since they have about nine people on staff for two thousand square miles and nothing ever happens."

I remembered what Vivvy said the other day about Joss's dad having been the sheriff. Then I remembered my story, and warmth stole into my cheeks. Texting it was one thing, but face-to-face...

Maybe Vivvy was reading my mind, because she asked, "Who hit Joss, Celeste? When do we find out?"

To hide my blush, I focused on her hands, which were pouring milk into a bone china creamer spiderwebbed with cracks. "I don't know if anybody hit him. I mean, you know, IRL. Maybe he fell, like he said."

"Who cares about IRL?" She handed me a full cup. The tea was smoky and strong. "I want more of that story. When I first told you my Joss/Seth fantasy, I figured you thought I was one messed-up little orphan. I mean, maybe you still do. Maybe you're just humoring me."

She might as well have been tugging my arm or tickling my neck, trying to get me to react. "I've never written about real people that way before," I said, keeping my voice neutral. "Only fan fiction."

"I don't read fan fiction. I don't watch TV."

"You can write fic about anything. I was mostly into *Les Misérables*—stories about Enjolras and Grantaire."

Vivvy looked mystified—clearly not a serious *Les Mis* fan. "They're doing that one this semester at school, a concert version."

There was no point in explaining to her about hurt and comfort or other slash tropes—all the reasons my Joss/Seth story wasn't exactly original. "The point is, I've written other stories *like* that. But this feels weird, because they're real. And the real Seth isn't into Joss, is he?"

"He could be. It's been so long since Seth and I really talked. But like I said, who cares? When do I get the second chapter?"

Footsteps clomped on the stairs, and Bram stepped into the kitchen, saving me from answering. His halo of candy-floss hair made him look monkish and angelic at once, and I blushed.

"Scram, Bram," Vivvy said in an exaggerated, sugary tone.

I shuddered, embarrassed on Bram's behalf, but he only sang back in a happy way, "Go shiv yourself, Viv," as if they were doing a call-and-response.

Vivvy swept out one arm dramatically, indicating me. "You may remember Celeste. She's from Montreal. You're not allowed to take her away from me."

Bram's cheeks went as red as mine already felt. "I was just getting a snack."

Why would she *say* that? Bram spent way too long rummaging in the fridge, muttering something under his breath that sounded like "weirdos," "spinsters," and "cardigans." I couldn't draw a deep breath until he was gone.

Then Vivvy burst out laughing. "He likes you."

"Doesn't look that way." I learned long ago I don't understand boys my own age, unless they're the boys in my stories. But Bram was more confusing than most. Since our first meeting, I'd paid more attention to him at school, where he was usually on his own or talking to one of the teachers. In the library, I watched him bend over Mrs. Tebbetts's shoulder for ten minutes, pointing at her computer screen like he was explaining something. When I finally gave up and googled "Bram Kray," I found a local newspaper article that said he'd coded an app for gamers that was in the App Store. So maybe he was just too brilliant to be hanging around with us.

"Oh, trust me," Vivvy said. "Next time he sees you, he'll be super friendly and ask you a million questions, or he'll ignore you. Hard to say. Anyway, what about my new chapter?"

Bram had upset the balance of the tea ceremony, putting me on the alert, sharpening my edges. Vivvy, it occurred to me, could show my story to other people. Could I be sure I trusted her?

It was time to test her. I tilted my head—casual, teasing. "I think writing the second chapter is *your* responsibility. You started this, after all."

Vivvy groaned. "I tried writing a novel in fourth grade, in seventh grade, and again in ninth grade, but after fifteen pages max, I got blocked."

"Well, this can be way less than fifteen pages. Send me a story, and I'll write one back."

Now

We have our alibis straight. Seth will say he stayed home Saturday. His mom will back him up—she's not a fan of the cops. Vivvy and I will say we were at my house the whole night—easy enough, since we were officially having a sleepover and my dad was locked up in his basement study.

"But you slept at your house that night," I remind her. "No one noticed you come in?"

"Val was on an overnight date, and Fiona was dead to the world. Bram was in his room playing one of those loud shooters. I'll say I came home before any of them were up. Thank God for eccentric dads and aunts and brothers."

Seth doesn't seem reassured. "It was barely twilight when we walked up that hill. What if someone saw us?"

"If they had, we'd know by now. *I'd* know."

Vivvy's inside track on the sheriff's office has put her in the driver's seat. It's hard to remember that she used to look to me before making important decisions about our Joss/Seth stories. I was the plotter, with a better sense of the overall arc. I *started* the whole thing.

When that black hole opened in my head on Saturday, I lost the thread. Turned into just another character.

Seth asks, "What if a witness IDs just one of us near the scene that night? And they question that person?"

"What are you saying, Seth?"

Each time she says that, Vivvy sounds more worried. *She's trying to protect me.* And with the realization, just for an instant, fear roars toward me like a locomotive, whistling and clanking.

Seth doesn't back down. "Do we tell them the truth—about how many of us were up there, and who left when? Or do we keep quiet?"

"The truth," I say before Vivvy can disagree. "It's too weird otherwise."

What would I tell Sheriff Palmer if I had to? *I got so close to Joss that night that we felt like one person? I could never have hurt him?* Sheriff Palmer is the kind of man who thinks all girls are squirrelly little lying S-words.

Vivvy says, "We can't throw each other under the bus."

Seth rises from the stone stairstep, kicking up the delicate yellow aspen leaves. "Easy for you to say, Vivienne Kray. Your aunt is the undersheriff, and the fucking town is named after you. And you"—he turns to me—"have a professor daddy with state government connections. Me? I'm the stoner dirtbag." He scuffs the leaves into a flurry. "I'm the one they're happy to have an excuse to haul into the station. I'm the one they all want to believe would kill their precious golden hockey star. But *I left first.*"

His pale face contorts. *His eyes flash, coldest blue steel.* In our stories, Seth sometimes flies into righteous rages at Joss, and Joss calms the fury by taking Seth by the shoulders and kissing him gently on the forehead.

I'm not trying that.

"Okay," Vivvy says. "How about this? If the sheriff or the state police call us in for questioning, we stick to our alibis. If they *arrest* us, we come clean. Fair?"

"They can lay some pretty heavy shit on you without arresting you."

"This is Kray's, Seth, not Guantanamo. You can take it."

Seth's shoulders straighten, and I feel the current pass through me, too. When Vivvy tells you you can do something, you want to believe her, even if she's really just telling you not to be a wuss.

"Okay," Seth says. "Fair. But if one of us is arrested, all bets are off."

"All bets are off," I say.

We stagger our departures the way we did our arrivals so we three aren't seen strolling out of the woods together. I leave Middle-earth last because I was the last to arrive. It's practically dark by the time I make my way down the narrow path, orienting myself by the anemic moon and the distant glint of the Krays' backyard floodlight.

It was overkill for Vivvy to make me leave separately from her, but maybe that's her way of saying she doesn't want me to come in for a pot of one of her musty teas. Everything's different now. The air has a metallic tang, the dark feels darker, and it's not just winter coming.

Why did inviting Joss to hang with us ever seem like a good idea? Fantasy. Reality. There's supposed to be a line.

He doesn't even really like you, slut.

A piece of darkness rises from the lawn and veers toward me. And suddenly I'm in full-on flight mode—the world wobbling, my lungs refusing to breathe, my stomach trying to squeeze itself up my throat.

Half-formed sensations swim in my head—*the dark maw of the cave. Hands all over me, lifting me. Cold wind on the mountainside blowing past me, raising each hair on my neck.*

"Hey. Hey," says the piece of darkness, who has emerged into the half-light and is only Bram. He speaks into the silence left by my sharp intake of breath, my almost scream. "Celeste, it's just me. You okay? You're trembling."

Then

"First for Everything"

"No more talking," Seth says. And he slides closer to Joss on the rock ledge of Middle-earth, grabs Joss's chin, and kisses him.

Joss freezes, then kisses back hard. He presses against Seth, his bulk making the ledge tip.

It's a rough kiss, all spit and gristle. Not exactly the kiss Seth's been daydreaming about for the past four years. He pulls himself free of Joss's iron grip.

Joss sits back, frowning. "Do you even know what you want?"

Seth rubs his face, remembering all the times he's fantasized about feeling Joss's hands on him, smelling the sweaty tang of his skin.

"It was an experiment," he says. "I kind of thought if I ever did that, you'd punch me in the mouth."

"Yeah, well." Joss isn't looking at him. "Been wondering for a while if you're into me that way. Now I know."

"Guess I know something, too."

Seth's heart is pounding. He reassures himself that Joss won't tell anyone what just happened. The entire town has already drawn their conclusions about Seth. Joss is the one with something to lose.

"Lucky for you I'm so good at keeping secrets." Seth tries to keep his voice breezy. "Who really messed up your face, anyway?"

Joss turns to look at Seth. His sea-glass eyes are hard.

"You know," he says, "we could do some more stuff. Nobody would know. It wouldn't have to matter."

It's not the sexiest or most spontaneous come-on. In fact, it's kind of creepy. "Are you trying to bribe me to keep my mouth shut about everything?" Seth asks.

Joss shrugs with studied indifference.

Every muscle and sinew in Seth's body screams as he slides off the ledge and stands up. And his heart screams, too—Stay!

"Be real with me or nothing, Joss Thorssen," he says. "Let me into your life or don't. Whatever game you're playing, I don't want any part of it."

Joss stares into space, stoic as an action hero, and the truth batters Seth with the cold wind of Kray Woods. Joss will never feel like Seth does—like something's been torn out of his body every time they part.

He's halfway out of the clearing when he hears Joss say softly to the wind and the whirling dead leaves, "I wasn't playing a game."

Seth shouldn't turn back. He knows that. He should keep right on walking.

He doesn't.

"Well?" Vivvy asked three hours later, letting the porch door snap behind her. "Did you hate it?"

"Did I...what?" Talking wasn't easy, because I was lugging a buttload of splintery logs from Vivvy's driveway to her back porch. I'd agreed to help bring in a winter's worth of firewood without realizing just what an endless, dirty, back-straining job it would be.

"My story!"

Oh right. But why was she asking now? "I love it," I said, struggling to keep a small, thick branch in place with my chin. "Like I commented on the doc when you shared it with me." I'd written *OMG, this is amazing, thank you* with three heart emojis, which is pretty gushy for me.

Vivvy snagged the branch before it could fall. "I thought maybe you were just saying that."

I hadn't expected her to be insecure. "Wait a sec." She held the door for me, and I tramped up the steps and dumped my logs inside. My hands and clothes were scaly with bark flakes. The gigantic heap in the driveway—"Only two cords," Vivvy had said—didn't look any smaller.

"It was just weird reading it at school," I said as I returned outside, where Vivvy was now staggering under her own load. "But good weird."

I didn't mention I'd spent all of health class staring into

space, Joss and Seth's awkward kiss playing in my head, because that kiss reminded me of Jerome, one of the college students in my McGill theater workshop. For Frank's audition class, we did a scene from *The Glass Menagerie*: Jerome as the Gentleman Caller; me as poor, awkward Laura. Jerome was blond and beautiful, like Joss. He was supposed to kiss me, so he did—my first kiss. A peck on the cheek.

I was ecstatic that day and mortified, standing frozen with embarrassment. I hoped Jerome didn't hate kissing me; I hoped he didn't laugh about it with his friends and call me *moche*— ugly. Maybe I betrayed my feelings then—a flush, a gasp, a quiver. Maybe the need to be kissed was written all over my face as it was on Seth's.

As I read Vivvy's story in school, I wondered if my face was betraying me all over again. If people could tell. "I totally wondered if the kids in health class could see how hot and bothered I looked," I said, trying to joke about it.

Vivvy laughed—a naughty giggle. "In their dreams. You *always* look calm and collected. Like a grown-up."

"I don't." Did I?

"You do so. I bet you never have breakouts."

What did that have to do with anything? "I wish I could wear outfits like yours," I said, wanting to tell her how calm and perfect she always looked to me. "But most of the vintage stuff is too small for me, and I sweat."

"Everybody sweats." Vivvy wiped her hands, glaring at the chaos of logs on the already-none-too-orderly porch. "Anyway, I'm glad you didn't hate it. I'm going to start stacking these.

Would you go upstairs and remind Bram he's supposed to be helping?"

Something quailed in my chest. It must have shown on my face, because Vivvy's was suddenly covered with a knowing grin. "Don't worry. He won't flirt with you—he's way too shy for that, plus being a gentleman."

"I am *not* worried he's going to flirt with me." I underlined the words by brushing wood debris off my jacket in brisk, businesslike strokes. Then I headed through the kitchen and living room and up the steep, creaky main staircase.

Bram's door had been closed last time I was up here, but now it was cracked open, emitting buzzy video game sounds. I took a deep breath—*I will not be intimidated by a "genius"*—and knocked.

"Come in!"

When he saw me, he rolled off the bed and leaped to his feet, scrutinizing me through his glasses. I froze. Behind him, the image on the screen was frozen, too: a flame-haired, armored avatar with what looked like double-D breasts.

For an instant, I saw us both from the outside, the way we'd probably look to Vivvy, and laughter rose in my throat. *He's as scared of you as you are of him.* "Vivvy asked me to say we need help with the firewood."

Bram took a moment to process this message, as if it were too mundane for his brilliant mind. Then he grunted, " 'kay, then. Be right down."

I took this as my cue to flee back down the stairs, a little light-headed, and told Vivvy, "He's coming."

82

"He better be."

Bram arrived in five minutes, wearing heavy work gloves. Despite his ranginess, he could heft stacks of wood half again as big as mine. Soon we were both panting too much to talk, which was a relief. When smaller branches tumbled off his overambitious loads, I chased them. The second time we crossed paths at the porch door, he held it open and nodded for me to go first, and we fell into a rhythm.

We carried wood till we were plastered with sweat and our backs and arms and thighs ached. Bit by bit the pile grew smaller. At one point, Bram paused to argue with Vivvy about stacking methods, and I stayed outdoors until I was sure they'd resolved it without yelling or throwing things. Maybe bickering was just what siblings did.

But it was all worth it when dusk fell and we went inside and built the year's first fire in the woodstove. "It's practically *hot* out, Bram," Vivvy noted, but that didn't stop her from serving tea and cookies, then sprawling on the hearth rug to gaze at the flames.

I sat between them, the warmth licking my face. I'd only built fires out camping, and the tame blaze behind its thick glass fascinated me, like a natural disaster shrunk to dollhouse size.

We talked about school. Then Vivvy said Bram would have to build up more cold resistance if he wanted to live in Antarctica, and I asked why Antarctica, and suddenly we were talking life plans—or, more precisely, dreams. Bram would work on a geological research station. Vivvy would work at a fashion house in Paris or Milan. I mumbled something about my animal sanctuary.

I expected Bram to tease, "Oh, so you can get an early start on being a cat lady." Instead, he said, "I brought a squirrel to wildlife rehab last week."

"Squirrels are just glorified rats," Vivvy objected.

And it was all okay, at least until Bram spoke into a moment of silence: "What about Joss Thorssen? He coming with you to Paris?"

I choked on my tea, my cheeks burning. Vivvy only said, "Yeah, him and his magnificent delts."

Bram made a face. "Ooh là fucking là!"

Those words made my stomach lurch sideways. And I was back in a musty apartment in Montreal, feeling a tickle of hair against my thigh. Hearing a man's voice tell me to relax. Watching a votive candle burn fitfully in a jam jar.

To a French speaker, "oh là là" just means "Wow, check it out." It's what my dad says to call my attention to a pretty sunset. But when Frank said it in his English-speaker way, drawing out the *ooh*, it suddenly became dirty, and Bram reminded me of that.

That memory was supposed to stay in a drawer that was hard to open, balky as an old-time card catalog. I slammed it again.

Vivvy was busy taunting her brother about his online-gaming BFF "Velouria Dawn" and her busty avatar. "At least Joss is real."

"Yeah, a real asshole," Bram said. "And I know Velouria isn't actually Velouria."

"I hope not, because she'd tip over with those melons." Vivvy tickled her brother in the ribs, and he swatted her.

Later, when the fire was dying and Bram was back upstairs, I said to Vivvy, "I did love the story, but I'm wondering: How did

Joss and Seth get out in the woods, kissing? Last we saw them, they were saying goodbye in the roadhouse."

"You said the story didn't have to be long, so I only wrote the good parts. Should it make sense?"

"It doesn't have to." But, to my surprise, I wanted it to. I wanted Joss/Seth to have a progression and an arc, just like a real romance, or how a real romance should be.

"How about you write the prequel? Set up my story?"

She was giving me permission. And in that instant, gazing into the embers of a dying world, I knew just what I'd write.

Now

S orry I scared you!" Bram uses his phone to light his face. "I was hiking in the pass. Are you coming in for tea?"

"I was just taking a run."

"Vivvy's pretty messed up," he says. "About what happened to Joss. If she's being weird, that's why."

"I guess we're all pretty messed up."

He just stares at me, the light from the phone making ghostly hollows of his eyes. "That's not how I'd describe my feelings. I mean, I'm sad someone died, but this particular person—well, I guess I wish I felt worse than I do."

You feed Bram the stuff everyone's supposed to say, the Wonder Bread of conversation, and he tosses you back something flavorful, strange, and true. "That makes sense," I say. "You barely knew Joss."

We head toward the house together, falling into step. I think about Bram hiking in the dark—nothing new for him—and the things he might see up in the mountain pass, at the trailhead. The cave runs straight through the mountains, Dad says.

"Do you ever explore the cave when you're hiking?" I ask.

"Sure, but only with the right gear. It can get dangerous."

Freak accident. Someone struck Joss in anger—wanting him dead, or not. Someone had to be in the cave that night, or close by; someone we didn't see or hear.

At the roadhouse, back in August, Tanner said the cave kicked Joss's ass. For all the stories I've written, finding ways to explain that remark, I still don't know what he meant. "Why do you think Joss was up there?"

I shouldn't pull Bram into this. He doesn't know where we were Saturday night, and that's a good thing. Vivvy always says he's a bad liar.

My question doesn't seem to faze him. "Those hockey players, they like to hang in the cave and get up to all kinds of shit."

"Oh?" I say over my accelerating heartbeat. "Even after it got posted?"

"The part that Fish and Wildlife posted, where they found Joss, that's just a little sliver of the cave. They have their own places."

"Like where? And what do they get up to?"

He turns toward the house. "Never mind. I was going to say something nasty about Joss and his jock friends. I keep forgetting he's dead. Don't want to be an asshole."

"I want to know, though. What do the hockey players do in the cave? Did you tell the sheriff about this?"

"He probably already knows."

"Knows what?"

He doesn't answer, keeps his face turned from me. Is he

worried he'll scare me or scandalize me? If anyone could have emerged from that cave and killed Joss on Saturday night, I need to know.

I need to know it wasn't one of us.

"Where's this other part of the cave?" I ask. "How do you get there?"

One of Bram's shoulders quirks in a shrug. "I could show you. But not in the dark."

"You can't just tell me?"

"Not really. It's complicated. And you can't tell Vivvy—she teases me about being a busybody."

Somehow I've already guessed that he doesn't want to include Vivvy, even though it's always been the three of us doing things together, or just Vivvy and me. Bram and I don't pair off, even in the most innocent ways. Vivvy made me promise I wouldn't ever think of him that way, and I don't, but this is different.

Anyway, Vivvy seems sick of me right now—of defending me to Seth, of making excuses for me. When you have to be each other's alibi, things change. "So you could show me tomorrow?" I ask.

"Sure." A grin. "I'll just check my social calendar....Nah, kidding. Tomorrow it is. We could even ditch school and go early, if you want."

"Sounds good—text me." I don't usually skip school, but avoiding further encounters with Vivvy, Seth, Patrick, and the anonymous note writer feels like the best decision I've made today.

Then

W hen Vivvy suggested I write the prequel to her story, I wrote it from Joss's point of view, because he deserved to have his side told. Because there should be more to Joss than the boy everybody wanted to kiss or wanted to be.

"There Is Thy Sting"

Joss Thorssen had never been in love.

Sure, he'd gone through the motions, with Halsey Halstead and other girls before her. But when you hate yourself, love isn't what you expect or want.

Sometimes you want comfort. Sometimes you just want punishment.

Today, on the way out of chem class, punishment arrived in the form of an incoming text. Joss deleted it, but not before his eyes caught words.

Please. Tomorrow. Once more. Cave.

When Joss was twelve, he disobeyed his dad's orders and explored the cave above Kray's Defile. He ventured too deep and got lost. After a terrifying night in the dark, full of the roar of flooding, he stumbled out into the glare of flashers, into the arms of his sobbing mother. She told him his dad had come searching for him, taken a wrong turn, and drowned in the swollen underground river.

The cave kicked Joss's ass that night, turning him and his mom into bruised, bleeding shells. It hated him. He hated it right back, and he kept going in there, learning its every twist and turn, refusing to fear it.

No one ever blamed him for his dad's death. But last week in English class, when Seth called him a monster, Joss heard an unmistakable echo of the accusing voice inside his own head: You hurt everything you touch. You need to be punished.

He'd gone in the cave again last week for a stupid, stupid reason, and he'd gotten hurt in there again. Now came this goddamn text, and he couldn't breathe.

Joss couldn't let anyone see him like this, couldn't do the usual school's-out backslapping and bullshitting and fist-bumping. In a daze, he grabbed his stuff and headed for the parking lot.

As he hauled the door of his truck open, a pair of blue eyes captured his attention across a half dozen snow-spackled car roofs. Seth again. Shit. Joss looked away.

Tears blurred his vision as he climbed into his battered pickup. He patted his phone to make sure it wasn't vibrating. Why the fuck had he ever gone into that cave? Had he wanted it to happen?

The memory was a blur: an argument. Pleading words and wandering hands. Then a panicked dash through a space that was too tight, too treacherous. Frenzied apologies that made him sick to his stomach. A dirt floor. A dizzying drop. Anger and hard stone and pain.

For the nth time, Joss swore on his dad's memory he'd never set foot in the cave again, but what was the point?

Someone tapped the window, and he realized he was sitting there like an idiot, keys unturned in the ignition. "What do you want?" he snarled.

Seth again. He motioned at Joss to roll the window down.

Joss remembered Richard III, and it all came back—the itching frustration of wanting to kiss Seth and slap him at the same time. He imagined stealing a kiss and then letting Seth slap him, pain like spring water on his cheek.

He knew he shouldn't want it, but he did, even as he asked, "What the fuck is your problem? Why are you always watching me?"

Seth looked taken aback, but he didn't turn and leave, only said in a surprisingly gentle voice, "Sorry. Just wondered if you wanted to have a smoke in Kray Woods like we used to."

Seth always had good weed, but that wasn't why Joss barely hesitated before saying, "Get in before someone sees us."

He wanted those curious, reproachful eyes on him again. He wanted Seth to call him a monster, wanted to be seen and known for what he was. Why did punishment sometimes feel so good?

Vivvy responded within ten minutes. *Poor Joss. Poor boys! But I'm confused. Who's the text from? How'd Joss get hurt? Who was he meeting in the cave?*

We'll see, I replied, then realized I was making it sound like the story was mine to tell. *I mean, we'll figure it out as we go.*

Maybe Joss met Halsey in the cave and she went psycho and hit him and now she's stalking him.

Maybe, I wrote, putting her off. I didn't want Halsey anywhere near this story; I didn't know her, but I already knew she was a character I didn't want to write.

That'd be kind of boring, though. Too close to real life. I bet you already have a plan. You're not going to tell me?

Vivvy felt like a friend I'd known much longer than two weeks. She made me laugh, sometimes with her and sometimes at her, but never in a bad way. She and Bram reminded me of bonsai trees, their growth stunted in ways both grotesque and beautiful. And so, for the first time in my life, I embraced the idea of teamwork. I wanted to know how she'd push the story forward.

It's your turn to write one.

Now

We meet at Middle-earth. Morning sun gives harsh angles to the spiny red pine trunks as Bram emerges from the boulders, a backpack on one shoulder.

At six thirty this morning, his call woke me from a dream in which Joss's shirt had escaped from my closet doorknob and flapped up to the ceiling like a bat, and I was trying frantically to snag it with a broom. I wished he'd texted instead, worrying he'd hear the panic clinging to my voice, but he sounded perfectly matter-of-fact. Now I'm glad to see him, glad to have something to do that reminds me of other, happier excursions with him and Vivvy.

"You'll get dirty," Bram says, giving me a once-over. "Just warning you."

"I'm fine. Is that a special caving outfit?"

He wears a black skullcap and a jacket and pants that might have been designed for a gas station attendant—a short one, since they leave his wrists and ankles exposed. He's made up the difference with wool gauntlets and socks.

"My crappy attempt at one. Real cavers have suits you buy online."

"I didn't know you were a caver." For a gamer, Bram knows his way around the outdoors, but I never considered the underground part.

"I'm no expert, but I did grow up around here," he says. "You know the cave system's way bigger than that little bat cave, right?"

"Of course." A chill passes over me as I remember the tragic backstory of Joss's dad's drowning—a story I made up that has come to feel true. I've only ever peeked inside the one cave chamber, at the mountainside entrance where Joss died.

That's not where we're headed as we leave Middle-earth and continue up the jogging path. Frosty grass crunches under my sneakers; I squint at streaks of bright sky between the pines.

"This better be good." Misgivings make my stomach jiggly and delicate, a soft-boiled egg. I should have eaten, not just grabbed a Pop-Tart.

"What better be?"

"Whatever you're going to show me that you couldn't just tell me."

Not that I didn't expect it, because Krays don't just like to tell stories, they like to set scenes. Bram's insisting on showing me the cave is like Vivvy's taking me to Joss's house back in August. If he's taking me on a wild-goose chase for his own amusement, I'll never trust him again, but I can't say I mind the distraction.

"It'll be good." His tone is deeper now, less flip. "If that's the right word."

"Would you stop being so cryptic?"

Bram shoots me a smile, then veers off the jogging path onto a narrower trail that zigs and zags uphill. Rusty needles slide under my feet like beach sand.

I keep seeing Joss's shirt clinging to my ceiling in the dream, trying desperately to hide itself from me. On Sunday, I didn't mind touching the shirt, but now it feels like a trophy. Evidence. Something I need to bury or burn.

"Why don't you want Vivvy to know where we're going?" I ask between heaving breaths, clambering over rock slabs. We have to be headed straight up the mountain. "You said she called you a busybody."

Bram pauses for me to catch up. He wears his contacts today, his enormous eyes blue and bleary in the sunlight.

"Takes one to know one," he says with a grin when we're side by side. "Vivvy told you about the security cams we have set up in the woods, right?"

I nod. The cams are supposed to be in case of prowlers, but Vivvy has other uses for them. She thinks she has a subtle claim on every citizen of the town named for her ancestor, a conviction I used to find adorably quirky. "You watch them, too?"

We pick our steps carefully as rock ribs start to warp the path. Bram says, "I can't help being curious when a motion alert comes in, right? You never know when it might be an ax murderer. Anyway, these woods do belong to my family."

"Not all the way up the pass," I point out.

Tall pines and firs give way to scrub and spindly aspen. Dark crags shoulder their way into the sky: the two mountains that form the sides of the town's namesake defile. Bram points to a thicket of chokecherry. "Over there's the trailhead."

He heads off-trail, holding back a low-hanging branch for me. "Maybe we are nosy, Vivvy and I, but it's a small town. Everybody spies on everybody. Anyway, I kind of—it's hard to explain, but I feel responsible for the cave. I've been exploring it since I was little."

My dad has his own kind of weird attachment to caves, but this is a side of Bram I didn't expect. "Vivvy never told me much about it," I say.

A dry laugh; I can't see his face. "She doesn't like it in there. I do."

We weave our way through calf-high grass and stinging thickets until a pile of boulders blocks our path. Behind them rises a sheer cliff pocked with fissures like an asteroid. Bram picks his way over the rocks straight toward it, and I follow. "Isn't this a dead end?"

Even as I speak, he slithers between the boulders and disappears from the waist down. "Look closer, Celeste."

Bram rarely calls me by my name; he wants me to pay attention. The dark hole in which he stands is roughly crescent-shaped, scarcely longer than my arm or wider than my hips.

"That's not a cave," I object. It's barely a fox's den.

Bram pulls off his pack, removes two headlamps, and holds one out to me. "You're going to need this."

"Seriously?" My heart begins to pound.

Rather than answering, Bram crouches and inches headfirst into the blackness, somehow managing not to bang his lamp. As if his entire body were a key he's fitting into a lock.

"It gets bigger quickly," he says from inside—his voice

hollow, his protruding feet kicking up gravel. "Look, I'll guide you every inch. We'll be there in ten minutes, and I won't leave you alone for a second. You're not claustrophobic, right?"

He asked me that question this morning, and I said no, because I knew I could handle a cave like the bat cave, big enough to stand up in. This is just a tunnel in the earth where desperate animals go to ground.

At least he was right—it gets wider. After the first, horrific moments when I'm not sure my shoulders and hips will fit through the gap, the passage releases its glovelike grip. We're still crawling, and I can't raise myself a few inches without bonking my head, but I can breathe.

The rock walls are dry and crumbly; no threat of flooding here. The whole place has an iron-tinged basement smell that reaches deep into my hindbrain and says *safe*.

Safe because it's hidden, as all burrows are. It's not the tightness of the space that unnerves me now, but the twists and turns. The headlamp keeps slipping sideways, disorienting me, making me smack into walls.

Bram scrambles too quickly ahead. I want to cry out: *Are we almost there?* I want him to stop, wait for me, remind me I'm not alone.

This could be a sick joke, or a test. But something about the way he moves—deftly, sinuously, like he's finally found a place he feels at home—keeps me going. Just a little farther.

I'm not surprised Vivvy doesn't like this place. But I wonder why she never talked about it, even just to make fun of Bram for choosing to worm around underground.

My headlamp glares on a wall of gray. Straightening it, I see no passage ahead, only Bram's legs disappearing into a crack no wider than a hand.

He calls to me, muffled by the wall of rock. "You okay? I'm right here; I'll wait for you."

"I—I don't know if I can do this." My voice shrills as I feel along the fissure between two boulders, trying to work out how my skull will fit, let alone the rest of me. Maybe Bram has a smaller head.

"Two steps and we're there. It gets wider."

Where's *there*? My throat constricts at a whiff of something sharp in the mustiness—stale liquor—and suddenly I'm desperate to get closer to Bram. I poke my head into the crack, but the lamp catches, sending a spray of gravel into my eyes. Is this how dying feels? Like being pulled through a barrier that smothers and breaks you?

Something tugs at my hoodie, and I yelp, but it's just Bram reaching through the gap. He has long fingers and delicate knuckles like Vivvy's.

"It's okay. You're okay. Give me your headlamp, then turn sideways and put your head through here"—slapping the rock— "and your hips through here." A lower opening. "Your waist will clear the tightest squeeze."

I bite my lip hard. "Who's been drinking in here?"

"Jocks. Like I said before. Here, I'll hold your hand while you go through."

The placidity of his voice makes the whole scene unreal,

transparent, like a story I'm plotting with Vivvy. As I catch his hand, I think of a poem we read in school: *This living hand...I hold it towards you.*

Keats wrote that right before he died young.

First the head. *What if I get stuck or the boulders shift?* As panic punches my lungs, Bram's hand squeezes mine. I drag myself forward on my elbows, rotating. My pelvis catches, and I almost scream.

Bram kneels before me, his face intent in the ghostly light. "No, other side. That's right. Just like a puzzle piece."

At last my hips slide through the cavity. Delivered, I crouch and breathe, head on my knees. My clothes are gritty, my hair full of dust. The stink is stronger.

Bram stands before me—hunched but *upright.* When he helps me to my feet, the ceiling has retreated to a reasonable height.

I look back the way we came, my left hip and shoulder throbbing. I know he didn't mean to terrify me. He tried to warn me, but I didn't know what to expect. "Is that the only way out?"

"Depends," Bram says.

"What's that mean?" Headlamp back on, I follow him down the rock corridor. "Kids party in this death trap? *Joss* partied here?"

His name echoes too loudly.

"Not here. There."

Bram aims his headlamp at the rock wall to our left, now actually a rampart of slabs like a kid's clumsily made fort.

Through a fissure, maybe three feet wide at its largest, we

gaze down into a high-ceilinged chamber. My headlamp picks out pale stalactites dripping from the roof, and I think of a gallery overlooking a castle's throne room.

"Cool"—but the rest of my thought dies in my throat as Bram swings his light to the chamber's wall.

Words loom there, stark and white. THIS PLACE IS DEFILED.

Then

Taking a shortcut to Vivvy's house, across the scrubby grass of the elementary school playing fields, I watched it happen from far off.

First, I saw Vivvy's blond head, bobbing in a bunch of those girls in blue powder-puff football jackets. She was walking through them in the same direction I was, her darker coat making her more visible. Then came a purposeful kind of shouting, singling somebody out. A girl's voice, then a boy's. Vivvy's head whipped around. She called something back, but I heard only her tone—scared and defiant at once.

My instinct was to turn and take a different route, but it was Vivvy. She was in trouble.

I started walking again, faster—past long strips of canvas drying on the yellow grass, hand-painted with messages like MOUNTAINEERS SLAY YOU and DODGE WEAVE CRUSH. More school spirit stuff. The boy's voice rose above the others. "What about it, Viv? You gonna show your new friend *all* around town?"

It was a redheaded boy in a letter jacket—Tanner McKeough

from the roadhouse, Joss's friend. The words seemed innocuous, but he made them sound obscene as he blocked Vivvy's path, looming over her. The air thickened with danger as he added, raising his voice, "Hey, I'm talking to you. You gonna pretend I don't exist? Not cool, Viv."

A blond girl—Halsey?—pressed in close to Tanner and said something I couldn't hear. Telling him to stop, maybe, but in that fake, prissy way you do when you're really egging somebody on.

I wanted to run to Vivvy's defense, but an old reflex iced my muscles. The mismatch between Tanner's words and tone put me back in the center of a circle of taunting girls. *I love your dress, Celeste. Soooo cute, did you get it at Goodwill? What's wrong? Why are you ignoring us?* The words so close to sweet until you heard the sarcasm.

It doesn't make you special, being prey, but it teaches you to keep your guard up. It teaches you to freeze. Sometimes it even makes you a bad friend—like me right then, because Vivvy was backing away from Tanner, and he was advancing on her, and I couldn't seem to take a step.

And then, out of nowhere, a tall figure charged into the group in a whirl of arms and legs. Before I could sort anything out, he was winding up and landing a punch that sent Tanner staggering backward.

Tall, blond. Bram. My heart stuttered, and suddenly I could move again.

I dashed toward them as Vivvy grabbed Bram's hand and yanked him away from Tanner and the rest of the group, onto the sidewalk. I expected Tanner to lurch after them, but he stayed put, swiping a bloom of red off his upper lip.

Thank God, I thought, and then, *Bram decked Tanner.* He'd really done it, and all for her. I quaked with silent joy as I followed my friends up the street, giving Tanner and his powderpuff friends a wide berth.

Vivvy and Bram were moving fast; I didn't catch up with them until we all reached the Krays' iron fence. Then I saw that Vivvy's face was pink and corrugated, silverfish tears on her cheeks.

"Are you okay?" I'd never seen her even close to crying before; the sight squeezed my throat. What else had Tanner and Halsey said to her before I arrived? What had they done?

"She's overreacting." Bram tugged himself free of Vivvy's grip. "Tanner was being an asshole, picking on a girl half his size, so I gave him a little tap. It's all gonna be fine."

"*I'm* overreacting? He didn't lay a hand on me, and you punched him! His dad could sue us!"

Bram shook his head in a resigned way. "He won't cry to his daddy. He was standing in your way, being a menace." And then, to me, "She's just shook up. I bet she'd like a pot of tea."

"Do *not* patronize me!" But Vivvy allowed me to lead her into the kitchen, while Bram headed upstairs. Her thin arm was shaking, and today she seemed very small in her plaid vintage schoolgirl jumper.

She washed her face in the half bath, and then she sat at the table while I made the tea. She said, "It's always Tanner. He tormented Bram in second grade, and when Bram fought back, suddenly it was *his* fault. Tanner has this big, toothy grin that wins all the teachers over. I hate him."

"Me too," I said soothingly. Bram had been defending her, not himself, but I could tell she didn't want to talk about that—or why Tanner had confronted her in the first place. "I'm sorry."

She blinked at me. "For what?"

"I was there, too. I should've done something."

"What, silly?" Vivvy grabbed my hand and pulled me down into the chair beside hers. "There's nothing *to* do. You just have to ignore them."

"But they were..." In the roadhouse, Vivvy had seemed so friendly with all those people. "They were talking about me, too."

"What?"

"He said *your new friend*." The kettle shrilled from the stove, and I got up again. "Never mind." I didn't really want to know what Tanner had been insinuating, and it was almost reassuring to see this side of her, to know she wasn't as perfectly in control of everything as she wanted me to think.

"Oh, that," she said. "They're just jealous because they're curious about you. About anyone from outside this stupid town."

"They should be jealous of you," I said, pouring water into the pot. "You're going to Paris with Joss Thorssen."

She smiled, but it looked like an effort. "I don't really believe that, you know. Not about Paris specifically, but that I'm ever getting out of here."

That surprised me. "But you're going to college, right?"

Vivvy wiped her face. "I guess. You can't imagine how hard it is, though, when you're from somewhere like here, to imagine leaving. I feel like, if I get on a plane, I might die like my parents."

"You've never been on a plane?"

"Pathetic, right?"

"Of course not!" I took the pot to the table and sat down with her again. "Everybody has things that scare them."

"I guess," Vivvy said.

"Sometimes you just need to ease into new things." I was the last person who should lecture anyone on facing their fears, but that *was* how it worked, right?

After a moment, she smiled at me. "You can be my personal cheerleader."

It took a fire on the hearth and two cups of tea to get Vivvy back to normal, to dry her last tears and steady her voice. By the time Bram came back downstairs, she was her normal self, teasing him for eating everything chocolate in the house, and nobody mentioned Tanner all evening.

Now

W hite graffiti cover the cave walls from floor to ceiling, the letters lean, crooked, and angry. THIS PLACE IS DEFILED. SEE US, HEAR US, KNOW US, FEAR US.

There are more messages, and stick-figure drawings, all so pervy or violent that I have to look away. The word "defiler" appears over and over: DEFILERS WERE HERE; HOME OF THE DEFILERS; DEFILERS OWN YOU; DEFILERS RULE; DEFILE NOT, LEST YOU BE DEFILED.

"Who did this?" Our school's team is the Mountaineers, not the Defilers. The words and cartoons glow silver-white like quartz, as if a single unhinged mind produced them all.

"This is why I had to show you," Bram says.

I can't let him see me fall apart again, not so soon after the embrace of the cave passage, so I pull my fear in tight. If Bram is right about Joss and his friends hanging out here, then they drew these demented doodles, not some serial killer, and I bet they did *not* wriggle in through that foxhole. They strode upright.

Which means there's an easier way out somewhere.

"I'm going down there." I hook my elbows over the edge of

the gap. The drop is doable, maybe nine feet, less a wall than a steep slope.

"Don't do that," Bram says.

Now *he* sounds scared, and annoyance-fueled adrenaline floods my veins. "What do you mean? We came to explore, right?"

"They might notice footprints."

"They who?" I grip the edge and haul my feet over. "I thought you weren't scared of people like Tanner McKeough."

The drop is bruisingly uneven. Trying to avoid protruding rocks, I half slide, half fall to the dirt floor—rattled but intact. "C'mon! There's another entrance, isn't there?"

"Yeah." His voice sounds distant now. "But I don't use it. It's theirs."

"What do you mean, 'theirs'?" I rise from a crouch, blood pumping in my temples. Fear of that tight squeeze has given me courage. "Come down here—it's easy."

"I can see plenty from up here." But after a moment, Bram lands beside me in a cloud of dust.

"God, it stinks." I take a step on the soft earth and bump up against a rendition of a couple doing it doggy-style. One stick figure is a crude caricature of an Indigenous woman with a feather headdress, her mouth open in a silent scream. "This is offensive and wrong on so many levels. The whole place is creeping me out."

"That's why I usually stay up above," Bram says. "All the view, less of the stink."

He's right, but now that we're here, how can we not look around? "There are footprints all over." I sweep my light across the cave floor. "No one's going to notice ours."

I rotate my lamp again, catching a torn and filthy mattress, a broken bottle, a line of several intact liquor bottles, a scrap of salmon pink—are those *panties*?

Before I can bend to check, something stabs my ankle and makes me yelp. I've upset a pile of kindling—sharp branches roll across the floor.

"Shit," Bram says. "We need to put all those back."

I shine my light on the debris—not branches after all, but white, stripped bones. Ribs and legs and a skull, smaller than a human's—a dog's?

I lurch toward Bram, feeling that Pop-Tart rise in my gullet. "Is it some kind of satanic thing?"

Bram takes me awkwardly by the elbows, his breath warm on my hair. "I think it's a couple of sheep, mostly. Maybe a pig."

"They kill them here?" My voice wobbles. "Jocks do this?"

"The bones are old. I've never seen them kill anything."

His presence is so reassuring that I edge closer, into the shelter of his chest and strong arms. His caving suit stinks of mothballs. Fingers close on my elbow, steadying me, but when his breathing quickens, I lurch away. I promised Vivvy, and anyway, the last thing I want is for Bram to think I'm a "slut," too.

Why am I even thinking that ugly word? It's this place.

I wheel to the far wall, where a benchlike outcropping free of graffiti tempts me to sit down. Something incongruously white catches my eye—the spine of an ordinary three-ring binder, wedged behind a stone.

"Oh, look, someone left their crap here. Maybe their name's in it."

It's like clickbait. You know you shouldn't want to know why "What Was Hidden in This Cave Will Shock You," but you do. I wrestle the hubcap-sized stone sideways to uncover the binder, which is spotted with black mold. "Bram, help me."

"We have to put everything back the way it was." Then Bram sees the binder, too, and his expression goes queasy.

He gets a good purchase on the stone, and I unwedge the binder, pull it out, and open it.

The pages hold a gallery of photos of various vintages—some stiff and colored, others grayscale printouts on flimsy paper.

They show boys and girls, younger than we are, all apparently snapped while lying on their backs looking at the camera. Or not looking, because some have their eyes shut tight. Others squint. Only a few face the camera head-on, and none smile.

Below their faces, you can see roughly half their bare torsos. Some have their shirts pushed up into their armpits; others wear no shirts at all.

Something was happening to them when these photos were taken, just out of frame. How can I tell? Maybe it's in their braced posture or the hard set of their mouths, scared or resolute. As if they're telling themselves it's almost over.

Why did I want to see any of this? What does it have to do with Joss?

I'm breathing through a tube, each exhalation tinny and dizzying in my ears, as I flip through perhaps thirty images. Some look ancient, like they were developed in a darkroom.

The last page in the binder is flimsy notebook paper covered with wavery signatures in rusty watercolor. No, too lumpy for paint. Too red.

I should decipher the names, but the photos keep drawing me back. A boy with wild hair and freckles bites his lip like he's trying not to laugh or cry out. A blond girl, delicate-featured, turns a death glare on the camera—a glare I saw just yesterday in the school hallway.

It's Halsey Halstead. It can't be, but it is. Someone did this to her. My cheeks burn as my glance veers away. She looks so *young*.

Bram says in a low voice, "Oh shit."

"What?"

"Last row. Third from left."

The boy can't be older than thirteen or fourteen. Dark hair sticks to his cheeks, as if they're wet. His full lips grimace, and his eyelashes—

"That's Seth." The world sways, and I dig my nails into my palm. *It's all right, it's all right, you'll get out of here.*

I will get out. Unlike the stick figures on the walls or the kids in these pictures, I'm not trapped in a moment of shame and misery that will never be over. *Am I?*

"I don't understand. What happened here, Bram? What *happens* here?"

Bram runs his fingers through his mad-scientist hair, agitated. "I don't know! I've seen Joss and Tanner and their buds partying in here, but that's all! Drinking, smoking. None of this messed-up shit."

My glance flies over the bloody signatures on the tattered paper. Names I know from the roadhouse, from school, from watching them react to Joss's death. Tanner McKeough. Gibsy Arnesen. Cammy. Halsey—who signed her full name, Melinda Halstead. I don't see Seth's name.

Then I come to it, wobbly and almost unreadable: *Joss Thorssen.*

I've never seen his signature, but I know it's real. Even before I lower my head to fight the mounting nausea, and my light catches on a fleck of silver, and I spot the ram's-head belt buckle winking on the cave floor, half buried—even before I see that, I know.

Bram was right; I had to see this place for myself before I could understand. Joss has secrets, all right. Just not the ones we thought.

Then

keep expecting something to happen," I said. "Something to change."

Joss Thorssen and his teammates were holding court at the round table by the cafeteria window, as always. Halsey sat beside Joss, her arm a boa constrictor around his waist, while he traded fist bumps and guffaws with his friends and barely looked at her.

"Tell me about it," Vivvy said.

But nothing will change.

For the past week, we'd been filling a shared doc with daily drabbles: stories of a hundred words each in which Joss and Seth exchanged smoldering glances in the hallway, or Joss drowned his yearning for Seth in tequila, or Seth drowned his yearning for Joss in weed. We seemed to be stuck on yearning.

The curve of Joss's shoulder. The shadow of lashes on his cheek. They're burned on the back of Seth's eyelids.

*Those blue, blue eyes of Seth's. One glance could keep
Joss going through another miserable twenty-four hours.*

He is the only real thing.

The only true thing.

*A sweet-burning itch under the skin. A reason to get up
in the morning.*

A daily dose of steamy glances and angst, right there on my
phone. My hand creeping in front of my mouth to hide my secret
smile, my knuckles nudging my lower lip. I took another bite of
tuna on rye and tried to go back to Vivvy's latest drabble—*Joss
picks up the fallen notebook and hands it to Seth, not meeting his
eyes*—but now all I could think about was Vivvy sitting right
there watching me, and beyond her, the real Joss sitting with
Halsey.

I put the phone away.

Vivvy's leg jiggled under the table. "Kind of fuels our thesis,
doesn't it?"

I glanced around, half expecting to find Seth gazing smolder-
ingly at Joss, but Seth was nowhere to be seen.

"No, I mean Halsey. *Look* at her. She's seriously overcom-
pensating."

I looked at Halsey again and flinched. She was staring at Joss
with moon-eyes, an expression I knew too well. My mom always

looked at her boyfriends that way in the early stages, when they could do no wrong.

For a second, I felt sorry for Halsey, but then I remembered her taunting Vivvy on the playing field or not stopping Tanner from taunting Vivvy, and I didn't feel sorry at all. "Ugh," I said. "I thought they'd been together forever."

"They have." Vivvy fidgeted, her eyes gleaming as if she'd just thought up a new way to torment fictional Joss and Seth. "Halsey's feeling a little insecure, that's all."

She had more to say; she was practically bursting with it. "Why? You know something I don't, don't you?"

Vivvy buried her head in her hands. "Oh God, I shouldn't."

"You have to." She'd been teasing me with this ever since she showed me that pic of Joss and Halsey on her phone. "C'mon. Important source material for our stories."

"Can you keep a secret?" She didn't wait for me to say yes (of course, yes), just held out her phone, huddling close so our bodies hid the screen.

"My aunt Val put up a bunch of motion-sensitive security cams after Fiona got neurotic about prowlers. The footage gets erased every twenty-four hours, but I saw this back in July and saved it 'cause...well, just 'cause." She hit play. "I guess I couldn't help myself."

The video clip was soundless, with the weird artificial light of night vision. A tree branch dipped into the foreground, vanished. A boy stood with his back half-turned to the camera, his Mountaineers letter jacket swimming out of the murk. At first,

I thought he was wearing an elaborate kilt of some kind, until I realized a second person was kneeling on the ground facing him, too close. A blond, ponytailed head—

Oh. *Oh.*

My face went hot. "Um. Her and Joss?" It wasn't a private moment I particularly wanted to see, but why such a secret?

"No!" Vivvy froze the image, pointed at the screen. "Joss is number seven."

The jacket in the image said 12. My heart lurched in that way it does when you feel a little piece of your world come apart. "Who is..."

"Tanner," Vivvy whispered. "It's Tanner McKeough."

I tore my eyes away from the greenish-lit otherworld. In our reality, Halsey beamed at Joss as she rose and hoisted her handbag to her shoulder. She kissed him full on the lips, and both of us winced.

"But...why?" I kept my voice low. "If she wants to be with...the other one, why can't she just be with him?"

Vivvy shrugged. "She and Tanner are second cousins or something."

"That's not such a big deal. Are you sure Joss doesn't know? Maybe they're polyamorous. Maybe it's a thing." Joss seemed so bored with Halsey that I couldn't imagine him being jealous.

"That could be a 'thing' in Montreal, Celeste. But in Kray's Defile? With three nice Christian kids from nice Christian families? Whatever's happening, it's not a 'thing.' It's a secret."

Vivvy's voice deepened and throbbed on the word, and I knew

she, too, was thinking of our imaginary Joss's still-unrevealed secrets. Of bruises and caves. Of Joss and Seth in the woods.

Joss knows about Tanner and Halsey. He has to. Why does he stay with her? As we headed toward the din of the tray drop-off, I was already writing the story in my head. I knew how to get beyond the yearning now. I knew what came next.

Now

Caves make their own time. They kill phone signals. They replace all the things that normally offer clues to the hour—sunlight, birdsong, insects—with moist dirt, distant trickling, and darkness. They put you out of reach, even when aboveground is only yards away.

We cover up all traces of our presence. Gather the animal bones into a neat pile. Replace the rock that hides the binder. Sweep the dirt clean of our footsteps.

Bram points to a lightning-jagged crack between boulders. "You sure you want to use the exit *they* use? It must get wider quickly, 'cause they bring all kinds of crap in here."

"Yes, please, let's use it," I say.

He's right. Once we've navigated the saw-toothed opening—my heart thumping as I remember nearly sticking in the other passage—things get easier. A wide, wending, nearly head-high tunnel leads us into a dishwatery twilight.

At first, I think I'm imagining the distant sunlight, but with each step it grows stronger, yellower. The passage gains shadows, corrugations. Bram switches off his headlamp.

Then we're climbing a short flight of natural steps out of the cave, into a teardrop-shaped green hollow surrounded on three sides by cliffs.

Out. Light floods my eyes. The birds are still chirping morning calls. The sun is high overhead, east of noon.

I collapse onto a rotting log and breathe, trying to settle my stomach. Remembering how young Joss in my story spent a night in the cave and stumbled out to find his father dead, I feel his horror and dislocation in a way I couldn't before.

What if some part of Joss, the real Joss, is trapped here? But I don't believe in ghosts.

Bram is stowing the headlamps in his pack. He still looks a little shaken by what we saw in the binder, but he asks, "Are you okay?"

All I can do is point to the cave mouth we just emerged from—a decent-sized gap, no foxhole. "Why didn't we come in that way? Why did you take me through that..." *Tunnel? Birth canal? Death trap?*

"This is their entrance," Bram says. "The other one's mine. They don't know about it, so I don't have to worry about getting caught."

"They're not going to hike up here and 'catch' us during school!"

"It's not like they've never cut before." He lifts the pack onto his shoulders. "Anyway, I wanted to show you my way in. Because I found it. Because no one else knows about it—except now you."

I scramble to my feet, struggling to process the possible

meanings of what we saw. "We should've taken pictures of that binder."

"Want to go back?"

His face is dead serious. If I asked to go back into that underworld, he would.

I laugh—and, remembering how I almost fell into his arms down there, how solid and warm he was in the dark, I feel a flush of gratitude toward him for being sensible when it counts. "God, no. Let's go somewhere with a lot of people and eat greasy food and just be alive."

Bram's smile starts tentatively and spreads. "Sounds good to me."

Then

O h my God," Vivvy said when we met for tea at her house, as we now did several afternoons a week. "You wrote a *long* story, Celeste. Finally, my prayers are answered."

I'd worked up the courage to hit share during health class; pleasure and embarrassment crept hot down my neck. "You haven't read it yet, have you?"

"No, but I've been dying to. Now?"

I held my tea close to my face so the blush could be blamed on the steam. "I'm going to sit in the living room and do my trig problems."

"You're so silly. I won't laugh or make faces, promise."

"It's just easier this way." I grabbed my backpack and fled.

And spent the next ten minutes staring unseeing at sine and cosine curves, trying not to remember what I'd written:

"Secrets"

Seth had to get out of the roadhouse before he started doing something unspeakable like yelling or crying.

Pounding footsteps and heavy breathing followed him out into the parking lot, where he ran straight into sharp gusts of wind from the mountains. Not fast enough—strong arms grasped him from behind.

Seth went limp and let Joss shove him up against Joss's truck. "What's your problem, dude?" he asked coldly.

Backlit by the neon, Joss was a glitter of eyes. "You were following me again. How come?"

Seth tried to ignore Joss's fingers digging into his forearms, the knee tantalizingly grazing his thigh. They hadn't touched since that afternoon in Kray Woods, weeks ago. They'd barely spoken.

Their crushing kiss was just a memory—if Joss even remembered it.

"Following you?" he said. "Don't flatter yourself. I was doing...business."

Seth had been meeting his supplier in the road-house john as he usually did. Only this time he'd stepped out and found Joss hooking up with Halsey up against the ancient, busted cigarette machine.

Her tongue down Joss's throat. Her fingers hooked in the back pocket of Joss's 501s. His hand in her blond hair.

No big, right? Joss and Halsey probably did this every day. But still, to see it—

Joss had raised his head, and for an instant, their eyes locked over Halsey's shoulder. Then Seth bolted. He hadn't expected Joss to follow.

Seth's whole body was tight with rage. For the length of that kiss in the woods, he'd opened himself up to another person, imagined he could be loved. He'd thought—well, he'd hoped—that Joss just needed time to figure out what he wanted. Now he knew he'd been living in a dream world. Humiliation crashed like surf in his sinuses, a black curtain wavering over his vision. Screw you, meathead jock prick.

He made his voice hard. "I know you get around, dude. But does Bitch-Face Prom Queen know how much you get around? Does she know about me? Or about whoever bruised you up that time?"

Joss's arm was a flash of liquid power. He caught Seth's chin and lifted it till they were eye to eye. "You don't own me," he said, fingertips digging into Seth's flesh. "One kiss doesn't give you a claim on me. Nobody owns me—got that?"

Seth squirmed. "Yeah. You're hurting me."

Joss released him, and Seth inched backward, his heart pounding with something that wasn't entirely fear. "What's the point of all the secrets, though? Do you even like Halsey? I heard a rumor about her and your buddy Tanner."

He expected Joss to come for him again, maybe hit him this time, but Joss only sagged back against the truck.

"Look," he said, "my mom wants me to marry somebody like Halsey. My mom's been through hell with what happened to my dad. I have to do something right."

"So, because your dad died, you have to carry the weight of the world on your shoulders? And your mom doesn't care if Prom Queen's cheating on you?"

"That's all none of your fucking business."

"It is my business." Seth heard his own voice shaking. "You knelt right down in front of me in AP English and you screwed my brain, Joss Thorssen. You messed me up good, big hero. Because that's what you do."

Joss flinched at the words. Then he moved.

Seth was off-balance before he could object. Next thing he knew, he was inside the truck, his back pressed against the vinyl seat.

Joss's tongue was in his mouth, blond stubble scouring his cheeks and chin. Joss's hectic breath was on his cheek. It was hot and wet and stinging and good, and Seth struggled at first under Joss's weight, then wrenched his hands out from under him and threaded them through Joss's hair, pulling him closer.

And closer.

Half the night seemed to have passed, though it was probably less than an hour, before either of them could speak again.

"I don't want to be your secret."

"We all have secrets here." Joss ran his fingers through Seth's lank dark hair, over Seth's sensitive scalp. "Halsey has a secret, so why shouldn't I? Maybe that's what defiles are for."

*Seth closed his eyes. I shouldn't be doing this. This
will end badly. Stupid, stupid.*

*"But you," Joss went on, "are more than just a secret.
You're someone I care about, and I won't give you up.
Ever."*

I was focused so furiously on feigning interest in math that I
didn't notice Vivvy until, quick as a cat, she knelt before me on
the Persian rug.

"You took it up a notch, Celeste," she said, pressing both
hands to her heart.

"Is it too dark?"

"God no; it's just right. That's almost exactly the way I imagined them getting together."

I blushed, but it was a good kind of warmth, spreading from
my cheeks to my toes. A warmth of being understood.

If Vivvy really had imagined it like that, why hadn't she written it? I wouldn't have minded getting a little more credit for
originality, but this *was* a team effort. Creating a shared world
was the point.

"So," she asked, "is Joss going to break up with Halsey
now?"

No, my story-brain said. Joss didn't want to be "owned"
by anyone, which meant he'd try to keep both Seth and Halsey
as long as he could. In their different ways, they both protected
him. "He explained why he can't. His mom—"

"I know, but is Seth going to just accept that? I mean, it's
Joss. You can't share Joss."

She was right. If Joss pushed me up against a parked car, if he kissed me like he kissed Seth, I would go mad with needing him to belong to me. I would burn for him, a glowing ember. I wouldn't care that he didn't want to be owned.

I don't even know him.

Vivvy's dry little voice brought me back to reality.

"They should break up," she said. "Joss and Halsey. She doesn't deserve him, she's practically begging to be caught cheating, and a pretend relationship isn't good for anybody."

Something about her voice made me look up from the faded pattern of the carpet. She was rocking gently, arms around her knees.

"You mean they should break up in the story, right?"

Vivvy's gaze flicked to me, still and thoughtful. "Maybe. But also in real life."

We don't control that. I said it with my eyes in case she'd forgotten, living in this town named after her ancestor, that she wasn't the center of the universe.

Then I remembered she couldn't forget. There on the playing field, Tanner and Halsey had reminded her. Was it so wrong for the two of us to indulge in a little fantasy?

Vivvy looked away from me, but she said, "Seth would make it happen. Our Seth, if he were real. He'd find a way."

Now

W e should tell somebody, Bram." I spear a french fry with the tasseled toothpick from my BLT and dangle it in midair. "Whatever's been going on in that cave is seriously wrong."

I'd ordered carbs to settle my stomach. Whenever I close my eyes, I still see those photos in the binder: Seth's dead eyes; Seth's bare, narrow chest; Seth so much younger. A Seth who's been living in the cave all this time.

"Do you think it's related to what happened to . . . you-know-who?" Bram twirls the pencil he's been using to sketch a map on a paper napkin.

He's right, we probably shouldn't say Joss's name in public— even though Weiner's Diner is dead in the afternoons, the vinyl-and-Formica booths unoccupied except for ours by the bay window. From the bowling alley in the back comes the occasional thump of pins hitting hardwood.

"I don't know. But he signed his name in that binder."

Sitting here, it's easy to forget the dread I felt in the cave, the cold that got under my fingernails and behind my eyelids. Now all I feel is a queasy relief, because Joss *did* have a secret life—maybe a dark side, maybe even enemies. The sheriff will ferret them out. In the story I told Vivvy, I left him at the cave mouth, and anything could have happened next.

Maybe my story's not a lie so much as a half memory. An attempt to make sense of something I didn't understand. "Are the different caves connected?"

Bram flicks his napkin-map toward me. "Sure are. Check this out."

The map looks considerably bigger than what we explored, but it doesn't tell me much. "How long have you known about it?"

"Years, but I don't come often, and they're only there at night. *Him* and his hockey bros, drinking and talking bro talk." Bram rolls his eyes. "They call themselves the Defilers, like it's a secret club. I've heard them mention an initiation."

He digs his fork into a slice of blackberry pie, the only thing he ordered, though he insisted on paying for us both. "And here's the weird thing. Those creepy-ass photos—they're *of* the club members. The Defilers. I recognized Tanner McKeough and Ashley Mathis and Gibsy Arnesen and a bunch of others."

"Halsey."

He nods. "They're younger, but it's them. In fact, there's only one pic I *don't* think is a Defiler."

"Seth Larkin." My face flushes as the memory repeats: Seth young, half-naked, exposed. He can't have been there by choice. Unless—is posing for the photo part of the initiation? The Seth I know would never submit to that, but kids are different in middle school, more vulnerable and eager to please.

"There was no pic of, um, you-know-who," I point out. Only the signature in blood.

"He sure seemed like a Defiler to me."

"Somebody needs to report this." *And it has to be you.* Approaching the sheriff would call attention to me, not to mention breaking my pact with Vivvy and Seth. But telling Bram why I want him to go to the sheriff would break the pact, too.

"It's not that simple," he says through a mouthful. "You and Vivvy worshipped you-know-who like he was a golden god. Every signature on that paper you saw—they're *all* golden gods. Hockey players and cheerleaders and powder-puffs. Am I supposed to go tell the sheriff they're doing kinky weirdness in the cave?"

"Why not? Say you stumbled on the binder while you were exploring the cave, and you're wondering if that signature could have anything to do with what...happened."

"What if Palmer asks why I didn't report it earlier?"

He's being reasonable, but I can't stop. "Say you thought it was just a bizarre joke until now. You didn't care what those guys did at their underground parties. They were jerks to you, right?"

"Sure. Maybe." He frowns. "I *didn't* really care till now."

"Bram—you never saw them *taking* those photos, right?"

"No! I watched them get wasted and high and talk shit, but I never saw...that." His blue eyes lock on mine, panic-pale. "Look, if I tell Palmer, he'll wait a week and send some idiot deputy to check it out. He tolerates Val and Vivvy, but he hates me; he calls me 'his lordship' and...other things. I don't fit his idea of how a teenage boy should be, which starts and ends with decking people with hockey sticks. Anyway, the instant the Defilers get a whiff of trouble, they'll clean the cave up."

I wince, thinking of the sheriff saying nasty things about Bram. In the real world outside the Defile, Bram's already somebody, making money off his app, but here he can't compete with people like Tanner McKeough—a Defiler, a golden god. The Defilers have the strength of numbers, and Bram and I are just two people, and I don't know if I can count on Vivvy's or Seth's help.

"This town's priorities are so far out of whack," I say.

"Sure." Bram threads his hands through his halo of hair so it stands on end, trapping the light. "But there's another reason Sheriff Palmer might not care if I tell him—he might already know. Check this out." He hands me his phone. A lurid red font spells out *The So-Called Cave of Defilement*.

"Fun fact about Josiah Kray, my ancestor: He was pure evil. He liked telling tall tales about Indigenous people almost as much as he liked stealing their land and killing them. Anyway, according to Josiah's diaries, when the Crow guided him through the Defile, they showed him a cave stacked with animal bones and decorated with strange drawings. He claimed that every year they brought a virgin there and, er, defiled her, as well as sacrificing an animal. Then the spirits that lived deep in the cave gave them a good harvest."

A chill raises the hair on my arms. *The dark maw of the cave. It draws Joss.* "Did Josiah make that all up?"

"Oh yeah. It's typical colonizer bullshit, according to the tribal elders, but it stuck and turned into a local legend."

"So the Defilers are just carrying on the messed-up tradition your ancestor invented?"

"Not just carrying it on—making it into reality. Like when an urban legend inspires a real crime."

Like Vivvy and me with our stories. A memory flashes before my mind's eye: Joss in our English classroom, kneeling in front of Seth as if he were begging for mercy—or for forgiveness. How much have we not known all this time?

"We have to tell somebody, Bram," I repeat. *You have to. I can't.*

Bram lets out a long breath. "Celeste, I'm not like you and Vivvy, always wanting to be the hero of a story."

Before I can object, a sharp tap sounds on the window. I jump, but it's only Vivvy peering through the glass, her mouth a crescent of annoyance.

"Speak of the devil." Bram cackles in a deep, spooky way, while his eyes say, *Don't tell.*

The doorbell jangles, and Vivvy strides up to our booth, the old floorboards creaking under her Fryes. "Celeste, can we talk? Outside."

Bram waggles his brows and digs the fork into his pie. "Don't mind me."

He's playing a part for her—the head-in-the-clouds brainiac, overdoing his eccentricity so she won't ask him inconvenient questions. And it's me he's protecting, because he senses something weird's up with Vivvy and me.

I used to think he really did have his head in the clouds, like my dad, but now I know better.

I follow Vivvy outside, the cold hitting me like a slap, into the

130

alley between Weiner's and the Sewly Yours dress shop. I can't tell her about the cave—I can tell Bram wouldn't want me to, not to mention she might get the wrong idea about why we were off in a desolate place together.

Seth is the one I really need to ask. The one who might know something.

Vivvy's face is pinched, nervous. "Since when do you ditch school to hang out with my brother?"

"I didn't tell him anything." My eyes scan the alley. "I just couldn't face school today."

I fear she's going to grill me about spending time with Bram, but instead she launches into a monologue, her words jostling one another aside. "What I was coming to tell you is that I heard Val talking on the phone. They've questioned everybody who lives on the hill except old Mr. Knudsen. He lives alone in that ratty double-wide at the base of the path. He left for a hunting trip to Amelia Island on Sunday. He's way out there without a cell, so they have to wait for him to get back, which his nephew says will be Thursday."

A tremor, not just from the frigid air, creeps from my shoulders down my spine. "No one else saw us on the hill Saturday night?"

"Nope. Sounds like they were all plastered and glued to a Bobcats game."

We're almost in the clear, assuming we didn't leave any evidence by the firepit—or anything big enough to notice. I shudder as I remember the saliva I shared with Joss, the long brown hairs I must have left festooned on his jacket. If the sheriff ever gets a reason to swab for my DNA, I'm in trouble.

Please don't let him get a reason. Please don't let someone suggest it to him, like whoever wrote the note.

"So we're just waiting for Mr. Knudsen to get back?"

Vivvy nods. "I already told Seth. If anything happens—if they bring in one of us, or all of us—it'll be Thursday or Friday."

Two days max to figure out what happened that night. If Mr. Knudsen saw me on the hill, I'll need a story to tell Sheriff Palmer—a true one.

Vivvy must see me shivering, because she tugs off her long angora-blend scarf and twines it around my neck. "It's okay, Celeste. We just need to be careful, right? Go to school tomorrow. And please, don't play detective with Bram. He doesn't need encouragement."

I let her tie the scarf under my chin. "Why would we be playing detective? Maybe we were having a hot date." Normally I know better than to joke about that, but this is not a normal day.

Vivvy doesn't laugh. Dry flakes of snow drift from the oatmeal-colored sky; she brushes one from her suede lapel. "I know Bram. Being smart can be a curse—your brain wants to get to the bottom of everything. He has stories he tells, things he gets obsessed with. When he can't solve a mystery, he starts making things up."

I've been lying to Vivvy since Sunday. She's done nothing but defend me, but she needs to control things, and she'd think it's stupid and dangerous to pry into Joss's secret life. I can't explain that I *have* to know who hurt him.

Have to know it wasn't me.

She buttons her faux-fur coat high against the rising wind.

"Look, Celeste, if Bram thinks I'm in trouble, or you are, he knows just enough that he could let something slip to Val that he thinks might help us, but he could end up hurting us by accident."

Bram knows better than that, but maybe she needs to think he's less worldly than she is, more naive. I say, "I would never try to pull him into this. Promise. I'll sit tight."

"I know you will."

All at once she seizes both of my hands, and I feel the iron of the muscles that wind around her bird bones. "This whole thing is a mess. But we didn't do anything, and we're going to be okay. Trust me?"

I squeeze back.

Then

I f you were a character in Kray's Defile—*our* Kray's Defile—who would you be?"

"I don't think of myself as a character." I licked my lips uncomfortably, trying to decide what Vivvy meant. Some people wrote self-insert fics, infiltrating their own stories as idealized heroines. Not my thing. "I don't want to…come in and break Joss and Seth up."

We were lying on our backs on the mushy Persian carpet in Vivvy's room, a stack of index cards between us, teacups in saucers on either side. But now Vivvy popped up. "I would *never* break them up."

Her eyes darted away from me to the leaded window, where marigold-yellow leaves shivered against clouds heavy-bellied with rain. "I don't want to be the star, just a recurring character. The eccentric girl who lives in a haunted house with her weird twin and makes wise-beyond-her-years remarks. I think I'd be a *good* recurring. I'd offer comic relief and help ground things when the romantic angst gets out of hand."

Vivvy as a sensible, grounding type? It didn't square with the wild mischief I so often saw in her eyes, but I didn't say so.

She kept pestering. "Who would you be?"

"I'll be the mousy new girl who speaks French and hangs out in the library. Every time they want to translate some French, they'll come to me."

Vivvy rolled her eyes theatrically. "Is that the kind of character you try out for in plays? The boring one?"

"Of course not." But the whole point of acting was to be *not* me. To be Juliet, Antigone, Lady Macbeth, Blanche DuBois, not someone who turns to ice when a boy looks at her.

"So you'll be the *glamorous* new girl who auditions for the school play. She sings a sappy song from *Les Mis*, and Joss falls in love with her."

"I don't want him to fall in love with me!" Was she trying to trap me into admitting that, on some level, I wanted to be the main character?

"*Briefly*. After which he reaffirms his love for Seth. I'm pretty sure our Joss is bi." Vivvy sprang to her feet. "C'mon, let's see if Val or Fiona has clothes that fit you."

We both knew I wouldn't fit into Vivvy's clothes; I was too tall, with actual hips. "I don't need clothes to write stories."

"Well, I like dressing up. And I don't think you realize how pretty you could be."

I'd heard things like that before, usually from older women who wanted to give me makeovers, but from Vivvy, it stung. "Ouch," I said as I followed her into Val's room, which smelled of spicy perfume. I tried for playful, but my voice shook. "You make it sound like I'm a troll."

"Oh my God! I didn't mean that." She collapsed dramatically onto a bed with a crimson satin duvet cover, as if I'd mortally wounded her. "You're gorgeous, and you have great style, but it's subtle, that's all. It doesn't say 'Look at me.' "

And that's the point. If I dressed to show off, people would stop seeing wasted potential and see one more girl trying to look prettier than she actually was. One more girl asking to be kissed.

It was safe to show off here, though, in this room that reminded me of a theater's wardrobe, with somebody else who understood how it felt to be singled out. Vivvy hadn't let the Halseys of this town stop her from dressing however she wanted.

As we flopped clothes out of Val's walk-in closet and tried them on, we listened to the *Les Misérables* tenth-anniversary soundtrack on my phone—"For inspiration," Vivvy said. She giggled when the songs soared operatically, and I tried to forget I knew every word, every note.

But when I heard the unmistakable intro to "On My Own," I couldn't help it. I stood stock still, wearing a drop-waist dress that looked terrible on me.

"You know, in the original French version, this song is called 'My Story.' It's about a girl who invents a romance with a boy who doesn't love her, and every night she writes a new chapter."

I remembered the first time I saw this song performed live by a pro. No karaoke vibrato, no faltering pitch, just my own loneliness embodied in pure, naked notes.

I made it all up. He's not really with me. My lips moved in

Vivvy's mirror, forming the French lyrics instead of the version we were hearing.

Vivvy was staring at me. "This is Éponine, right? She kicks total ass, and then look what happens to her."

"Yeah." I tugged the dress back over my head. "She gets to sacrifice herself for the boy and die in his arms, but he never loves her back, not really."

"Self-sacrifice is the worst plot arc. Why is it always the girl doing it?"

"Wish I knew."

"Tryouts are next month," Vivvy said. "What if you sang that song in French? Everybody would stare in awe."

"Everybody would stare like I was Carrie at the prom."

Thanks to her, though, I was already imagining myself in a dark red velvet dress, standing on a stage that was professionally lit despite being part of a high school auditorium. Joss sat in the front row, his eyes glistening. The camera pushed in on him as he leaned forward, mesmerized by my singing.

Stay in reality. But Kray's Defile never felt like my real life.

By the time we'd chosen our favorite outfits, it was dark out, whirling leaves blanketing the wet street. I pivoted before the full-length mirror, transformed by a black sheath dress and carmine lipstick. Vivvy had blown out my bob and draped sultry bangs over one eye. She wore a high-collared, lacy dress accessorized with tall suede boots and hoop earrings, a look she christened "gothic disco."

"You should grow your hair out, Celeste."

"I don't know." Having long hair felt scary, like an invitation to stroke and pull. My mom's hair used to be so long she could braid it.

"You have long lashes. Bedroom eyes." She turned to stare directly at me. "You should use them."

"For what?"

"To make guys fall all over you."

With me, they didn't fall. They lunged. They took over, or tried to. "I just don't think that's me. Me is more...elegant. Aloof."

Only Vivvy knew I wasn't aloof, I realized with a jolt. She'd read my stories. Did she guess that every time Seth gazed at Joss, or Joss gazed at Seth, that was me gazing at...someone? Both of them, and neither of them?

"Aloof" was a good word for "pretending not to feel anything," and Vivvy probably knew that, too.

Back in her room, she threw herself onto the four-poster bed. The tinny music of Bram's video game echoed through the wall.

"It isn't fair," she said after a long silence. "Halsey being a main character. It just isn't."

I thought about Halsey as little as possible, but I understood why Vivvy did. We all have our demons. "She isn't a main character. She's barely in our stories."

"But in real life, she's with him, so she *is*." Vivvy rolled over to pin me with her lichen-colored eyes. "Maybe she doesn't even really like Joss. It's bad for both of them to be together. They're living a lie."

"They'll figure it out eventually. They're probably only together for popularity reasons."

"But it's *wrong*."

Vivvy believed in true love. She believed in lying for love, in sacrificing for it. I did not, but I said, "I do wish Joss/Seth were a real thing," with a dizzy sense that I was egging her on.

"Oh God, me too." She spoke in the dreamy voice she always used when we started talking about Joss/Seth, staring up at the lacy antique valentines taped to her ceiling. "Which do you think you're most like? Joss or Seth? Do you want someone to grab and overpower you? Press you down? Or do you want to be the strong one who learns to be gentle?"

"I don't know." Didn't my stories answer that question? I was Joss and I was Seth, and each of them was powerful and over-powered by turns. No need to choose, because they were both boys. No matter how hard I tried, the girl characters in my head were sweet and gauzy and yielding and not exactly empowered.

Not Vivvy, though. One moment she was sappy and wistful, and the next she was hard as a nail, sharp as a tack, and I needed that about her. I wanted to tell her to stop worrying about Halsey, that Halsey was nothing, but she wouldn't want to be reminded of that day when I saw Tanner and Halsey taunt her on the playing field.

"Well, I want to be Seth," she said, "and I want a beautiful, perfect moment with Joss, like holding hands at sunset, and I want to live in it forever. I don't know how I feel about the rest of it—the sex. I can take or leave that. But I want that moment."

"What if you couldn't have it without the sex?"

She batted me playfully on the shoulder. "Let me have my fantasy, dah-ling."

I changed clothes before Vivvy walked me home—she liked rainstorms, she said. We splashed on slick pavements, kicking up the season's first fallen leaves.

The clouds spat cold rain. A gust of wind seized me, whirled me toward the curb, and she held me fast. "Don't blow away. I need you alive."

It was something a recurring character on a very silly TV show might say. "I need you alive, too."

Once you acknowledge a bond, even jokingly, it's so easily broken.

"Maybe I will audition for *Les Mis*," I said, watching for signs that she'd just been kidding when she suggested it. I told myself I was testing her, but the truth was, I wanted to be big and bold, too. I wanted to be the special guest star who would graduate and vanish into another world, untouched by anything that had happened in Kray's Defile.

Vivvy yanked my hand. "Yes! I'll help you rehearse—coconspirators! Bursting through the barricades! You have no idea how boring it is living here. Or *was*."

That wild look was back in her eyes as we dashed down the sidewalk and slithered through a puddle, shrieking, speeding up instead of slowing down. When we skidded to a stop under my porch light, she kissed me slowly and solemnly on both cheeks. "That's right? That's French?"

It wasn't at all how we do that, but I laughed, because right now I wouldn't care if my phone buzzed with a text from Frank, not now when I was dizzy with being alive, and I said, "Yeah, perfect."

Now

've texted Bram three times since I got home. *That was so awkward. I'm sorry. I didn't tell Vivvy anything.*

Then: *Could we maybe meet and figure out what we're going to do about this cave thing?*

Then: *I'm not saying you have to go to the sheriff.*

No reply. Maybe Vivvy figured out we were, indeed, "playing detective" and persuaded her brother to ghost me for his own good. In my experience, though, Bram doesn't obey Vivvy's orders unless he thinks *her* good is at stake.

Dad and I are eating pizza in the glow of cable news, muted with captioning. That never stops him from reacting with head shaking and choking noises, inventing his own insults for the politicians and pundits: "jerkaholic," "dimbecile."

During the ads, he flips past local news without a glance. Does he even know about Joss? Last night he stayed late on campus, busy as usual.

"Did the school send you an e-mail?" I ask.

"Mmm?"

I check my phone again—nothing. I don't want Dad to know

about the shadow looming over my life, but it would be weird not to mention Joss, when he's all the town can talk about. "A boy died this weekend. Up on the mountain. At the mouth of the cave."

My father comes to life instantly, speaking fast French. "I heard. Those idiot kids and their keg parties! Someone was bound to get hurt sooner or later. And now the idiot cops are trampling all over the place—disturbing the hibernating bats, ruining the habitat."

I draw in my breath. "He died. The boy."

"Very sad. Yes. And if the wildlife department had posted cameras at the entrance, or the imbecile sheriff had patrolled it occasionally, the cave wouldn't be a playground, and the boy might still be alive."

I say a silent prayer of thanks that there are no cameras at the cave entrance, something that had never occurred to me.

Dad adds a few of his choicest curse words, then switches to English. "This state is led by jerkaholics enabling other jerkaholics."

The word makes me wince. Dad thinks I'm like him, all lofty principles and hard work. But if he knew where I was Saturday night, if he got a call from the sheriff about me, I'd transform into a sordid, small-town news item. Another jerkaholic, partying teen and, worse, the girl who fell for a local hockey god and might have killed him.

Bruises on my neck, still covered with a scarf. Bruises on my arms. If Mr. Knudsen remembers me climbing the hill, will I tell the cops what I told Vivvy? Or will I try another story to fill the black hole, a story in which Joss attacks me and I fight back?

If Joss hurt me, if I hurt him, the impact should still be reverberating through me, part of my body's silent memory, just like the queasy terror that grips me when I hear a phone buzz. It shouldn't be possible to kill a person and feel nothing at all.

I dig my nails into my palm. "People are freaking out. We had a special assembly yesterday."

"Did they lead you all to a safe space where you could wail and beat your breasts?"

"It wasn't like that, we—no, wait, stop. Go back to three."

Joss is on the screen.

They've put together a montage: There he is with his teammates, holding a trophy aloft. Wrapping his arm around a blond woman—his mom? At Vivvy's Halloween party, dressed in his half-assed, last-minute Indiana Jones costume. Always grinning at the camera with gleaming eyes and teeth, pure sunshine.

"This is him? The boy who died?"

The many Josses disappear, replaced by two sober-faced local news anchors. The scrolling captions answer Dad's question. I draw a breath that hurts my lungs.

I want Dad to change the channel now, but I can't let him know how the pictures make me feel—as if I've dived off a cliff and I'm still falling, wind shearing my cheeks. *Lips. Cheek. Thigh. Glint of eyes in the firelight. Arms wrapping me in a chamois shirt.*

I need to get rid of that chamois shirt. Bram needs to talk to someone about the cave.

"You know that boy," Dad says. A furrow has appeared between his brows, like he's trying belatedly to be sad about Joss.

"Not well."

"But he came to the house. Just this weekend—Saturday."

Everything in the room has gone brighter, harder. The Batman clock that my dad keeps on his "kitsch shelf" ticks like a pile driver. "No, he didn't."

"You were at Vivvy's when he came, Celeste. I remember the hockey jacket. The blond hair. He said he needed to speak with you about a school project."

"But we weren't—" I swallow the words. Why would Joss lie about a project? Why would he drop by in the first place? He didn't say anything about it when we saw him that night.

Then I think I understand. "He kept asking me to translate French stuff from a Canadiens forum, posts by his favorite player. It was probably about that."

I try to imagine Joss walking right up to our front door. What did he say to Dad? Did he call him "sir"? My Joss would say "sir."

Did anyone besides Dad see him? Anyone like Patrick, who somehow thought we were together?

"I meant to leave a note for you." Dad rises, cradling the grease-stained pizza box, trying to apologize in his sheepish way. "But I had a Zoom that day with a news program in Vancouver."

"It's okay." I swallow, willing myself steady, and right then the phone buzzes.

Thank God, it's Bram. *Meet me in the orchard at the end of our backyard. Ten minutes ok?*

I tell Dad I'll be back by ten, though I know once he's in his cinder block basement lair, crunching his research data, he won't

144

notice the time. Sometimes he emerges blearily well after midnight, tosses popcorn into the microwave, and doesn't bother to ask why I'm still up.

Outside, a slick layer of snow coats the front yard. Reaching the sidewalk, I find footprints and faint indentations that look like letters traced in the slush with a finger, facing our house: a *C*, an *O*, two snaky *S*'s. Crosswalk? But there's none there.

I hurry up the block, through the wet, fitful flakes, trying to remember if any kids live nearby. I barely know our neighbors, any of whom could have seen Joss at our door on Saturday.

Behind me, an engine purrs, then brakes with a harsh wheeze. Adrenaline shoots through me, quickening my pace, till I see the shabby sedan is only turning at a stop sign.

I need to be calmer, less jumpy. Less guilty-looking. How am I going to persuade Bram to tell his aunt about the binder?

He could end up hurting us by accident, Vivvy said. It's true Bram doesn't know the facts about the night Joss died, can't know them, but doesn't that just make him a more reliable witness? He doesn't know his sister could be in danger—or me.

The letters in the slush keep bugging me. Compass? Compress? I cross Route 722, which leads downtown, and veer onto the street that dead-ends at Vivvy's house at the foot of the mountains. Below me, the glossy sidewalks of the main drag are deserted; everything closes by nine except the roadhouse and the mini-mart out on the highway.

Should I tell Vivvy about Joss stopping by my house on Saturday? Maybe I owe her the information, but all I want to do is fold myself around it like a shell until it shrivels up and disappears.

Cosset? No, there were melted-together letters in between. Congress? Concuss?

Behind me, a horn honks long and loud, tearing a hole in my thoughts. A car sweeps past, wheels swooshing in the slush, looking like the same sedan I saw a few minutes ago.

It'll have to turn and head back when it reaches the end of the cul-de-sac. Pass me again. I start to run, boots skidding, pulse thundering in my ears. *Don't fall!* Past the dirt road that leads to Joss's house, past the tiny park, past the bench where I woke up on Sunday morning, till I reach the iron gate and the looming Victorian.

The sedan is pulling a U-turn. I hear the whine of spinning wheels, that braking wheeze again, the spitting of slush.

It's probably just joyriding farm boys, stir-crazy in the long winter night. But my city instincts won't let me slow down, and I jump the low fence and hurtle toward the safety of the Krays' orchard.

The sedan's headlights spear me as I dash around the corner of the tall, dark house—straight into Bram. He stops my headlong progress with his solid bulk, long arms extended in surprise. This time I don't bounce away but let my forehead rest on his puffy coat as I catch my breath, trembling with relief.

He folds one arm tentatively around me. "You okay?"

"Fine. Fine." The street is silent now; the sedan is gone. I step away from him, not too fast. "Just thought somebody was following me."

"I should've walked you," Bram says.

"No, it's okay." Only a five-year-old would be afraid to walk around Kray's Defile by herself at night.

But as we cross the backyard, I remember the note in my locker. The cold flourish on the *S* in *slut*. A shiver grips me hard as I see those paired *S*'s in the slush again, and just like that, I know what the word is:

Confess.

Then

Do you trust me?" Vivvy asked.

"Sure. Why?" We faced each other across her favorite booth at the roadhouse, homework fanned out around us, though Vivvy barely seemed to have glanced at her trig problems. I preferred tea in her kitchen, but she'd heard the roadhouse was attempting pumpkin spice something-or-other and insisted we needed to document this trend fail.

So why'd she driven here swerving at cloud shadows? Why hadn't she snapped a single photo? Why was she ignoring her nearly full cup of syrupy foam, her gaze focused over my shoulder?

When I started to turn, she whispered, "Don't!"

My throat tightened, and I lowered my voice, too. "You're acting like you're waiting for something. Is it..."

"No! Not him. It's like you and that audition, okay?" She looked ready to crawl out of her skin. "I want to do something, finally. I *need* to do it, but I'm scared."

"And you won't tell me what—"

Before I could finish, she was on her feet and sliding out of the booth, her eyes still following something in the distance. I got up, too, and saw a pale-blond ponytail disappearing through the door to the restrooms.

Halsey. I'd noticed her when we came in, squeezed into a booth with four of her friends. A few of them had finger-waved to Vivvy, but Halsey hadn't even raised her eyes.

Now Vivvy weaved her way among the empty tables to the door, and I followed. "What's going on?"

She stopped and gave me a ferocious glare, though I'd barely spoken above a whisper. "Come if you want, for moral support, but if you do, you need to trust me. You can't ask questions or anything. Okay?"

Were we going to ambush Halsey in the restroom? An uneasy feeling sprouted in my gut. I didn't know the specifics of Vivvy's problem with Halsey or vice versa, and I didn't like her ordering me around. "Maybe we should talk first."

"No time." After a quick glance toward the booths, Vivvy pushed the swinging door open and marched into the musty hall beyond. "You'd say no," she called after her, "and you don't know all the facts."

"No. I don't." The self-conscious throb in her voice made me think of movie heroines flaring their nostrils to fight injustice. What had Halsey done besides dating Joss and egging Tanner on?

Instead of veering into the restroom, as I expected, Vivvy strode past the antique cigarette machine, swung open another door, and stepped out into a day that kept sporadically spitting rain.

We were following in the tracks of Joss and Seth in my story—only, instead of a dark parking lot, we found Halsey leaning against a loading dock, wearing Joss's letter jacket and a pissed-off expression as she sucked on a cigarette. And I doubted any making out was going to ensue.

"Hey," Halsey said, looking bored but not exactly hostile. Up close, she had pretty gray-blue eyes, and I wondered if her seeming sneer was actually an illusion created by her curly lips and broad forehead.

"Hey." Vivvy shivered a little in her black turtleneck and pencil skirt, clutching her phone behind her back. "Researching for that sociology project, huh?"

"Yeah." Halsey's eyes flicked to me. "I don't know you."

I started to speak, my spine stiffening, but Vivvy broke in, "This is Celeste. She's from Montreal."

So far we were all being civil, but Vivvy-plus-Halsey was still a recipe for disaster. I watched closely as Halsey's gaze moved between us. "Oh yeah. The Canadiens. Joss is, like, super into them. So what's the occasion? You start smoking, Viv?" She tugged out a pack of cigarettes and brandished it first in Vivvy's direction, then in mine.

Vivvy actually danced backward, her whole body vibrating with repulsion. Halsey laughed—I almost did, too—but Vivvy didn't smile. Then Halsey said in a careless way, "Tanner's still pretty steamed about what your brother did to him. Been meaning to tell you, though, he's sorry, too. We all are. We were just horsing around that day."

Blood rushed to my face. I didn't dare look at Vivvy, but when I heard her suck in her breath, I knew she wasn't going to accept the apology.

She said, "Tell me something, Halsey. Does Joss know yet?"

My uneasiness cycled into full-blown dread. The air seemed to harden, to stick in our throats, as Halsey's smirk faded. She exhaled smoke and tipped ash onto the asphalt. "Pardon?"

All in one movement, Vivvy stuck her phone in Halsey's face. She had that pinched look she got when she was scared, but her hand didn't waver.

Though I couldn't see the phone from my angle, Halsey's reaction told me what Vivvy had queued up. First came confusion, then a deadly stillness. And then, after a way-too-long moment, Halsey raised the cigarette to her lips again, too slowly, and said, "I don't know what the fuck that is."

Vivvy lowered her hand. She was shaking. "I know what you're thinking."

Halsey repeated in that deadly still way, "I'm thinkin' I don't know what the hell that is."

"I'm not your enemy, okay? I would never post this." Vivvy glanced at me like she expected backup. "Never."

I nodded, but my pulse was a hectic drumbeat. *What are you doing?* Going up against girls like Halsey, in my limited experience, always led to more trouble than girls like us could handle. I understood Vivvy's wanting to see her sweat, but couldn't we just drink tea by the woodstove and write her out of the story?

"You're sick, Viv," Halsey drawled, as if Vivvy had commissioned the video for her own personal enjoyment.

Vivvy's lip trembled. "You can guess how I got this. Like I said, I would *never*. The thing is, my brother saw it first."

The glowing butt tumbled from Halsey's hand. She bent to

scoop it up, then seemed to change her mind and crushed it under her duck boot.

"So, luckily, Bram told me." Vivvy took no notice of Halsey's disarray. Her voice was earnest now, almost supplicating. "You know how he feels about...the other person in the video. He *did* talk about posting it somewhere, and I had to talk him down because I didn't want you to be collateral damage. I made him delete it from his hard drive."

I couldn't believe that—Bram had lashed out at Tanner, but only to protect Vivvy. A stealthy and spiteful attack didn't seem like his style.

But maybe Halsey didn't know Bram very well. "You better have," she said in a snarl.

"I swear." Vivvy's nervous gaze said she was 100 percent on Halsey's side. "The thing is, Bram's actually kind of a computer genius, and, well, I can't be *sure.*"

Two pink spots had appeared on Halsey's cheeks, but she looked less furious than lost, like a little girl abandoned by her friends at recess. "Tanner would kill Bram," she said in a small voice. "If he ever posted it...he'd kill him."

Vivvy looked almost as miserable as Halsey. "Look, I tried, I did what I could. But you should maybe tell Joss. Now. Just tell him."

Halsey's eyes had started to mist over, but when she blinked the moisture away, the look on her face went dark.

Vivvy continued, still in that nervous way, as if she were one of Halsey's hangers-on: "I mean, Joss *loves* you. I've seen how he looks at you. So maybe it's better for him to find out from you, and he'll forgive you."

Halsey didn't answer. She looked like a wounded bird of prey, wings flailing in the dirt but talons fully operational.

"But you'd have to *tell* him," Vivvy went on. "Yourself. Soon. So that's why I came—to give you a heads-up."

Halsey stared at the ground, as if she were considering whether to retrieve her crushed butt and try to smoke it. She didn't appear to have anything more to say, so Vivvy stepped toward the door, and I followed.

And then Halsey spoke in that same cold, nasty voice I remembered from the playing field: "Yeah, you've been a *big* help. You've always been such a pathetic little suck-up, Viv."

The words hit me like a slap in the face, but Vivvy's expression didn't change as we went inside. Maybe she'd gotten exactly what she wanted.

And I understood Vivvy's secret weapon now: her weirdness. People assumed she was like Bram, too busy with thoughts of strange or brilliant things to notice much of what was happening around her. Once they realized they were wrong, it was too late.

"You're pathetic, Viv," Halsey called through the crack in the door. "You act so special, but that night you didn't make the cut, huh? You ran away and cried like a little baby, and your brother won't always be around to deck people for you—"

The door snapped shut. As we hurried through the foyer, Vivvy pressed her wrist to her mouth as if to stifle a laugh or a scream.

One stop at our booth to collect our stuff and leave some bills for Rayette, and then we were outside, dashing through the clammy dusk to the Impala. Clearly, Vivvy didn't crave a rematch with Halsey any more than I did.

We collapsed in our seats, breathing in sharp, painful gasps, and locked the car doors, though the lot was practically empty.

"What the hell was that?" I asked.

"Justice," Vivvy said. It must have sounded as absurd to her as it did to me, because suddenly she was laughing so hard she almost couldn't turn the key, and I was laughing, too, against my better instincts, till I blinked back tears.

As we drove back toward town, adrenaline still fizzed all through my body, tightening my throat and clenching my fists, making me feel powerful and dirty at the same time. I said, "That wasn't true about Bram, was it?"

She shook her head. "Nobody's seen the vid but us. It's all psychological warfare."

That was a relief. "It's like you kicked a hornet's nest. What's she going to *do*?"

Vivvy giggled nervously. "We'll see, right? Look, I'm not sorry, and I'm not scared of her or her stupid friends."

"I'm not, either. I'm not scared of anyone here."

Easy for me to say. I was the guest star. But the problem with being a guest star was that you learned everything jumbled and out of context. I asked, "What was she talking about? The whole thing at the end about how you didn't 'make the cut'?"

Vivvy groaned. "It's so embarrassing."

"You don't have to tell me if you don't want to." *But I hope you tell me, or I might not trust you.*

"Oh, it's just middle school stuff. Halsey and I were friends back then—not good friends, but we were at the same sleepovers. All those girls were doing powder-puff football, and I wanted to do it, too, and—ugh, can you forgive me for being a horrible little toadie wannabe of a thirteen-year-old?"

I could forgive her. Her steaming breath wafted over me, through me, along with the wet-wool scent of her coat. "Just tell me."

"So the powders let me in and everything, but they have an induction ceremony. It happened at an older girl's house." Vivvy pressed her knuckles to her lips, and I knew for once she wasn't enjoying telling a scandalous story. "We drank all this sugary hard cider, and there were older boys over. The senior girls called us, one by one, and they told us to go lie down in this dark room, on our backs, and *wait*. They kept telling us, 'Don't worry, only *over* the underwear.'"

Something twisted in my stomach—a too-familiar nausea. "Oh God."

Vivvy's fingers drummed on the wheel. "Yup. I saw the other girls go into that room, and I saw how they looked when they came out, and I was just like, no, this is not for me. So when it was my turn, I up and bolted all the way back home."

"Good." I wasn't sure I could have faced knowing Vivvy had gone into that room; I didn't want things like that to touch her. "But...Halsey?"

"The next day at school, she and her friends kind of surrounded me and made me swear not to tell anyone what I'd seen. They called me a wuss and a loser. They said if I snitched, the sheriff would just laugh in my face and say the whole thing was a misunderstanding. And I knew they were right. Who wants to be stuck in a town where everybody hates you?"

I released my breath slowly, then inhaled for four-count. So much for the idyllic town of Kray's Defile. "So what happened on the playing field a few weeks ago, when Tanner went after you... was it related to that?"

Vivvy looked at the road, not at me. "Who knows what goes through Tanner's pea brain? But yes. It started with Halsey asking me about you. When Tanner asked if I was going to show you all over town, he was digging to see how much I'd already told you. He was smiling like he was joking, but he wanted to catch me looking guilty. And to remind me they haven't stopped watching me."

I'd had only a postcard view of Vivvy's reasons for hurting Halsey; now I could see the complete relief map. And I was in it.

"I'm sorry," I said. "For what happened in middle school. For them still using that against you. For them using *me* against you."

She laughed, but it was thin and nervous. "I told you, people get riled up when a stranger comes to town. It's not your fault."

"I know. But..."

Vivvy turned to me at last, her eyes glittering through the gathering dusk. "I'm so much happier with you here, Celeste. *So* much happier. Because now I finally have the courage to stand up to them."

"Me too. I'm happy." Embarrassment made me change the subject. "But do you think Halsey's going to tell Joss about Tanner? And do you really think Joss would forgive her?"

Vivvy just laughed, and this laugh wasn't nervous. Or nice.

Now

B ram looks different to me than he did when we set off for the cave this morning, taller and more solid. Without Vivvy around to tease him, he feels less like a brother and more like a—well, like a guy.

We're in the orchard, where Vivvy won't see us from her window. Bare branches claw at the sky, and downed apples give the air a vinegary stink. I try to breathe evenly as we sit side by side on the crumbled brick wall, snow feather-floating around us. Only the tips of the grass blades show.

"Who would follow you?" Bram asks.

"Nobody." A note in a locker and a word traced in the snow have nothing in common. Who even writes a message in falling snow if they want you to see it? "All this Defilers stuff has me kind of rattled," I go on. "I'm sorry I ran off earlier, but Vivvy made me promise to stop 'playing detective' with you."

"Figured. You didn't tell her what we found, right?"

"Right."

The instant I say it, something changes between us. A relaxing of his shoulders, a slight inclining of his whole body toward me, a leveling of his breathing. I feel my body start to close the distance, too, as my pulse returns to normal.

"That's good," he says. "She might not have believed you anyway. She's too stuck on Joss."

How does Bram think *I* feel about Joss? But that's not the point. I raise my eyes to his. "So Joss was mixed up with the Defilers. Could somebody in that binder have wanted to hurt him?"

Two possibilities are obvious: Halsey and Tanner, the other points of the triangle. But Seth's in that binder, too.

"I don't know." Bram lets out a frosty breath, his voice cello-resonant like a male version of Vivvy's. "When I saw Joss in the cave, he was usually with Tanner and Gibsy. And from what I could tell, there was no bad blood between any of them. But what I do know is..."

A hand bursts from his pocket, clutching what looks like a dead moth. He unfolds it on his thigh—the napkin map—and uses his phone to light it. "There are three ways into the Cave of Defilement. The one they use, near the trailhead. The upper passage I showed you, where I watched them. Then there's this third passage that runs underground, all the way from the Cave of Defilement to the west-facing cave where Joss died."

"The Defilers' cave connects with the... bat cave?" Realizing I almost said *death cave*, I shudder.

His finger traces a long, squiggly line. "Yeah. It gets narrow in places, and there's a river that's dangerous during the spring thaw, but you don't need climbing equipment or scuba gear. I did it a couple times, just to see if I could."

This whole time I've been wondering whether someone was lurking in the bat cave all those hours we were up there. But the bat cave isn't a dead end; it's the entrance to a labyrinth. "So, if he was killed where he was found, whoever did it could have come from the Defilers' cave."

Bram nods, his shoulder nudging my side.

"We need to tell somebody, then. The sheriff, or your aunt Val. Maybe *you* need to tell her."

If someone crept out of the Defilers' cave on Saturday night and killed Joss, that person could have seen me with him. That person's face could be in my memory—and mine in theirs.

A snowflake melts on my lip, and I push down the panic that buzzes in my head, blurring my vision. If someone or someones ambushed Joss and me, how did I get safely to the bottom of the hill?

I need to know more before Mr. Knudsen comes home from his hunting trip on Amelia Island. Before Patrick tells the sheriff Joss talked about me, or one of my neighbors remembers seeing Joss on my street, or whoever wrote the note does whatever they're going to do.

"You're shivering, like, a lot," Bram says. "Can I give you my gloves?"

"I'm okay." My fingerless gloves are useless, but that's not why the tips of my right thumb and pinkie have gone numb.

That's how my anxiety always starts. After I told her I thought I was having a heart attack, the school counselor in Montreal taught me breathing exercises. I try them now: short in, long hold, longer out.

"We need to find out who was pissed off at Joss," Bram is saying, "because the passage by itself doesn't prove anything. Celeste, your fingertips are dead white. Can I, like, get the circulation going?"

"Okay." I say it automatically, but as I offer my hand to him, I shudder at the thought of being touched.

When Frank touched me, I left my body behind and just watched. When Joss touched me, I was so drunk my body didn't feel like mine. Maybe it was Seth's. Maybe it was Halsey's. But when Bram wrapped his arm around me in the yard, not holding me too hard, it was okay.

Now, as Bram takes my hand, I manage to stay here again. I expect a nervous grip, but he massages my fingers with a steady, reassuring rhythm. He's warm through the loose knit of his gloves.

He and Vivvy are always touching each other—they shared a womb, after all, as she likes to remind me—but he's barely touched me before today. Vivvy has suggested more than once that he might have a crush on me, but I never believed her.

Which made it easy to promise her I'd always treat him as if he were my brother, too. Now, though... There's nothing obviously flirty about what he's doing, nothing suggestive, but I want him to keep doing it.

Bram sets my right hand on my knee and takes the left. "I keep thinking I shouldn't have shown you."

"What? The cave? Of course you should have."

"But... You liked him, right? You shouldn't have to worry about this stuff. You're in mourning."

I imagine myself kneeling beside Joss's grave, like Bram and Vivvy at their parents'. But no, it's nothing like that, because Joss is still with me (*his hair grazing my cheek, his lips, his fingertips*). And he is a threat branded on the air, following me wherever I go. *Confess.*

No, I'm not mourning for Joss. I'm mourning for Vivvy and me: for the warm wave of excitement that crested when she texted to share a new story with me. For the time when our stories were just stories, enjoyed without guilt, before Vivvy started to test the strength of our words against reality.

Bram's hair tumbles in his face, its blondness catching the house's floodlight, and his thumb rubs my palm through the glove, *warm,* and *Joss bends his head, his wavy hair so pale on his forehead, and he says, "I just see him lying there, and I can't forgive myself."*

My head snaps up. When did he say that? Could it be a memory from Saturday? I try to latch the moment to a context, a story, but it's just there.

"Your phone's buzzing," Bram says.

Who could it be at this time of night but Vivvy telling me to leave her brother alone—or Frank? I pull out the phone, knowing from experience that it's better not to wait and wonder.

Celeste, this is Valerie Kray. If you're still up, can I swing by? I need to talk to you.

My head goes wobbly, turning the world into a kaleidoscope. *Patrick. The neighbors. The note leaver.* One of them has done their work.

"What is it?" Bram asks.

"Your aunt..."

Before I can finish, the businesslike crunch of heavy foot-steps approaches over the icy grass. "Ah, this is convenient." Valerie Kray towers over us, her dark form silhouetted against the house's bleary lights. "I thought I heard voices out here."

Then

The cobbler came warm in a fluted china vessel. When my teeth cracked the crust, the sweet-tartness of black-berries exploded on my tongue. Tiny seeds caught in my teeth.

"What did I tell you?" Vivvy watched me intently across our diner booth. "Lacey Weiner uses fresh berries. Her cobbler is the only thing anyone should ever eat in this town."

Beside her, Bram said through his own mouthful, "It's too sweet. Her pies are better."

"Wasn't asking you."

Outside, the sky and pavement were gray, unforgiving, except for a strip of hazy blue behind the Baptist church. Soon it would be Halloween, and Vivvy was planning a party.

First came the *Les Mis* auditions, though. I hadn't promised Vivvy I'd make a spectacle of myself. But she'd basically dared me to do it, and some stubborn part of me wouldn't back down, especially after I'd watched her face her own fears in the road-house with Halsey.

No one cares, anyway. No one knows me here.

I swallowed my second bite. "I still don't understand why it's called cobbler. It's got nothing to do with shoes."

As Vivvy started to explain, the bell jangled. Five girls in powder-puff football jackets strode in, swinging their hips, talking and laughing. Bram rolled his eyes.

In the nearly empty room, the girls' voices carried like seagulls' when they're fighting over an abandoned sandwich. "Lacey, get your ass out here!" Cammy called, plunking herself down at the counter.

"There goes the neighborhood," Vivvy hissed.

"Taken over by pastel blue hoodlums," Bram said.

His sister stirred cream into her coffee. "Keep it down."

That felt unfair, because the powder-puffs clearly weren't listening to us; they didn't even seem to have noticed us, tucked in our corner by the window. "Tell us!" two of them singsonged at Cammy. "You promised!"

"What did he do?"

"Did he cheat on her?"

"Was she *really* the one who dumped him?"

Cammy held up a fork, tines pointed at the pressed-tin ceiling, and everybody went quiet as if she'd fired a gun. Her presence could have that effect. I once saw the assistant principal try to call her by her full name, Camille; one eye roll and a grunt made him correct his mistake.

"Nobody dumped nobody," she said, calm as a White House press secretary. "She wasn't with him after the rally yesterday because they're on a break."

I glanced at Vivvy before I could stop myself. She was listening closely, eyes glistening, head on one side.

Bram jogged her with his shoulder. "Quit eavesdropping!" She jogged him back.

Cammy's friends' voices were rising in a skeptical chorus, demanding to know what "on a break" even meant. Were they broken up, or weren't they? And whose idea had it been?

"It wasn't her," said a girl whose voice was almost as brash as Cammy's. "I mean, I love Hals and everything, she's one of my best friends, but no *way* is she dumping Joss Thorssen."

As the other girls made affirmative noises, a cat-got-the-cream grin spread over Vivvy's face. I stared at her, my brain whirling.

For a week after our face-off at the roadhouse, I'd watched Joss and Halsey hold court daily in the cafeteria, just like always. Nothing changed. If Halsey had followed Vivvy's advice and told Joss about Tanner, he appeared to have no issues with it.

Now, all at once, everything had come apart.

The other three girls were vociferously agreeing that *they* certainly would never initiate any kind of "break" with Joss Thorssen. Cammy's voice sliced through theirs like a shovel in a gravelly snowbank: "*I'd* dump his weak ass. He ain't my type. I want more in a man than pretty."

Bram shoved his plate of crumbs away. "Let's get out of here. I can't hear myself think."

"Okay, okay." Vivvy's triumphant grin had faded into an unreadable expression.

If Cammy was telling the truth, Vivvy's roadhouse maneuver had gotten the exact result she wanted, one way or another.

"Joss isn't weak," the brash powder-puff objected as we stood up. "He's sensitive."

Cammy snorted. "What do you care, Katie? Gonna make a move on him?"

Everybody giggled as Katie protested her innocence. No heads turned as we crossed the room and stepped outside, the bell jarring my ears. I'd finished the cobbler, but I hadn't savored it the way I wanted to.

Vivvy walked fast down the sidewalk, stiff-backed against the chilly breeze. I jogged to catch up to her and asked, once Bram was out of earshot, "What do you think really happened?"

"What do *you* think?"

"I think..." I just kept hearing Cammy say "weak ass." I wanted to protect Joss from her nastiness, though I barely knew him. "Maybe Halsey did tell him, and Cammy and Halsey are spinning a breakup as a 'break,' " I suggested, "and he's playing along to be nice."

"Maybe." We glanced back at the same moment, but Bram had disappeared inside the "junktiques" store. "I think that whole chorus of girls was too much for him," Vivvy said. "They were all, 'Tell us more, tell us more!' "

I reached for another musical reference. "And Halsey's just a girl who cain't say no."

"Oh my God, you're bad!" She grabbed my hand and pulled me into a sort of messy pirouette on the sidewalk, both of us trembling with excitement. "Halsey's wily, though," Vivvy said as we came apart. "Maybe she decided the best way to solve her problem was by dumping Joss first."

I tried to wrap my brain around this. "She'd give him up? Just to avoid a scandal? I thought she—"

"Loved him? This isn't actually a TV show, Celeste."

Laughter burst out of her, whirling and twisting in the cold air like fireworks—and before I knew it, I was laughing, too. "It's your fault," I said. "You made me care about this...this drama. I didn't even notice it until you came along."

"And aren't you happier now?" Her expression turned serious. "She does deserve it, though, doesn't she? I mean, not for being a girl who cain't say no. That's her business. But for the other stuff."

"She deserves it," I said, not because I was sure but because I knew she needed me to.

Vivvy's face relaxed. "Anyway, I give this 'break' a month, tops. Halsey's just lying low till she's sure nobody's going to post that vid. Maybe she'll play hard to get, too. But she'll run back to Joss."

I tried to imagine Joss waiting around for Halsey; couldn't. "And by that time, he'll have moved on." To someone pretty, sweet, and drama-free like Sarah Blessingham, no doubt.

Vivvy flashed a devilish smile. "You think?"

Now

Over the months I've known the Krays, it's been easy to forget Vivvy's aunt Val is undersheriff of the county. I've been in her bedroom and tried on her clothes; I've perused her collections of makeup and pro wrestling DVDs; I've heard the details of her tumultuous love life. When she's home, she sometimes wears the brown deputy's uniform, minus the jacket, but she never seems much like a cop. She's always grandstanding or arguing with her sister—one stalwart and the other scrawny, like an old-time comedy team.

Tonight, though, there's something different about the way Val moves, as if she's weighing every gesture. Her eyes focus watchfully on me, and my guts churn because I know that watchful look from Vivvy.

Whatever's going to happen, I'm not ready. Telling her about the Defilers could only make her think there's more I'm not telling.

Val leads us through the back door, the wood-stacked porch, and the kitchen into the formal dining room, which the Krays rarely use, with its long, bare table and staring windows. When I see an official-looking file folder and laptop, my stomach roils again. Bram stands at my back, a silent presence I'm grateful for.

Val shoves a basket across the table. "Muffin? Fiona made them this morning, and they're not quite rock-hard."

Her booming voice belongs to the old Val, but her smile is too fixed, her irises too blue. She smiles like a cardboard cutout of a cop, impenetrable.

She knows something. Is Mr. Knudsen back from his hunting trip? If he ID'd me, surely they'd want to talk to me down at the courthouse, where the sheriff's offices are, not here.

Bram pulls out the chair beside me, but his aunt stops him. "Would you mind giving us a minute, Bram?"

"A minute for what?"

Val holds the door open for him. "You know what I mean."

Bram exits with a furtive swivel of his index finger into the hall, as if to say he'll be waiting there. Val shuts the door. "I like your all-black outfit, Celeste. Very chic."

"Thanks." Black is my safe color.

"I called your dad just now to check on whether he'd be cool with us having this conversation. He said you came over to do homework with Vivvy. But Vivvy's already in bed." A theatrical furrow appears between her brows.

I jab my thumbnail into my index finger under the table, keeping my face placid. "I told him that, right. But I kind of came to see Bram."

I expect her to ask why I hid that from Dad. But she only says, "You like to walk around at night."

"I walked everywhere in the city."

"Is that where you got that pretty scarf you're wearing?"

I catch at the scarf, still wound around my throat. "Yeah. Thanks." Pilled acrylic, zebra stripes. I bought it in a thrift shop in the Plateau with two college drama students who said it made me look sophisticated.

"It's a unique choice. Around here, at least."

"I guess." Are we here to discuss my style?

Valerie cants toward me like a friend would do, but so focused, and again I'm reminded of Vivvy. She asks, "What were you doing on a park bench Sunday at three AM?"

The air congeals. The grandfather clock in the corner goes silent, drowned out by the pounding of blood in my ears.

The bench where I woke up. Someone saw me there.

"A park bench where? Do you mean *this* Sunday?"

My voice is level, yet I'm a plane struggling for cruising altitude, the air buoying me up and crushing me at the same time. If somebody saw me passed out in that tiny park on Sunday morning, I need an explanation, right now.

Val's lips scarcely seem to move. "Vivvy says you and she spent Saturday night at your house. But you got up a little early, didn't you?"

Morning. I woke on the bench at dawn. Three AM is part of the time I don't remember. At three AM, I was probably already passed out on the park bench like an idiot, wearing my unique scarf.

I open my mouth to deny I was there, but what's the point? Someone must have seen me. Could it have been Vivvy or Seth? Could one of them have traced those letters in the snow—*confess*?

I take a deep breath, and a cold wave of terror rushes over me, followed by a warm, queasy one of relief. Maybe it is time to confess, to stop lying. I can tell Valerie about our stories, about Joss and me, about the note, about the cave, about the Defilers—everything. Let her make sense of it. Better her than Sheriff Palmer.

"We were together," Bram says.

My head jerks up. His head is sticking through a crack in the door, and if I weren't so terrified, I'd laugh because it's like something out of an old sitcom.

Valerie's hawk eyes shift to him. "I thought I told you—"

"This is about me, too. It was me and Celeste on that bench."

My face burns at the lie—so obvious, even outrageous. Whoever saw me on that bench must know I was alone. "Please," I say.

Undaunted by his aunt's glare, Bram slips inside. "I know you're embarrassed about Saturday," he tells me. "But we were just talking."

You weren't anywhere near me on Saturday. He was home in his room playing video games. But Val doesn't know that. She was away overnight, Vivvy said, and Fiona was asleep.

Does Bram know something I don't? Could this maybe actually *work*?

I try to follow his lead. "I didn't want Vivvy to know. She doesn't like us to, uh, spend time alone together." That part's true, at least.

"That's why Celeste had to sneak out to meet me. It was my fault, Aunt Val. My idea."

"It's not your fault!" I try to follow the thread of the scene we're playing, to *feel* my motivation.

171

It's not that hard, really. Not that far-fetched. As she glances between us, Valerie's face changes, suspicion mellowing into understanding.

"Val knows I came here tonight to see you," I go on, my face flaming. My fingers still tingle with the sensation of Bram's rubbing them in the orchard. *Use your sense memory.*

It *could* have been Bram on Saturday night, rubbing my hand and snaking his arm around my waist. We could have done all the things I remember doing with Joss outside the cave—the kissing, the touching. We didn't, because Vivvy exists, and I promised her, and with Vivvy so very *there*, I couldn't look at Bram that way. But *could have* is a good enough basis for a convincing lie.

The question is, why is Bram lying for me? He must know he's obstructing a murder investigation. Does he like me enough to risk his own safety? Does he wish he *had* been on the bench? His face might give me a clue if I had the guts to look at him.

Val's eyes glint with something like sympathy. "You picked a hell of a time and place for that," she says.

I wince, mortified by the *that* that didn't happen, and could swear I feel him wince, too. Val goes on, "Not my business, not judging. Vivvy can be controlling sometimes, God knows. But now I have a question for you, Bram. Let's just imagine there's a witness who saw the two of you on that park bench, and let's imagine that witness is looking at a lineup of photos. Would she pick yours?"

Her voice has thickened with an ominous undercurrent. But Bram doesn't sound the least bit worried as he says, "Yeah. I mean, it was just the two of us."

172

Val looks at him. Finally, she says, "The two of you shouldn't have been roaming the streets that late. That's asking for trouble, even in Kray's."

I breathe out.

"Not roaming far," Bram says. "I can see the park from my bedroom window."

"No excuses." Val's eyes shift to me. "Is that what you two were doing outside just now? Skulking so Vivvy wouldn't see you?"

I glance at Bram. "We just wanted another chance to talk."

"Talk." Valerie hauls herself to her feet as if the holstered gun on her hip weighs a hundred pounds. "Well, I hope all that *talking* was worth it. I'm glad we got a chance to clear this up— for now."

In the doorway, she pauses. "But I should warn you, we're looking very closely at who was where on Saturday night. A boy died."

Val is going to drive me home, no ifs, ands, or buts. While she's putting on her outdoor gear, Bram drags me into the warm kitchen.

The blaze in the woodstove is dying slowly to embers. Bram looks as rattled as I feel.

"I didn't know Val was going to do that. I swear." He leans close, his glance darting toward the door. "I would've warned you. Do you believe me?"

I don't know if I believe him. I don't even know for sure that we *weren't* on that bench together, unlikely as it seems.

He keeps on talking, tripping over his words: "I heard Val on the phone earlier today, saying something about a witness who saw a couple on a park bench really late Saturday night. A tall, blond guy and a girl in a scarf with zebra stripes."

My heart rises in my throat. *Joss and me?* Of course. Joss is tall and blond. "Did she say who the witness was?"

Bram runs his fingers through his wild hair. "No, no names. I didn't think anything of it till tonight, when Val said she wanted to talk to you, and then I saw your scarf and it all clicked."

It's still sinking in: Someone saw me with Joss at three AM. "So you just said *you* were there because—"

"I'm tall and blond, right? It could have been me."

"But it wasn't." I remember what Val said about a photo lineup. A witness who was distant or drunk or high enough *might* mistake Bram for Joss in the dark, but they aren't exactly ringers.

Bram keeps fidgeting, fiddling with his shirttails. I step closer and reach for his hands, and he just barely flinches before clasping mine back. The amber light of the stove glints on his neck, his pulsing Adam's apple. "It'll be okay," he says.

My hands disappear into his, his palms reassuringly dry. Mine aren't. "Bram, you could get in serious trouble."

It must have been Joss that night. Who else?

"I don't care." Bram looks straight at me, the fire reflected in his blue eyes—wider and clearer than Joss's, like lake or sky. "I don't care what happened that night, Celeste. I don't care if you actually were out there with him."

I try to breathe, but my lungs have shriveled. "If you think I was, you should care."

"I know you didn't hurt him." His eyes are so confident. "That's not you, Celeste, and I think I know by now who you are. You're someone who'd never hurt anyone. That's one reason I like you."

The last words are a whisper. Before I can speak, he steps close and kisses me on the cheek—a brief, warm pressure, so fleeting it could be a dream.

Everything slows down and goes liquid—the firelight on the wall, the clock ticking, the sound of distant footsteps. Then we're standing apart again, and Val calls from the other room, her voice echoing on the old kitchen timbers: "Celeste!"

I remember Joss's kisses in the firelight—those first strange, ceremonial pecks. My head spins, mixing up past and present.

All I know is that Bram is taking a terrible risk. Maybe he doesn't quite understand what he's doing; maybe he does. "You think I was out there with Joss, and you still..."

His eyes are closed to me. Dark. "I didn't say I thought anything."

"Everybody's assuming things based on a *scarf*."

He opens his mouth, but the door bursts open. Val says, "Celeste, we need to get a move on."

Backlit by the stove, Bram has become a stranger. I want to touch him again, to kiss him back, to tell him everything I almost told Val, but all I can do is whisper, "Text me."

Then

"Stars and Sugar"

"This place has always been special, that's all," Joss says.

From the granite slab halfway up Mount Grogan, they can see the whole valley and the night sky. Seth is panting from the hike, and he feels dangerously light-headed. Joss takes hold of his waist and eases him gently down on the rock.

"Steady." Joss spreads a blanket over Seth's knees and tucks a thermos between Seth's hands. "Take it easy."

"I'm fine." Or at least Seth's not sweating and puking with the flu, like he was a week ago. He's felt okay for the past three days, just shaky. When Joss barged in and forced him into his coat and boots for an outdoor excursion "to see the stars," he was grateful.

Seth doesn't say any of that, doesn't need to. He opens the thermos, sips the warm cocoa, and pulls the blanket close.

The stars are so bright in winter. Seth thinks he could touch Venus, or whatever that especially vivid sky-blot is.

Joss is pulling stuff out of a backpack. "Here," he says, placing a fluted china vessel and spoon in Seth's lap.

The china is warm and smells of stewed fruit. "What the hell?" Seth asks. "Are you Rachael Ray now?"

Joss says in a low, embarrassed voice—so Seth knows he did cook the contents himself—"It's blackberry cobbler. My mom's recipe. Don't let it get cold."

Seth has never tried cobbler, isn't 100 percent sure what it is. Something pie-like that you eat at potluck church suppers with the nice Christian ladies, or at Weiner's Diner after school with your friends, if you have those. Or maybe your grandma makes it for you, if you have the kind of grandma who whips up anything more elaborate in her kitchen than Brandy Alexanders.

Now it's something Joss has made for him.

Seth eats the whole thing in a blink. And when he lets his body slump against Joss's, asking a silent question, Joss answers that, too, by wrapping a strong arm around him.

No kissing. No expectations. Just the warm food and this touch.

Seth rests his head on the sleeve of Joss's parka, and they stay there, looking at the stars.

Now

Can anyone tell me the difference between *jus soli* and *jus sanguinis*? Anyone?"

Under the desk I dig my nails into my palm, willing my eyelids not to drift closed. Staying conscious in seventh-period government is always a challenge, and I couldn't sleep last night.

Thrashing around, feeling like a fish in a tightening net. First the note, then Patrick, then Dad's story. Thread after thread connecting me to Joss. And now a witness who saw me with him on the park bench, perhaps right before he died.

Bram has saved me—for now, anyway—but he hasn't texted me, and I can't bring myself to make the first move.

Whatever he says, he knew he needed to lie for me. Maybe he overheard Vivvy and Seth planning Saturday. The whole time we were playing our little detective game, researching the Defilers, he knew I was keeping secrets about that night.

He helped me through that tight squeeze in the cave. He kissed my cheek. He said he liked me. But how can he like me when he *knows*?

So now I play the game alone. If I find out something, enough to make it safe to come clean myself, maybe I can minimize the damage to Bram.

Seth lurks in the corner of my eye—one row back, leaning against the wall with his hoodie cinched tight and his eyes closed. Not even pretending to be present. After this class, I'll have my one chance to get him alone and ask about the Defilers.

"That's right, Payton. Now, who can tell me the first step in the naturalization process?"

Two rows away, Halsey glances at me and bends to whisper something to Cammy. They both wear full powder-puff regalia: flippy skirts, letter jerseys, purple goop under their eyes. It must be intended as a parody of eye black, but it looks like bruising.

Halsey's heart-shaped face is diamond-hard, those .pink lips twisting into pretty, malicious bows. The shoulder pads of her uniform sit on her desk. What did she tell Sheriff Palmer about me?

Vivvy hasn't taken her own advice about not drawing attention by cutting school; I didn't see her at lunch or in English. Maybe it's better this way. I don't even want to know if she knows about the park bench.

Cammy's hand is up. "Mrs. Callifrey, Halsey and I have a pass for early dismissal. Powder-puffs are helping with refreshments for the memorial."

There's a memorial for Joss tonight on the elementary school green, where Tanner McKeough went after Vivvy and Bram decked him. I'll go and watch all the known Defilers carefully, see how they interact. But Seth is my only chance of actually pumping someone for info.

"Go ahead, you two," Mrs. Callifrey says.

Cammy and Halsey saunter down the aisle. As Halsey opens the door, Cammy turns to look at me. Eyes narrowed, forehead bunched like a predator's.

My breath catches as I remember everything Vivvy told me. These girls went through an induction ceremony that involved... things that happen in a dark room between young girls and older boys. And what about all the powder-puff inductions since then? Chances are, nothing's changed. They're the older girls now, forcing frightened thirteen-year-olds into that room, promising it won't be so bad.

Anger heats my cheeks—for younger Vivvy, who had the sense to run away, and for myself. *He doesn't even really like you, slut.*

The bell rings, and everybody who was comatose an instant ago leaps to their feet. I almost miss Seth as he glides past me to the door, a blur of olive-drab jacket and black hoodie. Then I'm on my feet, following.

He doesn't run, but he's quick—nimbly avoiding knots of people, not burdened with a heavy backpack like mine. I nearly lose him when a bunch of powder-puffs come to a roiling stop between us, arguing over how to distribute a load of boxes—but there he is, a lean, dark arrow headed for the exit by the chemistry lab.

I should be in my next class keeping a low profile, but I have two days left to do this, maybe one, so I shove open the door.

The chilly air attacks me, my breath steaming as I tail Seth around the side of the brick building. When he disappears into the juniper thicket, I hesitate, and he calls, "I can hear you breathing out there. Barley?"

Nic Barley, one of the more notorious stoners. I swipe aside the branches and step into the humid nook between the bush and the wall.

A pipe at knee level belches steam. "Oh shit," Seth says. Fingers fumble, almost dropping the joint he's trying to light. "You shouldn't be here. We shouldn't be together."

I hug myself to hide the shivers. "Nobody'll see."

"I'm not the only one who comes here." He braces himself against the wall and takes a drag. "And you don't cut class."

"I need to ask you something." No time to think about diplomacy. I glance the way I came, but the juniper hides us. "Seth, have you heard of the Defilers?"

"The what?"

His face betrays nothing, the cold drawing red spots on his pale cheeks. But the answer came too fast, like he didn't bother searching his memory first.

"It's a secret society. Jocks and popular kids—they meet in a cave. I've heard rumors at school, people saying Joss was a member."

Seth takes another drag. His nostrils flare. "I haven't heard those rumors. Guess I don't hang with the right crowd."

He could be telling the truth. Maybe he doesn't know where his photo ended up, or even that it was taken. But my actor brain analyzes his demeanor—studiously muted, with none of his typical nervous volatility—and tells me he's hiding something.

I remember how Val interrogated me last night. She didn't ask me about the bench. She told me.

"Something happened to you in that cave," I say.

Seth pushes off the wall and lurches into the space between us. "Did Vivvy send you here to talk to me? Is she the one feeding you this shit?"

"There's something weird between you and Joss. You can't deny that."

Seth rolls his eyes. "He and his friends were assholes to me. Nothing weird about that. Anything else is just a fantasy in Vivvy's twisted little head."

And mine. I'm treading on dangerous territory, but I can't stop. "Seth, are you a Defiler? Like him?"

"I told you, I don't know what the fuck you're talking about."

He muscles past me—not ducking under the bushes this time, just plowing through them. On the other side, he turns, his eyes huge and liquid, his brow drawn with rage.

"You tell Vivvy she can go fuck herself. And you too, Celeste. You're just desperate to point the finger at anyone you can."

That hurts, but I try to hold tight to my inner Valerie. "I don't think you hurt Joss, Seth. But one of the others could have."

"You're not making sense. What others?"

"Seth, I *know*—"

I stop short, because I can't ask him about the photo. It's too embarrassing, too intimate. Some detective I am.

Seth's still talking. "Your story about him staying behind for a smoke—that's bullshit, Celeste, and we all know it. I was all the way home by then, but you were there. You know *exactly* what happened that night."

A prickly branch has caught on his jeans; he swears, tugs himself free.

"I don't," I say too low, too late, as he disappears from my view.

Standing where Seth was, alone with the steaming vent and the lingering sweet stink, my cheeks burning and my lip caught between my teeth, I hear him say: "You can tell Vivvy I'm not breaking the stupid pact. Not yet. But if my ass is on the line, you're going down."

Then

This was a nightmare.

The intro ended, and I drew a frantic, inadequate breath and released it, sending my voice out over the auditorium, and I was singing "On My Own." Singing in front of people, accompanied by a pianist in her sixties who wore a sweater with a sparkly pumpkin on it and shot me a pitying glance as I faltered off-key.

The words tripped by too fast, garbled by my dry mouth. *Toute seule.* All alone. *Sans une amie.* Without a friend.

I didn't want a part in *Les Mis.* I was auditioning because Vivvy dared me to, and then Vivvy broke up Joss and Halsey (sort of), and somehow this performance became something I had to do to show her that I, too, could make things happen. Make things real.

There was no pro stage lighting here, nothing like my fantasy, only rehearsal glare and people propping their feet on chair backs and crunching chips and checking their phones and gossiping in quiet clumps.

At least I'd made Vivvy promise not to stand where I could see her.

In my fantasy—no, our fantasy, the one we spun together—Joss was in the audience. Unlikely as that was, I was afraid to look beyond the first two rows, just in case.

There was one part of this I could control. Just one. I gulped a deep breath, dug my thumbnail into the pad of my pointer, and closed my eyes, gathering all my breath for the loud part.

Tried to be Éponine.

I was walking by the Seine. Night had fallen, and my evil family was out of the way, so the sleeping city belonged to me. I could tell myself the story of the boy who wasn't here, walking beside me. The boy who didn't love me. The boy who was not, did not, would never, unless maybe . . .

The pianist pattered delicately out of the verse into the warm, throbbing notes of the chorus. I was telling a story—a love story that began in the fairy tales of my childhood. The story of a girl who dreamed of a prince and woke up and found him.

A fiction. A lie.

My natural pitch was good, people always said, but my soprano voice was prone to shiver and break under the strain of nerves. I wasn't nervous now, though. Not anymore. I was singing in my own language, one no one else here understood, and each note brought me closer to him, though he'd never know.

Tall. Blond. He gave me his hand, and together we walked along the silent quai in the rain, watching our shadows turn into giants wobbling on the black river.

Then came a wall. Slamming itself down between us, yanking us apart. The frigid stone of reality.

Frank's pleading eyes. Those horrible texts. When I reached out for love, *that* was what I found.

The piano changed key, from romantic bliss to a cold, angry lament. Mounting, mounting, pushing my voice to high, furious notes as I confronted the truth.

My lover wasn't here. Never had been. I'd invented him to give me what I needed—but he was a shadow, a phantom, an empty shell. A steady hand that would never touch mine. An arm that would never enlace me. A voice that would never say, *Let's write this story together.*

Joss and Seth were never together in the roadhouse parking lot, comforting each other, soothing each other's wounds. They never kissed furiously in the woods, never shared cobbler on a mountainside.

No one was here but me, alone with the things I didn't want to remember.

Except maybe, somewhere, Vivvy. She was braver than me, brave enough to run from that induction ceremony, but she understood being singled out and mocked. She understood not being able to trust. She told the story with me.

The last notes were hushed yet full of feeling, defeated and defiant at once. When everything else was gone, there was still my story. *Mon histoire.*

I opened my eyes into the glare.

A smattering of people clapped, the ones who clapped for

everybody and not just their friends. The pianist clapped, but she didn't smile.

I looked to neither side as I hustled down the stairs and up the aisle to the exit sign, my face hot and sludgy with tears. I'd done it, and that was enough. Right? Taking great gulps of air, I swung a door and a second door and stepped out onto the teal lino of the school lobby.

"Hey."

He stood half in and half out of the other door to the auditorium, a few yards away, leaning on it and lazily swaying. He didn't wear his letter jacket today, just jeans, a washed-out blue chamois shirt, and hiking boots.

"Hey, that was pretty sweet," he said. "You really know French, huh?"

Joss Thorssen. In the flesh.

I forced my lips into a smile. I nodded.

His legs were a little shorter than I'd been seeing them in my head. His hair was wavier. His chin was softer and less square. I needed to look at him more often.

"Somebody told me you're from Montreal?" A little tentative now, as if he thought I might bite him.

"Yeah." Who would have told him? Who even knew?

"I'm a huge Canadiens fan. Hey! Maybe you could help me out sometime. There's this fan forum where the players talk, but mainly in French. I use Google Translate, but it doesn't get the slang parts." He looked sheepish, like he wasn't sure he should admit to the degree of fandom that would involve reading a forum.

I gave myself a good hard mental kick, and a chirpy girl's voice came out of my mouth. "If you want somebody to translate, I could totally do that!"

"Sweet." Joss shoved the door wider. A snatch of "I Dreamed a Dream," painfully off-key, curdled the air between us. "I'm not, like, a big *Les Mis* fan. I just came 'cause my buddy's girlfriend's trying out."

"Celeste!" A bell-like voice behind us.

Vivvy. She twirled me around, hugged me in a blur of floral skirt. She smelled like musky perfume she'd probably stolen from Val's dresser.

"You were amazing!" She turned to Joss, her face so childishly animated that for a second I thought she'd start telling him everything. "Wasn't she amazing?"

"Sure thing." With a fist bump that didn't connect, Joss vanished back into the auditorium.

Vivvy hugged me all over again, tighter this time, her breath hot in my ear. "It happened! It actually happened!"

And I hugged her back, the two of us celebrating something no one else could understand. Just once in my life, my story came true.

Now

J oss Thorssen is dead, and I'm still learning new things about him: For instance, his favorite song was "Sweet Child o' Mine." Two student bands have performed it so far, neither of them well.

This one isn't exactly a "band," just two wasted hockey teammates with a guitar. The singing is painfully off-key, but the lanky redhead doing the playing gets the haunting chords right, and people around me begin to sway in time.

It's Tanner McKeough again—the Defiler, Vivvy's bully, Halsey's little secret.

I was on the fringe of the crowd when I arrived, but people keep pressing in, tighter and tighter, jostling me where I stand with hands in my pockets and scarf tight around my face (red wool, no more zebra stripes). People on either side hold candles with paper wax guards, their flickering heat on my cheeks.

Up front, bracing for the final chorus, Tanner McKeough whips off his shirt to reveal JT RIP scrawled in blue on his chest. A girl shrieks. An older woman beside me mutters, "Drunk as a skunk."

The whole town seems to have gathered on this frosty grass rectangle. No more than half the crowd is actually paying attention to the action on the improvised stage, but it's enough to give a somber feel to the candlelit gathering as the night and the temperature fall.

Wet-eyed jocks clutch one another's hands. Moms try to pacify whining kids. Old folks gravitate to the buffet tables, spooning canned beans onto plastic clamshells with the pursed scowls of people who aren't surprised by anyone's death.

Joss feels nowhere near this pulsing, shivering crowd. Joss is still halfway up the mountain, calling my name through the cedars. Still, how many hours did I spend with him, total? Four? Five? These people have known him their entire lives.

Tanner and his friend draw out the last chord and draw it out some more. Another girl screams; a boy bellows like a wounded beast.

As pandemonium looms, a twig of a bald man in a suit—the mayor, I think—steps onstage and begins slow-clapping. Boos from the crowd. Tanner truncates his chord with a fierce twang and stalks offstage.

Everything goes quiet, too quiet, until the mayor speaks again. The mic turns all voices into a churning burr.

Maybe that's why I feel so detached as I leave my spot and force my way through the crowd, looking for Defilers. They should all be here—Cammy, Halsey, and the rest.

When I glimpse the Kray family—Vivvy sandwiched between the two aunts, Bram towering behind his twin, all four of them with fur-cuffed coats and candles in tall blue-glass holders—I steer clear. Bram still hasn't texted, and I'm trying not to think about what he did for me last night, or what I might owe him in return, or his lips on my cheek in the firelight.

No time for all that. This afternoon, Seth lashed out at me the way people do when they have something to hide. His reaction to my question about the Defilers was a thread, a clue, and I have to follow where it leads.

I head for the buffet area, where the powder-puff girls are dishing out food and taking donations for a memorial plaque. I try to ignore how raw I feel, as if Seth and Val and Halsey and everybody else in this town have scraped away my skin and left my organs exposed to curious glances. *Is that her? The foreign girl? Did she kiss Joss? Did she kill him?*

But no, nobody's looking at me, not really—or nobody but Sarah Blessingham, clad in powder-puff periwinkle, who darts out from behind the baked-goods stall to give me a hug.

When we part, there are tear tracks in her faux eye black. She thrusts a chocolate chip cookie into my hand and waves away my dollar bill. "I just keep crying. I can't stop."

"Thanks." The gesture brings tears to my eyes, too. Clearly, the TV shows were wrong about every cheerleader being a snarky, mean girl.

But Sarah isn't a cheerleader. She's a powder-puff. The memory of Vivvy's story is a filthy rag I keep wringing and wringing, trying to get out the dirt but only succeeding in spraying it everywhere.

"You okay?" Sarah asks.

Words slip out of my mouth. "Do you like doing this

powder-puff thing?" *Do you still send little girls into dark rooms to be hurt? Do you think it's fun?*

"It's pretty silly, but we raise tons of money for charity. I love visiting nursing homes. The old men are so cute, they always try to—".

"What about the induction ceremony?" Another ragtag band has launched into a classic-rock cover, and the landslide of noise buries my words, freeing the part of me that doesn't want to be frozen anymore. That wants to speak up, to *do* something. "Vivvy told me about it, Sarah. Do you still make girls do those things?"

Sarah points vaguely into the crowd like she thinks I'm asking where Vivvy is. "Things?"

I should let it go, but I keep seeing Seth in that photo in the Defilers' binder. Instead, I yell in angry bursts: "When you induct new girls! She told me about the drinking, and the boys, and the dark room!"

Too late, I remember what Vivvy said—how they swore her to secrecy and told her no one would believe her. But I refuse to be intimidated by a bunch of girls in flippy skirts, or even by Tanner McKeough.

Sarah flinches. She looks more puzzled than pissed off, though, as the band's last chord trails off into half-hearted applause. "Vivvy tells the weirdest stories. Our induction's barely anything."

"Maybe you weren't there that time?" Another customer approaches, clutching a wailing toddler with one hand and a brownie with the other.

Sarah takes the woman's dollar bills, her broad forehead as smooth and guileless as a baby's. "I've been at every induction since seventh grade. They're G-rated. I've never drunk a drop of alcohol. And I wouldn't take Vivvy's word on it, because she's never even tried out for powder-puffs."

The whole scene swims before my eyes. If Sarah's telling the truth, then Vivvy lied to me.

Then

need your decision," Mom said from my phone's speaker.

"Can't I think about it for a few more days?" I grabbed a sparkly scarf from a hanger. I was due at Vivvy's in eight minutes, and she'd told me to expect a "surprise."

"I have to clear out the room *today*, Celeste."

"Why today?" Mom had warned me that if I moved out, my stuff might have to go with me or to storage, because apartment space is expensive. But I couldn't seem to take the final step of giving her the go-ahead to pack it up. Dad and I lived in a rental, too. Was I supposed to keep shuttling my stuff between storage lockers until I could afford my very own mortgage?

Vivvy would never have to worry about that. Her old house might be clammy, full of doors that stuck, but it was a fortress, a home base.

"Why the hurry?" I asked. "Are you already getting a roommate?"

A rush of breath from the speaker. "Erich is moving in next week. He needs space for his files."

The news shouldn't have been a surprise, but it felt like a

dunk in cold water. "You're moving a *guy* in? A stranger? You couldn't just tell me?"

"He's not a stranger. You've met him!"

Was Erich the sixty-something professional activist in the Peruvian scarf who helped clean up after Mom's political meetings, or the younger, hipstery professor? Whoever he was, my room and my window and my closet were his now.

"I guess you're in love with him." The words came out colder than I meant them to. "You've known him for what, months? Now he's taking my place."

"It's very serious with Erich, yes, but he's not taking your place. Of course not. Anyway, you chose to leave. Celeste—"

"Box it all up and send it here." I shook all over; the room seemed to have shrunk to the size of the phone screen. "I'll deal with it. But when I come home in December, don't ask me to act like this guy's part of my family. I'll stay in an Airbnb."

Her voice trembled. "You will not, and that's not fair. Do you expect me to spend my life alone because you're gone?"

Being alone isn't the end of the world. "You think he's the love of your life, don't you?" I knew I was being mean, but I couldn't stop. "Give it a couple years, and you'll find someone new to give my room to."

"Celeste! That's a totally unacceptable thing to say." The words came out shaky and awkward, like she'd learned them from some TED Talk on parenting with tough love. "I have as much right to happiness as you do."

She did deserve happiness, and I might be bitter, mean, and ungrateful, but I knew her track record. I hung up.

"Don't you want the surprise?" Vivvy asked.

Her look was uncharacteristically up-to-date today—short, tailored shorts; long earrings. Traipsing across the yellowed lawn with a thermos, she could have been a model in a hipster catalog.

"You have a boyfriend?" I said, my heart sinking. The conversation with Mom had left me feeling a little pummeled, and Mom always dressed up when she started dating someone.

"Oh my God, no, silly!" Vivvy took a gulp, splashing tea on her sweater. "You'd be the first to know, and I'm not even on the hunt. *You* don't have a boyfriend suddenly, do you?"

I laughed. "I'm not on the hunt, either."

"Power to the single ladies!" She led me uphill toward Middle-earth through the tangled, tired-looking vegetation. "When am I getting your next story?"

"Soon. When am I getting yours?"

She didn't answer, and for an instant, doubt iced my chest. Could she be over the whole thing?

As we reached our spot, she turned abruptly to me. "Don't say anything about them. I mean, I know you won't. But just in case—don't."

"Don't say anything about what?"

Then I saw him—behind Vivvy, Seth Larkin sat hunched on the widest ledge, his oversized army jacket harmonizing with the gray rock. Black hair spilled into his eyes as he raised a peacock-blue vaporizer to his lips.

My throat tightened, the stone ledges closing in on me. Now I got it—this was the surprise. I wasn't supposed to mention our stories to *him*.

"Stop being such a sullen teenage cliché, Seth!" Vivvy called.

Seth gave me a perfunctory nod. He clearly wasn't surprised—or impressed—to see me.

Vivvy rocketed up the stone stairsteps to him. She extended a hand to help me up after her, but I didn't take it.

I knew Seth was real, of course. I knew Vivvy had hung out with him and Joss in middle school, here in these woods. But it still felt wrong to be here with him. He was a stranger, someone who might judge us. A *boy*.

"This is Celeste." Vivvy bowed as if formally presenting me. "Gorgeous and cosmopolitan, *mais oui!*"

Seth took a drag on his vaporizer and stuck out his hand without making eye contact. *"Enchanté."*

I shook, reaching over Vivvy. Though I saw Seth most days in English and government, I didn't dare look closely at him. The real Seth was smaller and younger-looking than he was in my imagination, with two whiteheads marring his chin. He moved from one slouch to another, as if incapable of sitting or standing up straight.

"I'm sorry about that weird thing in English class." My words tumbled over one another.

His blue eyes opened wide. "English class?"

"Seth has selective amnesia for school," Vivvy said—flushed, happy, as if she were watching a fireworks display. And then, to him: "Celeste knows how to kiss on both cheeks. She's like a fine wine in a school full of...Coors Light."

197

"Fresh and surprising vintage with notes of oak," Seth said.

They didn't act like people who'd ever stopped being friends. Like Vivvy and me, they had a private language, a shared script for the imaginings in their heads, and I wondered how much she'd told him about me. I hoped not much, but then, *I* hadn't told her that much about me. As long as Seth didn't know about the stories…

Seth looked directly at me for the first time. "Oh right, English class. The girl who shut me down."

He didn't sound pissed off, just sort of curious, but I knotted the tails of my button-down and clenched my fist in the knot. Vivvy teased, "You needed to be shut down."

"Yeah, guess I was bullying poor little Thorssen. I'm amazed he recovered from the trauma."

I had to explain somehow. "I—it was an acting-class thing. I used to take these workshops, and the director would try to humiliate us on purpose, to get a reaction. It reminded me of that, I guess. It wasn't personal."

I felt his gaze on me, but when I looked up, he was looking away again, fiddling with the vaporizer, his hands jig-jogging. It came to me all of a sudden, in a rush of relief: *He's shy.* Not with Vivvy or Joss, but with strangers like me.

"From the city, huh?" he asked.

Vivvy said, "Tell him all about Montreal. How you went to bars and clubs and college classes. He's gonna die. Billings is a metropolis to him."

"Fuck you," Seth said, but it was a friendly one, if there's such a thing.

He started asking me questions—first tentatively, then in a steady volley. He wanted to know about neighborhoods and festivals and gay clubs and most of all restaurants, and he seemed disappointed when I didn't recognize the name of a trendy place on the Plateau.

"Seth wants to be a cook," Vivvy explained.

"Not cook, chef-owner. I'm gonna go out to LA, get a dishwashing job, learn from the ground up."

"What about college?"

"Do I look like I need four hundred K in student loans?" Seth dropped the vaporizer and grabbed a tree branch, trying to swing himself up. "School of life, man."

"It's not that easy," Vivvy said, and I remembered her fear that she'd never leave Kray's Defile. "You can't just pack up and go to a place like LA."

"Why not?" He grinned. "Put some gas in the junker, take a road trip, rent a crappy apartment."

"You can't make a life from scratch."

"Sure, you can." Seth flung out his arms to embrace the scene—yellow grass, aspens, mountains, big sky. "I mean, it's not like I'll be leaving much behind, right? Anyway, Celeste moved, so she knows it can be done. Right, Celeste?"

The opening made me flush with gratitude. He didn't hate me. "I moved with my dad," I admitted. "That's different. But it was...a big change."

Again that dazzling smile. "Change is good."

We—well, mostly they—kept talking. Seth succeeded in

wedging himself in a crook of the tree where he could look down on us. Vivvy passed me the thermos of hot tea. I could feel her trying to find a way to bring up Joss.

She mentioned hockey, which Seth had no discernible interest in. She mentioned Halsey, ditto. Finally, she came right out and asked, "Who do you think Joss's going to hook up with next?"

"Thorssen?" As if the name were an effort to remember. "I dunno, maybe the entire powder-puff team. At once."

"You used to be friends," Vivvy said.

"For like a week."

"He beat up Nate Carlsson for you."

"Bullshit." Seth's cheeks were red now. "You weren't even there. Carlsson attacked me, Joss stepped between us, Carlsson reached around him to try to clock me, and Joss made a lucky swing. He wasn't some hero."

As he talked, his face lit up again. "You girls and your obsessions with jocks. I mean, I get it, Thorssen's conventionally hot. No disagreement from me. But do you honestly think you could get through a conversation with him?"

"Celeste did."

Vivvy nudged me, and I wanted to sink into the ground. "He heard her sing at the tryouts yesterday and came up just to compliment her. He wants her to translate French for him."

Seth leaped from his branch and staggered to a stop between us. "Wow. Am I invited to the engagement party?"

"We barely talked," I said quickly, because Vivvy was embarrassing me. And Seth had a point. "It *would* be weird having a conversation with Joss. He's all about hockey. Have you ever even watched an entire game, Vivvy?"

She widened her eyes, as if to say, *You're off script*. "It's not about that. It's about connecting on a deeper level."

"Thorssen doesn't have a deeper level," Seth said. "I mean, don't get me wrong, he means well, but there ain't much to him. Mainly, he's a coward."

"Proof?" Vivvy snapped.

Seth just looked at her.

"Well, that was interesting," I said in my most cynical voice as we flopped down on the wrought-iron chairs on Vivvy's lawn. "But I still don't understand what happened in English. In fact, I think now I understand it less."

Vivvy dug her toes into the scraggly grass that Bram was supposed to mow. "You do understand, silly."

"Seth doesn't think Joss is a monster. He just thinks he's shallow." *And he's probably right.*

But Vivvy wasn't letting the dream die. "Seth called Joss a monster because he's in love with Joss. He'll always be in love with Joss."

"He told you that?" I couldn't keep the skepticism out of my voice; Seth didn't strike me as a secret romantic. I liked him, but he wasn't the anguished, pining Seth in my head. The only things he seemed sentimental about were haute cuisine and his vaporizer, and he was downright eager to leave behind the Defile—and, presumably, Joss—forever.

"Of course he didn't *tell* me." Vivvy's voice shook a little. "You know what they say about writing: Show, don't tell. If you ignore what Seth says and watch what he does, you'll see he's more in love with Joss than ever."

Now

'm still looking for Defilers, but it's impossible to find anyone in this chaos. People on the green sway as a girl on the podium drones a dirge, accompanying herself on an acoustic guitar.

The crowd eddies and swells like an ocean. An internal current catches me, trawls me away from the stage, and suddenly I'm on the verge of a ragged ring of people who've drawn back to give space to two big guys who are circling each other, shoulders tight and eyes locked.

One of them is Tanner McKeough—still shirtless, an angry streak of white. Facing him a couple of feet away, fists clenched at his sides, is another hockey player with a long, whey-pale face and ears like jug handles.

Patrick from physics. I try to step backward, away, but the crowd's packed too tight. People murmur, some voices raised in fear and others in anticipation.

"You're a fucking pussy!" Tanner yells at Patrick. "Say it to my face!"

Patrick answers, but his low voice is lost in the crowd. Then, suddenly, people scramble in either direction, parting to make way for a tall, determined shape. I catch a glint of badge as Valerie Kray plows past me.

I back away, but she doesn't seem to see me, thrusting herself between Patrick and Tanner. "Time to chill, boys! Turn around and walk the other way!"

Her booming voice sends a shock wave through the crowd, opening spaces for me to creep farther from the stage, toward the darkness. I push and dodge and weave between groups, eyes down, till a voice behind me croaks, "Celeste?"

It's Patrick, alone and apparently unscathed by Tanner's wrath. "Hey," he says, smiling crookedly in a way that's both friendly and extremely drunk. "You okay? That was messed up, huh?"

"Yeah." I try to smile, craning my neck to make sure Tanner didn't follow. In the distant din, Val is still scolding someone. "Are *you* okay?"

"Oh sure. McKeough just needs a time-out." He gestures at the crowd. "We're all kinda wrecked tonight."

Feedback from the stage jams my ears as I try to look sympathetic. *Don't freeze up. Use him for info, work him—do what Vivvy would do.* "Hey, I'm sorry I was rude in class on Monday. I was just surprised."

"Shit, Celeste, I barely remember yesterday." Patrick lurches toward me—foul breath in my face. "Everything since that assembly's a blur."

"I know what you mean." I need to know why he and Tanner were squaring off.

Patrick is off on his own track, eyes bright with tears. "I gave Joss a hard time about you. This one night after a game, he kept talking about you, and I was an asshole about it."

A chill ripples through my chest. "Are you sure he meant me?"

"'Course. The French girl. We don't have more than one of those around here."

"But I didn't know him that well." Why do I keep insisting that? Because I'm Éponine, singing a story about love that can never be? Because, if Joss really liked me the way Patrick seems to think, he wouldn't have left me on a park bench at three AM?

Unless I left *Joss* somewhere. Unless I hurt him. And the more I deny any connection to him, the more guilty I probably look.

"I mean, of course I *knew* him," I say. "Everybody did. But I think we only talked about six times."

"You counted?"

My face and neck burn, and Patrick laughs and says, "He only said good stuff about you, promise. Mainly how he liked your singing. And how he thought you liked him."

Waves of heat radiate across my cheeks.

"He was amazing, right? We were best friends since we were four, running sack races right here on this field." Patrick sways and staggers toward me. "He was so fast. Celeste, I'm in shock."

My body wants to shy away, but I let him latch on to my shoulder, using me to stay upright. "That's totally natural. Patrick..."

The speakers release a high-pitched barb of feedback, making us both jump. Onstage, the mayor hands the mic to a tiny, tense-shouldered blond woman.

"Oh shit." Patrick's fingers knead my shoulder. "That's Neely Thorssen. His mom."

The whole crowd goes silent, candles flickering. Joss's mom drops the mic—*squeal*—and yells across the crowd, "Better this way, right?"

High and nasal, her voice slices the dry air like a razor blade. "Yes!" people shout back. "We hear you, hon!"

"People told me I shouldn't get up here. Said I might lose my cool."

Patrick whispers in my ear, "She is *seriously* messed up."

I strain my ears to catch the frigid string of Neely Thorssen's monologue. Something about too many memorials, about drugs and drunk driving and young lives cut short.

"But my son didn't party too hard." She points into the crowd as if to accuse us all of saying as much. "He was murdered."

Candles waver, the crowd's silence throbbing in my ears.

"Murdered by someone in this town, or somebody from away. Somebody that don't belong here."

Patrick sucks in his breath. For an instant, Joss's mom seems to be looking directly at me—*the French girl*—before she goes on:

"And we all know there's certain people here that don't belong. One of *those* people beat my son and left him for dead."

The crowd murmurs in unsettling affirmation. From the edge of the stage, the mayor steps forward, takes Neely Thorssen's arm.

She doesn't resist, only raises her voice. "This was an attack!"

"Yeah!" a man's voice bellows from the front.

They could be talking about me, and the outrage from the crowd makes me sway on my feet, my head spinning. Then I hear somebody mention deportation, and I realize whom they actually mean—the undocumented people who work at the meatpacking plant. I feel relief for an instant and then a hot stab of shame, because "those people" are more vulnerable to these reckless accusations than I could ever be.

And no one from outside the Defile did this. I know it.

Patrick's arms hold me up, his whiskey breath on my cheek like Joss's that night. "Hey, you okay? You want a drink or something? I mean, water?"

"I'm okay." But I let him lead me out of the crowd. We head for the edge of the playing field, Patrick using his bulk to sweep people aside.

I breathe more easily as we plunk ourselves in the grass beside an equipment shed, where the podium is just a blare in the distance. Patrick takes a swig from a flask, offers it. "J&B?"

"No, thanks." I need to find my footing again, to be the one asking the questions. "Did Palmer talk to you?" *Did you tell him about me?*

"Yeah." Patrick tips his head back. "He was asking me about Saturday, mainly. Where I thought Joss was that night."

"What did you say?"

"I told him hell if I know. I had a hot date with a college girl after the game." A wide grin. "I told Palmer what happened on Friday, though, like that did me any good."

There's a dark note in his voice. "What happened on Friday?"

Patrick re-ups on his flask. "That's the reason Tanner's pissed off at me. Palmer asked when I last saw Joss, and it happened to be Friday in the lot after school, when he and McKeough were fighting about a cave party. So stupid."

Cave party. I sit up ramrod straight, blood pounding in my temples. "So you're a Defiler?"

"A what?"

I need cop composure like Valerie Kray's, not this whole-body tremor. "I've heard about those cave parties in the mountain pass. Joss, Tanner, Gibsy Arnesen—they were all there, right?"

"They do stupid shit up there, yeah. They invited me one time, back in middle school, but caves give me panic attacks."

Too bad, but he can still tell me about Friday. "So what was their fight about?"

Patrick sprawls out on his back, the flask resting on his chest. "McKeough wanted Joss to come to the cave party, and Joss couldn't make it with his ankle. It wasn't even an argument, just ragging on each other. McKeough said Joss was a pussy, and Joss said McKeough was a dick, and then some other guy said they'd carry Joss up the mountain, and Joss told them to fuck off, he'd find something else to do. Or some*one* else." He laughs.

Us. That's what he found to do. "So he didn't go to the cave."

"I dunno. McKeough was like, 'Well, if you're gonna be a dick about it, your traitor ass ain't welcome; maybe you should run and tattle to the sheriff,' and Joss was like, 'Whatever,' and he limps off, and that's the last time I saw him." Patrick's voice falters. "I didn't even tell Palmer all that; I just said they had words. Now McKeough blames me—what an asshole."

Light from the podium glints on his flask. The Milky Way fuzzes the space between the stars. "Why would Tanner call Joss a traitor?"

"Every single thing, it's the same: You're either with Mc-Keough or you're against him. Guess he decided Joss was against him—like me now, apparently."

"But why would Joss tattle to the sheriff?"

Patrick shrugs. " 'Cause the cave's off-limits?"

Or because of what happens in the cave. I scramble to my knees; frost has soaked through the seat of my jeans. Blood sings in my ears as I remember the passage Bram showed me on the map, stretching all the way from the Defilers' cave to the cave mouth where Joss died.

Tanner could have taken that passage. Maybe Joss was a "traitor" in Tanner's mind because he'd threatened to tell the sheriff about the Defilers. Or maybe Tanner's problem was that Halsey still loved Joss, break or no break.

"Did he end up coming to your house?" Patrick asks. "Saturday afternoon?"

"Joss?" Patrick knows about that, too?

The edges of his words are starting to melt. "He said he was gonna go over there and tell you not to worry about Halsey. Said she might start bugging you, being nasty 'cause she thought he liked you." A sad laugh. "I figured that was just his excuse for making a move on you."

That's why Joss came over—to protect me, to warn me? "But he and Halsey were broken up."

"Maybe not so much in her mind. Halsey's a piece of work, just like McKeough—cold one second, hot the next."

"Yeah, well," I say, pushing myself to my feet, "when he came over that day, I wasn't there. No moves were made. Did you tell the sheriff about that, too?"

I know he didn't before he shakes his head. If he had, Palmer would have questioned me long ago—unless the sheriff's biding his time, watching me.

As I turn to go, Patrick calls drunkenly, "I'm not some kinda traitor, okay? I'm not goin' around telling everybody's secrets. My friend's dead, and I just—I mean, when I said Joss talked about you, it wasn't in a disgusting way. He just said you were different, like you had this 'grace.' That's all."

Then

Besides AP English, Joss and I had health together. When ancient, pissed-off-looking Mr. Sporko—they called him the Mummy behind his back—wasn't lecturing us about abstinence, he had us sit at our desks and do worksheets. I finished mine in seven minutes, pulled out my notebook, and watched Joss.

He wasn't doing his worksheet, either. He stared at his desktop, shoulders hunched, and flicked a pencil in a wobbly circle. His eyelids drooped. His skin was so ashen it made his hair look dark.

Under the desk, I checked my mail. Nothing from Vivvy, only from Mom, begging me to talk to her, and a DM from a college girl I knew in Montreal named Bess McTeer. She'd written to tell me about an upcoming production of *Spring Awakening* at McGill with a part I might be good for.

I'd always felt bad about not saying goodbye to Bess.

I'm actually in Montana now! Moved here with my dad, not really acting anymore. Sorry I haven't been in touch.

Flick. Flick. Joss never hit the pencil hard enough to send it flying off the desk. His patience seemed infinite, until he gave a little shake of the shoulders, picked up the pencil, and started doodling—what, I couldn't see.

I was Seth watching him—not the real Seth, but *our* Seth. I closed my eyes and breathed in the closeness of Joss. The pent-up-ness. The twitching. The boredom.

Oh no! Bess wrote back. *Don't they have theater programs in Montana?*

My face flushed at the memory of the *Les Mis* audition. *It's not really the same.*

Joss stopped doodling and lowered his head to the desk. The Mummy didn't notice or care.

I hope this doesn't have to do with what happened in Frank's class that time. When he started asking you those questions about your sex life—I should have reported him.

The room went swimmy around me, and I concentrated on not dropping the phone. Joss napped peacefully while the Mummy drank a Diet Coke and grinned at something on his laptop.

It wasn't worth reporting. I'm fine.

I know it was a college class, I know directors are supposed to break down our boundaries, but you were fifteen, and he knew that! Ugh.

The usual excuses rushed to my mind: It was part of an acting exercise. Frank was just trying to push me to a place where I'd show real emotion. But he was also angry, because I wouldn't answer his calls or texts after *that* night, the night I went to his apartment—which was my fault, too, wasn't it?

That was why I couldn't tell Vivvy about him. Not because of what I did, but because of what I didn't do.

But Bess wouldn't agree it was my fault, and maybe she was right. I wrote, *Thank you for stopping him.*

It was the LEAST I could do. Celeste, don't let an asshole poison something you love.

I won't.

The Mummy glanced up, and I slid the phone back into my bag before his gaze could light on me. It passed over the sleeping Joss without interest.

Bess's vehemence hung in the air, refusing to dissipate. *Poison something you love.* Had I let Frank do that, or had I only found something new, something I loved better than acting?

I pulled my notebook toward me and started writing. Not homework, but a new story:

"Drowning"

"Thorssen, pick it up! You got skates on those feet or lead bricks?"

Assistant Coach Heyerdahl was in charge today, and he wouldn't stop riding Joss's ass. Every time he bellowed across the ice, the sound splintering into echoes, Joss bit down hard on his mouthguard and felt his cheeks flush.

That voice hadn't always been so angry. And those deep-set gray eyes...The first time they talked, after a chance meeting in the cave, Drew Heyerdahl had seemed so understanding. Drew had grown up without a

213

dad, too. He understood the pressure Joss felt to please his mom, to please the whole town, on the rink and everywhere else.

Like an idiot, Joss had opened up to him, wanting advice from somebody a little older who'd been there, and now the coach wouldn't stop acting like an asshole.

After practice, Heyerdahl followed them all into the locker room on the pretext of psyching them up for Saturday's game, lecturing them on avoiding drugs, booze, and especially "bitches." Joss pulled his clothes on in the shower as fast as he could.

When he emerged, Heyerdahl was teasing Tanner McKeough about having a threesome with Ashley and Cammy. Joss tried to slip by without attracting notice, but the gray eyes darted to him, and Heyerdahl crowed, "Good thing we don't have to worry about our Joss. He's straight as a board, clean as a Sunday school teacher. No distractions for this boy!"

Everybody roared, while Joss went beet red. And then Heyerdahl—Drew, Drew, his name was Drew—started asking the whole room why Halsey had dumped Joss. Did he not satisfy her? Could he not get it up? And that was enough, just enough, and Joss nabbed his duffel and stormed out, leaving his teammates to whoop and carry on behind him.

He wanted to punch something. Drew was a prick, but Drew had all the power, and they both knew it. Joss could bring him down if he wanted, but not without trashing his own rep, not without destroying the whole town's image of him.

In the parking lot, he practically barreled into Seth, who'd been waiting crouched in the shadow of Joss's truck.

"Someone could have seen you!" Joss hissed, furious. The next moment, he was yanking Seth toward him and kissing him like both of their lives depended on it.

* * *

The first few times Joss drove Seth home, Seth had asked to be let off on the corner. This time, though, he let Joss take the turn, and he said, "That's me, right here."

It wasn't that bad. Just a crappy apartment building.

When Joss pulled up, Seth distracted him by palming his knee where the denim had torn, and he kept his finger there, on the heat of Joss's skin, while Joss pressed him close and kissed him one last time on lips that already felt tender and bruised.

Seth wrestled himself free of Joss's grip and slid down from the cab. As he passed the driver's side, a hand shot through the open window and caught him by the sleeve, drawing him in for one last risky kiss.

Blond hair wan under the streetlight. Stubbled cheek. Husky whisper: "Tomorrow."

Climbing the steps of the building, Seth still tasted Joss, still felt that hot breath in his ear. It could end any time, *he reminded himself.* Joss is just like a kid with a new toy. Not much to him.

But a deep, hidden part of him wanted to believe Joss wouldn't let him go.

* * *

Joss's mom was up late, doing the bills at the dining room table. When she saw him, she pressed a finger to her lips. "Be quiet on the stairs, sweetheart?"

"I'm supposed to be quiet for Mark, when he wakes me up every fucking morning?"

"Please don't cuss, honey. Were you out with Halsey?"

At moments like this, when his mom was sitting around in her robe without makeup, Joss remembered how beautiful she was. Her beauty was all about vulnerability, and something curdled inside him as he realized how much they looked alike.

"Hals and I aren't together anymore," he said.

His mom went still, like a field mouse watching a hawk swoop overhead.

"Go on. Tell me how perfect Halsey is for me. Tell me what a crappy son I am. Tell me Dad would be ashamed."

His mom just sat, pen poised over her checkbook. She'd grown up in a household where cocktail hour started at breakfast, and survival meant enduring her dad's belt and fists. You could body-slam her, stick her

216

inside an iron maiden, and she'd probably pretend she didn't feel a thing.

Joss was not his mother. When Heyerdahl started baiting him, he hadn't fought back, but he hadn't just stood there and taken it, either. He'd run and tried to drown in Seth, kissing him like a wild man.

Before he could push the memories away, a buzz from his phone pulled every nerve and muscle to attention.

It wasn't Seth. It was him again. He did things like that, humiliate Joss and then call to try to apologize.

Joss shoved the phone into his pocket, wanting to crush it like a bug. "Sorry," he said, meaning it. "I know you liked Halsey's parents and everything. But it wasn't working out."

As he headed for the stairs, he barely heard his mother say, "I just want you to be happy."

Now

I f Bram hasn't texted by now, it's because he doesn't want to. He lied for me, he kissed my cheek in the kitchen, and now he's probably having very reasonable second thoughts.

Outside my room, something creaks, and I freeze. Footsteps in the hall. Then whistling, opening of cabinets—Dad's getting a midnight snack.

I tug Joss's chamois shirt out of its hiding place in the closet and slip it on over my Henley. It still smells like him—sweaty musk under the woodsmoke.

In the en suite, I brush my hair in front of the mirror, noting how much smaller and more feminine the shirt makes me look. Like a girl wearing her boyfriend's shirt, not like a girl who wrote disturbing stories about a boy she barely knew.

I've drafted five or six texts to Bram and deleted them all. Some were about what Patrick told me, and the suspicion it casts on both Halsey and Tanner McKeough. Some asked, in increasingly pathetic ways, if he'd be willing to go back with me to the cave tomorrow.

If a Defiler killed Joss, those photos in the binder could be key evidence. The sheriff knows Joss and Tanner were fighting, but he hasn't arrested anyone. And by tomorrow, a witness might place Vivvy, Seth, and me on the hill on Saturday night.

Again I see Tanner McKeough ripping off his shirt, striking the last chord on his guitar. A boy with a flair for drama. A boy who doesn't go in for half measures. A boy who bullied Vivvy for no reason, who considered Joss a traitor and wanted Halsey for himself.

For no reason. Except there was a reason for that incident on the playing field, or I thought so—the powder-puff induction that Halsey doesn't want anyone to know about. The powder-puff induction that Sarah claims was actually harmless and G-rated.

I'm sweating in the overheated house, suffocating. Why am I waiting for Bram? The person I need to talk to is Vivvy.

I leave the bathroom, pull on my coat and boots, and quietly open the front door.

She'll hit the roof if she finds out Bram lied for me, whether she believes the lie or not. But *she* lied to me about that induction ceremony; neither of us has been 100 percent honest with the other.

Maybe it's time for us both to come clean. Maybe she knows something about Tanner that I should know, too.

Outside, the night is clear, the stars diamonds. The snow where I saw the word "confess" has melted. The cold gives me a surge of adrenaline, like a plunge into a frigid lake, as I thrust my hands into my pockets and head for the Krays' house.

Before I've gone ten steps, there it is.

219

The sedan that followed me when I went to see Bram last night stands parked in front of a ranch house no more than fifty feet away. The street is spottily lit, but there's a shadow—someone in the driver's seat.

Is it the same sedan? *Get the plate.* I order my muscles to unfreeze, my legs to take another step.

And I realize I'm still wearing Joss's shirt.

By the time I can think clearly again, I'm back in the house, gasping for breath, my hands shaking almost too much to twist the dead bolt. Dad never bought curtains to cover the picture window, so I flick off the foyer light and press my back to the living room wall.

The shirt burns through my coat, through my skin. How could I forget I had it on? Do I *want* to get caught? Caught for what?

When I finally manage to peek outside, I find bare trees. Parked cars. Neighbors' porch lights. The ranch house where the sedan was parked is too far down the street to see.

It probably wasn't the same car, and I'm just scaring myself, and I *am* going to the cave tomorrow, with or without Bram's help. Once Vivvy sees what's in that binder, she'll understand why I had to "play detective." We can join forces again.

Still, I can't shake the feeling that someone's out there. Watching, waiting.

Then

can't believe you're going to Montreal over winter break. I'll go crazy here alone!"

We were spending an unseasonably warm afternoon on the mountainside, in the dim nook behind the cedars, with cool air wafting to us from the cave. Vivvy had brought a thermos of iced Moroccan mint tea and a croquet mallet that she joked about using to ward off "creeps." As we talked, she played with it, tracing the red rings around its bulky head.

Now I grabbed the mallet's handle and waggled it, feeling its smooth solidity. "You won't be alone. You're never alone here."

Vivvy had her big house full of people and her head full of stories. She had Bram. She had Seth. I was the one who needed her. A whole day had passed, and she hadn't told me she loved my "Drowning" story. She'd only sent the words *Thank you!!!* and heart emojis. It bothered me like a splinter in my heel, and I knew I'd grown dependent on her detailed praise, her speculations about how the story would continue.

But when I looked up, she was crying.

Or her eyes were wet, anyway. Not a full-on loss of control, like that awful time with Tanner McKeough, just a wobbly, accusing look as she said, "You're so insensitive sometimes. Like, maybe you could say you're going to miss me, too?"

"I am going to miss you." Blood rushed to my face. "But it's not even happening for two months, and it won't be for very long."

"It's the principle, Celeste. When somebody opens up to you, you should open up back."

We didn't really say those things in my family—*I love you, I miss you*. But maybe that was just my excuse. Maybe, in my own wimpier way, I was just as mean as Halsey. "I'm sorry."

"You remind me of Joss." Vivvy bit her lip like a middle schooler. "I mean, *our* Joss. You wrote him like you. It's so unfair the way he hides things from Seth. I think he takes Seth for granted, in a really toxic way."

Better to be Joss than Halsey, at least. "It's not that simple. Joss has had a lot of—"

"I know. *So* much angst. Poor wittle jock prince who has a mysterious past with the coach that you didn't bother to explain. Why doesn't he ever stop and think that maybe Seth has things worse? I mean, hello, homophobia!"

Heat spread over my face as I realized she was right—the thing with the coach could have seemed mysterious. But I wasn't ready to spell it out. "Joss knows he's toxic."

"That hasn't stopped him from hooking up with Seth."

The words were so crude, and when had Vivvy become Seth's

official defender? Had she stopped separating the fictional Seth from the real one? "Things can be complicated. On both sides."

Vivvy dug the heel of one hand fiercely into her eye. "Why'd you give my brother your phone number?"

Now I was totally confused. "I...He asked for it. I mean, sometimes we all go places together, so it makes sense to have each other's numbers, right?"

"Do you like him, Celeste?"

"Of course I—wait, you mean like *that*?" Bram and I had certainly gotten friendlier since we met, even comfortable enough to tease each other, but there'd been no touching or furtive glances. Had she seen me looking at him wrong? Did she guess that I was impressed when he punched Tanner? "It doesn't have to mean anything when you give someone your number." It had meant way too much to Frank—but I tried not to think about that.

Vivvy's lips remained pressed together. "You haven't answered the question."

Maybe she wanted me to apologize to her again, but this time I couldn't, so I turned it into a joke. "Actually, yeah, I'm bored of Joss. It's all about Bram now. When we decide to elope and consummate our passion, you'll be the first to know."

She didn't crack a smile. "Celeste, Bram and I shared a womb. If you dropped me for him, that would be some seriously gothic shit."

Was *I* toxic? When you're toxic, people leave you. People replace you. "I was kidding, okay? I don't feel that way about him. He's just a friend. And I'm not going to 'drop' you."

"Promise me both of those things."

"I promise." I patted her hand—once, awkwardly. Not daring to hug her, not sure how to do it right.

"Thanks." Vivvy used the mallet to pound a small hollow into the dirt. "Sorry if that seems harsh. I just worry about my brother."

"I get it." I couldn't imagine a reason for her to worry about Bram, but they had a bond I couldn't fully understand. If I couldn't respect that, I was a bad friend.

"And your story was good. It's just, I feel sometimes like you're being so cryptic, withholding so much info, and when you do that, I don't know how to add to it. It's not my story anymore, just yours."

She was right—I'd been keeping secrets. Focusing on my own problems when I should have been thinking about us.

I said, "It's still your story. It's always your story. You write the next chapter."

Before we left, we walked to the cave entrance, just as far as Fish and Wildlife's NO ACCESS signs. The cold breath of underground blew on our faces as Vivvy propped the mallet on a rock ledge at waist level and said with a twinkle in her eye, "Just in case we ever need it."

Now

When I leave for the cave, the whole world is fresh-painted: plum for the shadows, blister pink for the bare raspberry canes, saffron for the sun-tipped tree-tops. I don't give myself time to wuss out. I leave a note for Dad: *Having breakfast at Vivvy's.*

This time it'll be just me, taking the easy way in and out.

I wonder if the croquet mallet is still where we left it in October, at the other cave entrance. Was that what Vivvy meant when she said the murder weapon was "not a rock, and bigger than a hammer," being so precise about it? I didn't connect that description with the mallet, but clearly she did.

Just in case we ever need it. We left the mallet in plain sight of anyone exiting the cave. Anyone could have picked it up and hit Joss with it—Tanner. Anyone.

Me.

I give the Krays' house a wide berth, thinking of those security cameras, and follow the jogging path up the mountainside. Frost still coats the hardy shrubs under the tall evergreens.

I used to walk the path on top of Mont-Royal in the early

morning and imagine the whole park belonged to me. But I could always see the city through the trees. Here, silence has a taste and texture. Except for the chitter of a squirrel or the occasional scream of a jay, I'm utterly alone.

This time I don't veer off the way Bram took me. Not far past the sign marking the trailhead, the looming gray cliffs scallop inward. They shelter the glen that marks the Defilers' entrance to the cave, where the grass is still green, frost-crisp, and pristine.

I wish I could stay here in the sun. But there it is, in an alcove at the foot of the cliff—an oblong of darkness that a casual hiker would miss. A passage.

At first, navigating my way inside is like descending uneven stairs. Stone and cold rush to meet me, filling my eyes and nostrils and mouth, combining the silence of the forest and the granite-and-rot smell of old cemeteries. I swallow hard and switch on my flashlight.

I am not claustrophobic. The hard part is leaving behind the last pale streamers of daylight.

I will myself not to look back, even once. I need to adjust quickly to the reign of darkness. Bram's crawled through that tiny tunnel he showed me dozens of times—at night, even. He's not scared of the cave.

Joss in my stories wasn't, either.

It folds around you, this earthy darkness. One instant it feels snug and safe, almost maternal, and the next instant it's full of distant dripping and trickling and drafts and—did something just move over there?

I keep close to the wall. Try not to think about bats, subterranean cannibals, uncharted passages, floods. Defilers.

When the walls bulge inward, leaving only a hip-width, saw-toothed passage, I sweep my light around once, quickly, before angling myself inside. The bottleneck forces me to look back the way I came.

I'm blind. Anything could be waiting. A skinny hand could reach from inside to clamp down on my groping, fumbling fingers.

I wish Bram were here, says a traitorous part of me. But even if Bram still likes me, he deserves to know the truth about Saturday night, and I can't tell the truth.

Fear becomes an itch, turning my reflexes against me. Emerging into a wider stretch, I swing my light again, too wildly. The shadows of crags lurch like attackers, and I stumble backward, nearly losing my balance.

Stop it. Get hold of yourself. Go on.

As I reach the mouth of the Cave of Defilement, cold sweat plasters my hair to my scalp.

I back myself up to the wall, turn off my light, and listen. What if they trekked here last night after the memorial to booze away their grief?

So dark. From far in the distance—above? to the left?—comes a soft humming that occasionally jumps or sinks in pitch. Like a harp? Like a swift-flowing stream deep in the rock? Like human voices?

No, not voices. There's no whisper of breath here, no fresh

alcohol stink. I step forward, switching the flashlight back on. The would-be badass graffiti of the Defilers screams and blusters and hisses at me.

There's nobody here. Only the words and obscene cartoons and animal bones. My breathing levels a little, though my heart still pounds hard enough to make my ears ring.

This time I'm careful to avoid the heaps of sharp bones, the bottles and cans, the bedraggled futon and pink panties. Has no one been here since Bram and I?

The binder is right where we left it, wedged behind a heavy shard that probably broke off a stalactite. I liberate it and spread it open on the dirt floor, making sure to stay facing the cave entrance.

I'm shaking so hard that my phone takes a moment to recognize my face and unlock, but then I steady my hands and snap the first two pages in a single shot.

I will myself not to look at the faces in the photos as I frame and snap the second pair. The third. The fourth. And finally, the last page, the one with the bloody signatures.

Joss Thorssen. With a shaking finger, I tap his name on the screen to make it the focus.

Vibration disturbs the air. I listen hard, expecting it to resolve into more trickling or that lulling harp noise.

Instead, it hardens into voices—real people's voices leaping and echoing toward me from the cave entrance. Girls' voices.

Run. But where can I go? They're blocking my way out.

If I'm shaking now, I don't feel it. As if I've surrendered control of my body to someone more levelheaded, I hit the screen and take the final photo. Shut the binder, ease back the rock shard, careful not to let it grate, and wedge the evidence into its hiding place.

Hiding place. Obeying a desperate, fragmentary memory of Bram's map, I aim my flashlight at the wall just past THIS PLACE IS DEFILED. He said there was a second passage out of here—the one that winds all the way back to where Joss died.

Nothing. Just rough wall covered with silvery cartoons, and the moldy futon, and the animal bones, and—oh.

One piece of wall doesn't glint like the rest. Velvety shadows signal a dip, an alcove.

Voices bounce aggressively off the walls. "Can you believe he acted like such a dick?"

My phone! I left it on the floor while I moved the rock, and it's still there, bleeding light. I dive out, snatch it, and stagger back to the alcove, hitting the sleep button as I go.

The alcove isn't deep enough. I flatten myself into it, panicking—until my hand grasps the sharp edge of a crack running from floor to ceiling. I can't tell if this is actually a passage, but if I wedge myself sideways, pressing my palms to the ice-cold, earth-caked stone, I can squeeze just far enough in to hide.

No time to pocket the phone, so I clutch it tight.

Their laughter darts here, there, everywhere, like a trapped moth. I have no idea how close they actually are.

My forehead, my chin—they aren't going to fit. Rock presses on my brow, cool like my mother's hand when I'm sick. Rock cinches my hips.

Bram said to wriggle and turn until I fit like a puzzle piece.

Not to flail, not to panic. Bend my knees, ignore the rock scraping my ear—and there, my head is inside. I inch forward, willing myself to ignore the lips of rock that nearly meet overhead. Just far enough into the hole that no flashlight will reach me.

They're here. I crouch in the only position I can, head throbbing. Is my ringer off? Could I even get a call here?

"I could just kill that bastard Palmer." A chirpy voice with a hard edge. "Why won't he let me alone?"

" 'Cause he likes seeing us squirm. That's all he's been doing this whole time—playing with us." This voice is lazy, coarse and gritty as the pebbles beneath my palm—Cammy.

Which means the other voice is Halsey. I stop breathing.

"Where is it?" Halsey sounds nervous.

The binder? Their footsteps come closer. I gulp a breath and hold it.

A scraping sound. Somebody swears. "Right here where it always is, Hals. Sheesh."

The hiss of a zipper, then rustling.

I exhale as softly as I can through the ringing of my ears. They've come for the binder because it's evidence, which means they really are hiding something. If they find me now—

"This is driving me crazy." Halsey's voice breaks a little. "I cooperated, I *helped* him, and he's still treating me like a suspect. I told him to arrest her, and has he even called her in yet?"

A snort from Cammy. "They can't just arrest anybody. They gotta build a case. Anyway, we don't know for sure that was her on the bench. Or Joss."

The bench. Joss and me. They're talking about me.

My heart is racing, my breath a roar like the ocean. Any minute they'll hear it and drag me out. They know about the bench. *How do they know?*

They haven't heard. Their own voices are too loud, too shrill. "Bethany says—"

"Bethany Perry was high as a kite that night, Halsey. She's a shitty witness, and everybody knows it. Probably changed her story ten times since you and McKeough made her go to Palmer—which was a dumb move, by the way."

My jacket is soaked in sweat, my brain struggling to keep up. They know about the witness who saw me on the bench with Joss. Halsey and Tanner *found* that witness. And they want to know why I haven't been arrested.

Are they trying to frame me?

The crevice is as tight as a glove around me, closing in. When my fingertips rub the rock, caked mud from old floods comes off, and I'm not claustrophobic, I'm not, I'm not.

"How's it dumb?" Halsey asks. "If Bethany saw a girl with Joss that night, shouldn't the cops know?"

"We should be laying low. More we stick our noses in, more they think we have something to hide."

"That weirdo could actually have done it, though."

"Bethany didn't see her face," Cammy says.

The stone pulses around me, drowning out signals from my cramped muscles. My refuge is suffocating me.

"You think I'm jealous, okay, I get it. But her own friend told me she was practically stalking Joss."

My *friend*?

"Look, whatever. Maybe. She just doesn't seem like the type."

"You keep saying that!" Halsey's voice rises hysterically again, drilling its way into my ears. "How do you know? Anybody can do anything!"

"Yeah. Sure. Look, I know you're a mess right now, but you need to shut your trap before you say something stupid in front of the state police. We forget anything?"

For an instant, light wobbles on the lip of rock above me. I gasp another breath and close my eyes.

But there are no cries of discovery. I'm in the belly of the rock, too far back to see.

"C'mon. If I'm late for earth science again, Boblett's gonna give me detention."

Footsteps grate on pebbles, moving away. My phone buzzes against my palm.

My heart skips a beat, then batters my chest. I stuff the phone under my jacket and shirt, against my bare skin, holding my breath. *Please not now.*

More pebbles. More voices. More footsteps—getting fainter. They're still going. They didn't hear.

Relief hits me like nausea, drawing a curtain over my vision. Through the swimming of my head, I hear Halsey saying she doesn't see how Cammy can give a rat's ass about detention right now, and Cammy telling her she needs a Xanax.

The rest of the conversation is lost to the windings of the passage as they leave the Cave of Defilement—probably. I no longer trust my ears or my sense of direction, at least not enough to emerge any time soon.

Her own friend told me...

The words hang before me in the dark, as merciless as the silence. Vivvy. That's the only person Halsey could mean, because what other friends do I have? Seth is barely my friend, and anyway, he knows so little.

Vivvy told Halsey I was "practically stalking Joss." Vivvy betrayed me.

Then

ONE MONTH AGO
(MONDAY, OCTOBER 21)

Hey. Bonjour. Have a good weekend?"

A boy's deep voice. On my knees, I pivoted too quickly, banged my forehead on the open locker door, and found myself looking up at Joss Thorssen.

We hadn't spoken or made eye contact since the *Les Misérables* audition. A deep blush seared my face and neck as I scrambled to my feet. Joss took a step back into the end-of-day crowd, looking amused.

"*C'était pas mal, et toi?*" He looked at me blankly—oh no, did I just speak French? That *bonjour* confused me. "Um, I mean, my weekend was okay, how was yours?"

"Not bad. Hey, did you get the part?"

"The what?"

"The part in the play."

"Oh. Yeah. I mean, no." I was too busy noticing he wore no letter jacket today, only a tucked-in spotlessly white T-shirt and jeans. Very James Dean. "I got a part in the chorus, but I turned it down because I'm too busy with AP courses."

"Bummer. You were so good, you should've been, like, the main girl or whatever." Joss started to turn, then added, as if in afterthought, "Been meaning to bring you some stuff from that hockey forum. Think you could still translate for me?"

I nodded and smiled, not knowing how to be with him. I didn't have Halsey's scary bravado or Seth's don't-give-a-shit attitude or Vivvy's sleek confidence. I didn't feel like a girl, just a heap of mismatched parts.

"Hey, Thorssen!"

Thank every possible god—it was Vivvy, in a frilly blouse and vintage tweed skirt. As Joss turned to greet her, I breathed out. Vivvy couldn't mess things up like I would. Whatever she said, Joss would just smile in his twinkly, noncommittal way— and yes, there was the dreamboat dimple, at the left corner of his mouth.

I just wanted to watch him.

But he was talking to me again. "Vivvy said you're into creative writing."

The world lurched sideways like a fun house. *What did she tell him?*

I heard myself say, "I guess. It's just for fun."

Joss's knowing about my writing was a closed loop, a short circuit sending up sparks in my brain. Something that should never happen.

But here he was, leaning against the locker, bending toward me, and saying with earnest, bright eyes, "So you're really, like, creative, huh?"

"You should ask her to write a story about you," Vivvy said.

"You wouldn't believe how good she'd make you sound. You know Jack drawing Rose in *Titanic*? That's how she is with words."

What was she *doing*?

"Uh. Yeah, cool." Clearly uncomfortable now—but not nearly as much as I was—Joss reached out as if to fist-bump me, then withdrew his hand when I didn't move to reciprocate. "Okay, see you guys."

"Hey, Thorssen," Vivvy called after him. "You going to help out with my Halloween party? Use those big strong muscles to hoist some ghosts and witches onto the roof?"

I expected him to make an excuse that meant no, he never wanted to see either of us weirdos again, but he yelled, "Wouldn't miss it."

Vivvy unlocked the passenger side of the Impala first, but I didn't get in. "What was that?"

Woodsmoke spiked the air. I was still keyed up from talking to Joss, and my brain was drawing connections fast, not taking its usual fuzzy processing time. "You've been talking to Joss about our stories?"

"Get in, silly. Not our stories. I just said you're a good writer."

I forced myself to slide in as she started the car. "I wish you hadn't."

"What's the problem if it makes him like you?"

"It didn't make him like me. It weirded him out." But that,

236

I realized, wasn't the point. "And I don't *want* him to like me. I don't even really want to know him."

"You can't live in this town and not know everybody. Anyway, why not?"

I couldn't write stories from Joss's point of view if I knew him, really knew him. It would be like writing stories about Vivvy or Bram, forcing the smooth contours of an imaginary landscape onto wild nature. Like dreaming awake, like losing touch with reality.

This had all started with Vivvy's ambushing Halsey, driving her away from Joss. I shouldn't have encouraged her, shouldn't have laughed about it. But I'd felt so bad for Vivvy with the whole powder-puff induction thing.

She vroomed the engine, sending two freshmen skittering out of her path. "Look, yesterday I went to the rink for public skating, and Joss happened to be there. We were lacing up our skates, and we started talking. He asked about you. I told him a couple of totally innocent things."

You should have told me right away. Warned me. I almost said it, but she'd hear in my voice how much it hurt me that she hadn't.

We passed the field where girls were headbutting soccer balls and pulled onto the state highway. She asked, "What's your problem, Celeste?"

"I don't have a problem."

"Yes. You've been weird ever since we hung out with Seth. You have a problem with my being friends with Seth, and now you have a problem with my talking to Joss."

The highway took us onto Main Street—boarded-up stores

and Mexican and Greek restaurants that never caught on, bricks dark with decades of grime, so many churches. In the glare through the clouds, Weiner's Diner was an image from a "Dying America" photo-essay. The day when we ate cobbler already felt decades distant, swathed in nostalgia.

"I don't mind you having friends," I said. "I just wish you wouldn't talk to them about me."

"Don't you see what I'm trying to do, silly? I'm trying to bring *them* together."

The light shifted. The Defile transformed from a gritty relic back into the TV-ready retro town where Joss and Seth kissed and fought and made up.

But she still wasn't making sense. "Seth and Joss? I'm not seeing how you're getting them together by getting me involved." If they even wanted to be together, which I doubted.

"Look, you may not understand this, but you're *new*, and that means more than anything in a place like the Defile. All I did was tell Joss about the newness. He'll come like a moth to a flame. When he comes to my Halloween party, who will he see? You with Seth—an *old* friend, someone he outgrew. Because he's curious about you, and you're friends with Seth, Seth will look different to him now. Grown up. Like a cool person from the city with cool, creative friends."

"What if he doesn't like Seth that way? What if he doesn't like *me* once he gets past the whole 'new' thing?"

"All things are possible," Vivvy said. "But you don't know small towns, Celeste. You don't understand what the sheer depth of boredom will drive people to."

Now

How long does it take to leave the cave? All I know is that, in the end, I stumble out into the grass of the glen. The sun slants across me—pearly, caught under clouds, yet so bright I squint.

I still feel the cold. I still hear that hum. It winds among the bare trees, as if some of the cave has escaped with me. When I reach the jogging path, I run as if tendrils of darkness might reach from the cliffside and pull me back in.

This time I don't try to avoid the Krays'. I pause in the middle of the sunlit lawn, daring Vivvy to come out—if she's cutting school again. Then I remember the text I got in the cave, the one that almost royally screwed me.

Sure enough, it's from her. *Where are you? Sheriff talking to Seth right now.*

Alone in the diner, I dip my fries in mayonnaise instead of ketchup, as if I were back in Montreal, and eat and eat, trying to tether myself to the world. I haven't texted Vivvy back.

Instead, I made a stop at home, where I printed out several copies of the cave photos. They went under my mattress, except for the set I chucked into one of Dad's manila envelopes.

Everything I've learned from Patrick and Cammy and Halsey and Val and Bram and my dad rushes in my ears like surf, bites like salt water. Thanks to the perhaps unreliable witness who saw me on the bench, I may have a scrap of the forgotten time back. But the moments and hours that I thought I knew so well—all those weeks with Vivvy—have gone dark.

Where *was* I these past three months? Why did I trust her? It's not the first time Vivvy has talked about me to other people, but telling Joss I'm a writer pales in comparison with telling Halsey I'm a stalker.

A stalker and maybe a murderer.

Since Monday in the gym, that possibility has been flashing through my head like lightning—*I could have done it*—but I haven't let it come close enough for a good, steady look. Like the marks I cover with a scarf, it's something I haven't examined too closely. Maybe it's time.

Outside, the street is desolate, the marshmallow sky streaked with gray, snowflakes thickening in the air. I dip another fry. From the kitchen comes female laughter and a crunchy dubstep beat.

Cammy is related to the woman who owns this place. Do they all know I've been branded a "slut"? Maybe it doesn't matter who wrote the note; it could have been anybody.

The snow will fall long and hard, according to my phone, and I'm waiting for the roads to slick up. I have less chance of running into cops at the station, especially Valerie Kray, if they have problems to solve outdoors. I should go before school lets out, though, and kids pour in here, bringing their gossip and staring eyes.

Now that I'm a person of interest, now that Seth is very likely one, too, I can't walk up to Valerie and hand her what I've found without making it look like I'm trying to draw attention away from myself. I wanted Bram to do it, but now that he's put his own neck out to bear false witness for me, I can't ask him for anything, either.

Heat rises to my cheeks as I remember him kissing me in the Krays' kitchen. What he did was foolish and noble and possibly catastrophic, but he did it because, as he said, he doesn't believe I'd hurt anybody. Because he likes me, whatever that means.

It means I can't ask for his help again, can't get him in any more trouble, no matter how much I want to tell him everything. Anyway, if he knew about all of it, about our stories and spin the bottle, I'm not sure he'd like me anymore.

The photos may not cancel out my lies, but they could lead someone to the truth. The Defilers know it—why else would Cammy and Halsey have swiped the binder this morning?

Yes, we had a pact. But if Seth starts throwing around accusations at the very mention of the Defilers, and Vivvy tattles on me to one of them, what choice do I have?

I can't freeze in place and hope things work out. Someone has to fight for me.

Then

didn't look closely at the man following us. I didn't give him a chance to catch my eye. Sidelong glances told me he was on the older side, with blond or gray hair and a sport coat. Like Frank, only Frank wore a duster.

In Kray's Defile, older men who wear suits or sport coats don't hike up the hill at midday. They're busy doing business things in their offices, making their secretaries pick up their lunch from the diner. Either this guy had decided to get his own lunch or he was after something.

"Hey, are you listening?" Vivvy asked.

"Yeah. Fiona's figuring out where to rent a cauldron, and I'm going to help you pick up the cupcakes."

"You're walking too fast. My legs are shorter, okay?"

We trudged uphill past ranch houses and split-levels and the occasional Victorian, all with neatly raked leaves and proudly displayed American flags. The sun fought its battle with the clouds, and the distance between us and the man shrank. Had he been in the diner when we ate our pancakes? Or spotted us on the street?

Vivvy was wearing a skirt. Some men react to skirts, even when they aren't short. To them, skirts say *girl*; skirts say *follow me*.

My steps were regular; I could feel both of my thumbs. I wasn't scared yet, just alert and aware in an old, familiar way. This was not Frank.

Would I even recognize Frank now, given how rarely I'd looked straight at him? *Look me in the eye, show me your beautiful eyes*, he begged, but I couldn't or wouldn't.

I never said no out loud, because it was so important to him to compliment me. Because he wanted so badly to let his arm settle around my waist. I could feel his wanting like I felt the autumn wind playing havoc with the flags today, transforming each moment into a tense *right now*.

That DM from Bess McTeer was bringing things back. Like what she'd told me the last time I saw her.

Not long before I left Montreal, Mom and I went out for ice cream on Prince Arthur Street. While Mom was in the restroom, Bess strolled by on the pedestrian mall.

When I recognized her wild chestnut hair, dancer's body, and animal-print leggings, my thumb and pinkie went numb. As Bess spotted me and darted toward my seat on the terrace, I forced myself to inhale, hold, exhale.

"Celeste! How are you?"

"I'm really good." *Because I'm leaving.* Far above us, sunlight wavered fluidly on the gray stone facades.

"You *look* good! No, seriously, you look great. I missed you in workshop this summer."

"I'm taking a break," I said.

The smile faded from Bess's face. Then, to my surprise, she lowered her dark brows and clawed the air like she was channeling a tiger in an improv workshop.

"Frank was such a bastard," she said. "If a guy ever tries to make you uncomfortable again, you tell him to fuck off, okay? Tell him I'll kick his ass. Or *you* will."

The world was strobing—my glance flitting toward the restroom, then back to Bess. Too fast. Out of control. The words bounced around in the air, free. My mom might hear.

But Bess was so fierce that for an instant kicking someone's ass seemed possible. I said, "Okay," and we bumped fists.

Now, though?

"Oh look!" Vivvy veered toward the nearest yard. "The Seagrams' calico had kittens."

She whipped out her phone to frame the black, white, and ginger furballs tussling in a fenced enclosure. I stayed on the sidewalk, my temples pounding, as the stranger approached: fifteen feet, ten, five.

We weren't in danger, I knew that, but my muscles itched to grab Vivvy and run. The man was older than Frank, gray-haired. He looked straight at me with a twinkle in his eye, as if I were a kid and he had a cookie.

Tell him to fuck off. Again I saw Bess's tiger claws, and as he finally came abreast of me, I whispered, "Stop following us!"

Or did I yell it?

The man's eyes widened. "Something wrong, young lady? Oh hi, Vivvy!"

"Mr. Deaver!" Vivvy's cheeks were violently flushed. She grabbed for my arm, but I stepped out of reach. "This is my friend Celeste. She's new in town."

Mr. Deaver tipped an imaginary hat, while I went hot all over. He reeked of cheap spray deodorant.

I'd lost control just now. What if I'd lunged at him, tried to "kick his ass"?

Now that they were talking like old friends, I wasn't afraid of him. It was Vivvy who frightened me with her tight, mortified smile. I said, "I'll wait for you at the top," and turned and walked away as fast as I could, ignoring her cry of, "What's your problem, anyway?"

I jammed my hands into my jacket pockets and walked without looking to either side. *Right, left, right, left,* a ribbon of gray pavement blurring in front of me, and if Vivvy wanted to stop being friends over my being rude to some random old guy whose whole family she was probably on intimate terms with, well, fine.

I couldn't do this small-town thing she did, this lady-of-the-manor thing. I was unmoored in the world. I couldn't trust people.

"Hey!"

Seth came sauntering down the walk of a weedy duplex, the usual vaporizer in hand. I slowed down long enough to examine the building—drab but presentable—and wondered if he lived there. "Hey."

He didn't seem bothered when I didn't match my pace to his, just loitered after me. "You okay, Celeste?"

Then I did wait for him, because it seemed wrong not to. "Yeah."

"You lost Vivvy, huh?"

He pointed down the slope, where Vivvy had separated herself from Mr. Deaver and was striding toward us with ominously bright eyes. Something caught in my throat.

"She stopped to talk to this guy, Mr. Deaver or something, and he creeped me out."

"Yeah?" Seth took a drag. His eyes were bright and alert, too, but without judgment. "He owns the Harley dealership. I don't blame you for being creeped out; he's got those oily eyes like a perv."

He saw it, too. An unfamiliar warmth rose from my chest to my throat, and before I knew it, I was saying, "I'm kind of a perv magnet."

He didn't look away. "I know the feeling. It's like, 'Seriously? You're old enough to be my dad and you're giving me the eye?' What's that gonna accomplish?"

"I hate it," I said.

"But pervs gotta perv, right? It's got nothing to do with you."

It was such a simple thing to say, but something spasmed in my throat. "I know. I mean, obviously. But—"

Vivvy caught up. "What was that, Celeste?"

I'd started coughing. Seth patted my back.

"I'm okay," I said when I could talk again. "I'm okay, really."

Vivvy gave me her water bottle. "You sure? That was weird back there."

"Deav winked at her," Seth said, improvising on my behalf. "Guy's a goddamn lech."

"Seriously?"

As I raised the water bottle, Seth caught my eye, and *he* winked—a split-second communication that Vivvy couldn't have seen. *I get it. I have your back.*

"You don't notice these things, Viv," he said. "You're too used to being up there on your Kray throne. You wouldn't survive two days in a city."

"Neither would you," she shot back.

"I have street smarts," Seth said.

Vivvy rolled her eyes. "Oh right. I forgot you're going to pick up and drive to LA the day after graduation and become the king of nouvelle-fusion-whatever cuisine."

"Just wait. You'll see."

We walked on up the hill, Seth explaining the concept of his dream restaurant and Vivvy teasing him about it, and I just kept hearing what he'd said: *It's got nothing to do with you.*

Now

S now is falling fast and thick as I make my way to the town green, the envelope of printouts in my backpack. I didn't include a message along with the cave photos, just a caption with the GPS coordinates of the cave and today's date. That should be enough for Valerie to put together.

The courthouse faces the green, a bulky, Romanesque mansion with a modest addition housing the sheriff's department. Only one cruiser occupies the lot to the right of the building, which means the deputies are out directing traffic or answering calls about snow-related accidents, as I hoped.

The evidence needs to get to Val, not to Palmer or anyone who might give it right to him. It was a pleasant surprise to hear that Halsey thinks Palmer suspects her and the other Defilers, but I still don't trust him.

Whirling flakes hide me as I cross Main Street and climb the cinder block steps of the addition. I've been here a few times with Vivvy, bringing Val takeout from the diner when she worked late. I know where both cameras are, by the door and in the foyer, and it's easy to pull my hood low and give them the cold shoulder.

The single corridor holds three labeled doors: Sheriff Palmer's office, dispatch, and admin. I creep past Palmer's office and dispatch, where a woman's talking officiously on the phone about a downed tree. Val's desk is in admin. The door is closed, the office inside probably deserted, but rather than risk peeking in, I slip the envelope through the crack.

The front says ATTN: VALERIE KRAY in block letters, as anonymous as I could make them. That'll have to do.

As I straighten, a door down the hall bangs open. I slip into an alcove with vinyl chairs and a soda machine.

Footsteps. Sheriff Palmer's voice booms down the hall: "You go to school tomorrow, and you keep your phone on this time and answer when we call. Understood?"

"Yeah."

"And wait for your mom to pick you up. Wonder what's keeping her?"

"Maybe the Sunoco was out of her brand of smokes."

I recognize that small, sullen voice—Seth in a very bad mood. Did it take this long to interview him, or did they call him in a second time?

"Well, don't go beyond the green till she gets here," Palmer says, and Seth mutters his agreement.

I keep my back tight to the alcove until the door clicks and a single pair of footsteps trips down the hall. The weather-sealed front door hisses open and shut.

I count to a hundred before tiptoeing out of the building, as effectively as I can in rubber-soled Sorel boots. My breath catches as shadows dance behind the frosted-glass door of Palmer's office, but it stays closed.

Taking the cinder block steps two at a time, I nearly barrel into a hoodied figure hunched on the lowest one, vaping. Seth's actually staying put the way Palmer told him to.

He's on his feet instantly, following me onto the sidewalk. Black hair streaks his white, angry face, but his eyes look frightened as he asks, "What the hell are you doing here?"

I stop, turned into the wind, and let the clammy flakes bombard my face like weak spitballs. "Just bringing Val something. They've been talking to you this whole time?"

Seth swings so his back is to the courthouse. "What were *you* telling them?"

"Nothing! I made zucchini bread, and I told Val I'd give her some." The storm slants fiercely, turning the courthouse into a red blur. "C'mon. They shouldn't see us together."

Seth laughs as he follows me across the street onto the whitened green. "Like that matters now. Knudsen saw me climbing the hill on Saturday."

At last, Mr. Knudsen has returned from Amelia Island. I thought this was the news that would open an icy pit of fear in my stomach, but my morning in the cave has left me numb. "He saw *us*, you mean."

"Yeah, but I'm the lucky one. The only one the old man got close enough to ID. He must've seen 'some girls,' too, 'cause

Palmer asked me about them. But he didn't seem to be sure if there were two or three of you."

Thank God. Mr. Knudsen must not have a sharp eye—*he* didn't notice my scarf. "What did you say?"

"What do you think?" Seth moves like a pissed-off robot, feet stamping the slush and arms windmilling with agitation. "I said I was home that night. Just like we agreed. And you know what? I have a feeling Palmer doesn't believe me."

There's a small playground beside the bandstand. He plunks himself down on the slippery roundabout, shuffles his feet to make it creak back and forth. "He thinks I had a drug deal with Joss that went south. He told me this whole messed-up story, trying to get me to agree that was how it went down. Dude's been watching too much *Law & Order.*"

He raises one gloved hand. "They fingerprinted me and took a cheek swab. I had to let them. Celeste, I don't want to ask this, I don't even want to *know*, but things are getting serious. Did you do it?"

He looks directly into my eyes, his own as blue as gas flames. His body has gone still.

"No! Of course not! I would never hurt Joss, any more than you would."

I reach for my phone, for the pictures that could change everything. The pictures Seth should already know about. "Seth, what do you know about Joss and Tanner McKeough?"

But he just goes on talking. "Palmer said if I pleaded guilty and was remorseful, I could get murder with mitigating circumstances. That's like manslaughter." His voice has a new tone, less accusing than plaintive. Like he wants something from me. "Remember what Vivvy said? It was practically a freak accident. Whoever did it probably didn't mean to kill him."

"I know you didn't do it, Seth." Flakes are melting on my touch screen, and I can't seem to find the right icon. "I know—"

"So, if you did it, Celeste, and it was like that—an accident—it's better for you to tell somebody. Right now."

"Why do you keep saying that? It doesn't have to be any of us three. The cave—"

Seth's voice drops lower. "Look, you were, like, obsessed with him. Everybody knew it."

"What are you talking about?" Rage bursts like a firework behind my eyes, blinding me, because this is suddenly all too familiar. "Did Vivvy tell you that?"

"She told me about your stories."

She wouldn't. "What stories? What do—"

A car with a bad muffler roars up the street toward the courthouse, drowning out my words. Seth rises from the roundabout. "That's my mom. Gotta go before she starts worrying."

He can't say that and leave me with this shame and disbelief cinching my throat, pooling in my lungs, swelling my skull. *She wouldn't have. She couldn't have.* I can maybe forgive Vivvy for blabbing nervously to Halsey because she knew I was lying about Saturday night, and she's so scared herself. But if Seth has known about our stories this whole time, I can't forgive her for that.

I chase Seth back across the green, my boots slipping and sliding. The cold wind stings my lungs and makes my eyes water.

"You can't just say that! You have to tell me what you mean!"

As we reach the street, the car pulls in beside the courthouse and honks. Seth wheels around sharply, so I almost walk into him.

"Look, if you two wanted to write soft porn about Joss, even about *me* and Joss, that's none of my business. But you had a thing—a weird thing with him. I think he maybe liked you, as much as he liked any girl, but the way you liked him—it was like you hated him, too. You wanted him to hurt. And if they arrest me, I'll tell them the truth. Just like we agreed."

Before I can say another word, he makes a second whiplash turn and disappears into the waiting car.

Then

I n Middle-earth, the aspen leaves tumbled around us, as yellow and salmon and pale gold as the soupy sky overhead. Seth leaped off his ledge and chased a swirl of them. The air was unseasonably mellow, but I felt a storm coming.

Seth waded ankle-deep into the thick of the leaves and kicked them in all directions, sending them scurrying over the clearing. "I still won't come," he said. "Not if that asshole's there."

So much for bringing Joss and Seth together. No sooner had Joss promised to help out with Halloween party prep and cleanup than Seth had announced he wouldn't show.

I sympathized. Right now, I'd way rather hang out here with Seth and Vivvy, snarking on everybody, than go to a party the entire town was invited to and make small talk with a painfully handsome hockey star I barely knew.

"You're being such a child," Vivvy said in the same maternal, loving-yet-reprimanding voice I'd heard her use on Bram. "You've barely spoken to Joss in years. He's not an asshole. I think he's actually kind of lonely."

"I can see perfectly well the company he keeps." Seth scooped up a stone from the scree beyond the trees and hurled it toward the valley. "Anyway, you said yourself, Joss wants to see *her*. Not me."

When I realized he meant me, my back snapped straight against the rock ledge as if I were a puppet whose strings had been pulled. "He wants me to translate French, that's all."

Immediately I hated how apologetic I sounded. Even if I were Vivvy's puppet, her machinations were nothing but wishful thinking. "And Joss can have his pick of anyone," I pointed out. "For friends or...whatever. At least you two used to be his friends. I don't even know him."

"The unknown is always more attractive than the known," Seth said.

Attractive. It was just one word, but it made me wonder if he *was* attracted to Joss, despite all his protests about shallowness.

"Oh my God." Vivvy shot to her feet on the ledge, towering over Seth on the ground, arms akimbo. "The two of you, it's like you're jealous of each other. Like this is some bizarre love triangle."

"I don't like Joss that way," I protested, at the same instant Seth said, "I am *not* fucking into Joss."

Then Seth and I went still and looked at each other, for the first time really sizing each other up. His blue eyes, as vivid as chicory flowers, and my brown ones. His scornful mouth and my tight one.

I wanted to be back in the moment when he said that what "pervs" did had nothing to do with me, but things had changed.

"So let him choose between us," Seth said at last.

He didn't mean it. He was making fun of Vivvy, I was pretty sure—so sure that I smiled and said, "Okay. But then you'll have to come to the Halloween party."

"I guess I will." His voice was deadpan. Grave, almost, like he was laying down a challenge. "But I refuse to wear a costume. You, though—you should come as something sexy. Give yourself every advantage you can."

My face and chest burned. A male student of my dad's once told me I'd never have to worry about college grades if I wore short skirts to class—as if long, knobby-kneed legs were my only route to the dean's list.

"She's coming as Emma Peel from *The Avengers*." Vivvy was bouncing up and down as she always did when she got a brainstorm.

"There's no such Avenger," Seth said.

"From the old British TV show, dummy, not Marvel. She gets to wear a catsuit. And I'm coming as Alice in Wonderland."

I scrambled off the rock ledge and landed in the leaves, enjoying the crackles and crunches of countless tiny acts of destruction. "No, I'm coming as Death. In a long, concealing black cloak, with a scythe."

Now

I t takes ten minutes to get up the hill to the Krays' house, and the whole time Seth's words ring in my ears. *You had a thing. A weird thing with him.*

Rage is armor. It keeps me from feeling the snow melting on my face, the pack bowing me over, my calves and thighs protesting the steep climb. Rage turns me from flesh into a glowing icon of purpose. *Find Vivvy. Remind her of all the things you know about her.*

Seth says mockingly in my head, *The way you liked him—it was like you hated him, too.*

Seth can tell the sheriff whatever he wants; he isn't the biggest threat to me. Someone saw me on the bench with Joss, and Bram's lie isn't going to hold up for long.

Joss was still alive and sitting on that bench with me at three AM. And that, I realize, is no alibi for me. What Seth said about Joss's death being a "freak accident" reminded me of something I read a few years ago, about a pop star who died after a minor fall off a snowboard. She got up and seemed fine, talking and laughing and even hiking back to the ski lodge, but hours later she slipped into a coma and never woke up. "Talk-and-die syndrome," the medical examiner called it.

Joss could have been hit, walked down the hill with me, returned to the cave, and died there. Bizarre but possible. Maybe he walked down the hill with me after *I* hit him. Maybe we talked about it. Maybe he forgave me, both of us thinking he'd be fine.

A blow in anger. Lashing out, then regretting it. That is something I'm capable of, even if I usually only hit myself.

The Kray house looms through the dusk, all sharp gothic angles and intimidation, its square cupola like a battlement. Almost there, and Vivvy's car is in its usual spot by the curb.

You wanted him to hurt.

I could have done it. Seth is right—I did want to hurt Joss. But not the real Joss, only the fictional one, and I only wanted to hurt him because he was like me, part of me, *my* character—

"Hey!"

The shambling figure I just dodged turns out to be Bram. He's dressed as I've never seen him before, in an enormous buffalo-plaid jacket that obscures his outlines and makes him look like an old man.

He grabs me by the elbow and wheedles me toward the high-roofed carriage-house-turned-garage. "We need to talk. Vivvy's been acting weird. She actually stole my phone so I couldn't text you."

I shake him off, veer toward the house. "I'm going to see her right now."

"No!" Bram latches on to my shoulders and holds me fast. "I

told you, we need to talk. About the thing with Val and the stuff we found in the cave and the rest of it."

He wants to know the truth about why I was on that bench. My rage dissipates, my strength with it, leaving what feels like a gigantic stone in my chest. Cold, unforgiving granite.

The truth. I owe it to Bram, who's the only reason I'm not sitting in custody right now. And maybe I need to tell someone, finally.

"Okay." I wait while he hand-cranks the squeaky old door, then ushers me inside.

We step into roomy, dark mustiness. Bram reaches past me, his arm brushing my chest, and a bare fluorescent bulb comes to life, illuminating a semiorderly clutter of shelves and pegboards. I come in here only when Vivvy and I need a rusty old bike or equipment for a lawn game.

Unknotting my wet scarf, I see the croquet set hanging from the pegboard, missing the red mallet. Is it still propped on the ledge by the cave entrance, or if not, who has it now?

Words emerge in a groan before I can stop them: "Vivvy's been telling people I did it."

"Did what?" The light glints on Bram's glasses, making him look disconnected, as if he's seeing some more innocent, alternate-universe version of me.

"She's saying I was obsessed with him. That I had a weird thing for him. That I could have hurt him!" Tears swell and bead in my eyes, hot and humiliating. First Halsey, then Seth. It's all so absurd, and everyone will believe it. They'll believe it because they don't know that Vivvy, in her own way, was every bit as obsessed.

And I can't explain that I was obsessed with a figment of my own imagination. Never really with Joss at all.

A storm is churning in my chest, pressure building, and Bram will hate me now. He should hate me. His hands are reaching for mine, gently unclenching my fists and stroking my palms, because he pities me. Because he knows if he doesn't touch me, I'll fly apart. Slap myself, maybe even slap him.

He croons soothing words. "Vivvy would never say that, Celeste. She knows you'd never hurt anybody."

I shake my head, not wanting to face him. Knowing I should tug my hands away.

But he deserves the truth, and though I don't want to tell him, he guided me through that passage in the cave. If I can trust anyone, it's him. "Bram, I was with Joss on that bench on Saturday night."

His fingers tighten on mine. "You were? For real? Why?"

My gaze stays fixed above his head so I won't have to see his reaction, even through a veil of tears. "I must have been. But Bram, I don't remember. I was with Joss, up by the cave, drinking. It was him and Vivvy and Seth and me. And then I don't remember anything. I must have blacked out."

There it is.

Releasing the truth makes me feel so light I could float away.

Bram's grip is distant now, my own breathing louder and louder in my ears, as if I'm underwater.

"I did write stories about him." I'm not sure I'm speaking the words aloud. "Him and Seth. But they were just stories. They were never supposed to be real."

The churning won't stop. A dark haze covers my eyes, and I lean forward into something soft, remembering Joss's chamois shirt. How he peeled off his jacket to give it to me. *You were real. Just for a few minutes that night, we were together and you were real to me.*

"Celeste?"

I'm leaning against Bram. He's holding me up. "Are you okay?"

I lift my head from the buffalo-plaid jacket that isn't Joss's. Bram's arms are around me, and my back is braced against something hard—the garage wall.

He's standing here holding me because I need it, not doing anything else. Not pushing himself against me, not reaching for my face to kiss me. His hold doesn't feel robotic or indifferent, just steady, like he knows that's all I can handle right now. His breath warms my scalp.

"I'm okay." My legs are supporting me again, but I don't pull away, only bring my arms up to circle his back through the scratchy wool. It feels just like Joss's jacket did, but Bram is different—narrower and a little taller and more tentative as he leans down to rest his face, his lips, in my hair.

It's almost a kiss but not quite, and if Vivvy saw us, her voice would go ice-cold with anger. She never wanted us together. But this is happening, just as it happened with Joss that night, and hasn't she already done the worst she can do?

I could edge away. I could pretend it's not happening till he gets embarrassed and moves. I don't.

I reach up and hold his face to keep it close, my hands slipping into his hair.

"I'm so glad you showed me the cave," I say. His loose curls are soft, just as I always thought they'd be, and I can't believe my own daring, but I keep my voice level. "I found out some more. Joss and Tanner were fighting. Tanner called him a traitor because he didn't want to go to a Defiler party on Saturday."

Bram's breath speeds up as I stroke his hair. I feel him wanting to lower his head, to kiss me, but he doesn't yet. Maybe he's thinking of Vivvy, too. "Why would he be a traitor?" he asks shakily.

"Probably has to do with what's in that binder." My thoughts fragment as he leans closer. "Maybe Joss was going to tell."

When his lips finally brush mine, the stubble on his chin meets my cheek, sending a raw tingle of sensation all the way to my fingertips and toes. Our mouths flinch away, but only for an instant. I catch his bottom lip between mine, sucking it in.

Don't think about freak accidents. Don't think about Vivvy. This is a mystery, and we'll solve it together.

Bram gasps, too, his bulk pressing me harder against the wall. Something heavy shifts back there, digging into my spine, but it doesn't matter. His mouth is opening to mine, hot and wet; his glasses are slipping.

It doesn't have to be bad. It doesn't have to be scary. I can control it.

Or maybe not, and it doesn't matter. I'm standing in a strong wind, a summer storm, waiting for the rain and feeling the thunder in my bones.

I flick his glasses straight, smiling into his mouth, and then I lift the hem of his enormous jacket and slide my fingers under his button-down, under his T-shirt, until I feel the burning smoothness of his skin.

What happened with Frank was nothing like this. I turned my body off for it, the way you do at the doctor. What happened with Joss was wilder, hazier, like a sexy scene in a movie, the alcohol in my bloodstream making everything weightless. I don't even know what this is.

Something Vivvy will never forgive.

The thought makes me stop and pull back—do I *want* her to hate me? Is that why this all feels so good? But no, that's something spiteful Vivvy would say, that kissing Bram is a way to get back at her. This has nothing to do with her at all.

As I move, the bulky thing behind me sways perilously, and I have to let go of Bram to turn and steady it.

It's a ladder, the old-fashioned wooden kind, jointed and folded in half. It's so tall I can't quite see the top, only feel where it's fastened to a sturdy hook in the shadows of the eaves.

Too many memories come with the worn smoothness of the aged wood. "This is the ladder Joss fell from. At the party."

I pull the ladder straight, careful not to let it swing off its support. The broken rung is just low enough for me to reach on tiptoe.

"Yeah." Bram nudges me from behind, still careful not to crowd me. As I lower my arm, his hair brushes my bare wrist, tormenting me with another shower of itching, dangerous sensations. And we both stare at the ladder, at the place where the rung broke under Joss's weight and snapped off from the frame.

Then

The Krays' Halloween party was a bigger deal than I'd ever imagined it could be. A line of flickering jack-o'-lanterns stretched up the driveway and down the block, and not one had been smashed so far.

From the window of Vivvy's room, I watched as people of all ages milled in the front yard. Folding tables groaned under the weight of candy apples and popcorn balls and doughnuts and coffee and spicy cider and a pyramid of black-and-orange-frosted cupcakes from the best bakery in Billings, according to Vivvy. There was a tank for apple bobbing and a mammoth real iron cauldron sitting on a fake fire, full of fizzy, blood-colored cranberry punch.

"Do you see him?" Vivvy asked from her perch by the other window.

"No." We'd been prepping all day and most of yesterday, with Seth helping on and off, but Joss hadn't showed. Maybe he'd forgotten all about his tossed-off promise, though Vivvy said he'd reassured her twice at school he'd be here to help.

"Let's check the backyard again."

We pounded down the corridor to the guest room, which looked out on the rear of the house. The solid old walls swallowed the sounds of the crowd outside, but I heard tiny *pew pew* video game noises from Bram's room.

"Isn't he coming to the party?" I asked.

"Bram hates parties. You know that."

I did, but who could miss this? Down below, in the backyard, the storm doors gaped open. A small line of people snaked down the basement stairs toward the "House of Horrors," which was actually some sheriff's deputies proffering buckets of peeled-grape "eyeballs," rattling chains, and taking donations while creepy sound clips played in the background. The house's enormous basement was unsettling enough by itself, with its vaulted ceilings and rough stone walls.

"There's Sarah and Ashley—and Halsey." Vivvy knelt on a console table for a better view. "With Tanner McKeough! All Joss's freakin' friends are here, so where's he?"

Sure enough, a bunch of letter-jacketed boys and scantily clad girls—mostly sexy nurses and nuns—had formed a tight cluster around the backyard punch cauldron. Probably busy spiking it.

I gazed up the hill to the orchard, which had been all red and gold haze earlier today. Around four, gray-veined cloud banks had settled on both horizons, and now the trees were bony fists shaking themselves at the sky in proper Halloween fashion.

"He's here!"

Vivvy leaped from the table, skidded on the floor, and

grabbed the voluminous sleeve of my Death costume. "He's talking to that hot French teacher, Ms. Perrin. Celeste, you have to go down there and grab him."

"Why don't you talk to him?" She was so much better at it; my chest tightened at the thought of trying to be what Joss wanted me to be when I wasn't even sure what that was.

"Because you're new, remember? Tell him he has to stay afterward with us. Tell him we'll explore my grandpa's liquor cabinet, and there might be absinthe."

"What is that even?" If I didn't know, Joss probably didn't.

"It's a liqueur that used to be illegal. That makes it cool." She tugged open my black robe to reveal my jeans and T-shirt. "You look better this way. I'll go find Seth, and we'll meet you. Please?"

———

Joss must not want his friends to see us together.

Why else was he steering me down the basement steps into the musty gloom? Nobody our age was exploring this tame House of Horrors, but there were enough shrieking kids and long-suffering parents to rule out the possibility that he wanted to get me alone. *Don't think about that.*

He'd acted happy to see me, but he seemed to be under a spell that forbade him from reacting too strongly to anything. When I told him about Vivvy's after-party plans and the absinthe, he dimpled noncommittally, his eyes not quite meeting mine. He wore a half-assed Indiana Jones costume, basically just a leather jacket and fedora, that was way hotter on him than it had any right to be.

Say something to him. Say something now or you might as well leave. As recorded guttural groans and howls tore the air around us, my whole body trembled with the force of trying to be someone with him. Trying to be a girl who was breezy, fun, cool, and just attractive enough. That was what boys wanted, right?

"This basement would be perfect for a remake of *The Texas Chain Saw Massacre*," I said. "I mean, obviously, there's already a remake, so, uh, I mean a better one."

He stared at me, his blue eyes troubled reflections of the spooky orange lighting, and I added, "It's a movie. A classic."

"Oh yeah. I've heard of it."

I could be many things, but not breezy. Not cool. And not like Vivvy, who acted like her own strange self and damned the consequences. If she and Joss were running water, easy and flowing, I was a log wedged across the stream.

So it was a shock when Joss grabbed my hand and pulled me past the cringing kids, the eyeballs, the candles, and the chains into a darker part of the basement, where a single deputy stood guard before a closed door. DARE TO ENTER THE CRYPT? a sign inquired.

Joss tossed a dollar bill into the deputy's donation bucket. "Let's do it."

"Really?" Then I understood. Behind us, Halsey, Ashley, and Cammy were clomping down the stairs.

Why didn't he just make an excuse and leave? Tears of

humiliation stung my eyes as the door grated open, dragging on the floor, and we stepped inside.

"This is actually just a storage area," I assured him, and heard Vivvy's voice in my head say, *Duh, he knows it's not a crypt; you're boring him.* The door thudded closed, stranding us in the dark.

It was the kind of utter, bottomless dark where you start seeing stars. Joss could have been a mile away from me or two inches.

A stink of wet stone, earth, and something else burrowed through my nostrils and into my brain. It was a tangible presence, furry with an edge of organic rot—old apples? A dead rat?

"You should go if you want to go." In the dark, the words flowed from me, nothing to stop them. "You don't have to hang around with me. That was Vivvy's idea."

"So you don't like me?" The voice was closer than I expected, and it barely sounded like Joss. Less woozy and aw-shucks, more direct.

I couldn't answer that any better than I could reach out and grasp the strange smell. If I said no—or rather yes, I did like him—what else would I be saying a blanket yes to? Why had he really brought me down here, away from everyone?

"Of course I do. But I don't want you to feel—"

Buzzing vibration ripped the air apart. Lightning struck the masonry in front of us, illuminating a skeleton that leered through the gloom.

I screamed, and then his arms were around me—pulling me in, protecting me. He stank a little of weed, and he felt very solid, very real, and I expected his arms to keep tightening until I needed to get away, but they didn't. They held me just close enough to leave breathing room, as if my body had spoken and he'd heard.

This is how Seth feels with Joss.

The buzzing noise stopped. The lightning was just three strategically placed spotlights. The skeleton was plastic, dangling lifelessly on the rock wall.

The door opened. Joss released me, both of us laughing as we stumbled back out.

We laughed a little too long and a little too hard.

———

"The rain's coming!" Vivvy's voice shrilled through the front yard. "We've got to get the stuff off the roof!"

It was nearly eleven; most of the guests had left long ago for trick-or-treating or more private parties. The caterers and deputies were doing some cleanup, but Vivvy, Seth, and I had been filling trash bags and taking down streamers and paper skeletons for what felt like hours.

Joss had been helping, though mainly with tasks that involved carrying something enormous or climbing something high. When it was just drudge work, no physical prowess required, he got bored and drifted away.

When Vivvy sounded the alarm that the decorations perched on the house's peaked roof were in imminent peril, he reappeared instantly. "Where? You got a ladder?"

"It's going to take all of us to carry it."

Vivvy led the way to the garage, where we found an ancient, unwieldy wooden ladder folded in two and swaying from the eaves. Joss dislodged it from its hook, and the rest of us latched on and guided it downward before it could crash. We hauled it outside and unfolded it to its full length on the grass, then lifted it again and gingerly propped it against the house.

Joss had taken charge, shouting orders to us like a platoon leader in a war movie. Bram, who'd been MIA till now, showed up and more than pulled his weight. Seth glowered each time Joss told him to go over *there* or grab *that* end; if he had the slightest interest in winning a contest for Joss's heart, he didn't show it.

So you don't like me? Maybe Joss was just curious because he wanted everybody to like him. Because I didn't giggle or hang on him the way other girls did.

Cold rain was already sprinkling us as Vivvy returned from the house with a big flashlight. She trained it on the peak of the roof, sleek and treacherous. Up there huddled two dummies—a witch and a Headless Horseman—made of knotted sheets and gourds, looking profoundly unscary.

To me, they also didn't look precious enough to justify this daring rescue from the storm. But Joss, clearly happy for any excuse to be a daredevil, glided up the ladder, while Bram and Seth held it steady.

It was a long climb, at least thirty feet. Vertigo sent chills through my stomach and legs as I watched him.

We hadn't talked much since the House of Horrors. Back in the yard, I couldn't look at him, just nodded when he offered to get some punch. When he handed me the cup and disappeared into a group of senior girls, I was almost relieved.

Maybe if I kept semi-ignoring him, Vivvy would give up on forcing us all together, and Joss would melt back into fiction, where he belonged. Watching him dart around on the roof's peak, untrussing the dummies, I decided to write more stories where Joss performed physical feats. Maybe he could save Seth from a roaring brook or a deep pit in the cave, a situation that created lots of opportunities for pounding adrenaline and sweaty physical contact.

Joss's footing looked sure up there, his movements easy and graceful. Being a jock, I realized for the first time, wasn't just about social domination. It was about knowing exactly what your body could do.

"Throw the shit down here!" Seth yelled. "You're gonna break your neck!"

Joss was descending one-handed, the other arm clutching both dummies against his chest. "I'm good! Almost there."

With a sharp crack, the rung broke under his weight.

For an instant, Joss clung to the ladder frame, swinging nearly eight feet up, speared with the glittering raindrops in Vivvy's flashlight beam. Then he fell. Bram and Seth darted out of the way as he landed in the grass—on his feet, but staggering—beside the two piles of sodden sheets.

He took a step and collapsed, clutching his right ankle. "Shit."

Vivvy offered him a hand. "Is it sprained? Can you stand?"

Joss rocked, his voice coming out clenched. "Don't know. Hurts."

A new shape thrust itself into our circle. In the fractured light, through the increasingly dense rain, I saw a hip-high plaid skirt and blond hair—Halsey.

"Don't let him walk on it!" she cried shrilly, as if we'd been encouraging Joss to spring up and run a marathon. "If it's a fracture, you'll make it worse. I'll get my car."

"It's okay, Halsey." But when Joss tried to rise again, he grimaced in pain.

"Stay right there!" Halsey was already halfway to the street. Her eye caught mine, colder than I would have thought possible, and then she turned and dashed on.

Bram ended up toting the precious dummies indoors while the rest of us waited awkwardly for Halsey to bring her car around. Vivvy suggested getting Val, but Joss needed a doctor, not a sheriff.

Halsey returned and barked orders with the authority of an EMT. Bram and Seth supported Joss the few paces to her sedan and settled him in. When Joss protested that it could be just a sprain, Halsey glared at him. "A bad sprain can mess you up, too!"

She patted his knee, her hand resting there slightly longer than necessary. The fingers digging in, as if he might slip away. I felt Vivvy tense beside me.

Then Halsey turned to us. Her face was shuttered; she didn't meet anyone's eyes. "We need him in the tournament this year. He shouldn't be taking stupid risks."

"You'd rather have him get brain damage from a flying puck," Seth muttered.

Halsey ignored him. I expected Vivvy to contribute her own cutting remark, but she didn't say a word as Halsey buckled herself into the driver's seat and slammed the door. The engine roared. Vivvy's teeth chattered.

Not until the car roared off toward the county hospital did she say, "I'm so glad she's more concerned about his well-being than a stupid trophy."

"Maybe she's not done with him," I said, again seeing Halsey's grip on Joss's knee, protective and possessive at once. "Break or no break."

Now I wondered whether Joss had really been hiding from Halsey when he took me into the basement, or whether he'd wanted her to see us. To wonder if he was holding me the way he'd held her.

Vivvy snorted. "She may not be done with him, but I think he's done with her."

Val stormed out to ask us what was going on. We ended up abandoning the ladder and dashing inside as windblown rain battered us, as unforgiving as Halsey's eyes.

Now

No one has fixed the ladder. Now I can see exactly where the rung broke: not splintering in the middle, as I'd assumed, but snapping cleanly at one end. I run my fingers over the breakage point and, instead of splinters, find an even, sandpapery surface and a hardened bubble.

Dried glue. As if the rung was sawed out of the frame and then stuck back in. But not for long, or not well enough, because it broke under Joss's weight.

"Bram," I ask, "was the ladder already broken before Halloween? Did someone try to fix it?"

Bram is still so close that I feel him shaking his head, his breath wafting my hair. "It was fine when Val put up the decorations. Joss must have been just heavy enough to break it."

The sawed-off rung doesn't prove anything. Someone could have done that years ago and then tried to fix it—but sloppily, so that it broke under Joss's weight.

Everything followed from one weak rung. Because Joss couldn't resist a challenge, he sprained his ankle. Because he sprained his ankle, he sat out most of the season and didn't go to the Defilers' cave that night. He came with us.

"What is it?" Bram sounds genuinely baffled. "I can't see."

Before I can answer, Vivvy calls from outside, "Bram! Are you in there?"

She sounds angry and a little frightened—not like herself at all. Both of us go absolutely still.

"Shh," Bram whispers then.

But I came to find Vivvy, and I'm not going to hide from her. I slip between Bram and the ladder, brushing off his attempt to hold me back, and duck under the garage's half-open door into the red dimness and whirling snow of twilight.

Vivvy scrambles away from me. She wears sweats and an old cardigan, which isn't like her even if she did stay home from school. "Celeste, what the hell?"

"She came to see you, but I stopped her on the way in," Bram says behind me. "We were just talking."

We weren't, but it doesn't matter now. I advance on Vivvy, who doesn't have a coat or boots; she must have thought she wouldn't be outside long. She looks so small, so fey and childlike, with her pixie face and dreamy eyes. She played the clueless innocent to catch Halsey off guard, but I know her better.

"Someone sawed the ladder," I say.

Her eyes go bigger, way too perplexed. "Ladder?"

"You don't remember how Joss hurt his ankle?"

It would sound ridiculous to an outsider—who cares how Joss hurt his ankle, when Joss is dead? But Vivvy knows why it matters, and her eyebrows arch. "You came here to look at our *ladder*? When Seth could be arrested tonight or tomorrow?"

Again I'm on the town green, listening to Seth begging me to confess as if only I can save him. Believing the worst of me. And now, instead of explanations, I get angry questions from the very person who convinced Seth to believe that—this tiny, defenseless girl in glasses and a cardigan knitted by her dead grandmother. The past hour has been almost too much to process, but now, at last, I have a focus for my rage.

"You told Seth about me. And not just him—you told *Halsey* that I liked Joss. That I wrote stories. That I was obsessed and stalking him." The words are bitter and jagged; I spit them into the snow between us. "And now she thinks I did something to him. How could you do that?"

For a split second, Vivvy looks lost—a person air-dropped into the middle of Antarctica and told to survive. Then her expression hardens into sternness, as if she's regained a sense of where we both stand.

And where I stand is below her, in a basement full of broken, unsavory things. That's clear from the twist of her lip, the flare of her nostrils. She's looking at me the way Halsey or Cammy would.

"Everything I told Seth," she says, clipping each syllable, "was because I had to tell him something to make him hang out with us and Joss. And I *had* to tell Halsey, too, because she saw you by Joss's truck that time and came to me freaking out, asking if Joss liked you. I told her he liked you for a reason, because you were a writer and understood him better than she ever could, but I never said 'obsessed.' I never said 'stalking.' I tried to make you sound cool, actually. And I barely told either of them a sliver of it. I didn't tell them about all the creepiness in your stories."

"Cut it out, Vivvy. Don't talk to her that way," Bram says.

But his attempt to stand up for me is background noise, because after all, he doesn't know how creepy I am, either. My head has turned into a dark well of echoes, spinning and spinning until they merge into a single rushing roar.

How can she say my stories were creepy?

How can she say that *now*?

How can she?

"We wrote them together." The words slip out of me.

Vivvy shakes her head. The scolding expression on her face has loosened into something wilder that it takes a second to recognize.

Fear.

"It was always about you," she says. "Your past. Your issues. The things you wouldn't tell me. Celeste, you scared me. The things you did to Joss in your stories, the things *he* did—you had so much anger. I was scared to tell you. I was scared to ask— except through another story. And when you answered, it was like I was seeing a whole new side of you. A dark side."

I want to hurl the accusation back at her. What did I see in the garage, what was that cleanly sawed rung, if not *her* dark side? Only Vivvy or Seth could have done that on purpose, and though I can see him helping, I know it wasn't his idea. She's the one with the plans. She knew that if she exiled Joss from his team and his friends, he would be all ours.

But that bubble of shame is swelling in my chest and skull again, distorting the world—distorting Vivvy, whose fear seems real.

The furrow between her eyebrows is in the wrong place, drawing an ominous, upside-down V. Her fists clench at her sides. She's not just posturing for Bram to keep him away from me. I scared her, and I still do.

I remember the exchange of stories she means, and my gut twists, sending bile into my throat. Why did she hide what she was feeling? Why didn't she tell me?

Then

Two days after the party and Joss's fall, my phone buzzed while Vivvy and I were drinking tea in her kitchen. Crows cawed in the hedge outside, the woodstove crackled, and Bram and Val were arguing in the other room about his using his parents' trust to buy a car.

Sometimes you know you're due for something bad. There were days when I could ignore the alert, but today I dived for the phone, breath held, sweat already beading under my sweater.

Not him again, please. Not in front of Vivvy.

It was him. Words swam before me, a quote from some French philosopher. It didn't make any sense. It didn't apply to anything. It was just him showing off, trying to make me curious enough to respond.

The longer I thought about it, the tighter I'd be caught in his trap.

When I looked up again, across the teapot at Vivvy, it was like waking from a nightmare. Everything was so perfect and vivid: the steam drifting between us, the logs glowing in the square window of the stove, Vivvy's eyes fixed on me. In this light they were gray, not green.

"I should go soon." My throat wanted to gulp the words. "Dad's getting pizza."

"Okay." She held my gaze a few seconds too long.

When I checked my mail at home, after dinner, a story was waiting for me:

"Trust"

This time, when Joss's phone buzzes, Seth reaches for it. "Who keeps texting you?"

Joss snatches it from him. "Personal boundaries. Anyway, it's just my mom."

Joss glances at the phone, and his face falls. Just for a second, it's as if a gray curtain has lowered over the bright, wistful eyes and soft lips and everything that makes Joss Joss.

"It's not your mom. If it's Halsey, you can tell me." But Halsey doesn't actually scare Joss, does she? "Or is it your stepdad?"

"Nope." Joss stuffs the phone into his pocket.

Seth isn't going to let him slither out of answering questions. Not this time.

"It has to do with that time you got bruised, doesn't it?" he asks.

Joss doesn't answer. Stares straight ahead. It's too cold to walk in the woods—okay, to make·out in the

woods—so they've pulled off onto a logging road, noth-
ing around for miles but dark and trees and silence.

"Look, Joss, I love you." The words just slip out—Seth
can't take them back now. "But if you don't tell me what
the hell's going on with you—who hurt you, what you're
scared of—then this can't go on. It can't."

Joss keeps quiet for a while, his face turned away
from Seth, as if he's mesmerized by the snow that shines
ghostly between the trees.

Finally, he says, "Okay. If you're sure you want to
know, I'll tell you."

I wrote my next story that night. I didn't revise it—that would
have meant rereading it.

I didn't send it for three days. On Monday at school, everything seemed back to normal between Vivvy and me, and I considered not sending it at all. But then I started to feel something
between us again, a force field pushing us apart. It was getting
harder and harder to meet her eyes. She was so happy and animated when she talked with Seth, and so solemn and restrained
when she turned to include me in the conversation.

She was waiting. Like Seth with Joss, she needed to know I
trusted her.

Which didn't mean she loved me, of course—not that way,
anyway. Seth telling Joss he loved him was a sword pulled from a
stone, an ovation with red roses, something I'd been longing for,

but here in the real world, in my life, "I love you" was something people said to try to make you do what they wanted. "I trust you" meant more.

I told myself if she knew the truth, if she *sort of* knew, maybe she'd stop worrying about me. Maybe she'd understand.

And so I sent it:

"Better Left Unturned"

He'd been an idiot, Joss chastised himself, to leave his phone on the dashboard.

It was Assistant Coach Drew Heyerdahl's number again. A glance at the screen was all it took to transform a perfect evening—the world clothed in sparkling snow, the two of them far from everyone else—into a nightmare.

I keep thinking of you. Saturday at four in the cave?

Seth wouldn't stop asking questions, wouldn't accept Joss's deflections and lies. "It has to do with that time you got bruised, doesn't it?"

Joss stared out the window, anywhere but at Seth. In his head, he composed a furious response to the text: Why do you think I like you? Where do you get the fucking nerve?

Seth was still talking. He was using words like "hurt" and "scared." He was talking about breaking up, which was no surprise, and he was using another word that was a surprise, a word Joss couldn't, wouldn't process.

Love. I love you.

"Okay," Joss said without thinking, too focused on trying not to hear the echoes of the word love. "I'll tell you."

A tickle in his throat—and then, all of a sudden, Joss was choking, the roadhouse burger and fries threatening to come back up in a flood of acid. His breastbone ached.

"Joss. Joss!"

The gentle pressure on both of his temples returned him to himself. Seth's hands cupped his face, steadying him. Seth's eyes glinted in the snow-reflected moonlight.

And something in Joss surrendered.

"It's not what you think," he said. "I never answer him. I don't want to see him."

"Whoever it is, whatever it is, I'm not jealous, okay? It's just—well, I want you to be safe. And you don't look like you feel safe."

"I'm not scared of him." Shame burned Joss's throat like bile. "It's just, he won't stop."

"The texter is your ex?"

The word was so wrong, laughter bubbled up and threatened to choke him again. "It wasn't like that. He started out as just this guy I met in the cave."

"You hate the cave."

"I know."

Joss couldn't explain how the dark maw of the cave used to tempt him, night after night. How he'd found his way to the passage where his dad drowned and turned off his flashlight and sat staring into the dark.

One summer night a light came down the passage. A headlamp. A tall shape bent to ask if he was okay.

Drew Heyerdahl. It was their first meeting, and they started talking like two people whose differences didn't matter, because that's what the cave did to you. They talked about caves, the weather, beer, old girlfriends, and not having dads in their lives. When Joss mentioned hockey, Drew said, "Hey, I just got hired as the assistant coach at KDHS."

Joss stared down at his hands, pale starfish in the darkness, and told Seth, "We met there a couple more times. He'd bring beer and a joint. But I didn't think it was anything. I just liked talking to him."

Oh, they'd talked. Joss told Drew how his dad died and how he felt about it. Drew told Joss about a boy he'd loved back in college who died by suicide. Drew felt responsible for that, and it had taken years to feel less responsible. Hearing that made Joss feel less alone.

"How old is he?" Seth was clearly trying to keep his voice neutral, but Joss could hear the pinch of disgust.

"Old, okay? I thought—I don't know what I thought."

One night, talking became something else. And Joss went along with it because—well, who knew why? Because Drew seemed to understand. Because Joss was flattered by the attention and curious about how it all worked. Because he didn't dare be with the boy he secretly liked back in Kray's Defile.

He said yes to Drew, or anyway he didn't say no, and almost immediately he realized he wasn't ready, not with this person, not like this. But how do you explain that you changed your mind? Joss wasn't a guy who wussed out, whether he was climbing a rooftop or facing down an opposing team's enforcer. He went through with things.

So he went through with it.

"Nothing much happened," he said, reacting to Seth's expression. "Really." And it was true, technically, but "nothing much" felt like too much. "After that, he wouldn't leave me alone, though. E-mails. Calls. Texts."

Then school started. Practice started. And Joss realized that Drew Heyerdahl was now in charge of him on the ice and in the locker room, and in a position to be as much of an asshole as he wanted.

It was not a good time to have just broken up with Drew Heyerdahl—if that was even the word.

The mocking digs started coming—about Joss's laziness, his lack of concentration, his being a pussy, and worst of all, his sex life. Was Halsey keeping him satisfied? Clearly, he needed to do more fooling around in his truck and less on the ice. It could pass for typical locker-room talk, a coach trying to motivate a player by getting a rise out of him, but there was a nasty edge. And Tanner McKeough picked up every insult or backhanded compliment and amplified it.

Joss suffered through a year of this, and then he texted Drew.

"I thought if I met him in the cave one more time, I could make him promise to cut it the fuck out. I just wanted to see him with no one else there. To make him admit it. To scare him."

He remembered that day too well. The cold dampness of the cave, the smell of the joint he shared with Drew to be polite.

"Did he hurt you?" Seth asked.

"No! But he wouldn't admit he was doing anything wrong. I told him how messed up it was, how I could report him, and he said..."

"What?"

Joss could barely get the words out. "He said, 'You've always been in control of this, Joss. You're beautiful and you broke my heart.'

"And then I hit him. I hit him. He never touched me."

Joss remembered how his palm stung as he drew it back. How he wanted to hit Drew again and again and again till the older man collapsed on the ground, and maybe then start kicking him.

Drew didn't try to slap him back. He reached for Joss, and Joss ran. He ran and ran, from Drew and from his own murderous, unsatisfied rage, until he slipped in a narrow corridor and fell. His cheek bled, as if the cave itself were punishing him.

Joss wanted more. He bashed his forehead against the cave wall, eager for the pain. Eager for anything that would calm the monster inside him.

Drew had called him "beautiful." How beautiful would he be now?

He did it twice more, until the trickle of blood down his temple made him stop. He was supposed to meet his buds and Halsey at the roadhouse, so he went straight there, the pounding in his head keeping him from realizing this was a dumb idea.

Seth knew the rest of the story.

"Joss," Seth said, "this isn't your fault. I know he said you were in control, but that's bullshit."

"Do I look like a victim?" Joss said automatically.

Maybe he did—he honestly wasn't sure anymore. He just knew he didn't want the texts on his phone, the weird pleading, the claims of love. The locker-room ribbing. The queasy memories in his head.

"It's not about you being a victim or not," Seth said. "You told him to back off, and he kept coming, and then he tried to gaslight you into thinking it was your fault. Pervs gotta perv, Joss. It's got nothing to do with you."

Joss wanted to believe that. "I blocked him, but he got a burner. I should've gotten a new number."

It's not really Drew I'm afraid of, it's me. Of this weakness I have inside, and this anger.

"You should report him. He's a predator. I'd come with you."

Before the last words were even out of Seth's mouth, Joss was growling, "Not in a million fucking years. And if you tell anybody, I'll—I'll—"

When Seth tugged him into the circle of his arms, Joss crumpled. He rested his head on Seth's army jacket and breathed carefully—no hitches, so Seth wouldn't know he was fighting back sobs.

He wasn't worthy of this. He didn't deserve the way Seth listened to him, reading his body's signals, caring about what he wanted.

He deserved to be hurt. Gaslit or not, he was strong. He could take it.

Seth held Joss that way for a long time. Then he said, so quietly it took Joss a moment to understand, "I'd like to kill that bastard."

His face muffled against Seth's chest, Joss replied, "Not you. If he ever touches me again, I'll kill him myself."

Now

Like Joss in the cave, I am running.

I run because I can't bear to face Vivvy—her suspicion, her fear, her lies. Showing her the photos on my phone won't change her mind, and I don't know anymore if that's because I'm the guilty one or because she is or both.

I run through the twilight and the whirling, stinging storm. I pass the park where Joss and I sat on the bench that night. I pass the path up the hill.

The sidewalk's empty, just my footsteps making a crooked black line. Bram isn't coming after me. He did call out as I left the Kray house: "Wait up, don't leave like this!"

But he didn't follow. Vivvy's words must have shaken him, combined with what I told him about my missing memory.

He can't trust me when I don't trust myself.

The Defilers' binder, the ladder rung, Joss's bloody signature, my own missing time—they've all come loose in my head and started dancing like the phantoms you see when you have a high fever. There's no coherent picture, no solution to the puzzle.

Unless the solution is me. Unless I don't remember because I don't want to.

As I head downhill toward my street, wind whips icy tendrils of hair into my face, bringing tears to my eyes. Tomorrow—maybe even tonight—Sheriff Palmer will come for me, and it will be time to tell the truth.

I'm not surprised to see the familiar sedan parked practically opposite our house. Coming up from behind, in the waning light, I can see it was once bright red. A layer of snow on the windshield says it's been there awhile.

And now, with a warm flush of rage in my chest, I know I've seen this nondescript car before, and Joss riding in it. I can guess who's inside.

The cold is gone. There's a hot thudding in my head as I cross the street and stride up to the driver's window. Sure enough: bottle-blond hair pulled back from a tense little face, splashed by the light of a phone.

I tap on the glass.

The startled look on Halsey's face is almost worth the swimming vertigo in my gut.

I have no plan. I only know I'm done running.

She stares at me for an instant before lowering the window. All alone this time, no Cammy or Tanner for backup.

"Were you waiting for me?" I ask.

She opens her mouth and closes it. She looks like a trapped animal, but there's scheming behind her eyes.

"I know you never wanted to break up with him. I know you thought there was something between him and me."

Halsey's face turns to cement. The only sign of nerves is a slight widening of her eyes. I remember her at the Halloween party, rescuing Joss from us, buckling his seat belt and patting his knee possessively, and I wonder if she loved him just as dearly and madly as Seth did in our stories.

"I know you think I might have hurt him."

She opens her mouth, and I brace in case she spits on me. But she only glares like she doesn't trust herself to do anything else.

I say, "I didn't, but I want to know who did, too. I want to talk to the witness who saw Joss and me on the bench. Will you take me to her?"

My voice doesn't sound like mine right now, and my body doesn't feel like mine, either. I'm hovering several feet above the snowy pavement, watching us interact like two glowing arrangements of pixels in a video game.

When Halsey finally moves, it's like she's waking up. She hits her phone, darkening it, and opens the passenger door.

"I'll take you there," she says tightly. "She's in a trailer park just out of town."

When I get in and buckle up, she doesn't look at me. Just puts the sedan in gear, works the wipers, and screeches away, skidding a little, toward Main Street.

Something thumps in the trunk as if she's filled it with rocks.

I look back once at my dark house and think of Dad at the university, probably waiting till the storm tapers off to drive back. I rub my hands—remembering how Bram warmed them, trying to steady my breathing.

Nothing the witness says is likely to change Halsey's mind

about me, but that isn't why I'm going. *I* need to know what Joss and I were doing in the wee hours of Sunday morning. How we were sitting, whether we were talking or kissing or even shouting. I need to fill in the black hole before I face the sheriff.

She turns a corner. *Thump* from the trunk again.

"You've been following me this whole time," I say.

Halsey just nods, her shoulders bunched like she thinks I might hit her. I could—I'm bigger than she is.

I really did hit Frank, and he didn't even try to hit me back.

"You left the note in my locker?" As I say it, I have zero doubts.

Her head swings to me, her eyes glittering with a hint of that demonic scowl. "Yeah. You like it?"

It shows me how jealous you were. How desperate to have him. And it doesn't seem like a note she'd have written if she'd known already, before the assembly, that Joss was dead.

So maybe she didn't know. Maybe only Tanner did.

"I saw you go into the sheriff's office today," she says, her voice suddenly low and intimate like a friend's. "What were you doing?"

So she saw that, too. "Just returning something I borrowed from Val." Wait, she's missed the turnoff. We're gliding on toward Vivvy's house. As we reach the corner, Halsey eases on the brakes.

"This is a dead-end street." But she knows that.

I twist back, then forward again. Somebody's walking toward us through the gloom, too tall for Vivvy or Seth. "Who's that?"

As I crane forward, the tall figure starts to jog. And a dull bang sounds from the trunk, making the junker vibrate, even though we aren't moving. My body goes taut, my ears ringing. *Get out now. Get out—*

Freeze, my body says.

"Just a friend." Halsey clicks the locks open, slides down a window. "Hey, Tan," she calls, "look what I found!"

Another thud from the trunk. There's someone in there. Fear claws at my throat, and I grab for my door as it swings open.

Tanner McKeough towers over me, dressed in sweats and long johns, a crooked smile on his face. "Well, bonjour," he drawls, and he thrusts a formless darkness into my face like a bouquet.

Until he presses it to my forehead, I don't realize it's a handgun.

Then

The day after I sent Vivvy my story, we didn't talk for hours. It was me who lowered my eyes when we were in class together, me who couldn't face her now that she knew a form of my truth.

An exaggerated, dramatized version. I didn't see Frank outside of school as often as Joss saw Drew Heyerdahl. Our "caves" were the museum and then his apartment. Our locker room was the rehearsal room, where he pushed me for an emotional reaction, asking those awful questions in front of everybody, until Bess made him stop. But it happened only the one time.

And I didn't actually bash my head till I bled, just slapped myself because of "stress." That's what I told my mom, the counselor, and anyone else who insisted on asking. I was stressed out from city life and theater workshops. I needed a fresh start.

When the last bell of the day rang, I just sat. I ignored the flurry of gossip and packing up and leaving. I couldn't find the strength to get up and take the bus to my empty house, knowing I'd probably spend my afternoons alone there from now on.

Vivvy had Seth and Bram and the aunts. She'd be fine.

The teacher stepped into the hall to talk to another teacher, and when I looked up from my desk, Vivvy was standing there.

I got up—to explain or flee, I didn't know—and then I was in her arms. My head rested on the shoulder of her bottle-green crewneck. She held me tight around my waist. My arms fell slack at my sides—and then I raised them and hugged her back.

At first, it felt like nothing, my body stiffening as usual, but then her breath moved my hair, and I knew she was *here*, and I was here. I didn't want to touch her the way Joss touched Seth sometimes, the way I imagined touching Joss sometimes—desperate and dark and needy—but I did want her close, and I wanted her to stay, and she stayed.

The clock ticked. Outside in the hallway, a boy bellowed, "Yeah, sick burn!"

Because of the clock, I knew it was seven seconds before we came apart, and Vivvy said in a low, strained voice that didn't sound like her, "You don't hurt yourself, right? Not now?"

"No."

"Do you want to report him—the real person? If it is a him?"

"It's too complicated. He's not here."

Vivvy blinked, taking a moment to process this, but the story had prepared her. "You know it's not your fault, right?"

I nodded because, although I'd never feel sure of that, it helped to hear someone say the words. It helped every time.

She squeezed my arm. "If you ever feel like hurting yourself, if he's ever bugging you again, you call me, okay?"

I said, "Yes."

Side by side, we walked out of the classroom and down the hall. Out the doors of the school, through the parking lot to her car, like a couple in the last scene of a teen movie.

As we settled into the Impala, I was light-headed with relief.

I'd told someone, and I hadn't died of shame, and it was over now. No more questions. Like Seth with Joss, she understood I just needed to feel safe.

Silently I thanked Seth and Joss—the fictional ones—for saying what I couldn't.

Vivvy turned the key. "Want to hit the diner? I hear they have a cobbler special today."

A smile spread over my face, and for once it felt natural. No acting. *My* smile. "Yes, please."

Now

THURSDAY, NOVEMBER 21, ???
(THEY TOOK MY PHONE)

The thumping from the trunk continues. I can't see where we are because of the bandanna tied over my eyes, but I feel the car rumbling into a lower gear, tackling a sustained grade. We have to be going all the way up the mountain pass.

To the cave. Where else would they be heading?

"Who's back there?" I ask after my shaking has subsided enough for my teeth not to chatter. I'm in the back seat now, my hands tightly cinched behind my back with a bungee cord, a shorter cord manacling my ankles. Even if I get out of here, I won't be able to run far.

Tanner cackles from the front. "Wouldn't you like to know, mademoiselle."

I smell the liquor on him. The whole time he was tying me up, he was crooning—"That's it, there we go, just sit tight, you're doing good"—while that whiskey breath blasted into my nostrils. My stomach turned over and over, but I froze, as still as the dead, and he didn't hurt me.

See? Mom says. *Just go still.*

Now that he's farther away, I can breathe again. I can speak, though every time I blink, I'm still falling and falling into a cold abyss, screaming without sound. "Where are we going?"

Tanner laughs wildly—it's clear why he's not the one driving. Halsey's voice cuts through his, brisk and cold sober.

"If you want," she says, "we can go straight to the sheriff. It'll be easier."

My right thumb and pinkie are numb. I twist my wrists around and around, trying to loosen the cords, as gravel explodes like popcorn under the car's wheels. *Are we at the top, then?*

"Sure. I'll go to the sheriff." Right now, anywhere feels safer than this car.

"But only if you're ready to *confess*." Tanner draws out the last word, practically braying it, and I remember the letters in the snow.

Do they actually believe I killed Joss, or is that just what Tanner wants Halsey to think, or maybe even vice versa? Either of them could have done it, but somehow I don't think they both did.

"I don't have anything to confess." I say it crisply, the way Vivvy would, like it's the simple truth—like there *is* a simple truth. "Have you told Sheriff Palmer why you had a fight with Joss the day before he died?"

Tanner lets out a sarcastic yip, as if I've wounded him. "Joss was my best friend in the world. And one of you is the crazy bitch that killed him."

One of *you?* For an instant, I think he means Halsey, but

then that thump sounds from the trunk again, as the car pulls to a stop and the motor dies. My heart races, a hollow booming in my ears. "Is it Vivvy? Do you have Vivvy in there?"

Tanner just laughs again. I hear the car door open and shut, then footsteps on gravel going around to the back. The trunk pops. The thumping stops.

"You're not going to get away with it by playing dumb now," Halsey whispers. "You were telling Val lies about us. You wanted to talk to Bethany to shut her up, didn't you? Or because you don't even remember what happened that night. Vivvy told me all about you—you're crazy, and you killed him."

"Vivvy wouldn't say that." I twist my hands frantically as the back door opens, remembering Vivvy's denials and wanting to believe them. *Needing* to believe them.

Halsey's voice is poisonous. "Well, she told me enough, so I figured it out by myself."

I shy away, pressing against the opposite door, but Tanner's big hands are on me, sliding me across the seat. Unable to keep my balance, I land crouched in slushy dirt. An arm grabs my waist, tugging me up and forward like a mannequin, and I hear someone else nearby, breathing fast. Not Tanner.

"Vivvy?" I whisper.

"This would've been easier if you'd let me call Gibsy," Tanner yells in Halsey's direction. He drags me over slick grass, panting, and I realize he's trawling the second person with his other arm—those light, quick breaths are still close by.

A car door slams, then another, and Halsey's footsteps

stumble across the grass. "Can't trust Gibsy to keep his trap shut," she says.

"Well, keep the gun on them. Hear that, freaks? She's got a gun on you."

"Vivvy?" I ask again, and then the other captive says in a voice sharp with panic, "Celeste? You too?"

It's Seth.

Then

He says he was very frustrated by the decisions of the referee in the Red Wings game. He would have protested them, but to do that is like, uh—well, he uses an expression that literally means 'fart into the wind.' "

Joss laughed—a guffaw from deep in his chest that startled me. He slouched against the cab of his truck, supporting himself seemingly effortlessly on one crutch, while I read from his phone screen, translating a forum message from his favorite Canadiens player. He'd intercepted me on the way out of school, and now I wondered if I was really all that much better than Google Translate, but I wasn't going to say no.

"He says he's very excited—um, pumped up, I guess—for the next Maple Leafs game." Maybe I *was* his translation robot. Joss was clearly more interested in this tobacco-spitting puck slinger than he would ever be in me. "He wishes all his, er, homies in the Côte-des-Neiges neighborhood a happy holiday season."

I couldn't see the Impala from here, but wherever Vivvy was in the parking lot, I had a feeling she was watching.

She kept talking about how we needed to invite Joss to "hang out," just the four of us. She'd want me to suggest it right now, but even meeting Joss's eyes—so intense, so blue, so focused—took all the courage I possessed.

I finished the post and handed back the phone. "He sounds like a nice guy. Humble."

"Yeah." Joss launched into a monologue about the player's record—hat tricks and assists and bodychecking—while I nodded and tried to look understanding and enthusiastic, but all I saw was the starry glow of his eyes.

This was what he loved. Talking hockey was when he was most alive. I tried to imagine we were married and at the breakfast table, and I was gazing into his beautiful eyes and not hearing a word he said, just as he wouldn't hear a word when I talked about books and plays. Would that be enough?

Maybe not.

"Oh! Let me help."

He was fumbling the door open now, his weight on one crutch while the other leaned precariously against the truck bed. I caught it before it could fall, then nabbed the other crutch as Joss swung himself up into the seat. His arms took most of the weight, so strong the movement looked effortless.

"Thanks." He opened the passenger door, and I brought both crutches around and slid them carefully onto the seat. The engine thrummed, a deep-down vibration I felt in my back and thighs.

"Want a ride home?"

"Oh, thanks, but Vivvy's waiting for me." The words came automatically.

Vivvy might be furious with me, but too damn bad. Joss was already grinning and saying so long and putting his truck in gear—*he* didn't seem to care either way—and, in all brutal honesty, the last thing I wanted was to nod and smile through another hockey monologue when I could be with my actual friend, planning and scheming about fictional Joss.

This could be another of my ill-fated interpersonal decisions, choices that might lead someday to my living with zero humans and an entire sanctuary of cats, but right now I didn't care.

Now

E ven blindfolded, I know where we are. How could I not? When the slushy grass beneath my boots gives way to packed dirt and stone, when flakes stop hitting my face and the cold breath of underground settles around me, when water trickles in the distance, I know.

We're taking the "easy" way in, and I know we've reached the tightish squeeze between two boulders when Tanner stops and tells Halsey to go ahead. "Take it," she whispers to him, and I know she means the gun.

Bad idea. Tanner's breathing hard, hiccuping occasionally, and his smell is all over me, making me almost tipsy myself. Or is that fear turning me giddy? With his hands on me, I don't know my own feelings, don't know anything but limpness and dread.

"You gotta turn sideways," he says, tugging me forward. He doesn't have to tell me to rotate my head one way and my body the other; I know this passage by now. Stone walls close around me, pressing against my chest and tailbone.

But I feel no panic this time. Last time I was here, the cave hid me from Cammy and Halsey. Its embrace is tight, but it will only trap me if I fight it.

Seth doesn't navigate the crack so easily. As I stumble across the dirt floor, hearing my breath echo on the walls of the Cave of Defilement, I hear his aggrieved protests.

Halsey's small fingers close on my arm like steel. "Don't you dare try to run."

I don't struggle. I'm getting my bearings in the cave, hoping they take off the blindfold—hoping, too, that they can't tell I've been here before.

"What are you trying to do?" I pitch my voice just to her, hoping she's the more rational one. "All I want is what you want—to know what really happened."

Five talons dig into my flesh, sending pain shooting up my arm. "What happened is, you wanted him, and you couldn't have him. He hooked up with you, but he didn't really want you, and when you realized that"—she draws her breath sharply, almost a sob—"you killed him."

The accusation comes out in a hiss of anguished certainty. I know Halsey believes it, every word. She believes it because she knows how it feels to want Joss, and to think you have Joss, and to not really have him at all.

"You loved him," I say. "Even when you were cheating, even when you pretended to break up, you could never let go."

Halsey's nails sink deeper. Feeling them break skin, I kick out reflexively, trying to get her off me. But the bungee cord pulls tight between my ankles, and I topple backward.

Tanner's hands, far too familiar by now, catch me and set me upright. "C'mon," he says, giving me an impatient shove. "Let's start the treatment already. I want to get the hell out of this hole."

"What's the 'treatment'?" Seth asks in a dead, distant voice.

"No questions." Tanner drags me a few paces and pushes me to the ground. When he's drunk, his speech gets a chanting rhythm. He seems to be enjoying this the way some guys enjoy playing villains and thugs onstage, slamming into the scenery and manhandling fellow actors.

If he killed Joss, shouldn't he be scared shitless right now, or is he just too shit-faced? And if he killed Joss because of Halsey, can't he see it won't do him any good?

Maybe that's why he's so pissed off. I could shout out my suspicions right now, try to turn them against each other, but that gun...

"Look." Seth's voice is breathless but steady. "I can only speak for myself, but I didn't lay a finger on your precious friend. You're wasting your time, and if you let us go right fucking now and let Palmer do his job, we won't tell him any of this happened."

Tanner guffaws and starts repeating Seth's words back to him—only shriller, like a banshee. Echoing off the cave walls, the sounds are so unnerving that Halsey yells, "Shut up! Go sit outside if you can't take this seriously."

"*Take this seriously.*" He's mimicking her now. "You know what I take seriously?"

Thunder claps, making the cave sway like an earthquake until all the sound in the world blinks out. Blackness, silence.

Then my ears are alive again with painful ringing. Somehow

I'm crouched on my hands and knees, covering my head. Beside me, Seth mumbles, "Oh shit, oh shit."

"You idiot!" Halsey yells. "Give it to me!"

"It was a warning shot, okay? Got better aim 'n that."

"It could've ricocheted and killed one of us!"

Footsteps dance away from us, followed by scuffling and angry whispers. Seth breathes shallowly beside me, close to the dirt floor.

We have to get out of here. Tanner may or may not already be a killer, but he's definitely a loose cannon, wasted and armed.

I inch until I meet the cave wall, but instead of supporting me, it falls away, sloping upward at a gentle incline. Could this be the place where Bram and I slid down the first time I came here, when we entered from above?

Tanner's unhinged voice rings out across the cave. "So you wanna know what the 'treatment' is, Seth? You stay here in the dark till one of you confesses. Or both of you."

"You're a fucking moron," Seth yells.

I tense, half expecting another gunshot, but Tanner's voice thins as he retreats down the passageway. "Scream all you want, ain't no one gonna hear." A last jeering giggle. "Guess you already know that, Larkin."

At first, I think Halsey's gone with him, but then she kneels beside me and tightens the cords on my wrists, her hot, angry breath in my ear. "You thought you were so special because you wrote stories about him."

"Vivvy told you that, right?" My pulse thuds again, a sickening, hectic beat, and my muscles flood with so much adrenaline

I want to toss these cords aside like the Hulk. But my tensing is probably only making them tighter, and Vivvy doesn't matter right now. "Halsey, listen. Patrick told me Tanner called Joss a traitor. Tanner could've ambushed Joss that night because he wanted *you*."

"Oh, *Patrick* told me!" she mimics, her flashlight a fuzzy radiance through the bandanna. "So you think Patrick was into you, too? You don't know a thing about me and Tanner. You don't know *any* of my friends, you little bitch. You're just a tourist. You made Joss feel like a big hero, and he ate it up, but it was never about you. With Joss, it's only ever about Joss. I saw him come to your house on Saturday."

Of course she did. "I wasn't there. Nothing hap—"

She cuts me off, her voice grating. "He put the moves on you because you were easy. Because you were there."

And then, abruptly, she's sobbing. "And you know what? He deserved you. You deserved each other. But if he'd been with me that night, if he *cared*, he'd still be alive."

"I'm sorry," I whisper, but she doesn't answer. Footsteps crunch, the flashlight's glow receding.

Seth calls, "Goddamn, Halsey, what're you going to do, bury us alive?"

Her footsteps are a distant rustle now—or is that the trickle of water?

"Celeste." Seth's voice comes out choked, as if the oxygen has bled from the cave along with the light. "You need to tell them."

Rage rises in me again, but it's the pale, empty ghost of what

I felt this afternoon. The cave and the dark have pared me down to essentials. I draw up my legs, sit on my bound hands, and wiggle them under me and around to the front, looping my legs through my arms like a contortionist. Now I can get at the knots.

Halsey's reaction showed me I'm not going to convince anyone—not here, not now. But I can start to piece together the truth.

"If you think I killed Joss," I say in a voice that sounds too calm even to me, "why didn't you tell those two about Saturday? Why didn't you tell them I left last?"

Pebbles shift; he's trying to free himself, too. "Because they're assholes."

"It's not just that. I've seen the binder, Seth." I've got a knot between my thumb and forefinger. I worry it, trying to massage the loops apart. "I know you've been here before. I know something bad happened. Why don't you just tell me what the Defilers did to you?"

Then

Vivvy was practically skipping as we walked to the Impala. "*Tell* me," I said, sliding into the passenger seat, when I couldn't stand it anymore.

"He's coming!" She hit the gas, and the old engine vroomed in the frigid air. "Just now in class, I said we'd be up by the cave on Saturday night sampling vintage liqueurs, the three of us. I said it all casual, like not *exactly* inviting him but leaving it open, and he said, 'Cool, I'm there.'"

I ran the scene in my head, trying to hear Joss's tone of voice. "That's all he said? Nothing more when you left class?"

"No, but it was crowded, and he was busy." She squealed to a stop on Main Street, sparing a dawdling squirrel from certain destruction. "Stupid tree rat—just *go*, won't you?"

"Because that sounds kind of vague." My gaze followed leaves skittering into a frozen gutter as I tried to decide whether I really wanted to drink old liquor on a mountainside with Joss. "Like maybe he was just being polite."

"You're such a downer sometimes!" Vivvy hit the gas again, and we lurched forward. "You're being very Bram right now. Trust me, Joss will show."

Now

What are you trying to do, anyway?" Seth asks. "You know they're right out there. And they've got a gun."

"There's more than one way out of this place." I nudge at the knot that holds the cord around my wrists, trying to get a finger through the loop, telling myself I'm not just making it tighter. "Two more, actually."

One: the long way to the bat cave, the passage Tanner could have used to kill Joss. I'm guessing it starts in the alcove where I hid. Two: Bram's private passage, whose entrance could be right above our heads. It hasn't taken me long to weigh the options and decide that a steep climb and a tight squeeze are a better bet than a longer tunnel that could be flooded or blocked.

"If you tell me the whole truth," I go on, "I'll take you with me."

Seth laughs, short and sharp; the dark swallows the sound. "What makes you think you're going anywhere?"

"Tell me."

"Tell me how you ended up on a park bench with Joss. I heard them talking about that."

"We made out behind the cedars. I passed out. And then... I don't know any more than you do. I blacked out, I guess." I'm grateful we can't see each other's faces. "Okay, your turn. Why does Halsey think you'd want to kill Joss, anyway?"

It's a shot in the dark, but right now everything is. The first knot is loosening.

Seth groans. "I'm surprised Vivvy didn't blab to you. She seems to have blabbed everything else."

Tell me about it. But Vivvy's betrayal isn't the point right now—the reasons for it are. "Joss was a Defiler. But you're not, are you?"

"God, no." There's pain in his laugh, and something darker. "Look, we did try to set up Joss that night—Vivvy and me. It was halfway between a prank and revenge, I guess, but we didn't want to *hurt* him, just embarrass him."

"How?" My heart races; I have to dial it back, control my breathing, to keep from accidentally cinching the knot again.

"Cameras. In the cedars." Seth laughs again, as if acknowledging how silly it sounds. "We were going to get him to kiss me—which happened, right?—and get pics of it, and then post the pics on social. Expose him for what he was—a hypocrite and a coward."

The quiet rage in his voice sends cold creeping down my spine. This is not the love-hate Vivvy and I envisioned. This is hate, straight up.

And Vivvy knew.

"What did Joss do to you?" I ask again.

"Not just me. And not just him. Do you seriously know how to get out of here?"

"Yeah." *God, I hope so.*

"Good, because I never want to come back here again in my life." He pauses, his breath a rasp in the dark. "So Joss and I hung out in middle school. Not much, mostly just with Vivvy. Right before the end of eighth grade, we were smoking a joint, and he invited me to a party. A kegger in the cave with juniors and seniors. He said Vivvy would be there, too, and I figured, why not?"

"*Vivvy* was there?" Her photo wasn't in the binder—her signature, either.

"Yeah, she was kind of friends with Halsey and those girls back then. And me—well, maybe I did like Joss a little. So I went."

Vivvy was here. I can't focus on that, though, because my thumb is through the loop. Excitement makes me shake almost too much to attack the last knot with my teeth.

"They started giving me hard cider and whiskey shots, and long story short, I was nervous, so I got totally trashed. That's when they turned out most of the flashlights, and they started talking about an 'initiation.'"

I remember Vivvy's story about the powder-puff induction that never existed. The hard cider, the older kids. "Oh shit. Was Vivvy trashed, too?"

"Oh yeah. So Gibsy's older sister took a severed hog's head

and a bunch of organs out of a trash bag, all goopy and gross-smelling, and they plopped it down in the middle like a picnic, and then they called, 'Initiates!' I couldn't see straight by that time. The cave walls were swaying."

The second knot loosens between my teeth. "You were an initiate?"

A dark laugh. "I had no idea what was going down. They called names—Tanner, Gibsy, Cammy, Halsey, Vivvy—and everybody somehow knew what to do. As they got called, they came and lay down in a circle around the hog's head, arms at their sides like they were dead. Then they called Joss, but he didn't do like the others. He didn't lie down."

Seth's voice cracks, swerving from its deadpan. "Joss went and whispered to the senior who was in charge, this guy Akeman, and Akeman said, 'We have a request to use a proxy.' Everybody laughed in this weird, high, psycho way, and next thing I know, these two big juniors are grabbing me and dumping me in the circle."

"I don't get it." I pull the second knot free, my whole head ringing to a terrified, triumphant beat, and start unwrapping the still-tight loops of cord around my wrists. *I'm doing it. We're getting out.* But not till Seth's done.

"I didn't, either. The older kids started ragging on Joss, calling him a pussy, but Akeman shut them up by saying it was okay to use a proxy, it was in the 'rules,' and anyway Joss's dad was a Defiler, just like Vivvy's dad, and legacies are important even when they can't 'go through with it.'"

"Go through with what?" My hands free now, I toss the

bungee away and rip off my blindfold—not that it makes a difference, since I can't see a thing.

Whatever happened happened right here, in the dark that presses on us.

"So." Seth barrels ahead, his words tripping over one another. "There was just one flashlight left on, and Akeman went around the circle.... Maybe you don't want to know this."

But I already know it. I've seen the photos of kids with their tops pushed up, skewered by the flashlight. I've heard Vivvy's story about the dark room. I know how you freeze when those hands touch you, how you tell yourself you don't feel it, how you remember every detail afterward even as you tell yourself it didn't actually happen, it didn't matter.

"They giggled the whole time they touched us," Seth says. "When Akeman snapped our pictures—you saw the pictures?— that's when some of us freaked. Not me. Tanner made this whimpery sound, and Cammy said shut up, be a man. They didn't touch us inside our underwear, though; that must've been a rule, too."

What did Vivvy tell me? *Don't worry, only* over *the underwear.* Year after year of scared kids in the dark, lying still for initiation. Did they tell themselves they were special, Technicolor movie stars in this gray town? That it was a rite of passage, the price of joining an elite sect of people who'd always have your back?

I understand wanting to feel special. What else were we doing at the roadhouse, the audition, the Halloween party? But this...

I should be attacking the knots tying my ankles, but I can't move. "And Vivvy?" Just like the first time I heard a version of this story, I need to know she didn't lie still for that. I need to know she escaped.

"After they were done with me, right before they got to her, she started yelling, 'This is messed up!' and up and bolted out of the cave. Some of them tried to go after her, but Akeman called them back. Said they'd make sure she didn't tell."

And she didn't. I remember Halsey saying, *That night you didn't make the cut, huh?*

Vivvy didn't spill the Defilers' secrets, but when the time came, she found ways to get back at them. The video. The ladder. The "prank."

"So that's the big secret you wanted to hear. That's the initiation. Except I wasn't initiated like the others. While they were all signing their names in pig's blood or whatever, I was hurling in a corner, and next thing I knew, Joss dragged me outside. I was too freaked to ask questions. He walked me home and told me to keep my mouth shut or the seniors would kill us both.

"And I believed him. For a whole weekend, I thought we were both, I dunno, victims. But Monday at school, Joss was hanging with Tanner and Gibsy and even Akeman like nothing had happened. I googled 'proxy,' and then I got it."

Proxy boy, Tanner had called Joss in the roadhouse. Taunting him with a reminder of that night. "You were Joss's proxy. You did the initiation, but he was the one initiated."

Cold stiffens my fingers, but the knots around my ankles are giving way, sloppier than the ones around my wrists. "Why would Joss do that? And why didn't Vivvy *help* you?"

Stupid questions with no answers, like why Frank still texts me, or why I never told anyone but Vivvy. People do what they do. You survive it; you don't ask why.

Seth laughs, the sound an island in the formless dark, and I tug the cord free and hurl it away.

"They were both just scared," he says. "Scared to do the initiation, scared not to do it, scared to tell. You know, for years after that, Vivvy and I didn't speak. We couldn't even look each other in the eye. That didn't change until last summer—right before you came—and that's when she told me the Defilers made her swear not to say a word or they'd hurt her brother. They did a number on both of us."

"Turn around. Give me your hands." We crawl toward each other's voices. I find Seth's knee, his jacket, and finally his trembling fingers. He's loosened one of his knots, giving me a head start.

"There's a way out. I promise. The problem is finding it."

"I might have a light." He squirms against my fingers. "Hurry."

I was hoping Seth's story would supply a better motive for Tanner's killing Joss. But now I'm thinking that if anyone had a reason to kill him, it's this boy I'm unshackling.

"Revenge," I say. "That's what you said you wanted."

"It's not really like that, though, it's—"

He stops short as laughter sounds in the distance, male and female, refracted by the cave's twists and turns into ghostly howls.

318

We're both on our feet at once, the last stretch of cord kicked away. I hear the *tchock* of a lighter.

"Don't!" I cry, my palms slick and my heart galloping as an orange flame blooms in Seth's hand, leaping between us, sending shadows skittering over the revealed cave walls.

"It's okay! They're a ways off!" He dances away as I grab for the lighter, the sweat on my temples going cold as I imagine what Tanner and Halsey will do if they find us like this.

"Climb!" I jab a finger at the sloping wall, my gaze raking the top for the opening Bram and I used. Like a gallery window in a castle, I thought then, but I see only a jagged crack where the rock slabs don't meet.

Again that ghostly laughter, deceptively near or deceptively far. I hurl myself at the slope and grab a rock spine that protrudes from the dirt, hauling myself up while Seth boosts me from below.

My snow boots are big and clumsy, and I keep losing my footing, but I hug the slope with my whole body and repurpose my fingernails as crampons, my biceps burning with every inch. The lighter's flame flickers, vanishes, reappears, light and dark strobing, but I know where I'm going now. I'm a rat clinging to a ship's hull, just above the burning salt waves. I am Joss saving Seth from a spring flood in the cave, and I am strong, and I will not let go.

When I hook my fingers over the opening, there's a patter of dirt, and I wait for the ceiling to thunder down on top of us. But beneath the dry sediment is solid stone. With a final wrench, I get my elbows over the edge. Twisting my hips for momentum, I propel myself through the crack and into the hidden passage beyond.

It's tighter than I remember—did this really seem like the *wide* part? I manage to pivot, kneeling for stability, and reach through the gap to yank Seth up by his jacket.

"Thanks. Shit!" Scrambling over the edge, he's dropped his lighter. An instant more of wavering, burnished shadows, and then we're in darkness, rolling together back into the burrow that Bram showed me.

As our limbs entangle and flail, for an ice-cold instant, I lose my sense of direction. Which way is out?

Then harsh yellow twilight blinks in the opening above us—their flashlights, coming back—and I know.

Flat to the dirt, I press Seth down beside me. "Straight ahead, head down, *quiet*."

Beyond the rock wall, Tanner's mocking voice bounces off the cave's contours. "Yoo-hoo! How you guys doing? Ready to get defiled?"

I rise and tiptoe hunched over, keeping track of Seth by his ragged breathing. Behind us, in the Cave of Defilement, the jeers are turning to incredulous shouts. Then angry ones.

Seth freezes at the sound of blood in Tanner's voice, and I grab his wrist and pull him to his knees. If we can just get around this bend—

Flashlights play over the opening, sending bits of our burrow into stark relief. "Up there?" Halsey asks. "I heard something."

"That's not a way out. Check the alcove."

We crawl in single file, as quietly as we can, then slither in the dirt as the roof closes in. Around the first bend. "Shit," Seth moans softly as pitch-black swallows us.

I understand, but it feels almost good this time—my senses so awake, straining through the dark. My breathing levels out as the burrow bends again and again, the solidity of earth drowning our captors' voices. We're safer in the grip of the cave, enveloped in layer upon layer of sediment and silence, than we were with the Defilers.

I know what comes next. I know why Tanner thinks there's no way out. When our crawl ends at a seemingly impregnable rock face, I take a deep breath and run my hands over it, reading the surface, searching for openings.

"Turn sideways," I whisper. "Right arm over your head, left one by your side."

Seth breathes fast and shallow. I place his fingers inside the slender crevice so he can feel for himself. "You go first—you're skinny. Feel your way through, just like a puzzle piece."

"Shit," he hisses again, but he moves, floundering past me. I hear a thud, more muffled swearing, a shower of pebbles.

"Damn it, I'm stuck. I can't—"

"You're not stuck." My temples are pounding again, but I keep my voice steady—the voice of Joss helping Seth through a tight space. The brave Joss, the best Joss, the one he sometimes was. But, of course, the voice I'm really hearing is Bram's.

"Tilt your hip sideways and wiggle. I've done it. You can."

"I'm gonna die here." Panic sharpens his voice.

"You're not. Sideways and kick yourself through."

Gravel thrashes as he kicks desperately, sending dirt into my eyes. But a final burst of swearing and a loud yelp tell me he's made it through.

No time to think now. About how I could wedge myself in the wrong way and stick; about how Tanner and Halsey could be clambering up the wall after us. Blind, I read the crevice with my body, lead with one arm, and do what Bram told me to.

The passage takes a bite out of me, and maybe vice versa, but I emerge, my left hip and elbow throbbing as if someone smashed them with a hammer.

"You okay?"

We clasp hands again, a more meaningful communication than words. "We're through the worst. It *does* lead out. Promise."

And so we go on—sometimes on our stomachs and sometimes on our aching hands and knees, sometimes crashing into the turns and sometimes fumbling our way into them. Seth isn't Seth anymore, only a constant slither and scurry ahead of me, another small animal using the burrow as an escape route. Heavy breathing, slide of pebbles, faint whimper, scrape of rock, and then, and then light. *Light.*

It's faint and spectral, the light of a snowy night, but now we can see each other's scuttling forms. There's the rough black mouth of the cave, ahead and above, and *please don't let them be there waiting.*

Light glints on the toe of one of Seth's Doc Martens as he hoists himself into the open air. I brace myself for shouts and scuffling.

Silence, then rocks sliding, and then a hand dangles through the hole. I seize it, and Seth pulls me up.

Air. Light. Wind. The glaring snow, the skeletal black trees, the spilled-out jewelry box of stars. At our back looms the cliff; before us, the forest. The snow has stopped falling, and a dry, cold breeze ripples over us.

It sears the scrapes on my cheeks, my torn and filthy fingernails. I rise to my feet beside Seth, careful not to jar my hip.

"Where's the other entrance?" he asks—clearly wondering, as I am, whether Tanner and Halsey will double back and catch us on the way down the hill. Or do they think we've ventured deeper into the cave?

"Not too close, but we shouldn't take the path."

I pull him into the trees, grateful to the stinging cold for a burst of adrenaline. "Just head downhill."

Toward Vivvy's house, the place that has always meant safety.

Then

Vivvy pulled a dingy cobalt-blue bottle from the cupboard under the basement stairs. "Is this one too old?"

I dusted off the label and googled the brand. "They stopped making it in 1977. Sell it on eBay, but I wouldn't drink it."

"Okay, put it in the 'no' pile." She handed me a bronze-tinged bottle. "This?"

I sat on the bottom step on an old towel Vivvy had found for me because the Krays' basement was filthy and creeped me out, even without the horror-house decor. Room after dark room, dust-furred and spider-infested as a mad scientist's workshop.

The bronze bottle was a fifteen-year-old brandy, which Vivvy deemed acceptable. "Boys'll drink anything that gets them drunk."

I didn't bother to express any more doubts about Joss joining us tonight on the hillside. If he came, he came. The real question was what she thought would happen if he did.

"I'm starting to think Joss might be boring," I said, inhaling that deep-down basement smell.

"Boring?" She passed me a clear bottle with such an exaggerated expression of shock that I wondered, for an instant, if she was putting me on. But why bother? She knew all my secrets.

"Real Joss," I specified. "I'm starting to think maybe Seth was right—there's nothing there. I'm not sure Joss likes Seth that way, either."

"Then why did he *fall on his knees* in front of Seth in English class?"

"I don't know."

And, in the space of my not knowing, in this clammy cave of a room lit by a single bulb, the fantasies wove themselves again:

> *"Why did you fall on your knees that day?" Seth asked.*
> *Joss stared at him, his sea glass eyes full of too many feelings to express. "In that moment, I just had to. Because you were right—I did feel like a monster."*

I was curious about tonight, yes. I hoped Joss showed, even if the possibility gave me a constant tickle in my stomach. (*Because what if he doesn't like Seth? What if he likes me?*) Either way, though, my boys, my very own versions of Joss and Seth, would endure. I could give them new names if I wanted. I could make them vampires or demon hunters or eighteenth-century aristocrats or hustlers on Sunset Boulevard. Their story was mine.

Now

T hat's why Joss knelt," I say, making the connection at last. "In English class. Because he used you as his proxy at the initiation."

Seth's laughter comes back to me on the biting wind as we trudge down the mountain, dodging trees and wading through snow-dense undergrowth. Now and then, the woods part to offer a vertiginous glimpse of the town's glitter far below.

"That was pretty weird, huh?" he says. "And you made me stop. Vivvy and I didn't talk about it till later, after Joss and Halsey broke up, but she said that's when she knew you were important."

"Important to what—your plan?"

I remember what he told me in the cave, and the sense of betrayal chokes me again, as dank and foul as the ancient liqueurs she fed us that night. An icy patch sends me sliding, and I hug a tree to keep from barreling into Seth. Gripping it with fingertips black with cave dirt, I imagine sap pulsing placidly through the trunk, keeping the tree alive through the winter.

I did not kill Joss. I did not.

"Your plan and Vivvy's," I say, picking my way down the slope after him. "You plotted revenge on Joss together, right?"

"It wasn't like that. There was no master plan. I told you, it was more of a prank, and it wasn't even that until around Halloween." His jacket is a dark blotch on the snow, his voice surprisingly calm. "Last summer, Vivvy showed me that vid of Tanner and Halsey. She wanted to post it, to hurt them, but I told her Joss was the one who deserved to be hurt. Then, after the Shakespeare thing, she got this idea in her head that Joss was secretly in love with me, and I halfway believed her."

So did I. "She tried to trap us both, to make us throw ourselves at him. She told him I liked him, and then she told Halsey I was stalking him."

"I don't think it was like that. Vivvy told me Halsey came to her and demanded to know the deal with you and Joss. Vivvy said you were this amazing little snowflake and Joss was smitten and Halsey should just back off. Which Halsey interpreted as you stalking him, I guess."

The story matches what Vivvy told me, but it doesn't change the rest of what she did. "So was it a 'prank' when you sawed that rung off the ladder?"

Seth stops short. "I didn't! You know about that?"

"Yeah." He's just admitted he thought Joss deserved to be hurt, and I should be afraid of him, maybe, but we've been through too much together—Joss kissing us on the hillside, Tanner and Halsey's taunting, the tight squeeze through the cave. Once part of my story, now Seth's part of my life, and try as I might, I can't see him killing Joss on purpose.

"Vivvy told me she'd done something to the ladder." His voice has gone taut. "But I thought she was just talking, so I put it out of my head. After all, she never used that vid, right?"

"Actually..."

Before I can explain how she *did* use the vid, though, he goes on: "And whatever happened to Joss on Saturday, I was long gone by that time. Swear on my grandma's grave."

We've emerged from the woods on the top level of Middle-earth; the rock ledges spread below us, a canyon flattened by reflective snow. I clamber down the first two steps and hold out a hand for Seth. "I believe you. But you two did have a plan for Saturday, right?"

"Yeah." Seth ignores my hand and plunks down on the second-highest ledge with his legs dangling, gazing into the dark. "Like I said, we were just going to humiliate him. I had my doubts, like *serious* doubts, but Vivvy thought it would work, and you know how she gets when she's excited about something. The way she builds it up, it's like you're in a heist movie."

I nod. I know.

"She said she'd rig up one of her aunt's security cams in the cedars, and all we had to do was get Joss in a 'compromising position.' I actually bet her fifty bucks he wouldn't touch me, but she kept insisting he secretly wanted to."

He slides his butt off the ledge and leaps to the ground. "Guess I lost that one."

Betrayal is still lodged in my throat as we make our way down the jogging path, but it's less rank now, more like a flavorless wad of gum. "So when we made our pact, that's what Vivvy really wanted you to keep quiet about. Your plans."

"Right." He looks at me, a flash of pale face and eyes. "That's over, though. State police are coming to grill me tomorrow. I'm going home to find some cheap-ass ambulance-chasing lawyer, and then I'm gonna spill everything, including how Tanner and Hals tried to kill us. I'm done with sneaking around, looking over my shoulder."

His tone is defiant, like he expects me to protest, but I just follow him down the path to the Krays' orchard. "Do you think Vivvy could have done it?" I ask as we step among the gnarled trees, their branches velvety with snow.

"No." He doesn't look at me this time, his voice lower. "I mean, she wanted payback for the Defilers, for sure, but I don't think she wanted...that. Especially not for Joss. And it's not her style."

"I know." If I can't imagine Seth picking up a mallet and smashing it into Joss's temple, I can imagine Vivvy doing it even less.

"It was probably that psycho Tanner." Seth kicks a stone across the yard. "I mean, he wanted Halsey all for himself, right?"

The Kray house rises above us, a silent hulk against the stars. "Maybe," I say. "Or maybe it was me."

He turns to face me then—but only for an instant before he crosses his arms, shivering, and turns toward the street. "Yeah, well, I'm going to let the pros sort it out from here. You got a problem with that?"

Either he's changed his mind or our time in the cave has worked on him, too, making the possibility of my guilt shrink in the bigger picture. Or maybe he always thought Joss had it just a bit coming.

"Do what you have to. I'm going to go up and talk to Vivvy."

At this point I don't care if I have to pull her out of bed. There needs to be truth between us, regardless of what the "pros" decide.

Seth nods as if he gets it. "You can tell her I spilled. I don't mind."

"Okay. Good luck."

"You too." Halfway around the corner of the house, though, he stops and calls back, "If you want proof, look on her hard drive. I bet you'll find that footage from Saturday night. I bet she hasn't even thought about deleting it."

Then

He's not coming." Seth twisted a stick in the fire. "Wish we'd brought marshmallows."

"He's coming," Vivvy said. "The way he said, 'I'm there,' I could tell."

Seth snorted. The stick burst into flame, and he held it aloft, a torch flaring against the pool of darkness in the valley. We'd been on the mountainside for three hours, shivering and drinking and messing with the fire.

Now and then a bat wheeled over our heads, a deeper blackness against the stars. When the sky was still light, we'd seen dozens of them, presumably emerging from the cave. Vivvy asked why they weren't hibernating, and I explained that, for whatever reason, some Montana bats were active year-round.

Wind whistled, and I pulled up my collar and reached for the bronze-tinted bottle again. Fifteen-year-old brandy turned out to taste like cough syrup, and I was spacing it out with sips of tea from my thermos, but it was worth it for the distracting buzz in my ears and the warmth in my chest.

"Careful, Celeste," Vivvy said. "You don't want to pass out before he gets here."

I rolled my eyes. With just Vivvy and Seth, I felt perfectly at ease; with Joss here, I'd have to worry about everything from my wind-driven hair to my dripping nose to my blurred vision.

"The bats look healthy to me," said Vivvy as another one dive-bombed the hillside. "Why all this fuss about them?"

I started to explain that white-nose syndrome was slowly progressing across the continent, when Seth said, "Oh shit." He stared into the valley, his half-burnt stick forgotten in the embers. "I think it's him."

He and I both stood up at once, making Vivvy say, "Don't do that; play it cool." We popped back down like jack-in-the-boxes, but not before I saw a tall figure with a distinct limp coming up the path, less than fifty yards away.

"Can't fucking believe it," Seth said under his breath.

Joss must have seen the fire, because he waved, then stuck a finger in his mouth and whistled. Seth waved back and said, "Dude," and then we all shut up. The fire crackled, sparks soaring into black sky.

As Joss got close, we heard his quick, labored breathing. And then he was there—really there, blocking the lights of the valley, tall in his boots and jeans and barn jacket, the firelight turning his hair strawberry blond.

He circled the fire to the cave side and collapsed there, between Vivvy and me. "Longer walk than I remembered."

"You off the crutches, man?" In the firelight, Seth's face was sullen and indifferent, but his voice tremored.

"That's what I decided." Joss rubbed his bare hands over the fire. He didn't look at any of us, just reached for the bottle. "Hey, is this the special antique hooch?"

"It'll make you float," Vivvy said, though she'd had only a couple of sips.

Joss took two long swigs and scrubbed his mouth with the back of his hand. "Tastes like rat poison."

"How would you know?" Seth took the bottle from him. "Someone try to poison you?"

There was an edge to his voice, but Joss just belched amiably and said, "Many have tried." Then, for the first time since arriving, he turned to me. " 'Scuse me."

I couldn't speak. Vivvy giggled. "You're excused."

Joss kept looking at me. "How's it going, Celeste?"

He was just being polite, but there was something about having his full attention on me, even for a minute. "Okay," I stammered. "Not looking forward to doing my Shakespeare monologue."

"You kidding? You're aces at that acting shit." He reached across the listing fire to grab the bottle from Seth.

Seth held it out of reach, a playful glint in his eye. "Come get it."

"Seriously?" But Joss rose awkwardly and circled back to Seth, who jumped to his feet and dodged and weaved a few steps down the hill, sloshing the bottle and laughing. Joss followed him, limping but game, and they acted out a slow, wobbly stage fight— pulled punches, mimed kicks—that ended with Joss's grabbing Seth in a headlock and prying the bottle from his fingers.

I glanced at Vivvy for her reaction, but she wasn't even watching, just tapping her phone.

This was your idea. As the guys trudged back up the hill, I cleared my throat, and she put the phone down.

They were both panting. Joss chuckled as he eased himself down on the cold grass. "Got a smoke?"

Seth rolled a joint, lit it, and took a hit. He passed it to me, and I passed it on to Joss.

"You sure?" Joss asked me. The fire captured the lucent blue of his left eye, the hint of tropical sea.

"I'm good." To show I wasn't a buzzkill, I reached for the bottle. Joss passed it to me, and I drank without wiping the mouth.

When I handed the bottle back to him, everything was dancing a little in the firelight; the world was no longer fluid but stop-motion. One moment everything went still, and I was alone with the stars; the next, time lurched into gear again. Things kept jumping forward without my being sure how they got there.

Suddenly the bottle was empty, and Vivvy was saying, "Let's spin it like we're in middle school." And Joss was guffawing and saying okay, why not, while Seth said nothing.

And then Vivvy was spinning the bottle in the scrubby grass. It pointed back at her, more or less, so she spun it again.

It pointed at Joss. Seth came alive, making *Yeah, c'mon* noises, while Vivvy rose and knelt beside Joss and took his head in both of her hands.

The way she touched him reminded me of a priest, or a parody of one. She kissed him lightly on each cheek, then forehead, then lips.

"That's all you get," she said, and returned to her place, while Seth continued to catcall as if he were at a strip club.

Joss closed his eyes and spun the bottle. It pointed straight back at him, but instead of spinning again the way Vivvy had, he raised his palm to his lips and gave it a sloppy kiss, then hugged himself and did a surprisingly funny impression of someone feeling himself up.

We whooped with laughter, all of us sounding drunk although maybe not all of us were.

When he was done clowning like somebody in improv class, Joss handed the bottle to me. Vivvy said, "No fair. The next turn goes to the person you just kissed, and you haven't kissed anybody."

"Who put you in charge?" Joss gestured mock-imperiously at me. "Go on."

This wasn't a game I wanted to play, not a safe game, but Joss's silly approach had put me more at ease. I found a nearly bare patch of ground and gave the bottle a spin, willing it to point at me or at no one.

It pointed at Vivvy.

"Let's hear it for girl on girl!" Seth chanted drunkenly.

With everything flickering in time with my pulse, I couldn't get a good look at my friend's expression, and that was probably for the best. I crossed in back of Joss and knelt beside her.

I meant to kiss her solemnly on both cheeks, the way she'd done to me the night we ran to my house through the rain, but she turned her head abruptly, and somehow her lips were on my lips.

"Make it a *real* kiss," Seth said.

I remembered why we were out here—to get Joss hot and bothered, right?—and I tried to give her a real kiss, whatever that was. At first, her lips were cold and inert, like an uncooked hot dog, and I froze inside—this wasn't right. We wouldn't be able to look at each other tomorrow.

But before I could flinch away, she grabbed my chin and pulled me to her from a new angle. Now she was warm and alive, opening to me, or maybe I was opening to her, I wasn't sure.

So much of Vivvy was in that kiss—the slyness, the whimsy, and a hint of woodsmoke from her kitchen. I tasted brandy; her teeth clinked against mine. Her tongue darted between my lips just before we came apart.

It was just acting, I told myself, though I couldn't look at her, my face flaming as I returned to my seat.

And apparently it'd worked, because when I looked up, Joss was staring at me, eyes wide and lips slightly parted. "Now that's a kiss," he said, and heat shot from my chest up my neck, into my cheeks, all the way to the roots of my hair.

From there on, we followed Vivvy's rules. She spun and got Seth. The two of them made a big production of it, rolling around on the ground and pretending to make out, but from what I could see, their lips barely touched.

When Seth spun, the bottle wobbled to a stop with its mouth between Joss and me but distinctly closer to Joss. Joss inched away from it, and Seth said, "Yeah, I'm not into it, either."

"The gentlemen doth protest too much." Vivvy sounded excited but not out of control; she wasn't drunk like I was. "You can't just pass, Seth, you have to forfeit," she added.

Seth blew a scornful kiss at Joss across the fire. "That good enough?"

Joss reached over to grab the joint from him, took a long drag. "That'll have to do," he said, and spun the bottle so hard it nearly careened into the embers.

Around and around it went, its sleek bronze glass sparking once per circuit—nearly as old as I was, liberated from the basement's dark and dust. The play of light was hypnotic. I closed my eyes, blood thudding against the lids, and when I opened them, it was still spinning, and somehow I knew where it would stop, where Joss was willing it to stop. I knew, I knew, I knew—

The bottle came to rest with its neck pointing directly at Seth.

"Ah, fuck," Joss said.

Vivvy crept closer to him on hands and knees. "I think the bottle's trying to tell you something, Joss."

"Scared of me?" Seth asked.

Joss took another long drag on the joint. "I'm not scared. I'm just not into it."

"You're defying the spirit of spin the bottle, Joss," Vivvy complained, while Seth said, "Bet I know where you wish it was pointing."

I turned to ice.

"Kiss me first, and you can kiss her," Seth said, too hard and mean for it to be a come-on or anything but a taunt.

"You're making the rules now?"

Vivvy's knees were touching Joss's. She looked up at him shyly, a mouse appealing to a tiger. "You've got an unfair advantage, Thorssen. Everybody wants you, and you know it."

"Fuck that." He handed her the joint, but she passed it across to Seth. "Stop talking to me like you think I'm stupid."

His eyes darted to me then, and I saw a question in them, or maybe an appeal. Maybe he wanted to know I didn't think he was stupid, or maybe he wanted me to stop this like I'd stopped Seth in English class.

But I wasn't going to, not this time. I'd kissed Vivvy, after all.

"I want to see you kiss Seth, Joss," I said.

Seth said, "Hear that?"

"It's not an insult, Joss." Vivvy sounded very earnest, and abruptly very drunk. "You're special, and that means you owe it to us to spread the love around."

"You *owe* it," Seth repeated.

"Don't owe you anything." Joss scrubbed fingers through his hair.

"Oh?"

The word hung in the cold night, in the cellar smell of rotting leaves and the black of the cedars and the closeness of the cave. And at last, into the silence, Joss said, "Okay. Okay."

He started with Vivvy, because she was the closest. When his head dipped toward her, a fist clenched in my chest, but I forced myself to watch....

Now

The Impala isn't on the street where Vivvy usually parks it. Light shines in Bram's bedroom, I can see from the street, but not in hers.

I don't know where Vivvy would go this late, but it doesn't matter, because I remember what Seth said, that I should look on her hard drive for proof of his story. And I know where to find the spare key to the back door: on the porch under the rusty paint can that sits beside the stacked wood.

The key turns so loudly I tense, half expecting the house to come alive with lights and pounding feet. But nothing happens. The snowy hedges and raised vegetable beds reflect the light of downtown. No car swooshes by in the Defile's night; no plane unzips the sky's stillness as I ease open the heavy door.

I unlace my boots, still caked with grayish cave dirt, and leave them on the mat. A few steps take me to the kitchen, where embers glow in the woodstove. After a moment's hesitation, I tip-toe through the living room to the central staircase.

Stiff-backed sofas and fringed lampshades loom in the light that filters in from the front porch. All the rooms in this house smell just a touch like the basement—a textured, musty smell that makes you think you hear furtive footsteps and doors creaking.

On the stairs, I keep to the edges, quiet in my socks, trying not to think about my sore hip or my missing phone. Each steep step is a crag to my tired muscles. Halfway up, I trip and grab the banister. Century-old wood groans, but everything else is quiet except my raspy-loud breathing and the burble of a game from Bram's room.

He doesn't hear me. He's not coming out. Another step, another, and I'm in the upstairs hall.

The oak boards creak like a shipwreck, so I cross my fingers and count on the game to camouflage my steps. Or maybe he'll think I'm her.

There's no light under Vivvy's door, no sound when I press my ear to the varnished wood. I turn the knob.

The bed is a denser blot in the furry darkness. If she's here after all, I'll need to explain. I count to thirty, searching for the whisper of her breath. But all I hear is a clock ticking, so I gentle the door shut and hit the switch.

Light blazes—too much light, as stale as noon. She's not here. At the desk, I flick on the gooseneck lamp that we both prefer to the overhead fixture.

Her laptop sleeps innocently. What's the password?

Sitting in her chair, I close my eyes and rest my fingers on the keyboard. *Think like Vivvy.* It won't be anything obvious like her name or birthday or Bram's name. It won't be random. Passwords are secrets, talismans, and Vivvy wouldn't waste a chance to pick one that meant something to her.

Her mother's name? Her father's? No, too obvious. I sift through our time together, trying everything that sticks out. *Evergreen*, for the boughs on the grave. *Memento mori. Recurring character. Rat-brown*, for her car. *Flannery O'Connor. Éponine. Lapsang Souchong*, the tea she loves. I try phrases and titles and names from our stories.

Just when I'm ready to give up, I remember Joss cooking for Seth and the two of them gazing at the stars, and us in the diner, and I try *cobbler*, and boom, I'm in.

In the movies, the folder the amateur detective is looking for is always right out on the desktop with a suspiciously generic name ("Photos," "Saturday"). But Vivvy is prone to more cryptic naming practices. One folder is just "QL!" Another is "2019xxn." Another is "starshell." I scan them all for video files.

A folder marked "Guarding the Perimeter" holds a video dated last July—Tanner and Halsey. But it's not until I explore the folder "OTP" and then the subfolder "Assignments Now" that I find it.

Another night vision video, unearthly as a medieval engraving, date-stamped November 16. The camera must be behind the cedars, facing the valley. Dark boughs frame a bright, wavery gap—our flickering fire. That ghost facing me, with smoke wafting over his head, is Seth.

He bends sideways, out of frame. The camera shudders and follows him, and my spine goes rigid as I see how shaky the image is even when the camera isn't panning. It captures the action around the fire first through one hole in the cedars, then through another.

Someone's holding it.

This is no surveillance cam.

Someone was hiding behind the cedars that night.

Shooting us.

Less than three minutes left. I see Joss, his hair a spectral halo, lifting the bottle to his lips. Seth blowing out smoke. Vivvy's mostly out of frame, but her hair shimmers like Joss's. I have my back to the cedars and hence to the camera, until I get up and kiss Vivvy.

Oh. I did kiss her, didn't I?

Time moves slowly inside this window to the past, so much more slowly than I remember it happening. Our ghostly eyes glow. We look possessed, yet our movements are bashful and awkward.

Now Joss is arguing with us, his words lost to the breeze. It doesn't matter; I know what he said. He kisses Vivvy. He limps around the fire and kisses Seth.

The cameraperson lurches sideways to catch them in frame, because this is the part that matters. The zoom happens an instant late, but you can still see Joss Thorssen kissing another boy.

Whose eyes am I looking through? Faces flicker in my head: Tanner? Too loud. Patrick? Scared of caves. And then there's Halsey. I still hear her saying coldly, *If he'd been with me that night, if he* cared, *he'd still be alive.*

She wanted Joss to hurt. She and Vivvy weren't friends, but maybe Vivvy eventually grasped that Halsey was a victim of the Defilers' initiation, too.

I pause the video before Joss kisses me, because I'd rather remember it my way. Then I hit play again, just in case the camera captured what happened to Joss.

But the vid is almost over. It stops the moment before Joss's lips touch mine, and there are no more files in the folder.

Staring at the freeze-frame on the screen, I find my mind supplying the images now, sending them thick and fast. My memory isn't returning, but I think I know what *could* have happened.

When Joss and I went behind the cedars, whoever was holding the camera—Halsey?—must have ducked into the cave. Later, after I passed out, a noise could have alerted Joss to the presence of a spy. I imagine myself lying on the ground, dead to the world, as he stiffens at the sound of a snapped twig, a shower of pebbles.

Joss would have gone to catch the intruder, deft and athletic despite his limp. Vivvy, if she was still by the fire, would have tried to explain. Explanation would have turned to confrontation as Joss realized Vivvy and Halsey had teamed up to film him.

I imagine Joss saying the wrong thing, something to make Vivvy angry. Something about how she's a pathetic small-town voyeur, an old lady peering over the fence, and not an evil mastermind. I imagine her slipping into the cave entrance and coming out with the mallet.

Yes, she could have hit him—acting on a moment's impulse, out of shame and pent-up rage at everything the Defilers did to her and Seth and even Halsey.

I log out of her e-mail and into my own and send a copy of the video file to myself and log out again, and then I close my eyes, feeling the shaking run from my core to my fingertips.

Vivvy, you didn't. Please tell me you didn't.

I don't hear footsteps, only the door opening. "Viv?"

It's Bram. Thank God, it's Bram.

Then

Joss has pulled himself apart from me, one become two, and he's drinking from a flask but he won't let me have any more. Life has become a slideshow with jarring gaps, but I don't care because my arteries fizz with power, and the very darkness around me is alive.

I'm so alive. So warm. I will never freeze again.

Joss is talking. He sits with his elbows on his knees, and he bends his head, his wavy hair pale on his forehead, and he says, "I just see him lying there, and I can't forgive myself."

"Who?" I try to ask, but the word doesn't come out.

"I was his *friend*." His voice is edged with tears. "I mean, I could have been his friend. I was just so scared that night, Celeste, so I threw him to the wolves. I was *thirteen*. And now they all think I'm a pussy, whatever they say. All of them. Except Hals, maybe, and right now she wants my head on a stick."

"Who?" I manage to croak this time, and then everything goes black.

Now

I clap the laptop shut, but I can tell from Bram's face he's already seen the image on the screen. Sweat prickles on my neck. I look like I'm trying to destroy evidence, and he won't want to believe that Vivvy did anything wrong.

He comes to stand beside me at the desk, light glaring on his glasses. "Hey, are you okay? I've been texting you for hours. The way you ran off, I was worried."

I remember his hands guiding me through the cave, making it possible for me to guide Seth. The cool, chalky feel of his bare skin in the garage this afternoon. A sob rises in my throat. "You didn't come after me."

After the argument he overheard between Vivvy and me, I can't blame him.

"I tried," he says. "But Vivvy was upset, and I had to get her inside first. I walked down to your house after, but I couldn't find you."

He tried. I have this stupid impulse to throw myself into his arms and tell him everything that's happened, but I can only ask, "Is Vivvy okay?"

"She calmed down. Dunno where she is now, though." When he speaks again, there's a coldness in his eyes. "Does she know you're here? Why are you going through her stuff?"

"It's a long story. I was...looking for something."

I can't stop myself from glancing at the laptop, and Bram looks at it, too. When our eyes meet again, he says in a flat voice, "You found the video."

"You—"

"Yeah. I know what they planned to do to Joss. Did Seth tell you?"

"Yeah." The light makes a halo of Bram's hair, blond like Joss's, and I remember his Hail Mary pass to save me, his claim that we were on the bench together at three AM. He's known this whole time we were up there with Joss.

Maybe he also knows who killed him.

Outside, a throaty engine rumbles a path through the winter silence. Slows down, stops. "That's her, isn't it?"

He nods. Strong Bram, sweet Bram, awkward Bram. Too loyal Bram.

A car door slams. I rise to my feet, something sliding inside me as if my guts have turned to sand, and hold tight to the back of the chair.

"Did she tell you what happened?" This explains so much— Vivvy keeping a leash on Bram, hiding his phone. "She and Joss had a fight, didn't they? She didn't mean to hurt him?"

He shakes his head, a strange, stony blankness on his face, as I go on. "I understand. She's your sister. But, Bram, Seth could—"

"You *don't* understand."

His mouth twists, and I take a step away from him. Below us, a key turns in a lock, crystal-clear through the stillness, sounding not like something fitting into place but like something falling, falling, falling with a hard jolt at every step.

"Whatever Vivvy planned, whatever she did, it was because of the Defilers." Bram's eyes flash behind the glasses. "Back when we were in middle school, she went into that cave with them. I followed her, but I was scared to go in. She came running out and wouldn't tell me anything." His lips tighten. "That's why I spied on them. I needed to know. I found the binder a long time ago. She made me promise not to tell. But when she asked me for help giving Joss some of his own medicine—"

He breaks off as we both hear footsteps on the stairs, as sure and soft as cat feet. Steps in the hall.

The air has thickened between us, squeezing my windpipe. I want to move, to run, but I'll have to face Vivvy either way. "You helped her?"

"Yeah." The words seem to come from very deep in his throat. "And you're wrong. She didn't hit him."

"Then who—"

The footsteps stop. Together we look up at Vivvy standing in the doorway, small in her baggy sweater and sweats. It's hard to believe our fight was hours ago and not days—both of us wearing these same clothes as she did her damnedest to convince me I'd murdered Joss Thorssen.

She's taking in the situation—her expression soft with confusion, then hardening. "What a surprise! I went to see Seth, but he wasn't home, and here you are!"

"Seth's going to the sheriff," I say. "Vivvy, we should, too. I saw the video."

Vivvy freezes. I know the signs—stillness, shallow breathing, too wide eyes. For a moment, she seems to hibernate within herself, and then she emerges with a forced smile.

"There's nothing on the video you don't already know," she says. "But you *do* know, don't you? Have you remembered?"

I want to tell her that yes, I have, but blackout memories don't come back. And now that I know what happened, now I understand, I'm not angry anymore. I feel sorry for her, because she'll have to live with this for the rest of her life.

"Who else knows?" I ask. "Who was the person hiding with the camera?"

I reach for her hands, but she shies away from me, looking like she did when Halsey offered her a cigarette. "I know you didn't want to do it," she says breathlessly. "I know you didn't mean to do it."

It's like a comedy routine—*that's my line!* I stand stock-still, my hands still outstretched. I didn't want to come right out and say it, but— "Vivvy, you set Joss up. You planted somebody to take that vid. When Joss figured it out, you panicked."

Her face has gone blank like Bram's. "You're saying *I* did it?"

Facts shift uneasily in my brain; instead of a pitch-dark hole, that night has become a fractured kaleidoscope. "I don't remember it. I'm not saying that. But—"

"But you won't face the truth." Her face is a mask with burning dark holes for eyes. "You really want to know? Everything? I was there when it happened. I heard Joss yell, and I came through the cedars. He was holding his head, and you had the mallet, Celeste. He said you two were kissing when suddenly you freaked out and hit him. I didn't believe him at first. I tried to get your side of the story, but you just lay down and passed out, and then Joss..."

It's such a plausible story, but I don't believe it anymore. "You've been trying to make me think that the whole time. When you mentioned the mallet, you knew I'd start wondering if it could've been me. But you knew where it was, too, and you—"

"Stop!" Bram shouts.

As one, we turn to look at him.

"Both of you, just stop it." He's collapsed in on himself, his face shiny with sweat. "Neither of you hit him." He spits out the words like lumps of sludge, things he's desperate to expel. "I did."

"Bram." Vivvy's voice is a warning. "Stay out of this."

But two words are already reshaping the air between us, ricocheting in my brain. "You?"

Bram sits down heavily on Vivvy's bed. "Told you I helped. I was there the whole time with the camera. When you and Joss went behind the cedars, I hid in the cave and I...listened. It got quiet really suddenly, and I snuck out just enough to see. You were lying there, not moving, and he was on top of you, and it was so dark. I thought—"

My face is fiery hot. "No!"

His eyes meet mine, and they're so sad. His shoulders hunch. "I know. But you were so out of it, and you looked wrong. You looked dead. I thought he was... Anyway, I'd found that mallet in the cave, and I yelled at Joss to get away from you. He got up. He was still pretty drunk, I think, but he grabbed for the mallet, and I just...reacted."

"That's not what happened, and you know it." Vivvy's voice is a hiss. "You're trying to protect her."

He doesn't look at her. His voice is dull, as if a weight presses on his chest. "You're trying to protect me, actually, but it's over now. I can't let any of you three get in trouble. I didn't want to believe it at first; I told myself it wasn't real, because I didn't *mean* to kill him. But now..." His hand reaches for mine. "This isn't going away."

I take his hand, my own quivering. Nothing he's said feels real to me yet, but I do know one thing. "You have to go to the sheriff. We all do."

"I didn't want to leave you on that bench, Celeste. I walked you down there and I stayed with you for hours while Vivvy was up by the cave with Joss. But she was worried we'd get in trouble if we brought you back like that, so we left you at first light. Joss told Vivvy he wanted to stay up there and clear his head. We didn't even know he was dead until they found him on Sunday. I swear."

Vivvy stands like a statue. I'm still, too, holding the hand that killed Joss, the hand that rubbed life back into mine in the cold. His fingers are the chilly ones now.

"He was walking and talking when I left." Bram's voice wobbles. "Then he just passed out, Vivvy said. But we never thought...Will you go with me?"

I squeeze his hand. "Yes. Right now."

"Celeste." Vivvy's voice is small but firm. She's not giving up. "You know he's trying to take the fall for you because he cares too much about you. You can't let him."

"No." She's trying to manipulate me like she manipulated Halsey in the roadhouse, like she badgered Seth into going along with her plan. I know her too well to fall for it.

I may have lashed out at Frank and myself; I may not remember most of Saturday night. But I didn't hit Joss with a mallet. I may not love Joss, but the memories I have of that night are good.

And I believe Bram. My palm is damp against his, my temples pounding. The light seems to blur as Vivvy keeps talking, faster and faster, desperate to make me believe:

"It's all in your stories, Celeste. In your head, *you* were Joss—so special that everybody was in love with you, and you just couldn't choose! You played with Seth and me, and you played with Joss, and then you played with Bram. When Joss in your story said he'd kill that coach for touching him, that was you—a powder keg. The next person who tried to reach out to you was going to get an explosion. And that person was the real Joss."

Bram tugs at my hand. "C'mon. Don't listen."

"You were jealous," I say, realizing it at last. "You were jealous of me."

Together we step toward the open doorway, but Vivvy's tight voice follows us:

"I have all our docs and texts saved, Celeste. If I show them to Val, if I tell her you were obsessed with Joss and writing stories about him getting sexually molested in a cave, how's that going to look?"

Bram pulls me another step, and she says, "Everybody else will see them, you know. Everyone will know."

I can imagine it, all right—my stories floating out there online for the whole population of Kray's Defile to see. "First Aid" and groping in the roadhouse parking lot and tender confessions and Joss hurting himself the way I did.

It'll be like having my heart ripped out of my chest and displayed in a butcher's window, bloody and veiny and slimy. It'll be like getting stripped naked and paraded down Main Street.

For a moment. But in the end, what other people think won't matter, because the stories weren't written for them. They were written for Vivvy, the way hers were written for me.

Girls get hurt every day. Girls make up dark stories to deal with their hurt every day. Sometimes they share them with people who understand. And the world keeps turning.

I'm not afraid, and I'm not ashamed. "Let's go," I say.

I drop Bram's hand and walk fast, eyes straight ahead. The stairs open before me, black and steep as the cave wall that Seth and I scaled. Behind me Bram shouts, "Stop!"

I turn just as white hands emerge from the darkness and latch on to my elbows. Vivvy's face hovers in midair, haloed by the light of the corridor, so angelic for an instant, and then her weight is slamming into me and pushing.

One of my knees buckles, the foot finding empty space. The cold air of the stairwell rushes to meet me, to carry me all the way down in a flailing tangle of limbs.

But because I turned at the last second, because I saw her, my right hand has a death grip on the banister. I sway wildly, get my footing, and shove her backward. "What are you doing?"

She doesn't answer, only barrels forward again, crushing me with her entire weight. She knocks the breath from my chest, and I kick out, my left hand grabbing for her right while my other keeps me from falling.

Something jolts my shin—her foot—and then I'm losing my balance in the near dark; up is down is sideways. I stagger backward and grab out randomly as I start to free-fall—and my back finds the opposite wall.

Breathless, I sink to my knees and hold tight as if to a pitching ship, waiting for the next kick. It doesn't come. Through the pounding in my ears, the shuddering that blurs my vision, I see that Bram has pinned Vivvy to the wall, holding her hands fast.

"It's over!" he says as if for her ears alone. "No more!"

She fights him, her pale, spidery limbs twisting. And then, with no transition, she's as limp as a Halloween scarecrow, a bundle he's holding in his arms, her head buried against his shoulder.

She's crying and saying something about not wanting to lose him, not letting him go, so frantic that tears spring to my own eyes.

She loves him, and she doesn't want him ever to hurt. Not for a second. Not if she can throw herself in the way.

A door bangs down the corridor. A sleepy voice calls, "What's going on?"

Aunt Fiona. Which means this scene is about to end. But in

the two seconds it takes Fiona to stride down the passage, I fix it in my memory forever: Vivvy with her arms around her twin, the one person she would have died to protect, the one person she would have sacrificed me for. Bram restraining and comforting her at the same time.

I don't belong in this scene. I'm the force pulling them apart. And I wish so badly it weren't true.

Now

The sheriff's office doesn't have a waiting room, just four vinyl chairs flanking the soda machine. Fiona sits opposite us, her eyes vigilant. All Bram would tell her was, "I need to talk to the police about Joss." At first, she gave me worried glances, hoping I'd spill, but now her gaze has turned flat and suspicious.

While she checks her phone—she keeps texting Val, though Bram has warned her he won't talk to Val, either—Bram slips his hand into the crack between our chairs. I do the same, and now we're not exactly holding hands, but I feel the sweaty warmth of his palm.

Waiting for the sheriff and the state police detective, we've slipped into *The Twilight Zone*. Bram is right here, the light limning the curls on his forehead, and at the same time he's receding from me like a sky diver tumbling out of a plane.

When Fiona started asking questions about the scene on the stairs, Vivvy yanked herself from her brother's grip and walked back to her room without a word. Fiona was too distracted by Bram to call Vivvy back. The last thing I heard from her was the door clicking shut—not a slam, but somehow more final.

I know without being told that Bram will not tell the state police about the plan to embarrass Joss, or the video footage that Vivvy is probably erasing right now, or how Vivvy forbade him to confess and hid his phone and badgered Seth and me into not talking. The slight pressure of his hand against mine says he knows I won't talk about any of those things, either.

And I won't. I won't lie, exactly, just stick to what I knew before the revelations of this endless day. If they ask why I didn't come forward, I'll tell the truth: I was afraid.

There's the shutting door, and then there are Vivvy's words, also running on my personal loop: *In your head,* you *were Joss . . . everybody was in love with you.*

Could she be right? I don't write self-inserts or wish-fulfillment fantasies about being swept away by Prince Charming or a viridian-eyed gym-rat half-vampire. But in a way, I was Joss, and I was Seth, and their love was my love, and their hands on each other soothed the forces that were working under my skin, tearing me apart.

I don't think the real Joss was in love with me. Halsey was right about that. The only person who's maybe in love with me is beside me, touching my hand, and I understand why Vivvy tried so hard to shield him.

We had a moment together while Fiona got the car out of the garage, just the two of us with our breath steaming in the dark.

"I'm sorry," Bram said. "For not telling you right away. For lying."

I felt his gaze on me, but I couldn't meet it. "You had me almost convinced the Defilers did it."

"I wanted so badly for that to be true." His voice broke. "I wanted things to go back to the way they were. But then, when you told me you couldn't remember that night, I realized you were blaming yourself, and Vivvy *wanted* you to, because it would help me. I couldn't stand that. I told her it was time to tell you."

Behind us, the garage door ground open. "You could have told me right then."

"I know." He talked faster as the car pulled out. "You need to know I made a wrong assumption. That night. I made a split-second decision because I never liked Joss, and maybe because I could tell *you* liked him and it pissed me off. But the instant afterward, when he explained, I—"

Fiona honked the horn. "I did like him," I said, going around to the passenger door. And almost to myself: "I liked you, too."

Now, in the sheriff's office, Fiona is giving us both the stink eye, so we can't talk, not really. They'll have us in separate rooms soon enough.

But Bram does say, while Fiona's busy on her phone, "Vivvy was wrong about you."

I tense. Vivvy's said so many awful things about me tonight.

"She used to say you reminded her of a house with the lights turned off. Like in a war, during a blackout."

Vivvy told me that once, too. I imagined her breaking a window in the house that was me and forcing her way in and making me blaze with light.

"But I never thought that." His voice is stronger now. "To me you're a house with one candle burning on the bedside table. Most people outside can't see it, so they think the house is dark

358

and empty, but there's just enough glow, just enough flicker, and—well, for the people who *can* see it, it's a beacon, leading them home."

I curl my fingers around his and let the image bloom in my head.

Outside, a car pulls up, the engine roaring through the pre-fab walls. The sheriff.

As a door bangs at the end of the hallway, I say, "Thank you."

Now

TUESDAY, FEBRUARY 18, 12:27 PM

When I open my locker, an envelope slithers out. Heavy and cream-colored, with my initials written in a calligraphy I recognize too well.

I drop it as if it burns. Then I pick it up gingerly and turn it over, thinking about bad things that fit in envelopes. Hexes, anthrax, compromising photos.

She doesn't have any reason to hate me now. My carefully circumscribed testimony, and Seth's, saved her from the charge of witness tampering she may have deserved. But I don't open the envelope, just slide it into my backpack the way you might slide a spider into a jar, and I go to lunch, feeling a hot tightness settle behind my eyes.

As usual, I choose the most isolated spot. Since Bram's confession went public, every minute at this school has been like standing alone on a brightly lit stage playing a role I didn't choose: the girl who is sort of halfway responsible for the death of the boy everyone loved. Hard glares followed by eyes cutting quickly to the side—this is my life now.

When I put myself in their place, I understand. Joss was part of the Defile, just as Vivvy and Bram were. Uprooting Joss changes the landscape, and it doesn't matter if he wasn't quite the hero people imagined, because who is? Only the Defilers know that for sure, anyway.

If there still are Defilers. After she checked out the photos I left for her, Val got the sheriff's office to raid the cave. The whole place has been cleaned out and posted, and some tearful confessions about "small-town hazing" have made their way into the pages of the Billings papers.

I'm so busy thinking about the envelope that I almost don't notice when Seth sits down opposite me. Another boy settles beside him, wolfish with wild sideburns and brows and a T-shirt advertising an indie band I vaguely remember from posters in Montreal. I've spotted them together a couple of times before.

"Hey," Seth says, and I say it back, neither of us smiling. He has a new haircut, kind of a Beatles mop-top, and it works on him.

"This is Will," he says. "Will, Celeste."

The wolf nods at me and attacks his shepherd's pie. His shoulder almost touches Seth's but not quite, and I remember Bram and me in the sheriff's office.

"So I hear you're getting out of here." Seth is eating his Jell-O first, not looking at me, using his bangs as camouflage.

We saw a lot of each other, Seth and I, after the DA decided to press kidnapping charges against Tanner and Halsey. They ended up pleading to lesser offenses and getting probation, by which time we were pretty used to sharing space in waiting rooms, trading glances before returning to our respective books or phones. Seth hasn't been downright unfriendly, just distant.

"Yeah," I say. "My dad got a new job studying the progress of white-nose syndrome in Washington state, so we're moving to Seattle in June." Which can't come fast enough.

The wolf comes alive, his dark eyes fixed on me. "Seattle? I'd kill to explore that scene."

"We're going out west after graduation," Seth says. "Will's all about the Northwest, but I'm like, c'mon, screw the granola, and we've had enough nature to last us our whole lives. It's all about LA."

"Seattle's got a restaurant scene," the wolf objects in a rumble. "Something for both of us, like I've told you a million freaking times."

And then I'm grinning without knowing why. The cold outside is still bone-chilling, the sky through the wide windows still dandruff gray, the cafeteria still full of self-righteous eyes.

"What's funny?" Seth asks.

"Nothing." I stare down at the wasteland of white rice and teriyaki sauce on my plate. "I just like that you're getting out. I like that you're going together."

While the wolf looks perplexed, Seth rolls his blue, blue eyes. They cut like switchblades, nothing like Joss's bleary, apologetic ones. "Nice to know we have your stamp of approval."

"I don't—I didn't mean that." For a moment, the air is pregnant with all the stuff we can't say about fictional Joss and Seth.

Seth may not know anything beyond their existence, but I can see the awareness in his eyes. "I'm just glad you're happy."

"Are you going to start writing stories about us now?" His shoulder nudges Will's, the playful curl to his lips removing the sting from the words. "Because I don't need anybody fetishizing my actual relationship, thanks."

"Fetish what?" Will asks as they both get up.

Seth exchanges a glance with me. "You know what I mean. Hey, want some fodder?"

Then he grabs Will by the shoulders and dips him back a little, Lifetime movie–style, and gives him a real, deep kiss that lasts at least four seconds. I hear high-pitched laughter from one table, and grunting and shushing from another, but Seth doesn't cut it short.

I'm blushing when they're done, and so is Seth. I know he was brave to do that, and the moment belongs to him and Will, not to me.

"It was good to see you," I say, meaning it, as they pick up their trays. And then I can't stop myself: "Have you seen her at all, Seth? Do you know if she's...back?"

He doesn't ask whom I mean. "Not for a while. I thought she was living pretty much full-time with her aunt."

Fiona has an apartment in Billings now, because it's on the interstate and a straighter shot to Miles City, where Bram is serving three months in the juvenile correctional facility. Last I heard, Vivvy was staying there and homeschooling.

"Why?" Seth's face has stiffened. "Have you seen her?"

I shake my head.

But she is back, of course, at least for a few days. I know that even before I get up the courage to open the envelope and pull out the heavy card inside.

The whole thing is covered with tiny, dense hand-printing. For a moment, it makes me dizzy, trying to figure out where it starts.

There's no salutation. *I thought you might want a recap of the missing scene. The part I didn't talk about because they didn't ask.*

When I got back there, behind the cedars, it was basically just shouting, Joss being all "He fucking hit me!" and Bram insisting he wouldn't leave you and wanted to take you to a hospital. Somebody had to be rational, so I checked your vitals, and I made them team up to get you on your feet, and I ordered Bram to walk you down the hill while Joss sobered up.

Joss didn't like that. He wanted to stay with you. Were you wondering about that? His dad died of alcohol poisoning, apparently—no, he didn't drown in the cave, I keep forgetting you made that part up—and Joss learned CPR because of that. When Bram saw him on top of you, Joss was trying to check your breaths per minute. He was relieved when you opened your eyes, but still worried, so I said, "Don't you think you've done enough?" Joss knew I was really talking about the Defilers, about Seth, about me, and he let you and Bram go.

We were alone. "Nobody's ever gonna forget what happened

in eighth grade, huh?" he said when you two were out of ear-shot. The blood on his temple was dry, and his voice was weirdly empty. He tried to vape, but his hand shook and he dropped the pen.

I sat down beside him, because why not? "Why'd you do it? Why didn't you just go through with the stupid pervy initiation like everybody else?"

He didn't answer for what felt like half the night. I listened to his breathing, watching bats against the stars. My eyes closed, and maybe I slept for a few minutes.

A buzz woke me. Text from Bram: We're getting cold.

Wait, I'm coming, I texted back.

But then Joss started to cry.

At first, I couldn't believe it was really him, sobbing aloud. "I'm sorry," he said in between his sobs. "I was just a kid, and after what happened with my dad, it was like everything could break apart any second. I thought those people would be my friends for life. Always have my back. But now they laugh behind my back instead, and I want to leave, to get out, but it's so hard...."

I'm not sure how, but I ended up holding him. I stroked his hair. He cried. He shook. It was like a story.

But it felt wrong, and I realized something. Earlier that evening, when he kissed each of us, when you kissed me, that was right. We were a triangle, perfectly in balance—okay, no, a square. No, cooler than a square, maybe a rhombus or some-thing. Seth was part of the equation, too. We did a ritual that fixed us together forever in that moment, under the stars.

That was over now. "I'm sorry, too," I told him. "I'm sorry about everything—all the lies, and all the true things I said when I shouldn't have."

I don't think Joss understood. He went quiet against me, but he was still shaking.

"We should go back down. You should get home," I said, and that's when I realized he'd passed out.

I thought it was just the booze. I swear. I checked his pulse and it seemed normal, and I couldn't exactly carry him down the hill, so I left him.

When I found out he died up there, I did blame you, for a while. I blamed me and Seth, too, of course, and Joss for being Joss and starting this whole thing. Anyone but the person who actually hit him.

I don't even know why I want you to know this; it just seems unfair that you don't. If you're at Middle-earth before Friday, in the afternoon, I'll see you there.

Now

I haven't been back to Middle-earth since Seth and I stood there in the snowy night. The closer I come to it, walking up the path, the more the memories expand in my head and crowd out everything else. Seth kicking the yellow leaves, Vivvy swearing us to secrecy, Bram and I hiking up the hill toward my first glimpse of the cave. I remember his "caving suit," and then I see him in an orange jumpsuit and thrust the mental image away.

The day is bitter cold, but the snow is sparse, a dusting that barely pads the cracks in the boulders. The sky is a retro filter turning everything to sullen grayscale, emphasizing each scabby ridge on the tree trunks.

I expect to have to wait for her, but she's here, sitting on the stairstep where the sunny spot would normally be at this hour, wearing her glasses and a puffy coat. Her hair is longer now, brushing her collar, ash-colored in this light.

She says "Hey" first, tentatively, and I say it back.

"I didn't think you were coming. You didn't yesterday."

"No," I say.

Even though I remember her face twisted in rage and the hard shove of her hands, it's still her. Even on a day like this, when all the hope in the world seems dead, her spirit still twitches inside her, bright as a flame. I felt that restless warmth when we exchanged our stories, and I felt it on the hillside when I kissed her, and I think I'll always carry some of it with me.

"How's Bram?" I ask.

She sips from a thermos, her gaze resting on the valley. "He's okay. He'll be okay."

"Do you think he'd like me to write to him?"

"Yeah. I think he would."

And finally, I ask the question I've come to ask. "Is it true what you wrote in that card? Or is it just another story?"

I don't mean whether she really held Joss before he died. I mean whether she's really sorry, the way she told him that night.

Vivvy takes a long sip, her gaze on the horizon. She removes her glasses and examines them as if for smears. "It's true," she says.

I turn first, and then she turns, and we're looking straight at each other. In this light, her eyes are nearly as gray as everything else, but there's the barest hint of green in the left one. She blinks, and a film comes over her eyes, and I imagine I see my reflection in them.

"I never showed anybody our stories," she says. "I never told anybody any details. I said some stuff about you and Joss, some stuff I shouldn't have said, but I never did that. Because they're ours."

"I know," I say. "I know you'd never do that."

Something crumbles in her face. "And the thing I said that night on the stairs. About the stories being all about you."

The memory makes my throat close. "You don't have to—"

"No! I mean, I did think you were Joss in the stories. But I could tell you needed the stories and they helped you, and I understood. They helped me, too."

"You still wanted revenge."

She almost smiles. Not quite. "I guess that's how you and I are different. It was like a thorn under my skin, and I needed to hurt somebody. You...you hurt yourself, didn't you? But you also made something—those stories—and you made them real for me. It was a whole world we had, and we were safe there, and...I miss it."

"Me too." I get up, careful on the icy ledge, and start to climb down.

"So don't let anybody ever make you ashamed of that stuff. Just don't."

"I won't." I remember her crying, the day that Tanner picked on her. "Don't ever let anybody make you feel like you're stuck here. Like you're not brave enough to leave."

The ghost of a smile. "I've already left, haven't I?"

"I guess you have." I want to believe she'll be able to stay away from Kray's Defile at least long enough to see more of the world. I want her to ride on a plane and not be afraid.

"Hey," I say as I reach the ground, "you know when Seth told Joss he loved him? And Joss didn't say it back?"

"Yeah," she says. Behind her I see the ghostly forms of Joss and Seth tangled in their first kiss. "I remember that."

"For a long time, I didn't think I could love anyone," I say. "And now maybe I do."

It wasn't Joss by himself I felt that way about. It was all of them. It was Seth-Joss-Vivvy. It was Bram. It was my mind mingling with Vivvy's, and my body waking to Joss's kiss, and my hands on Bram's waist, and a firepit on the hilltop, and cobbler in the diner. I wanted the whole equation, and I wanted to belong, and I wanted a lead role, and she showed me I could take one. Whatever else she did, she did that.

In a small voice she says, "I miss you so much already."

"I miss you, too," I say, and I mean it as I walk away from her for the last time.

ACKNOWLEDGMENTS

While I'm not sure there's ever just one "book of your heart," this one certainly belongs in that category for me. Huge thanks to my agent, Jessica Sinsheimer, for giving me the confidence to show her *We Made It All Up* and for championing it every step of the way. Thank you to Rachel Poloski for seeing its potential, and to her and Liz Kossnar for taking it to the next level. Thank you to Tracy Koontz for the sharp eyes, to Peter Strain for the breathtaking cover art, to Jenny Kimura for the wonderful design, and to everyone on the Little, Brown Books for Young Readers team.

Before all that happened, though, Dayna Lorentz and Rachel Carter read countless drafts of this book and helped hammer it into shape. It wouldn't exist without them.

Back in 2013, Ken Moore of the Vermont Cavers' Association showed this non-caver through a tight passage like the one described in this book. Big thanks to him, and to the Montana lawyer who walked me through some points of criminal law.

Jennifer Mason-Black, Grayce Lombard, Nicole Lesperance, Jesse Q Sutanto, Marley Teter, Vikki Ciaffone, Grace Shim—your support has meant so much.

Thank you to Mom and Dad for believing in me, and to

Kirsten for being my storytelling friend during those hard teen years. Eva, thank you for being the sister Celeste should have had.

Finally, Rosie (2005–18) and Minx (2005–21) were the best cats a writer could have, day after day. They are missed and remembered, always.

Matthew Thorsen

MARGOT HARRISON

lives in Vermont, where she reviews books
and movies (especially horror) for the newspaper *Seven Days*. She is also the author of
The Glare and *The Killer in Me*. She invites
you to find her on Instagram and Twitter at
@MargotFHarrison.